Carrington Elsewhere

A Novel

Justine Fernandez

Carol,
I really hope you enjoy this tale.
Thank you so much for your friendship
and support!! Justine Fernandez

iUniverse, Inc.
New York Bloomington

Carrington Elsewhere
A Novel

iUniverse books may be ordered through booksellers or by contacting:

iUniverse
1663 Liberty Drive
Bloomington, IN 47403
www.iuniverse.com
1-800-Authors (1-800-288-4677)

ISBN: 978-1-4401-2313-9 (pbk)
ISBN: 978-1-4401-2314-6 (ebk)

Printed in the United States of America

iUniverse rev. date:2/10/2009

For Lulu.

You will always be my “seester-een-law,” and I will always be your “bo-neena.”

Nothing can erase that.

Special thanks to Uschi K., Linsey S., and Craig D.

Part I

Chapter One

"I have no idea," Joan bellowed in Carrington's face, "how you made it to fourteen! You are the stupidest damn kid I have ever laid my eyes on! Did you think these dishes were going to wash themselves? Huh?"

Though Carrington was tall for her age, Joan still had to lean down to glare into her oldest daughter's eyes. It was only three in the afternoon, but already Joan's breath reeked of rum. Carrington shook her head.

"No, I didn't think that," she answered her mother in a near whisper.

"Then get your ass in front of that kitchen sink and wash them!" Joan shouted.

She fought not to, but Carrington winced. She couldn't help it.

"Aw, you gonna cry?" Joan taunted. She stood upright to her impressive height and looked down at her daughter. "Go ahead; see if I give a shit! Goddamn little whiner!"

Joan glowered at Carrington for another moment before sauntering away. Carrington waited until she heard the creak of the screen door before wiping her eyes. She bit the insides of her cheeks to keep from making any noise as she cried. After a few deep breaths, she filled the sink with warm water and added a squirt of dish soap. She sighed as she looked around the kitchen, appraising the grimy stove, the counters littered with dry bits of cereal and bread crumbs, and the splotches of coffee, alcohol, and cigarette ash on the warped linoleum floor. Carrington cleaned the house on a regular basis, but her mother and her younger sister, Missy, didn't seem to care how long it took to undo their slovenly habits. It never crossed their minds that sometimes Carrington had to scramble to do her homework at the one in the morning after tidying the house and dealing with her mother. Some nights, when Joan came home from the bar too drunk to be belligerent, Carrington had to walk her mother from the front door to her bedroom, remove her shoes, and help her lie down. If Joan was sick when she came home and didn't make it to the toilet in time, Carrington was expected to clean that up, too.

Joan wandered back into the kitchen and settled at the small dinette table to go through the day's mail. The only sound besides envelopes being ripped open and the occasional clink of dishes was the smoke Joan noisily exhaled. She coughed in between sips of beer. Carrington had noticed earlier in the year that her mother's cough was becoming more and more pronounced. She grimaced, relieved that her back was to her mother. She loathed the stench of cigarette smoke almost as much as she loathed Joan.

"He expects me to raise a kid with forty bucks?" Joan exclaimed. "What a joke!"

Carrington stole a look at her mother, but she already knew what the complaint was about. The pastel-colored envelope and cheap greeting card in her hand confirmed her assumption. Since Carrington's own father was never in touch, Joan was talking about Gary, Missy's dad. He, too, was largely absent from his daughter's life, but Gary occasionally sent cards to Missy with money orders tucked in them. There was never a return address, and the postmark was often from a different state. The money orders ranged in value from thirty to sixty dollars. Joan always responded with a combination of outrage and relief when she saw Gary's handwriting in her mailbox.

The money orders were cashed immediately and spent on booze, cigarettes, and groceries, in that order. Joan may have been peeved to hear from Gary throughout the years, but Missy's face shone with a huge smile whenever she saw one of the flimsy greeting cards waiting for her on the table. Joan never waited to let Missy open the envelopes herself, but Missy didn't seem to care. She became a different girl when she saw that her dad had written to her. She'd gloat for days, snidely pointing out that Carrington never heard from her own father. Carrington had long ago learned how to sulk without letting it show on her thin face. She was pretty sure that her father's name was Arnold. Whenever her mother spoke of him, she referred to him as "Arnie" or "the asshole." Carrington had no memories of her father. Whenever she asked her mother about him, Joan flew into a rage. Neither Gary nor Arnold ever married Joan.

Carrington glanced again at her mother, and this time Joan caught her.

"What, you suddenly think you have all goddamn day to get your chores done, Carrie? I guess the laundry's gonna do itself, right, just like you thought the dishes would, huh? Do I have to tell you how to do everything? Your teachers keep sayin' you're so damn smart, but I've had to keep on you as long as you been alive just to make sure you can wipe your own ass! And you sure as hell better not start slacking off just 'cause it's summer break," Joan sneered.

Carrington ducked her head, a deep shade of crimson spreading across her face. This day, being her last day in the eighth grade, should have been a happy occasion. She knew that some of classmates were having parties to celebrate. They couldn't wait until the final bell rang. This had never been true for Carrington. Leaving school was like leaving an old friend to go to a place where she knew no one. She wished desperately she could stay in school all day. The summer loomed before her, long and ominous.

She quickly finished the dishes without glancing in her mother's direction again and was relieved that Joan was too absorbed in the mail to yell at her anymore. The one bright spot this afternoon was that Carrington anticipated a brief reprieve. Joan would send her to the small corner store two blocks away to cash the money order.

Carrington rushed through the house, collecting dirty laundry. It was tempting to dawdle, as she would rather be occupied with the laundry for as long as possible than risk further interaction with Joan. It was better, though, if she hurried. Joan would accuse her of being lazy if she saw Carrington doing her chores slowly.

The bedroom she shared with her sister was narrow and dark. The view from their small window was of the side wall of a house identical to their own. The other house was so close that if she shoved the broom out of the window, she could easily tap on the neighbor's window. She knew this was true because the year before, a family who had a boy Missy's age lived there, and Missy and the boy spent several weeks passing notes back and forth by tying them to a broom and extending it out of their windows, the notes dangling from the broom handle.

Their bedroom wasn't terribly messy. Carrington always made sure their beds were made in the morning, and when Missy neglected to put her dirty clothes in their shared hamper, Carrington did it for her. The room had a musty smell, though, as did the rest of the house. It was the carpet, Carrington thought. It was as old as the house, threadbare in some spots, and riddled with ugly stains. Carrington tried to make her side of the room as pleasant-looking as possible with a couple of posters, silk flowers, and the occasional knickknack, but she never really sought or found solace in her room. Sometimes, when Joan was especially out of control, Missy retreated to their bedroom. But to Carrington, the entire house was just a series of compartments comprising one prison cell. No corner of the house felt safe.

She bundled her shirts and pajamas with Missy's and hauled them to the cramped laundry room off of the kitchen. A flash of bitterness made her jaw clench. She resented Missy's obvious position of favor. It wasn't just that Missy never had to do any work around the house. Sometimes Carrington wished that, just once, Joan would belt Missy across the face for spilling a glass of juice or for forgetting to bring the newspaper inside in the morning. She was ashamed of these thoughts, but they never strayed far from her mind. Her guilt was partly assuaged from knowing that nothing like that would ever happen. Joan occasionally scolded Missy and had even threatened her a few times, but she reserved her wrath solely for Carrington.

Joan was mixing a rum and Coke when Carrington passed through the kitchen again. A fresh cigarette hung from her red-painted lips, and the layers of black mascara on her lashes were clumped together and crusty. *God, you look like hell,* Carrington thought. Joan seemed to think that the more makeup she piled on her face, the better she looked, but nothing could have been further from the truth, Carrington often silently observed. She focused on the list of household tasks that lay ahead of her and tried not to let her gaze stray to Joan.

"Hey," Joan said just as Carrington passed through the doorway that led to the living room.

Carrington stiffened. "Yes?" she responded, turning around but not meeting her mother's eyes.

Joan pointed to the table. "Go get that money order cashed. Get me a couple packs of smokes, a bunch of those microwave soup cups, some bananas, shampoo, tampons, and a box of cereal. Oh, and milk, too."

I only have two arms, Carrington thought darkly as she reached for the money order. In a small way, though, she was grateful. The task, as she'd hoped and predicted, would take her away from Joan for a little while, and there would be food in the house for a few days. Buying cigarettes was never an issue, despite being underage. The old man who owned the corner shop didn't care who asked for them as long as he was paid in cash.

"Oh, and Carrie?" Joan called after her.

"Yes?"

"You better bring me the receipt and whatever change is left. You got that?" Joan barked.

"I will," Carrington answered, her voice trembling slightly.

Joan didn't even look at her daughter as she returned to the table to flip through the newspaper, but Carrington flinched as her mother passed her.

The pre-summer heat swallowed her the moment she left the house. In spite of this, Carrington shivered. Sometimes she wondered if Joan knew her secret. Carrington had been sneaking a few dollars out of Joan's wallet for months. Although she felt sick to her stomach each time she slipped her fingers into her mother's purse, she rationalized that the effort and anxiety were worth it. Not once in the past few months did Carrington have to find her mother at a bar and try to cajole money out of her so that she and her sister could eat. As far as Carrington could tell, Missy also had no clue about the stolen money, which was for the best. If Missy knew, she might demand half in exchange for not snitching or simply steal it all for herself.

Carrington was careful never to take too much money at one time, and she figured that the best time to do it was the morning after Joan cashed her paycheck or a money order from Gary and had holed up in a bar for most of the evening. Joan would wake up hung over and unsure of how much she spent the night before. Sometimes Carrington was only able to take a dollar or two at a time. Hiding it was easy, since she was the only one who ever did any work around the house. Carrington had plenty of places to hide things: under the bathroom sink in an empty Ajax can, on the very back of the tiny shelf in the broom closet, or tucked carefully behind the bottle of bleach in the laundry room. Sometimes the fear of being caught was even worse than the icy panic that tightened her chest whenever Joan came home from the bar.

Carrington walked slowly to the corner store, even going a block out of her way to visit with the small, brown puppy someone on the next street had recently acquired. She leaned over and let the tiny dog lick her fingers, wishing, just for an instant, that he belonged to her. There was nothing pleasant to see other than the puppy. Chain link fences sagged around small, weed-filled yards, and most of the houses had not been painted in years. The sun had bleached many of them to a dingy blue-gray or a dull, muddy orange.

At the corner store, she filled a hand basket with the things her mother wanted. She had to wait until she was at the counter to ask for the cigarettes. The grouchy old man who sat on a stool behind the counter was there, and as always, he didn't question Carrington's request for cigarettes. He did leer at her, though. This was new. She felt his watery eyes travel up and down her long legs as she walked past him. His gaze gave her the chills.

She didn't stop to see the puppy on her way home because the grocery bags were heavy enough that their plastic handles cut painfully into her fingers. Too soon, she was once again on the cracked sidewalk that led to her front door. The collection of small, drab rooms that Carrington called home was actually half of a duplex. Joan owned the house and rented the other half whenever she could, although for the past several months the space had been vacant.

Carrington opened the rusting screen door gingerly, steeling herself in case Joan was waiting for her in the living room. She half expected to see her mother passed out on the couch, an empty bottle by her side and a cigarette still burning on the coffee table ashtray. She heard her mother before she saw her. Joan was on the kitchen phone. Carrington gently set the grocery bags down on the floor. Joan hated being interrupted when she was on the phone.

"Well, it's got to be him," Joan snapped. "The obit says Arnold Browne, age thirty-nine. That's the right age, and that's the asshole's name. Doesn't say how he died, though." She paused to take a long drag off her cigarette. "He died almost two months ago. Don't know why the hell it was only printed now. Hell, probably 'cause that loser was shot to death or died of an overdose," she guffawed. "The obit says he's survived by his mother, Mrs. A. C. Browne. Figures that old bitch would be snooty like that and have 'em print just her initials," Joan snarled. "Anyway, he was Carrie's dad, and since my kid's got Browne blood in her, I think we are entitled to half of whatever was in Arnie's bank account, half of any property he had, all that. Don't you think so?" she demanded. "The sonofabitch never paid me a dime of child support, and Carrie's already fourteen. That's fourteen years worth of back payments! And hell, it's another four years 'til Carrie's eighteen, so Arnie's damn mom should pay me support for the next four years!" Joan was furious.

Carrington had to lean against the couch to steady herself. *Arnold Browne,* she thought, *my father. And he's dead.* Her palms began to sweat. She rushed to the small bedroom she shared with Missy, leaving the door open a couple of inches—just enough to hear more of her mother's conversation. Ever since starting middle school, there were many afternoons Carrington was annoyed that she had to come home an hour before Missy did. It was unfair that she had to face Joan by herself, she thought. Today she was glad that Missy wasn't home yet. Missy wouldn't be quiet enough to let Carrington hear the rest of Joan's conversation, and even if she was, she'd pester Carrington with questions or brag about her own dad.

Carrington could tell by the sugary coo her mother's voice had become that she was talking to one of her boyfriends. Carrington hated that voice more than anything. She would rather hear Joan hollering the most vile words imaginable than hear her pretend to be sweet and coy. It was sickening. Carrington closed the bedroom door, cringing as the latch clicked into place. She hoped her mother didn't hear it.

The sound of her mother on the phone became a muffled buzz that was easy to ignore. *My father,* Carrington thought again, her heart beating wildly in her chest. *And my grandmother,* she remembered with a start. *A. C. Browne. Her middle name must be Carrington,* she thought. She sat on the floor and leaned against one of the beds, tucking her feet beneath her. It would be simple enough, Carrington considered, to look for her grandmother's name in the phone book. If the number was unlisted, she could sneak a look at Arnold Browne's obituary and find out where the service was held. If she had to, she could even send a note to the funeral home to be forwarded to Mrs. Browne.

Carrington's right eyelid began to twitch as it always did when she was especially nervous or worried. What would she say to her grandmother? "Hi, I'm your son's long lost daughter. My mother is a hopeless drunk. Can I come and live with you?" Carrington shuddered at the thought. *How could she not know about me?* she wondered, feeling a rush of tears come to her eyes. *Arnold must have known about me,* she thought. *They just didn't want me.* Tears spilled over her cheeks, and she pressed her face into the faded comforter on her bed. Wisps of her long, reddish hair became soaked, and her bony shoulders shook as she wept. Carrington hated herself for crying. She pounded the side of her mattress with one fist.

"What the hell are you cryin' about?" Joan's gruff voice suddenly filled the small bedroom. "And why the hell didn't you put the groceries away?" she demanded.

Carrington looked up, startled. She'd been so upset that she hadn't heard the door open. Her mother's body filled the doorway. Joan watched her daughter with narrowed eyes and blew out a stream of smoke. Carrington felt like an animal in a steel trap. A familiar panic churned in her belly and spread to her chest. She jumped to her feet and wiped her face as well as she could with the backs of her hands. She started to say that she hadn't been crying, but there were still fat tear drops sliding down her cheeks.

Instead, she shrugged and tried to sound nonchalant.

"I just had a sad day at school."

"You get in trouble?" Joan demanded.

Carrington shook her head.

"No, I'm just going to miss some of my friends over the summer," she lied.

Joan scoffed, blowing out more smoke.

"That's nothin' to cry over," she said, snuffing the cigarette out in her empty glass.

She set the glass down on a small table in the hallway. Carrington didn't answer. She knew she wouldn't be able to keep the emotion out of her voice.

"Listen, I wanna talk to you about somethin'," Joan said, sounding awkward. She walked briskly into the room.

Here it comes, Carrington thought. *She's going to tell me about Arnold Browne. My father. My dead father.* She felt a fresh wave of tears and fought to keep her expression neutral.

"Yes?" she asked meekly, afraid to meet her mother's eyes.

Joan stared at her oldest daughter with determination. The uneasiness was gone from her face and her voice.

"I just found out that your dad is dead," she stated flatly. "He died a couple months ago. You and I are gonna pay a visit to his mom, and we're gonna get all the money I would've had if the sonofabitch had been paying child support all along."

Carrington began to cry again. Huge sobs shook her body. Joan stared at her as if Carrington had suddenly sprouted wings.

"What are you carryin' on about?" she demanded at last. "You didn't even know him!"

Carrington winced at this. She took a huge gulp of air and shuddered as she exhaled. It had been a long time since she cried so hard. She glared into her mother's eyes. The fear she usually felt in Joan's presence drained away and was replaced by searing anger.

"And whose fault is that?" Carrington shouted into her mother's shocked face. "You kept me away from him all these years! You didn't want me to know about him. You never told me anything about my dad. My own father!" she screamed, tears streaming down her face.

"He didn't want to know about you!" Joan shot back. "You think I wanted to raise an ungrateful kid like you with no help? He didn't care about you!"

"You're lying!" Carrington screeched. "You didn't want me to have any choice but to live with you and put up with your drinking and your laziness and your boyfriends! I hate you!"

"You little bitch!" Joan hissed.

She closed the gap between them in one step. The backhanded slap she delivered to her daughter's face was so hard that Carrington stumbled backward. Joan wasn't satisfied. She continued to slap Carrington across the face while cursing at her.

"I should've had an abortion when I found out I was pregnant with you," Joan growled, her face red and twisted with rage.

The stench of Joan's breath was nauseating, a blend of nicotine-rotted gums and alcohol. Carrington tried her best to shield herself, but Joan was too strong and too angry to be stopped. Through blurry tears and her own arms, she could barely make out the shape of her mother's hand, again and again landing on her face, her arms, wherever she could make contact. Carrington's lip began to burn. The blood was thick and salty on her tongue. Joan grabbed her daughter by one shoulder and shook her hard, trying to get the girl to drop her hands and arms.

"I hate you! I wish you were the one who died!" Carrington managed to gasp.

Neither of them heard the front door open and close or the footsteps that approached the bedroom.

"Stop it! Mom, stop it!" Missy cried.

She stood in the bedroom doorway, looking pale and frightened. Missy had seen her mother hit her older sister plenty of times before but never with such frenzy. She was shocked at the sight of blood that came gushing from Carrington's nose and lip.

Joan's face snapped toward Missy, teeth bared and cheeks flushed. She finally released the vise grip she had on Carrington's arm and took a step back.

"Clean yourself up, Carrie," she snapped without looking at Carrington. "We're going to see that bitch, and I don't want to hear another goddamn thing about it!"

Missy managed to scramble out of her mother's way as Joan stalked out of the room. She fished a towel out of the clothes hamper and thrust it at her older sister. She stared lamely at her feet and the walls as Carrington wiped her face.

"What happened?" Missy finally asked.

Instead of answering, Carrington once again burst into tears. She pressed her face into the grimy towel. The towel made her cries sound like the desperate yelps of a small animal being smothered to death. Missy gaped at her. She'd never seen Carrington cry like this.

"What happened, Carrie?" she asked again, her voice urgent.

"My dad," Carrington managed to say at last. "His name's Arnold Browne, and he's dead. Mom wants to get money from his mother."

She blew her nose into the now filthy towel and quickly folded it into a tight bundle, hoping Missy didn't see the bloody gobs that had come from her nose and mouth.

"Holy shit," was all Missy could say.

She sat on her bed and scooted her knees up to her chin.

Carrington deposited the towel back in the hamper and walked unsteadily out of the bedroom. She locked herself in the bathroom and washed her face, gritting her teeth against the pain around her eyes and mouth. What she saw in the mirror above the sink made her gasp. Joan had never given her a beating so severe. Carrington suspected that her mom knew better than to leave marks that could be seen by anyone. This time was different.

There was a slit in her lower lip that stung terribly when she touched it with her tongue. The skin around her left eye was puffy and purple, and there was a small gash near her hairline. *I could have her arrested,* Carrington thought, blinking back more tears.

Carrington sat on the edge of the bathtub and tried to think of what to do. The house was silent. If Joan was still home, she would no doubt be yelling at both girls. *She must have gone to the bar or to stay with one of her stupid boyfriends,* Carrington thought. If she called the police, she and Missy would probably be placed in a foster home. How would she ever get in touch with her grandmother then? She realized that Joan must have been drinking all day. She had been too drunk to consider what would happen if Carrington showed up at Mrs. Browne's house looking like she'd had the hell beaten out of her.

Her gaze wandered around the cramped room and finally settled on the small cabinet below the sink. Her money! She was certain that she had well over sixty dollars stashed around the house. Again she realized how simple it would be to find out where her grandmother lived. If A. C. Browne wasn't in the phone book, Carrington could write to the funeral home that handled Arnold Browne's death. His obituary had been listed in the local paper; that probably meant that her grandmother must not live very far away.

She jumped at the sound of the TV coming to life in the living room. God, what about Missy? What would happen to Missy? Her younger sister had nowhere to go. How could Carrington possibly bring her to Mrs. Browne's house? *My grandmother may not even want me, let alone my half sister,* Carrington thought, pursing her lips bitterly.

Back in the bedroom, she pulled her hair into a ponytail and changed into a clean T-shirt. The sound of a game show blared from the living room. Carrington could never understand how both her sister and mother could sit for hours watching mindlessly as people clapped and cheered over guessing simple word puzzles. The money people won on game shows was something to get excited about, but she could never endure sitting through an entire episode.

She was starving. The groceries were in the living room where she'd left them. Carrington put them away and made two servings of soup, filled two chipped juice glasses with milk, and brought everything into the living room.

She slurped down her soup noisily and was surprised that Missy didn't join her.

"Aren't you hungry?" she asked her younger sister between gulps.

Missy stared at the television screen with glassy eyes.

"Nah," she answered. "Not really."

"You should eat, anyway," Carrington suggested.

"I'll eat when I feel like eating," Missy snapped, still staring at the TV.

Carrington set down her spoon and turned to face her sister.

"What's your problem?" she asked.

"I don't have a problem," Missy answered, flipping through the channels. She finally glanced over at Carrington. "God, you look like crap, Carrie," she blurted, studying Carrington's battered face.

Carrington felt tears rush to her eyes. She turned away from Missy's cold gaze and sucked down a mouthful of milk. *I will not cry,* she told herself, swallowing hard.

"Gee, thanks," she muttered. "And I hate being called Carrie; you know that," she complained.

Missy scoffed. "Of course. How could I forget? Her royal highness wants to be called Carrington!" She adopted a bad imitation of a British accent and rolled her eyes.

"Knock it off!" Carrington snapped. "Why are you acting like this? Isn't it pretty obvious that I've had a really awful day? Get off my case, Missy." She sighed in disgust.

"Isn't it pretty obvious that I've had a really awful day," Missy mimicked snottily, still using the would-be English accent. "You brought it on yourself," she said in her own voice. "Why do you always have to piss Mom off?"

Carrington couldn't believe her ears. Missy was usually callous but never like this.

"What do you mean, I always piss her off?" she demanded. "So I deserved to take a beating, is that it?"

"What's the big deal if she wants to get money out of your dad? I mean, he owes her anyway since he's never paid any child support," Missy answered. "My dad does that, at least," she added smugly.

Carrington snorted. "Yeah, Missy, your dad is so responsible he mails you about eighty bucks a year. And I guess he's just so busy and important that he doesn't have time to write his address on the envelopes."

Missy flinched, and Carrington immediately regretted her words. A subtle change shifted Missy's face. Her eyes and mouth went from annoyed to enraged. Carrington had seen this look many times before, but usually it was on Joan's face, not Missy's.

"Fuck you!" Missy spat. "At least my dad never pretended like he doesn't know I exist. Your dad was too ashamed to admit he ever had a kid like you! No wonder Mom kicked your ass! No wonder she hates you! I would hate you, too, if I had a bitch daughter like you!"

Missy's face darkened with a deep flush of color in her cheeks. Her eyes shone like polished obsidian. She held Carrington's gaze for just a few seconds more before jumping up from the couch and stomping outside, slamming the door behind her.

Carrington was suddenly overwhelmed with exhaustion. If not for the bruises on her face, she would have felt nothing at all. She was startled at how numb she felt. The weight of Missy words registered but didn't sting like they normally would. Too much had happened, and Carrington did not have the energy to be hurt again that day.

She forced herself to finish her soup and drink her own glass of milk and the glass she had poured for Missy. Her movements were mechanical and mindless as she washed the dishes and wiped off the coffee table. *Well, I know one thing for damn sure,* she thought. *I'm not going to worry about leaving Missy here.* Even as she thought it, she knew that at some point she would probably lose sleep over what happened to her younger sister, but it wasn't going to be that night.

Carrington pored through the newspaper that had been abandoned on the kitchen table until she found the obituary for Arnold Browne. He had died nearly two months prior, just as Joan said. Reading the details made her stomach nervous, especially when she saw in print the name she had heard her mother mention: A. C. Browne. *That's her,* Carrington thought. *That's my grandmother. I'm going to meet my grandmother. And get the hell out of here.* She was relieved to find that there was a listing in the phone book for A. C. Browne. Carrington jotted down Mrs. Browne's information on a piece of notebook paper, as well as the name and address of the funeral home where Arnold Browne's service was held, just in case. She hurried through the small house, anxiously going back to the spots where her pilfered money was hidden. She was relieved to find that none of it had been touched. Behind the safety of the locked bathroom door, Carrington counted the money. Eighty-one dollars. *Plenty of money,* she thought, *to leave early in the morning, have breakfast somewhere, and wait for a decent hour to take the bus to Mrs. Browne's house. My grandmother,* she thought, her eyes welling with tears. She slept in her jeans and kept the money tucked in one of her front pockets.

Chapter Two

Joan Coyle was a tall, stocky woman. She was thirty-eight but looked several years older. Tight jeans, clingy T-shirts, and push-up bras were her favorite clothes. She strutted around in spike-heeled boots even when her feet and knees throbbed in protest. Her ash blond hair was nearly down to her waist. Her natural hair color was dark brown, but she'd been bleaching it for several years. She loved layering her face with makeup, favoring bright, bold lipstick, heavy blush, thick mascara, and sparkling eye shadow. Joan didn't have the patience to shape her eyebrows, so most of the time she either plucked or shaved them until there was barely any hair left and then penciled dark brown lines over what remained. When friends at work or boyfriends teased Joan about how much makeup she wore, she would laugh and tell them they were just jealous or too dumb to know beauty when they saw it. Both of her daughters had inherited her height, but only Carrington had her jade green eyes.

Other than being tall for their ages and Carrington's eye color, Joan's children looked very little like their mother. Carrington was fine-boned; she reminded Joan of a porcelain doll. She envied her daughter's smooth, clear skin, her long, perfectly shaped eyebrows, her small nose, and her curved lips. Carrington had a smattering of freckles across her cheeks that Missy, when annoyed with her older sister, called "stink spots." It was just as well that Carrington showed no interest in wearing makeup or styling her long, reddish-brown hair. Joan preferred that her oldest daughter kept her appearance plain. *Don't want her gettin' cocky about her looks,* Joan often thought about Carrington.

At twelve, Missy was already too confident about her appearance. Joan told her youngest child that she was not allowed to wear makeup until she was thirteen, but relented when Missy began sneaking lip gloss and mascara to school. It was just part of growing up, Joan figured. Missy could and frequently did spend at least an hour drying and brushing her wavy, dark hair. She usually wore it in a meticulous pony tail, shiny from so much hair spray. Missy had her father's tan complexion, rounded features, large, dark eyes, and dimples. She had just finished the fifth grade for the second time at the same elementary school that Carrington had attended. To Joan's relief, she'd passed this time, but barely.

Unfortunately, Missy did not share her older sister's appreciation for school. At least, that's what Joan was used to hearing from Missy's teachers. They remembered Carrington well: a bright, pensive girl, tall for her age, with enormous green eyes and long, often tangled, ginger brown hair. They shook their heads sadly at Joan when she was forced to come to the school for parent-teacher conferences about Missy's poor grades and matching attitude. Their most common complaints were about how chatty Missy was and how much time she wasted teasing the boys in her class. Missy's grades, at best, were only mediocre. Joan worried about how Missy would fare in middle school. But it was a worry that was easy to shake. *After all,* Joan considered, *I only went to the eleventh grade, and what difference did it make? I still got a house, a job, two kids, and a man whenever I want one.*

Joan worked part-time in a secondhand store, and she received disability payments because she claimed to have near crippling arthritis in her knees. It was true that she'd had knee problems since her late teens. As a high school student, sometimes the pain and swelling were enough to excuse her from gym class. At first, she managed the pain with aspirin, but it wasn't long before she discovered the relief that alcohol offered, usually coupled with prescription painkillers that she obtained however she could. The night before the hearing that would determine if she was eligible to receive disability benefits, Joan went dancing. She wore the highest heeled shoes she could find and spent hours pounding the dance floor in Fensen's lounge, one of her favorite bars. Her knees were stiff and swollen for days afterwards, but her plan worked. She was granted partial disability. Joan felt no guilt when she stood in line every month to cash the check she received from the government. The money was a relief, and on more than one occasion, she wished the judge had granted her full disability. One of the conditions of receiving her monthly check was that she could not legally work more than twenty-five hours per week, which suited her just fine.

Sometimes, when Joan had to meet Missy or Carrington's teachers or parents of their friends, they would ask what she did for a living. She loathed that question. It was none of their damn business, she figured. But she played along, answering vaguely that she worked part-time in retail. She often quickly added that working only part-time allowed her to spend more time with her girls. Joan despised the way some of the teachers and parents looked at her. She could feel the judgment in their gazes and see the doubt in their pursed lips. *Who the hell do they think they are to look down on me?* she often wondered.

Not surprisingly, Carrington seemed to have few friends, so Joan rarely had to deal with other parents because of her eldest daughter. Missy, on the other hand, was something of a social butterfly. She was outspoken, grinned often, and at the age of twelve, already seemed to have a hint of the overt sensuality that Joan remembered well from her youth. It was a quality Joan believed that she still commanded, even though her skin would never be as taut and fresh as it once was. Missy was going to be a handful in a few more years, Joan knew.

Carrington's insistence that she be called by her full name had started when she began middle school. She complained that Carrie was childish. Joan had rolled her eyes and told her daughter to shut up and stop being such a whiner. Joan had never liked the name Carrington. Arnold only wanted to name her after his high and mighty mom to rub it in Joan's face that he came from money while her background was firmly working class, she figured. He'd had no contact with Joan since Carrington was an infant, so Joan saw no reason to call her daughter by such an uppity name. Her teachers called her Carrington, but at home she was still Carrie.

Missy was indifferent to the name Melissa. She didn't mind having a nickname. This was just one of the many reasons Joan favored her youngest child. She could tell early on in Carrington's life that the girl would be a snob, like her father and his parents. And though Missy's father was a deadbeat and a drunk when they were dating, at least he was down-to-earth, not like Carrington's arrogant father.

What neither girl knew was that during the past several months, Gary, Missy's father, had been calling Joan at work and first requesting, then demanding, to have contact with his daughter. Joan gave him the same response each time he called. "You pay up all the years of child support you owe me, and I'll think about it." This answer usually quieted him down, although lately he'd been more insistent. He claimed he had been sober for over a year and was entitled to parental rights. During his latest phone call, Gary even said he was willing to meet with a lawyer if Joan would pay half the fees to work out a payment plan for all the years of financial support he should have been paying for Melissa. Joan was dubious and balked at the notion of paying legal fees. "That's bullshit!" she told him. "I been takin' care of Missy all these years by myself, and you want *me* to pay so you can do what you shoulda been doin' all this time?" Gary huffed that she couldn't keep him away from Melissa forever, and she had not heard from him since. Joan figured there was no reason to tell Melissa about Gary's calls. Her dad would only be a disappointment in the girl's life. But she filed away his recent interest in Missy in the back of her mind. He could be useful to them somehow in the future. She would be damned, though, if she gave into Gary's, or anyone's, demands. Joan called the shots in her life and in the lives of her children.

Joan was often furious with herself for not actively pursuing child support from both her children's fathers. She wasn't sure how to go about it when the girls were born, and she never really looked into it as they grew up. Money was always an issue. The men she dated were carefully selected; only those with steady employment and a generous streak were considered. When she managed to score a renter for the other half of her house, things were easier, but it had been a while since anyone was interested in the place.

The section of houses where Joan lived spanned a couple of miles and was originally developed to accommodate factory workers employed in the textile mill and plastic manufacturing plant, both of which had long since closed down. Her parents, Doug and Maria Coyle, met in a factory and married just out of high school. Joan's mother died just a few days shy of her twenty-second birthday. Doug Coyle dealt with the death of his young wife by taking a second job and drinking himself into a stupor on his rare days off. Joan was often left with neighborhood families, even on holidays. Doug drank and smoked himself into an early grave when Joan was just twenty years old. The only things she had left of her parents were a small collection of old photographs, her father's old foot locker filled with some of his belongings, and the house. Sometimes, when she drank at home instead of with a boyfriend or at a bar, she would look through the photographs and weep. Joan saw crying as a weakness. She blamed her brief crying spells on the alcohol. Occasionally, she entertained the idea of burning the old photographs, though she knew she would never do it. Maybe she would give them to Missy one day.

Chapter Three

Carrington slept fitfully and woke up around eight o'clock from a nightmare in which Joan and Missy took turns throwing dishes at her. Her face was wet with tears when she opened her eyes. She had no idea when Missy came home, but her younger sister was asleep in her bed, the blanket covering the lower half of her face. The door to Joan's bedroom was open, the bed unmade as usual. Carrington doubted that her mother had bothered to come home at all.

She crept through the house, not wanting to wake Missy. Carrington showered and borrowed a blouse from Joan's closet. It was one of Joan's few shirts that didn't have a bright print and wasn't low cut. It was a mid-sleeve button-up in royal blue, with a slightly cinched waist and breast pockets. Carrington eyed herself critically in the bathroom mirror. The blouse was too large for her and kind of old fashioned, but it was better than any of her own clothes. She also borrowed some of Joan's makeup to mask the sickly bluish bruise around her left eye. She found a small bandage in the bottom of a drawer, which she used to cover the gash along her hairline. There wasn't much she could do to hide the cut in her lower lip. She just hoped that anyone who noticed would think it was only because her lips were badly chapped.

It was half past nine by the time she was fully dressed and ready to go. Carrington was so nervous that she would have vomited if her stomach hadn't been empty. Even though she doubted that her mother would be home any time soon, she was terrified of what Joan might do if she came home and found Carrington dressed in her clothes and wearing her makeup.

Carrington decided to take a bus that would drop her off in the general vicinity of Mrs. Browne's neighborhood. She knew there was a shopping center in that area. Although the mall wouldn't be open for another hour or so, she planned to stake out one of the outdoor benches. She thought that, once the mall opened its doors, walking through the stores might help calm her nerves. She could also figure out what to say when she finally came face-to-face with the woman who quite possibly was her grandmother.

She took one of Joan's old purses—a cheap, imitation suede bag with a long strap. For a few moments, Carrington considered bringing along the binder that was filled with all of her school report cards and certificates of excellence, but ultimately decided it would be a mistake. It would be annoying to carry it around, and it would seem especially desperate and childish to show it to the grandmother, who may not even know of Carrington's existence. She wore a fresh pair of jeans and kept the cash in her pocket.

Carrington walked a half mile to the nearest bus stop. She glanced over her shoulder every few seconds, expecting Joan to come chasing after her. She knew that Joan was probably passed out in some strange man's bed and most likely wouldn't be awake for several more hours, but she couldn't help feeling anxious. Carrington was too nervous to sit on the concrete bus stop bench. She stood behind it, almost as if the bench was a shield, and watched the neighborhood with worried eyes.

The morning was still cool, and Carrington was pleased that she didn't have to walk in the heat. Many of the people who lived in the area had already gone to work. The kids on summer break were still in bed. An occasional stray dog trotted through the streets, and a handful of retirees and the otherwise unemployed people sat on crumbling porches with steaming mugs of coffee in their laps. A surge of relief flooded through Carrington when she saw the huge city bus come barreling toward the bus stop.

She paid the fare, regretfully handing over her money, and chose a seat in the middle of the bus. If she sat up front, the driver may try to chat with her, Carrington reasoned, and sitting all the way in the back might seem suspicious. There were only a few other riders on the bus: older teenagers dressed in uniforms for fast food restaurants, a young mother with two toddlers in tow, and a couple of elderly men who talked excitedly about which of them might come home with a bingo jackpot. Carrington's fear of being seen by Joan melted away as the bus merged onto the highway.

She tried to put together a timeline. Joan usually came home from one of her dates around noon. She would probably be angry to find that Carrington wasn't home, but she wouldn't suspect anything right away. If Joan had to work that afternoon, she'd leave the house around two, and when she came home some five hours later, she would expect Carrington to be home. If she wasn't scheduled to work, which is what Carrington hoped, then Joan may not come home at all, at least, not until very late in the day. And when she did finally stumble through the front door, she would probably be blind drunk and stay in bed for nearly ten hours straight.

Missy had no idea where Carrington was, so Joan would learn nothing by interrogating her youngest daughter. Missy probably wouldn't stay home that day, anyway. Most summer vacation days, Missy left early, stayed at friends' houses all day or wandered the streets with a pack of kids, and came home when it started to get dark outside. Often, she would call late in the afternoon to tell Carrington (because Joan was seldom home in the evening) that she was spending the night at a friend's house. The next day, Joan might yell at Missy for not coming home, but she was never very hard on the girl.

Carrington spent a lot of time at the public library during the summer. When she became sick of reading, she would walk to a park and bring a sketch pad or a notebook for doodling. She rarely had money, but if she did happen to have a couple bucks, she'd walk to the corner grocery store and treat herself to an ice cream bar or a ham sandwich.

Carrington thought of those ice cream bars and ham sandwiches as the bus pulled into the mall parking lot. She was fiercely hungry. The half sleeve of crackers in her purse would make for a dismal and unsatisfying breakfast, she knew from experience. *What the hell, I'm going to splurge. How many times do I run away from home?* Carrington mused with a wry half smile. She decided to treat herself to a sausage biscuit and orange juice at one of the burger joints that sold breakfast.

Most of the passengers shuffled off the bus with Carrington; the teenagers dragged their feet toward the fast food restaurants that shared the mall parking lot, and the young mother half dragged, half carried her squalling children to a nearby family clinic.

Carrington chose the restaurant that advertised the cheapest combination meal. The only other customers were mall employees and elderly people. She chose a table next to one of the plate glass windows, where she could watch the mall come to life. Neon signs lit up, and employees' cars trickled into the outer regions of the massive parking lot. Carrington finished her breakfast and slowly counted the money in her wallet. After bus fare and breakfast, she was down to seventy-six dollars and change.

A knot formed in her stomach as she tried to imagine knocking on Mrs. Browne's door and introducing herself. Several weeks had passed since Arnold Browne's funeral. She didn't think it was likely that Mrs. Browne would have a houseful of guests so long after the service. People came to mourn and stayed no longer than a couple of days, she imagined. Those who wept at the funeral would be Carrington's own relatives, and they had no inkling that the late Arnold Browne had a daughter out of wedlock. Carrington blushed. No one called illegitimate children *bastards* anymore.

Would it be worse, she wondered, *if Mrs. Browne had no idea about me or worse if she knew but pretended not to?* She suddenly had a very clear picture in her head of an older, distinguished-looking woman shutting the door in her face, and she knew, without a doubt, that it would be far worse if Mrs. Browne already knew that she had a granddaughter but wanted nothing to do with her. What would she do then? Go back to Joan's house as if nothing had happened? Would Joan still want to demand money from the Browne family once she sobered up? The greasy sausage gurgled in her stomach. *This was a stupid idea,* she thought, fighting back tears. *What the hell am I doing here?*

Another image crept into her mind. She saw herself timidly knocking on a door and being let inside. It was hard to see

Mrs. A. C. Browne's entire face in this picture, but Carrington had no trouble envisioning a kind pair of eyes and a soft voice asking questions. There would have to be blood tests, no doubt, to determine whether or not Carrington was related to Mrs. Browne. There was a chance, she allowed herself to think, that Mrs. Browne would be interested in her. She had nothing to lose. There was no point in going back home. For what? Another beating? Four more years of hell and then leaving for good with nothing to show for it other than a handful of school certificates and a high school diploma? If she was forced to go back to the duplex either because Mrs. Browne didn't want her or wasn't her real grandmother, she would think of something then. But for now, Carrington reasoned as she pushed through the heavy glass door of the fast food restaurant, her plan was all she had and she would see it through.

The mall was finally open. She walked across the mostly empty parking lot, slowly at first, taking the cautious steps of someone not used to her surroundings. She stopped only once to look back at the bus stop bench, briefly considering turning around and heading home. Again, Carrington called to mind the vision of entering Mrs. Browne's house, sitting down with the woman, and telling her story. She continued toward the mall, quickening her pace as she went.

Chapter Four

A. C. Browne brushed her hair briskly and pulled it into a neat bun. At sixty-six years old, her hair was still thick and smooth, although most of the reddish chestnut color had long ago faded to near white. A. C. often received compliments about her hair from women who were several years younger than herself. However, her younger sister, Regina, had been nagging her for years to get it cut. A. C. usually wore it in a bun or a chignon, but occasionally brushed it out and let it fall naturally to her shoulders. When Regina saw it down, she would cluck her tongue and remind A. C. that she wasn't a young woman anymore. Regina's own hair, once a luxurious honey blond, had turned completely white within a few years of her forty-fifth birthday. Along with its pigment, her golden mane had lost its shine and strength, becoming coarse and brittle. She gladly cut it short and permed it when she reached what she called "the menopause years." For nearly two decades, Regina had maintained the helmet of white curls. Neither A. C. nor Laurence, Regina's husband, ever said it, but secretly they both thought that the hairstyle made Regina appear much older than she really was, and certainly much older than her older sister, who was, in fact, four years her senior.

My Arnold has been dead seven weeks now, A. C. told herself silently, eyeing the pale woman who stared at her from her dresser mirror. *I look like a ghost,* she thought, reaching for her rouge. Her hand trembled as she applied the creamy pink powder to her cheeks.

It had been over a year since she'd seen her only child, Arnold, alive. The last time he came to the house, he had wanted money, as usual, and he looked awful—worse than ever. He had hollowed cheeks and sunken eyes, and he reeked of stale cigarettes and God knew what else. She had told him, as she always did, that she loved him and that the only financial assistance she was willing to give him would be to pay for his admittance into a rehabilitation clinic. He didn't even try pleading. Looking back, she wondered if that was a sign that he was near the end. It must have been too much effort for him to try to make her feel guilty. All he said was that she was wasting her breath. He gave her the name and phone number of a friend of his she could call if she changed her mind about the money. She called the number a week later, to see if she could appeal to him again, but when he realized that she wasn't going to just hand over a check, he hung up on her. She tried calling one more time, around the holidays, but the number had been disconnected.

Years before, A. C. had gone on the warpath to try to force Arnold into rehab. She made the rounds with his former friends and even a couple of his past girlfriends. She managed to gather six people, including her younger sister, Regina. There were three young men who had attended high school with Arnold and two of his old girlfriends—only six people other than herself who didn't want to see him drink and drug himself to death. Arnold came to the house one afternoon, thinking that his mother was going to give him a check to help him buy a car. Instead, he was confronted with faces he hadn't seen in years, everyone pleading for him to get help. First, he was stunned. He sat quietly, listening and watching as they told their stories. They loved him, and they missed the Arnold they once knew, a happy-go-lucky guy with a big heart. Please get help, they all begged. Even his icy Aunt Regina had been emotional: eyes wet, mouth drawn tight. When it became clear to him that he would not be receiving a check that afternoon, he stormed out of his mother's house, cursing them all and smashing his coffee mug to the floor as he left.

And now it's all over, A. C. thought, still seated on the small padded bench in front of her bureau. *My Arnold is gone.* The familiar gasp that always preceded her crying spells rushed through her lips, but no sobs followed. A. C. closed her eyes and lowered her head to her chest. *I don't think I'll ever be able to cry again,* she thought, both surprised and relieved by how numb and cold she felt. She imagined herself as the dry husk of the woman she had once been. If a strong wind blew through the house, she would be caught in the gust and whip through the air like an empty paper sack before disintegrating into dust.

I never got to say good-bye to my husband or my son, A. C. thought, the tears at last spilling from her eyes and ruining her fresh makeup. *Everyone I love is gone.* She rose on shaky legs and stumbled to her bed, where she let herself fall back on the mattress. A. C. pulled her knees up to her chin and wept into her bedspread for what felt like hours. She cried herself into a deep and dreamless sleep.

Chapter Five

Regina shook her sister's shoulder gently. "A. C., wake up, honey. It's past brunch time," she coaxed, trying to sound cheerful.

She shifted awkwardly from one foot to the other, impatient for A. C. to open her eyes. She never felt quite right when she tried to comfort anyone, even her own sister. She remembered all too well the same sense of helplessness and unease she felt when Calvin died nine years prior. She threw herself into making arrangements for Calvin's family to attend his funeral, cleaning up around A. C. and Calvin's home, and making sure A. C. had something to eat at least once a day. Regina was so exhausted after Calvin's funeral that she fell ill and had to stay in bed for nearly a week. But it had been worth it, she thought. At least she hadn't been forced too often to search for the right words to say to her grieving sister. What was there to say? A. C. had the perfect husband for over thirty years, and then one day he suffered a massive heart attack, lingered in a hospital bed for a short while, and was gone forever two days later. What could be said to console someone after such a loss? And what could she say to her sister now, with both her husband and her only child buried?

A. C. groaned and stirred beneath Regina's hand.

"Regina?" she asked groggily.

"Yes, dear, it's me. Want me to help you freshen up?"

A. C. blinked her eyes, trying to clear the sleep from them. She seemed confused for a minute, but then a sad realization settled on her delicate features. She peered up at her sister, who loomed tall and imposing over her. Regina had once been a lovely waif of a girl, but her sharp features had become birdlike over the years. Most people thought Regina had a unique beauty when she was young, but the lines around her eyes shrunk them into hard, beady pellets, especially when she smiled or cried. Her long, pointed nose, inherited from their father's side of the family, once resembled the noble profile on a Roman coin, but now it jutted from her face like a sharp beak.

"No, thanks," A. C. answered. "Just let me wash my face and put on a little powder and lipstick. I'll be ready to go in five minutes. You want a cup of coffee? The pot's probably still warm from this morning."

Regina suppressed a sneer. *Who wants stale coffee in the middle of the day?* she wondered. She never could stand the way A. C. didn't wash her breakfast dishes immediately after breakfast.

"I'll pour myself a glass of water and wait for you in the kitchen. Take your time," she responded in what she hoped was a soothing tone.

Regina strolled leisurely through the upstairs hallway and down the long staircase, admiring the paintings A. C. had chosen for the walls and the antiques scattered throughout the home. *Even if she doesn't keep house as well as she should, I have to give her credit for her taste,* Regina thought, frowning at a layer of dust on A. C.'s china cabinet. In the kitchen, she dumped out the lukewarm coffee, washed the coffee pot, and rummaged through the refrigerator, pulling out eggs that were past their expiration date and half a bag of shriveled oranges.

"What a mess," she muttered with a sigh. She threw out the stale food and tried to arrange everything in the refrigerator tidily.

"What are you doing?"

Regina jumped at the sound of her sister's voice. She hadn't heard A. C. come down the stairs. She closed the refrigerator door and spun around to face A. C.

"Oh, nothing much, just straightening up a bit for you," she said with a nervous little laugh.

"I didn't ask you to straighten up," A. C. said coolly.

"You don't have to ask! I'm your sister; that's what I'm here for." Regina flashed a gracious smile. "And you don't even have to thank me for washing your dishes," she teased, nodding toward the freshly scrubbed coffee pot that sat in the dish rack. "In fact, I was just thinking that I'm going to talk to Sonja, the woman who cleans for me, and get her to start coming over here. At least twice a week," she added, appraising the kitchen with narrowed eyes and pursed lips.

A. C. grimaced but didn't otherwise acknowledge the coffee pot. "What did you just throw away?" she asked.

"Oh, just some spoiled food. Really, you shouldn't just let old food sit in your refrigerator. It will start to smell, and then everything else in there will smell."

A. C. glared at Regina for moment before stalking over to the waste basket and snatching the lid off the top. She rummaged through the bin and yanked the egg carton and bag of oranges from it.

"What are you doing?" Regina cried. She hurried over to A. C.'s side. "You're getting yourself filthy!" she scolded. "It's just old food! Leave it in there. You'll get sick if you eat it, especially now."

She tried taking the egg carton and netted bag of oranges from her sister, but A. C. jerked them away, her eyes blazing. Damp coffee grains clung to her wrists and the cuffs of her blouse.

"I am not your child, Regina, and I am not so old and feeble that I can't decide what I should and should not eat. This is my house, and I'll keep whatever I want keep in my own damn refrigerator!"

They stared at one another, A. C. furious and Regina shocked. Finally, Regina closed her gaping mouth and seemed to recover somewhat.

"A. C., honey," she began gently, trying to sound as relaxed and confident as possible, "you're overreacting. I know it's the grief talking. Why don't you just set those things down, go upstairs, wash your hands, change your blouse, and I'll clean this up and then take you out for lunch. We'll get a nice big meal at whatever restaurant you want. I can even make you a cup of tea while you're upstairs, okay? Doesn't that sound lovely?" Her words were slow and syrupy, as if she was prodding along a fussy child. She attempted a smile, but it looked more like her mouth was twitching.

A. C. was quiet for a moment and seemed to be considering her sister's instructions. Regina was hopeful. *A. C. just needs someone to be firm with her*, she thought. Without a word, A. C. let the food she was holding slip from her grasp and land on the kitchen floor with a splat.

"Oh, dear," Regina sighed. "You could have just set them on the counter, you know," she scolded. "Just as well. Take your time getting ready. I'll take care of this." She began to make her way to the cabinet where the cleaning supplies were kept.

"You'll do nothing of the sort," A. C. announced. "In fact, what you're going to do right now is find your way out of my house and leave me be for the rest of the day. No, the rest of the week! You helped me get through Arnold's service," she paused, fighting not to break down, "but then I had to tolerate that miserable reception you insisted was necessary—you and your in-laws parading through my home and gawking at me like I'm a Goddamn museum exhibit!" She ignored Regina's gasp and continued, "As for the food on my floor and whatever else is in my kitchen, it's my business! I'll leave it on the floor for an entire year if I want. Maybe the next time you come over, it will be so rotten it will have melted into the tiles and become a permanent part of my house. I am not your child, Regina. I am not your charge, and I can keep my house however I please."

She paused to catch her breath, her eyes never moving from Regina's stunned face.

Regina's voice trembled when she finally spoke. "Fine," was all she could manage. She snatched her alligator skin handbag from the counter and stomped out of the kitchen and out of the house.

Chapter Six

A. C. stood absolutely still for a few minutes after Regina slammed the front door behind her. She heard Regina's car start and speed away. Her heartbeat slowed down after a minute but seemed too loud in her ears. She looked around her kitchen, feeling dizzy and weak.

"Damn her," she cursed, glaring at the coffee pot that Regina had washed. A. C. could have used a cup of coffee just then. She often enjoyed having a cup of what was left over from breakfast. The flavor of the coffee grew stronger after a few hours, and she drank it sweet and dark.

She filled up her tea kettle and set it to boil on the stove. Purely out of spite, she left the oranges and eggs on her kitchen floor. A strange thought entered her mind as she waited for the water to boil. *At least Arnold isn't going to rot like that food.* She felt guilty and relieved at the same time. *What kind of a person am I,* she wondered, *to think such a thing?* But at the same time, there was comfort in knowing that Arnold's grave held an urn filled with ashes and not a box with a decaying body in it.

"My baby," she whispered, tears sliding down her face. "My poor baby."

While she waited for the water to boil, she wandered into the living room to look at her picture wall. There were dozens of them, each photograph in a carefully chosen frame, some dating back to her parents' grandparents' lives. At the moment, A. C. was interested only in her late husband. She gazed up at Calvin's handsome face. Her favorite picture of Calvin was the one of him carving their first Thanksgiving turkey and smiling like a madman. A. C. couldn't help but grin at the photo in spite of her tears.

"I miss you so much, Cal. God, every minute of every day! But," her voice broke and she had to pause for a few seconds, "as much as I need you by my side, I wouldn't wish enduring the death of a child on my worst enemy."

She took slow steps to examine the entire collection of family photographs, paying special attention to the shots of Calvin and Arnold. Grief was a strange beast. Sometimes, she laughed out loud as she remembered the funny stories that went along with certain photos. The next minute, she found herself weeping uncontrollably. It was too painful to look at Calvin's pictures for very long, even nine years after his death. A. C. returned to the kitchen and prepared a large mug of tea for herself. She brought her tea into the living room and stretched out on her favorite couch, thinking only of Calvin and Arnold.

Calvin Browne was the first in his family to pursue higher education. After earning his bachelor's degree, he found a job as a foreman in a plastic manufacturing company a couple of towns away from his hometown. He was bright and hardworking, and over the years he worked his way up through the ranks.

At the age of twenty-eight, Calvin was promoted to personnel manager. His mother worried that he would never settle down and she would never have grandchildren because he was always working. She commiserated with a family friend whose daughter, Augustine, at the ripe old age of twenty-five, seemed more content being an elementary school teacher than finding a husband. After much cajoling, Calvin finally agreed to go on a date with Augustine, hoping that it would quiet his mother's nagging for a while. Dinner and a movie but no coffee afterwards, he told himself as he knocked on Augustine's apartment door. After his mother had repeatedly described Augustine as "sweet and attractive," Calvin expected a dumpy looking woman who probably had an annoying laugh, bad teeth, or worse, but he found himself immediately smitten when Ms. Augustine Carrington answered the door. She preferred to go by A. C. because Augustine sounded like an old woman's name, she said with a laugh. Her laughter was lovely and delicate, just like the rest of her. She had large hazel eyes, which were both kind and wise, thick, auburn hair that she wore in a smart French twist, and a generous handful of freckles sprinkled across her face, which she said she hated, but Calvin found adorable.

A. C. didn't immediately find Calvin handsome, but when he smiled, a large, somewhat crooked grin, his light brown eyes turned up in the corners and his face became the irresistibly charming face of a young, mischievous boy. He was very tall, and although he was on the thin side, she admired his broad, strong-looking shoulders. He kept his sandy brown hair short and neat and could easily grow a full beard, but he preferred to be clean shaven. A. C. found the shadow of a beard on Calvin's face sexy but was glad he preferred not to grow one. She liked seeing his strong chin and well-defined cheek bones. A. C. had dated men who were more handsome than Calvin, but none of them gave her the little jolt of electricity she felt the instant she shook his hand for the first time.

They had only been dating four months when Calvin proposed to her. He hadn't even meant to ask her to marry him that May afternoon when they went on a picnic in the foothills. The proposal just slipped out. A. C. had surprised him with a homemade peach pie, and he kissed her on the nose and blurted out, "You would make the perfect wife, A. C. I want you to marry me." For the longest moment, A. C. simply gazed into his face with her warm, olive-colored eyes.

Calvin was on the verge of apologizing and taking back the impromptu proposal when she finally whispered, "There's nothing I'd like more, Calvin, than to be your wife."

Friends and family alike speculated that Calvin must have gotten A. C. *in trouble*. "He's a good man, doing the honorable thing and marrying her," they all said. Calvin's mother was secretly thrilled at the idea of finally having a grandchild. People barely managed to conceal their surprise when seven, eight, finally nine months after the wedding, there was no baby.

Two years later, when A. C. and Calvin did have a baby, both sides of the family were thrilled. A. C. and Calvin were in love with their son. He was a beautiful baby. A. C. knew that all mothers thought their babies were the most gorgeous children ever to grace the face of the earth, but she also knew that her son was genuinely handsome. His was not a face that only a mother could love. Everywhere Calvin and A. C. took their little boy, people complimented his thick reddish-brown hair, just like mom's; his big golden brown eyes, inherited from Calvin; and the infectious laugh that was all his own.

Arnold was a friendly child, outgoing and popular in school. His grades weren't the best, but that was only because he put more effort into becoming the most well-liked boy in his class than he put into studying. Girls began to notice Arnold when he was a teenager, and he noticed them right back. A. C. was proud that while other fourteen-year-old boys were awkward, gangly things covered in pimples, her son was already tall and muscular, with a clear face and a firm, deep voice. *Just like his father,* she often thought when she looked at him.

Arnold was athletically inclined and played varsity football when he was only a sophomore in high school. The coach told Calvin and A. C. that their son could win a football scholarship to the college of his choosing, no problem. His parents could not have been more proud. He dated the prettiest girls, took the football team to the state championship two years in a row, and even brought up his grades. Then it all came crashing down. Arnold's senior year of high school was the beginning of the end, A. C. realized many years later.

His problems, at first, seemed like ordinary high school problems. He went to a party one weekend, which was nothing unusual. His classmates often had weekend parties. Calvin and A. C. weren't naïve; they had been teenagers once. While the hairstyles, slang, and music may have changed, the kids remained the same. They imagined their son had been alone with girls, kissing and possibly more, but so far, he had been responsible.

This particular party was to celebrate the football team's homecoming game victory. Arnold didn't come home that night. By Sunday morning, A. C. was in tears, and Calvin was quietly frantic. They called his friends' parents, and Calvin was just about to broach the subject of calling local hospitals, when a cab delivered their still drunk son to their doorstep. Arnold reeked of stale alcohol and marijuana. Calvin gave his son a long, loud talking-to, and A. C. said her piece, as well. Arnold seemed contrite enough, or maybe he was just too intoxicated to put up much of a fight. After they were all talked out, A. C. and Calvin sent their nearly full-grown son to his room, where he slept for much of the rest of the day.

Things went back to normal in the Browne household for a while. A. C. and Calvin believed the nasty episode was just something that all teenage boys went through, especially during their final year of high school. Everything seemed fine for several weeks. Arnold was still one of the football team's star players. He was attending all of his classes, and his attitude at home was satisfactory. After four straight weekends of staying home, A. C. and Calvin felt their son had learned his lesson and allowed him to spend Saturday night out with his friends. That evening turned out to be the first time they bailed him out of jail.

He'd been caught trying to break into his own house after losing his wallet and keys. The police didn't believe Arnold when he'd insisted, in a drunken slur, that he lived in the house. Calvin and A. C. had to wait for hours at the precinct while Arnold was booked and processed.

A. C. cried several times, soaking both her own and Calvin's handkerchief with makeup and tears. Calvin alternated between saying, "We should leave his butt in here and teach him a lesson, damn it," and, "Where did we go wrong? I can't believe our boy is in jail. We have to get him out of here." Calvin paced the small waiting area and barked at the police officers who manned the phones and front desk. They paid him little mind. They were used to dealing with irate, bewildered parents.

At home the next morning, a sheepish, red-eyed Arnold promised that he wouldn't bow to peer pressure again. He volunteered to give up football as his punishment. Calvin and A. C. were taken aback by their son's outpouring. They had expected him to be sullen and defiant, not contrite and tearful. They both immediately nixed Arnold's suggestion. Football was, after all, a possible ticket toward a college scholarship, if the arrest on his record hadn't ruined that. Instead, he would have to get a part-time job to pay back the money, and he would not be allowed to spend time with his friends after school or on the weekends for three months. Arnold was reluctant to agree to this, but Calvin began to raise his voice, and A. C. made it clear that she agreed with Calvin. Arnold gave in and promised to report for duty on Monday after school. He would work at the plastic manufacturing company where Calvin had recently been promoted to the board of directors. Arnold complained that his co-workers would take an immediate disliking to him because he was an executive's son. Calvin didn't disagree with Arnold. In fact, he knew that Arnold was probably right, and he thought of it as part of the punishment.

Arnold worked as an errand boy at Plasti-Corp for the next several months. To Calvin's disappointment, Arnold wasn't resented because of his status as a director's son. On the contrary, Arnold made fast friends with several of the employees, just as he always had in school. His grades slipped considerably, but he maintained them just enough to avoid failing any of his classes. Both Calvin and A. C. suspected that their son was still drinking and possibly even doing drugs, but they couldn't prove anything. They felt helpless as they watched their once peppy, ambitious son transform into a surly, indifferent young man who rarely spent time at home.

By the end of his senior year in high school, he'd been thrown off the football team for missing games and cutting classes.

His shot at a football scholarship was gone. He was just barely eligible to graduate with his class, but neither Arnold nor his parents attended the ceremony. Arnold slept in on the day of his graduation, completely uninterested in going through the motions with his classmates. A. C. and Calvin were too ashamed and distraught to play the parts of enthusiastic parents at their son's high school graduation ceremony.

By then, Arnold had alienated most of his high school buddies. He was an embarrassment to his old crowd. They were headed for college or a year in Europe, and he was working in a factory and hanging out with people who were arrested regularly and partied on a daily basis. Arnold met lots of other people through his new friends. A. C. and Calvin didn't approve of any of their son's new associates. They were all too old for him, his parents insisted, and they didn't have any plans for the future. Some of them even had criminal backgrounds. Calvin eventually fired his own son as a last-ditch effort at keeping Arnold away from the unsavory people who now dominated his time. The plan backfired. Arnold was furious with his father, and after a heated yelling match with Calvin, he stormed out of his parents' house and moved into a shabby apartment that he shared with several of his new friends. A. C. begged Arnold not to leave, but Arnold insisted that he wanted nothing more out of life than to get away from his father's control.

Calvin and A. C. fought bitterly the night that Arnold moved out of the house. It was, perhaps, the worst quarrel of their entire marriage. Each blamed the other for Arnold's downfall. A. C. accused Calvin of pressuring Arnold into a mold that was wrong for him. Just because Calvin wanted to be a football star and go to college on a sports scholarship, that didn't mean that Arnold should, she told him. Calvin was trying to live vicariously through his son, she tearfully charged. For his part, Calvin lambasted A. C. for always being so easy on Arnold. She babied him, spoiled him rotten, he accused.

Calvin slept in one of the guest rooms for nearly a week after Arnold left. He and A. C. didn't speak a single word to each other for three days. He came home from work one afternoon and found A. C. in the backyard, dressed in her gardening clothes and sobbing over a bed of flowers. The resentment he'd been harboring against her since the night that Arnold left melted away. He gathered his wife into his arms and carried her inside their house. She didn't resist. They wept together in their bedroom, wondering aloud where they had gone wrong as parents and apologizing to each other again and again for the mistakes they each believed they had made. They made love that night, a tender and strangely bittersweet encounter, and then both fell into a deep sleep afterwards.

A. C. and Calvin managed not to fall out of love with one another as Arnold continued his steady decline into the world of hard living and constant partying. Once in a while, in weak moments, they gave him money, even though they knew he was only going to spend it on booze and drugs. Arnold worked unsteadily throughout the years. They saw him most holidays, and after a while, they all tried to pretend that nothing was wrong. Even Regina, A. C.'s self righteous, prudish younger sister, went along with the charade that they were a normal, happy family.

Over the years, A. C. and Calvin occasionally met a few of Arnold's girlfriends. They all seemed to live the same lifestyle that Arnold lived, so A. C. and Calvin never truly felt happy about their son's relationships. Privately, A. C. used to pray for Arnold to meet a straight-laced young lady who would win his love and inspire him to change his life. It never happened.

A. C. remembered one of Arnold's girlfriend's in particular. Her name was Joan Coyle. Arnold brought her to the house for his parents' twenty-ninth anniversary party. A. C. had planned a fancy, catered dinner. She wanted it to be a celebration for Calvin, who was not only turning fifty-seven that month, but had just been promoted to vice president of the company. It should have been a jubilant time for them, but every occasion that should have been a happy one for the past several years had been overshadowed by Arnold's behavior.

Arnold did show up for the celebratory dinner that A. C. had taken such pains to plan. Much to his parents' delight, Arnold appeared to be sober, recently showered, and dressed in clean clothes. He'd brought someone with him. He never actually introduced her as his girlfriend or even his friend; he simply presented her as Joan. It was obvious to A. C. and Calvin that Joan was more than a friend to their son. They were both ashamed of the long, deep kisses Arnold and Joan shared throughout the evening. At one point, A. C. even saw Joan nibble on Arnold's ear. She was annoyed with Arnold and chagrined by his vulgar behavior, but the lion's share of her wrath was focused on Joan.

From the moment Joan Coyle stepped foot in the Brownes' home, A. C. disliked her. It would have been a struggle, but she may have been able to look past the younger woman's badly dyed hair, garish makeup, and skin-tight clothes. What really bothered her was that Joan was so obviously fixated on the furniture and décor in their house. Joan was even brazen enough to ask how much they'd paid for certain items.

A. C. tried to divert Joan's bold questions with small talk. She asked Joan where she was from and if she came from a large family. Simple and safe enough questions, she thought at the time. Joan seemed to take A. C.'s inquiries as a personal attack.

She snapped that both her parents were dead; her mother had died when Joan was a baby, and her father, she claimed, worked himself to death on the assembly line of a factory. A. C. muttered an offer of condolences and excused herself to greet more guests.

Months passed, and the next time A. C. and Calvin saw Arnold, he had a new girlfriend and hardly seemed to recall Joan. He looked more run-down and haggard each time his parents saw him. It broke their hearts to witness their once handsome, strapping young son decay into a languid, gaunt drug addict who cared for no one, not even himself. More than once after his visits to the house, A. C. noticed that a piece of her jewelry was missing, or sometimes it was a knickknack. She never told Calvin about the missing items. What good would it do? she reasoned. They hadn't seen him for more than six months when Calvin had his heart attack.

A. C. never left Calvin's side for more than a couple of minutes at a time while he was in the hospital. She hardly slept, ate very little, and was only away from her husband long enough to use the restroom. It was up to Regina to track down Arnold. A. C. gave her younger sister a list of all of the names and phone numbers she'd compiled over the years: his wayward friends and girlfriends, the various places where he'd worked, and even a couple of homeless shelters where he spent the occasional night. Regina finally acquired a solid lead on the whereabouts of her nephew by offering cash to one of his former girlfriends. In exchange, the woman told Regina about a seedy bar where Arnold was a regular.

Regina drove by the bar just once before deciding it was too dank and frightening an establishment for her to enter, even though her brother-in-law was on his deathbed. She enlisted the aid of her mousy husband, Laurence. She ordered him to go into the bar, find Arnold, and bring him back to the hospital. Laurence, as always, complied with his wife's wishes, but Arnold wasn't there. The bartender, after being persuaded by a twenty dollar bill, claimed he hadn't seen Arnold in nearly a week. Regina and Laurence returned to the hospital empty handed, but at least they were with A. C. when Calvin passed away.

To a great extent, A. C.'s life ended when Calvin's did. She became nearly catatonic for several days following his death. Regina immersed herself in making plans for the funeral, and Laurence, for his part, continued the search for Arnold. He finally managed to track him down at construction site where Arnold was temporarily employed.

Arnold seemed stunned by the news of his father's demise. He went with his Uncle Laurence to his mother's house with no fuss. By then, Calvin had been dead for nearly a month. A. C. was finally out of bed and moving around and, in fact, was waiting on Regina, who had fallen ill after overexerting herself after Calvin died. A. C. spent several days in Regina's house, taking care of her. Regina reluctantly agreed to let Arnold stay for a little while, too. She didn't trust him but couldn't bear to admit that to her sister after everything A. C. had gone through.

A. C. didn't know what to say to Arnold, and Arnold, it seemed, felt the same. She was furious with him for not being around while his father was in the hospital, but she also longed to hold him. If she could just touch him, run her fingers over his face and through his hair, and look into his eyes—his father's eyes—then she would have a little bit of Calvin back. She wanted to cry into his chest the way she had cried into Calvin's so many times, usually about Arnold. The guilt Arnold felt was obvious, but it meant little to A. C. She never outright asked him where he had been while his father was dying in a hospital bed. She knew the answer. He had been living his selfish, drug-hazed life, thinking of nothing more than his next high.

Arnold kept his mother company at her own house and Regina's house for three agonizing days. He tried to go through the motions of grieving and helping his mother take care of his aunt. He told A. C. many times that he was sorry, so terribly sorry, for not being there when she needed him. She said little to him during his short stay. She kept herself occupied caring for Regina and running errands. During those three grueling days, Arnold would disappear for hours at a time and would reappear at the house somewhat calmer, his eyes glazed over. When Arnold didn't return after dinner one evening, A. C. felt an odd sense of relief. It didn't escape her that his departure was just the same day she'd meted out a considerable amount of cash to him. It was a small portion of his share from Calvin's will. It was against her better judgment to give cash to Arnold, but it was rightfully his. She realized that whether or not she gave him the money, he wasn't going to change and would only find other means to feed his addiction. But it was the last time A. C. ever gave her son cash.

She didn't see him for nearly a year after that. During those months, she hated herself for giving him money at all. *What kind of a person am I? What kind of a mother?* she berated herself. *Not only did I raise a drug addict, but I'm helping him kill himself by just handing over his father's hard-earned money*. She thought of Calvin and the pride he took in his career and in providing a comfortable life for his family. *I wasn't in my right mind,* she thought often. *I wasn't thinking straight when I gave Arnold that money. Calvin was only just buried, Regina was sick, and I could barely manage to dress myself in the morning, let alone worry about what Arnold was doing. He took advantage of me. That's all he's been doing for years: taking, taking, taking.* A. C. could go on like this for hours and often did. For several months after Calvin's death, she was torn between loathing herself for what her son had become and loathing her son for the anguish he'd caused his family.

Although it was one of the most frightening decisions A. C. had ever made, she went to see a psychiatrist shortly after Calvin's death. Talking to an educated stranger about one's most intimate thoughts, fears, and experiences was unheard of for A. C.'s parents' generation. "Shrinks are only for nutcases and perverts," she once recalled her father remarking when he learned that a second cousin had been to a therapist. A. C.'s mother generally went along with whatever her husband said. Some of A. C.'s friends had tried therapy, but even then, it was a very hush-hush thing. People she knew only went when their marriages were on the rocks or when they had crawled into a bottle and needed help getting out of it.

She found a doctor in a city several miles away, and she made sure the psychiatrist was a woman. Her first meeting with Dr. Meyer was strained, but not because of anything Dr. Meyer did or said. At first, A. C. sat rigidly in the armchair across from the doctor, smiling politely and making small talk. Dr. Meyer encouraged her to relax and just say whatever came to mind or to talk about what prompted her to make the appointment in the first place. Their hour was nearly up by the time she was finally able to bring up Arnold's drift into a lifestyle of drugs and crime. Dr. Meyer, a kind woman with dark, intelligent eyes and a warm smile, let A. C. continue talking long after their hour had expired. A. C. was her last patient of the day, and she could tell the woman needed time to get used to the idea of seeing a therapist. A. C. saw Dr. Meyer steadily for several months, and then periodically for a number of years.

It was under Dr. Meyer's guidance that A. C. arranged the intervention for Arnold. A. C. remained skeptical throughout the planning, but she felt she owed it to herself, to Calvin, and to Arnold, to try. Dr. Meyer was a firm believer in the power of interventions. Some people didn't realize how much they actually wanted help and wanted to live a clean and sober life unless they were directly confronted by people who know and love them, she told A. C. several times. She also told A. C. about the many intervention success stories she had witnessed over the years.

When the intervention that A. C. had precariously undertaken fell flat on its face, she was crushed. Dr. Meyer told her not to let the setback beat her. They could try again, she insisted. But A. C. didn't have the energy or the faith to organize another intervention for Arnold. She also didn't think she could get any of Arnold's old friends to go another round. It had been difficult enough to coax any of them to participate in the first one.

Her visits to Dr. Meyer's office dwindled and finally lapsed completely in the months following the failed intervention. For a while, A. C. felt very bitter toward Dr. Meyer. She lamented that all the time and money spent in therapy was a waste. Regina echoed these sentiments. "I don't know why you bothered seeing a shrink in the first place," Regina often said. "It's not as if you're a crazy person. Imagine what Mother and Daddy would say!" At that point, A. C. didn't care what her parents would think about her decision to try psychotherapy. She was disappointed, although not surprised, that Regina's biggest concern seemed to be what people would think if they found out her sister was seeing a counselor.

Over time, A. C.'s resentment toward Dr. Meyer waned. It wasn't the doctor's fault that Arnold wasn't receptive to getting help. She had gone to Dr. Meyer for herself, and that part of her treatment had been a success. A. C. felt better about herself than she had in a very long time. Therapy had refined her strength and given her the tools she needed to get through some of the darkest days she had ever known. In spite of this, when Arnold died, A. C. realized that all of the therapy in the world could not ease the deep and constant ache within a mother's chest after the death of her child. She had been in mourning for the loss of Arnold's potential for years, long before his physical death. But that grief seemed trite when compared to the grief she felt when his life ended.

The memory of the evening when A. C. learned of Arnold's death would never fade as time passed. She had been watching the evening news when a uniformed policeman came to her door. His loud knock had startled her. She wasn't expecting anyone, and it was dark outside. She had the strongest urge to call out, "Cal, honey, will you see who's at the door?" Looking back, she thought it was appropriate that she should think to call out for Calvin, considering the news the policeman brought. Maybe Calvin had been with her when she heard that their son was found dead from an overdose in a seedy motel room.

She imagined sometimes that Calvin watched over her. It was usually a comforting thought, but nothing could have soothed A. C. that night. The officer gave her a lift to the hospital morgue, and she was given the option of seeing Arnold one last time. He wasn't in an advanced state of decay, the coroner told her. Arnold had been dead less than a day when he was found by a maid. A. C. knew that many mothers would demand to see their children one last time regardless of the condition of the body. She was about to nod her consent to viewing the remains, but she hesitated for a moment and suddenly found herself murmuring, "No. That won't be necessary." The voice seemed to come from someone else. She remembered feeling oddly disconnected in the chilly office. No matter what the coroner thought her son looked like, A. C. knew that Arnold would, indeed, be in an advanced state of decay to his mother's eyes.

A. C. could lie on the couch no longer. She'd had two cups of jasmine green tea, her favorite. The room, though spacious and airy, was beginning to feel like a like a cave. She swallowed what was left of her tea in one gulp and took her mug back to the kitchen. With a sigh, A. C. rolled her eyes and cleaned up the oranges and eggs from the kitchen floor, feeling both incredulous and wryly amused that her little sister still managed to get on her nerves, despite the fact that they were both in their sixties.

It was a gorgeous day outside, and A. C. decided that she needed fresh air. *I've been indoors too much lately*, she thought. *I need sunshine; to hell with melanoma*—although she sprayed herself liberally with sun block and donned a straw hat and sunglasses. There was a nice park just a few blocks away from her house: Mastic Crossing, nestled snugly between the section of large, majestic homes where A. C. lived. There was also a shopping center less than a mile away; if she became hungry, she could stop for lunch at the food court. She packed a bottle of water, a bag of chilled grapes, a couple of magazines, and a word puzzle book. The instant warmth that enveloped her when she stepped outside felt wonderful. There was almost something affectionate about it, like an embrace from an old friend. She ambled toward the park at a relaxed pace, her step considerably lighter than it had been in a while.

Chapter Seven

Browsing in the mall was a pleasant experience, especially when it was early enough that very few customers were out and about. Carrington felt less self-conscious when there were fewer people around; she didn't have to worry what they thought of her clothes and shoes. Most of the sales clerks seemed too busy or too tired to take much notice of her at all, and she was grateful for it.

She wandered through the collection of shops slowly, taking time to look at the clothes, perfume, shoes, and jewelry that she rarely had time or opportunity to admire. It made her feel both hopeful and deflated. Maybe one day she would be able to wear attractive, high quality clothes and jewelry, but it was difficult to imagine living any other way than the way she had been raised. It wasn't that she didn't realize that some people were filthy rich or even comfortably well off; at school, she had a glimpse into the lives of kids whose families were well-to-do. What was next to impossible for Carrington to imagine was how *she* would ever be able to rise above her past and live a life where she didn't have to scrounge for money and feel ashamed of the way she looked.

While she was admiring a sundress in the juniors' department, she overheard a brief exchange between a middle-aged woman and one of the sales ladies. The older lady wanted assistance in picking out a bracelet, a graduation present for her niece, she explained. *A gift*, Carrington thought. *I should bring a gift when I introduce myself to Mrs. Browne. It might help break the ice, and it would just be an overall nice gesture. She's my grandmother, after all. Probably.*

But what should she buy for an older woman whom she'd never met? What would be neutral enough that most anyone would appreciate it, but not so impersonal that it would be dull? And what could she reasonably afford? She wasn't about to spend every last penny on any one thing, certainly not something as frivolous as a present. But it couldn't be a cheap trinket, either.

She continued wandering around the mall, beginning to feel frantic. *Maybe it's a dumb idea to buy a present for Mrs. Browne*, Carrington thought sadly. It was going to be strange enough showing up on this woman's doorstep, claiming to be her long lost granddaughter. Wouldn't bringing a gift only make the situation even more awkward? She was about to give up on the mall entirely and head toward Mrs. Browne's house when something caught her attention. The women who worked behind the makeup counter in one of the more upscale stores were having trouble erecting an enormous cardboard sign on a flimsy stand. Emblazoned on the sign were the words "All Mother's Day Gift Baskets Reduced 70%." Carrington gazed at the large collection of perfume and bath sets arranged on a counter. Seventy percent off? Even if she found one that originally cost as much as forty dollars, it would be less than fifteen dollars with tax.

Carrington had received a body wash and perfumed lotion gift basket once. Her seventh grade homeroom teacher, Mrs.

Florenz, gave it to her for her birthday. She asked Carrington to stay after school and then presented it to her after all the other students had gone home. Carrington's eyes had filled with tears when she saw it, and Mrs. Florenz gave her a big hug. It was one of the nicest presents she'd ever received, but when she brought it home, Joan thought it was shady. "What is she, some kinda lesbo pedophile?" she had demanded. Carrington tearfully suggested returning it to Mrs. Florenz, but Joan decided that wouldn't be necessary. Instead, she kept the creamy, perfumed body wash for herself. She gave the miniature soaps shaped like roses to Missy, and allowed Carrington to keep the bottle of lotion and the empty basket.

Carrington face burned at the memory. Mother's Day had come and gone with no notice in her house. She wouldn't have bought Joan a gift even if she had all the money in the world. Missy didn't mention it, and Joan never brought up the subject. A gift basket for her potential grandmother would be the perfect present, Carrington decided. If and when she ever did have to return to Joan's custody, she would somehow let her mother know that she'd given Mrs. Browne a Mother's Day present.

She sampled all of the different fragrances in the discounted gift baskets and found that she didn't really like any of them. They were too flowery or too musky; some even smelled like cheap deodorant. A dull ache began to throb behind Carrington's forehead. She thought that if she sniffed one more bottle of scented lotion or perfumed body wash, she would vomit. She meandered toward the food court, where she purchased a chilled bottle of a green tea energy drink from one of the restaurants. It was her favorite thing to drink, and she bought one from the corner grocery store in her neighborhood whenever she could manage it. She had always loved the aroma of green tea.

Carrington sat for several minutes at one of the tables in the food court, sipping her tea and watching a wave of customers—lots of young mothers, older women, and a handful of teenagers—fill the mall. *Maybe a gift basket is a bad idea*, she considered. *Maybe this whole thing is a bad idea.* Soon, she was on the verge of tears. *I could catch a bus now and be back before Joan ever gets home*, Carrington thought. *She would never know that I had even considered going to see Mrs. Browne on my own. Neither would Missy.* She imagined creeping back into the house while Missy slept and scrubbing off the makeup. She thought of what was beneath the makeup, and the drunken expression of rage on her mother's face. *There's no going back now*, Carrington decided, finishing her tea.

There was a man setting up a display on one of the nearby kiosks. She watched curiously as he arranged dozens of bottles, all different sizes and colors, and a sign that read "Green Tea, Mango, Apple, and Lilac Lotions, Perfumes, Shampoo, and More!" Carrington dropped her empty tea bottle in the garbage and strode over to his setup. He was busy arranging everything just so, but offered her a smile of encouragement when she lifted a bottle of green-tea-scented lotion to her nose. She unscrewed the cap and inhaled. Heavenly! Carrington decided then and there that someday, when she had her own house, she would buy green-tea-scented everything: hand lotion, shampoo, even dish soap. She gladly handed over enough money for the bottle of lotion and a bottle of shampoo. The man seemed so pleased to have a customer that he added a small gift bag, free of charge. *If Mrs. Browne doesn't like it, I'll use them*, she decided, feeling somewhat cheerful.

Carrington stopped in the mall restroom to comb her hair and touch up her makeup. Her black eye was still fairly obvious, even with Joan's liquid foundation smeared over it, and there was a line of dried blood on her lip. She picked away the blood on her lip, flinching at the sting. *It's now or never*, she thought. *The earlier I get there, the better. The more time I'll have before Joan realizes I'm gone, and the more time I'll have to talk to Mrs. Browne before Joan tries to talk to her*. She took one final look at herself in the restroom mirror, adjusting the too-large blouse and parting her long hair so that it covered the bandage on her hairline. *I guess it's time to find my grandmother's house*, she decided, forcing herself to leave the restroom.

Outside, she dug through Joan's purse until she found Mrs. Browne's address. She walked toward one of the side roads off of the mall parking lot and squinted against the sunlight to read the street sign. This was it. This was the road that would lead to the street where Mrs. Browne lived.

Chapter Eight

Carrington decided to rest for a few minutes in a park, Mastic Crossing, which was roughly halfway between the mall and Mrs. Browne's house. She regretted wearing one of Joan's blouses. The cool morning had long since become a hot afternoon. Her back was soon sticky with sweat beneath the heavy fabric. She longed for one of her own T-shirts, worn out as they were. At least she would have been comfortable.

The park was lovely. It was filled with giant trees that had probably been around longer than many of the houses in the area. The lawn was well manicured and boasted dozens of brilliant flowerbeds. A well-shaded bicycle path wove its way through the park, even looping around the park's twin ponds, one at each end.

Carrington was torn. She longed to find a quiet place under a tree, far away from the happy sounds of children in the playground—a shady spot where she could close her eyes for a few minutes and just breathe. She was tired and nervous, and the grass looked cool and soft. On the other hand, she knew that she had come too far to wait much longer. Her gut began to ache with the growing, gnawing fear that Joan would soon be looking for Mrs. Browne, too. And for Carrington.

She compromised with herself. She spotted a row of wooden benches a few yards from the playground area where only a few other people lounged. She could have a bench to herself, but she wouldn't be completely isolated. She would have preferred a picnic table, but the mothers who brought their small children to run and scream in the open air dominated the shaded picnic benches, and they were more likely to be chatty, Carrington thought. She wouldn't refuse conversation, but she didn't want to answer questions about herself at the moment. She would soon be doing a lot of explaining, she figured.

She sat on one of the benches and stretched her legs across the length of the seat. The bench to her left was occupied by a woman with a funny-looking straw hat and sunglasses. The woman had a small bag of grapes next to her, and she absentmindedly popped one into her mouth every once in a while. Carrington was envious. She hadn't realized how hungry she was until she noticed several people in the park enjoying picnic lunches and snacks. She wished that she had thought to buy a sandwich at the mall food court. The crackers in her purse would be too dry to eat without anything to wash them down. *I'll save those for when I really need them,* she thought, hoping it wouldn't come to that.

"Do you know the capital of New Jersey?" the woman in the straw hat asked suddenly.

Carrington looked over at the woman, startled.

"Excuse me?" she asked.

The woman had a kind smile. "I'm sorry, dear," she said. "I didn't mean to scare you. I used to do these crossword puzzles all the time, but it seems I've become rather rusty at it," she chuckled. "I figured someone of school age would probably have a stronger grasp of geography than an old lady like me. Oh, and would you care for some grapes?" She lifted her half-full plastic bag of grapes and held them out to Carrington.

The bag was moist with condensation. Carrington's mouth began to water. She had to suppress an urge to dip her hand into the bag and pull out as many grapes as she could. *I must look awfully needy*, she thought, instantly filled with shame.

She crossed her arms across her chest self-consciously and offered the strange woman a wan smile.

"No thanks," she said. "And it's Trenton. The capital of New Jersey is Trenton."

"Oh, no, they'll go to waste," clucked the woman, the bag of grapes sagging in her hand. "Do you think the birds will eat them? I packed way more than I should have. Trenton, you say? Thank you! I was going to guess Hoboken. Lucky for me you sat down next to me!"

There was something about the woman's voice and smile that put Carrington at ease. She wasn't condescending the way so many adults were, and there wasn't a trace of pity in her tone. Carrington smiled back, a real one this time.

"Well, if you're just going to throw them away," she said shyly, nodding toward the grapes, "I guess I'll take them." A warm flush of color crept into her cheeks.

The woman grinned and handed over the sweaty bag.

"I don't think the birds would have liked them," she admitted. "I used to come to this park all the time, and I spoiled them with Ritz crackers and Wonder Bread."

She giggled, and Carrington immediately loved the sound of the woman's laugh. It was the giggle of a much younger woman, a girl even. They sat in amiable silence for several minutes; the woman continued to work on her crossword puzzle, and

Carrington gratefully consumed the grapes. They were cool and soothing in her throat. She ate them slowly, not wanting resume her walk to Mrs. Browne's house. Her palms were sweaty, and she knew it wasn't because of the grapes or weather. She was terror-stricken. She couldn't believe that she was so close to where the woman who might very well be her grandmother lived.

"Oh, this one's kind of unpleasant; what's a word for a castrated male horse?" the woman asked, once again startling Carrington.

She gulped down the grape she'd just put in her mouth, choking a little.

"A gelding," she managed to say, in between coughs.

The older woman looked sympathetic. "I'm so sorry. I didn't mean to frighten you again, dear. You seem a little jumpy. Are you okay?"

She removed her sunglasses to look Carrington directly in the eyes.

What lovely eyes she has, Carrington thought. She was touched by the genuine look of concern on the woman's face. She was older than Carrington had originally thought she might be. There were deep lines etched into the pale skin around her hazel eyes, but her voice was clear and strong. She felt shy about looking at this strange woman eye to eye, though not intimidated.

"Well," Carrington began hesitantly, "I am a little nervous," she admitted.

The woman laid her crossword puzzle book and pencil down in her lap.

"Why is that, dear?" she asked.

The woman gazed at Carrington with such a gentle expression of patience and sympathy that for a few seconds, Carrington was tempted to tell her the whole sordid story. She opened her mouth to speak but fell silent. *I can't tell her why I'm here,* she scolded herself. *She'll think I'm nuts. What if she lives around here. She may even know Mrs. Browne! She'll probably think I'm some kind of troublemaker.* She snapped her mouth shut and looked away.

Carrington resurrected the flimsy excuse she'd told her mother. "I'm just upset that I won't be going to the same high school as some of my friends," she said without meeting the woman's eyes.

There was a long silence, and then she finally looked over at the woman in the straw hat.

"Ah," said the woman softly. "I remember well how difficult a transition it can be. You're going to have to start preparing for college and making a lot of important decisions." Her voice suddenly became very sad.

She glanced at the children in the playground who were noisily engaged in the beginning of their summer vacation. "Those little tykes have it easy, don't they?" asked the woman, sounding rather wistful.

Carrington was relieved that the woman didn't press her for details, but she felt guilty for lying. There was something about the lady that made her feel like it would be okay to talk about what she was going through. She didn't want their conversation to end.

"They really do," Carrington responded, looking at the younger kids. "They don't have to think about writing papers or getting undressed in front of a bunch other kids for gym class. Or boys." She blushed.

The woman turned to face Carrington once again and smiled.

"I may be an old woman, but I remember those times, too. And you're right, junior high and high school are kind of universally miserable. I've often wondered if the boy-girl thing is easier for young people today. Boys of all ages can be a pain in the you-know-what, believe me, dear," she said with a giggle. "But I wouldn't guess that you're going to suffer from a lack of male attention and invitations in high school. You're a lovely young woman, and from what I can tell, smart as a whip."

The scarlet flush in Carrington's cheeks became darker, but she couldn't help the grateful smile that spread across her lips. There was a twinge of pain in her lower lip where the flesh was split.

"Thank you," she murmured shyly.

Worry flickered on the woman's face. "Oh, no, your lip is bleeding," she announced in a concerned tone. She rooted around in her handbag until she came up with a travel pack of facial tissues. She passed the packet to Carrington. "Please help yourself, dear. Are you sure you're okay?"

With trembling fingers Carrington pulled a small square of tissue from the pack and dabbed it gingerly against her lower lip. She was horrified at the blood she saw on the tissue. She began to imagine what she must look like to this nice woman sitting on the bench next to her. She closed her eyes to fight back tears and saw a very clear image of herself in her mind: she was too thin, with plain, long hair draped around her face; she wore ill-fitting, old-fashioned clothes; and worst of all, her lower lip was bleeding and there were poorly disguised bruises on her face. *I must look like some kind of teenage bag lady*, Carrington thought miserably. *She probably thinks I'm homeless or a juvenile delinquent.*

She was only able to nod in response because she knew she would begin sobbing if she tried to speak. She passed the small packet of tissues back to the woman. Her face felt very hot. At that moment, she wanted nothing more than a glass of water and a cool, dark room where she could lie down and sleep away the rest of the afternoon. She sucked in a huge breath of air and expelled it in a long, shuddering sigh. This was no time to have a breakdown, she knew. She'd been gone from home most of the morning, and she still needed to find Mrs. Browne. *I'm so close,* she thought, *yet it feels like I'm still so far away. I don't know if I can go through with it.*

She managed a small nod. "I'm okay," she said.

The woman was silent for a few beats. Then she asked in a cheerful voice, "By the way, what's your name, dear? You've helped me so much with my word puzzle, and I've had such a nice time chatting with you, yet I don't even know your name. I must be getting senile; you'd think I'd have better manners at my age," she added with her pleasant little laugh.

Carrington smiled back. "You don't look old to me," she said, her voice timid but sincere. "Not at all. And my name's Carrington. What's yours?"

The woman seemed slightly startled. "What an unusual name," she said at last. "I've never heard it before as a first name, but it's lovely. It suits you." She grinned at Carrington. "My name is a good, old-fashioned name that belonged to my grandmother, and my mother saw fit to pass on to me," she said, chuckling. "I couldn't stand it as a girl, and I'm still not fond of it," she admitted. "It's Augustine, and unfortunately, I, like most of the people in my generation, didn't receive a middle name, so I'm pretty much stuck with my first one," she said with another laugh. "But no one has called me Augustine since I was a child. As soon as I was old enough to speak, I convinced everyone to use my initials, A. C. My mother was the only one who still called me Augustine, but she was also the only one who could get away with it." She smiled in a sad sort of way.

This nice woman with the funny straw hat called herself A. C.? What were the odds that two women around the same age as a potential grandmother lived in the very same neighborhood him, um, Arnold. She believes that he's my father." She choked a little as she finished her sentence.

She was frightened to meet Mrs. Browne's eyes, but she forced herself to anyway. Even tearful and quite obviously alarmed, Mrs. Browne's expression still hadn't become unkind or angry.

"What is your mother's name?" Mrs. Browne asked.

Carrington hesitated for a moment, fighting a sudden urge to bolt away from the park and never turn back. She fought another wave of nausea.

"Her name is Joan. Joan Coyle."

Mrs. Browne's face went slack, and then her brow furrowed slightly. She took another deep breath and set her mouth in a firm line.

"I think we have much to talk about, you and I," she said to Carrington. "Would you let me take you to lunch?" she asked.

Carrington considered. She wasn't entirely sure what she had expected to happen at this moment, but this was certainly better than being turned away brusquely or being accused of lying. There was a seed of disappointment in her heart, but she shrugged it off as much as she could. *It would be too weird,* Carrington realized, *and unnatural if this woman just hugged me and asked me to call her Grandma.*

"Okay," she murmured in agreement.

They began to walk in the direction of the shopping center, eyeing one another self-consciously and not saying much. They were simply too stunned to make small talk. The afternoon loomed ahead of them, full of questions and possibilities.

Chapter Nine

She was surrounded by icy water, several feet of it, in some kind of enclosed tank. She treaded frantically, looking around to find a bank or a ladder. There was nothing. It was too dark to see much farther than a few feet at a time. A blazing white light momentarily blinded her. Someone had come to save her! She started to wave one hand and tried to scream for help, but couldn't form any words. A wave of water, even more brutally cold than the water already in the chamber, gushed forward.

Joan awoke, gasping then coughing, a sob strangled in her throat. There was filmy sheen of sweat on her face. She heard the toilet's rumble settle into silence. *Stupid dream,* she thought angrily.

The bathroom door opened with a rusty groan, and Abel padded sluggishly back to bed. He was nude, as was she. In the morning light, the dark thatches of course hair on his body looked strange against his pale skin. Despite the thick hair that covered most of Abel's body, the top of his head was almost completely bald. The bald head and his weight made him seem much older than forty. His considerable beer gut reminded Joan of the way her body looked when she was several months pregnant. *Abel's no prize,* she thought as he slipped underneath the sheet and rested one arm across her midsection. This thought often occurred to her when she woke up in his bed. But he made decent money as a plumber, and he was generous with it. Whenever they went out together, he paid for everything, and he didn't ask her a lot of probing questions about her kids. She hated the guys who questioned her about her daughters; some of the bastards even had the nerve to hint that she didn't spend enough time with her kids. Worse were the creeps who seemed more interested in her girls than in her. *Carrie and Missy are lucky,* she thought, not for the first time. *I keep the weirdoes away from them.*

"Mornin', babe," Abel said, his voice still thick with sleep.

"It's too hot in here. I feel all sweaty," she complained, wiggling free of his arm.

He sighed. "Want me to turn on the fan?" he asked.

"Well, yeah," she drawled, rolling her eyes. "And hand me my cigarettes. I think they're on your dresser."

Abel rolled out of bed with a grunt. He stretched on tiptoe to yank the cord of the ceiling fan. It whirred to life and sprinkled a shower of dust motes over the bed. He stumbled to his dresser and sifted through the pile of odds and ends for Joan's cigarettes, finally locating a half pack of Marlboros and a plastic lighter, which he dropped next to her on the bed. He disappeared into the hallway and returned carrying two cold cans of beer.

Joan claimed his pillows and leaned against the stack of them, smoking in bed. Her breasts hung free, partially covered by her long hair. Abel placed her beer on the TV tray that served as a nightstand. He took a long slug from his own can and set it down on the floor.

"You look real sexy like that, with your hair kind of covering you up," he murmured, gazing intently at her breasts.

Joan ignored him. She glanced around his bedroom, a scowl forming on her face.

"Your place is a dump, Abel," she said at last. "I thought I was going to choke when you turned on that fan—all the damn dust it kicked around. You should clean this place up."

Abel chuckled and settled next to her on his back, making a cushion of his hands since she had his pillows.

"Okay, I'll clean it up if you help me," he told her. "You could dress up as one of them French maids."

"Shit," she scoffed, laughing. "That'll be the day!" She took one more long drag off her cigarette and stubbed it out in a nearly full ashtray. "I could make Carrie come over here and clean the place up for you … for a price," she teased.

Abel rolled onto his side, propping himself up on one elbow. "Did you already get in touch with your ex's mom?" he asked, suddenly serious.

Joan sucked in a sharp breath of air, closing her eyes as if in pain.

"No," she said as she exhaled. "I told Carrington about it yesterday, but I ain't sure when I'm gonna go see the old bitch. Soon, that's for sure."

Abel was quiet for a long moment. "I been thinkin' about that," he finally said.

Joan's face whipped toward him, her bright green eyes narrow with suspicion.

"Yeah?" she demanded.

"Yeah," he said. "If you had gone to see her right after he died, it might have been easier to get her to do what you want, but it's been a little while. She's had time to think, to go through his papers, whatever he had; she probably even talked to her lawyer. Rich people always have lawyers." His voice became bitter. "What you should do is get a lawyer yourself and then contact her through your lawyer. If you just go charging over there, makin' demands, she could call the cops and tell 'em you're harassing her, trespassing, whatever. Then you'll never see a dime. But if you scare her with a lawyer, what is she gonna do? You're entitled to the money anyway, but if you go through the same system she uses, there'll be no way she can keep it from you." He smiled at her, clearly pleased with himself.

Joan's first thought was to tell Abel to shut his trap and quit trying to boss her around. She hated when anyone told her what to do, especially boyfriends. But she knew he was right. Things would get ugly if she simply showed up on Arnold's mother's doorstep, insisting that the old bag hand over all the child support that Arnold never paid. It was going to get ugly anyway, she figured; might as well go about things so that she stood a genuine chance of actually getting some cash.

She thought of Carrington and their fight the day before. *Goddamn, that kid is becoming more and more of a pain in the ass every time I turn around.* A twinge of guilt made her suck in a deep breath of air, but the feeling was short-lived. *She deserved it,* Joan thought. *Shouldn't be talking back to me; I don't care how old she gets or how smart she thinks she is. I'm her mother. I know what's best.*

Joan turned her attention back to Abel. She eyed him warily, not wanting him to see that she thought his point about getting a lawyer of her own was a good one.

"Well?" he prodded, the self-satisfied smirk still on his lips.

"Well, what?" she asked, knowing full well what he was talking about.

"You gonna get a lawyer or not? See, my sister happens to be good friends with someone who knows—"

"*If* I hire an attorney, I'll be the one to choose him," she interrupted him.

Abel pressed his lips together, looking hurt.

"It was my idea, Joan," he whined.

A wave of disgust washed over her. *How do I always end up with these losers?* she questioned silently. *Never mind. Abel's fine for now, but that doesn't mean I have to let him have any say in my business. I'm getting tired of him, but he could be useful to me for a while longer.*

It was a struggle to keep a sneer from her face. She gave him what she thought was a placating smile.

"You're right, honey, and thank you for it," she said softly. "I guess I'm just really stressed out over this, y'know?"

Abel was momentarily stunned by the sudden tenderness, but a smug smile soon settled once again on his lips. He reached out and stroked one of her breasts. When he spoke again, his voice was husky with yearning.

"Why don't we celebrate your decision?" he whispered, drawing closer to her.

She felt him against her leg, hard already. A look of revulsion flickered on her face, but Abel was too focused on her breasts to notice. Joan sighed, which Abel took as the heavy breathing of an excited lover. She closed her eyes when his warm mouth found its way to one of her breasts. She pictured all of the money she would soon have and imagined what she would do with it: all the clothes she would buy, a nice car, and a trip to Vegas … without Abel. She relaxed into the pillows as he climbed on top of her, her eyes still shut tight.

Chapter Ten

Missy Coyle blinked drowsily, opening her eyes to the late morning light. The house was silent. Carrington's bed was already made. Missy sat up and yawned, stretching her reedy arms high above her head. She kicked off the blankets and wandered into the living room, peeking into her mother's bedroom as she passed it. It was empty, same as the living room and kitchen. She had the house to herself—for a little while, at least.

Missy sighed, relieved that she wouldn't have to face her sister immediately. She felt guilty for the things she'd said the day before. Carrington was irritating and uppity, but a lot of the time she tried to look out for her younger sister. Missy couldn't understand exactly what made her want to hurt her sister's feelings. Carrington was nagging her, as usual, but Missy could have just blown her off like she usually did, without saying anything really mean. She cringed, picturing what she'd walked into the day before: Joan's face flushed almost to a shade of purple, and blows slamming into Carrington's face and body at an alarming speed. Seeing Joan smack Carrington wasn't a new experience for Missy, but what she witnessed the day before was one of the worst episodes she could recall. It made her shiver to think of it, even though the house was uncomfortably warm.

It was unclear to Missy why their mother was so hard on Carrington, but it had been that way as long as Missy could remember. She occasionally wondered what it was like before she was born. Joan wasn't much for collecting photographs, and there were only a handful of pictures from Carrington's early years. Her older sister was remarkably unchanged throughout the years. She looked the same as a young child as she did now: tall; skinny; long, auburn hair; freckles, which Missy secretly envied; and a solemn smile that didn't quite reach her green eyes. Missy was also jealous of Carrington's eyes. They were just like Joan's eyes, beautiful pools of emerald green, although Missy didn't become nervous when Carrington's gaze was on her as she did when Joan's was. Missy often felt impatient and annoyed with her older sister, but never frightened. *It isn't fair,* Missy thought, as she often had in the past. *Mom likes me, so I should be to one who looks like her, not Carrington.*

She took a cursory glance at the few items in the refrigerator and in the cabinets. *What crap*, she thought, her upper lip curling into a sneer. Today would be a good day to spend with her friends, she decided. Tanya in particular always seemed to have a lot of good food in the house, and Tanya's mother seemed to enjoy when Missy joined them for meals. Missy pretended to be oblivious to the pity she often saw in Mrs. Guzman's eyes.

She showered quickly, dressed, and sneaked into her mother's makeup drawer to borrow eye shadow and tinted lip gloss. Joan wouldn't know, and even if she saw it on Missy's face later, she wouldn't do anything about it, except maybe complain and throw out one of the idle threats that she reserved for such occasions.

Right before she left the house, Missy ran back to the bathroom and fashioned two balls out of toilet tissue, which she stuffed into her bra. She stood in front of the bathroom mirror, molding the lumps of tissue to achieve what she thought was a believable size and shape. *Perfect*, she thought, eyeing her newfound bust. She wore a satisfied grin on her tan face as she slammed the front door behind her.

Tanya had two older brothers: Michael, who was sixteen, and Alex, who was fourteen. Both boys, like the rest of the Guzman family, were muscular and compact, with olive skin and thick, brown hair. Alex had already given Missy the impression that he liked her as more than just a friend. The last time she spent the night at Tanya's house, Alex sat around with his younger sister and Missy, chatting for a while even though Michael teased him about hanging out with little kids. Tanya went to the bathroom at one point, leaving Missy and Alex alone together. They were silent for a moment, and then Alex asked Missy if she had ever kissed a boy. She had kissed a few boys, but she had the impression that Alex wanted to be her first kiss. She hoped that was the case. She shook her head and smiled at him. Then he asked her if she had ever "done it." A ripple of fear washed over her just for a moment, but she shook it off and managed to giggle as if he had just challenged her to a burping contest rather than inquired about the status of her virginity. Tanya returned from the bathroom before Missy could answer his question, and she began talking immediately. She didn't seem to notice or care that both her brother and friend were blushing furiously.

That was two weeks ago, and several times since then, Missy replayed the scene in her mind. It never failed to give her a strange tingle in the mysterious region beneath her belly button. Some of her friends claimed to have done it already, including Tanya.

In the last months of school, Missy heard the rumor that a girl who was three years older than she was, Olivia Irwin, had to drop out of the eighth grade because she was pregnant and starting to show. Olivia, like Missy, had been left behind a year in school, so she was one year older than the rest of her class. She should have been in her first year of high school. Missy and her friends knew Olivia casually from the neighborhood and school, but she wasn't in their circle. It was hard to know for sure what the truth was, not that it mattered much to the girls if what they heard was more than just gossip. It excited them. They all proclaimed Olivia to be the biggest slut in the neighborhood who got what she deserved, but secretly, more than a few of them were intrigued and even infatuated with the idea of having their very own baby.

The girls didn't talk much about it with each other, in spite of their preoccupation with intercourse. There was an unspoken law that it was okay, cool even, to talk about sex, but admitting that you wanted to get pregnant would be too strange, too taboo. Sometimes they heard older sisters or young aunts who were only a handful of years older than they were talking openly about having and wanting babies, and they would listen, rapt.

Missy remembered going to a baby shower a few months ago, for Tanya's cousin, Vanessa, who had been sixteen at the time. How she envied Vanessa! The teenager had been surrounded by food and gifts piled everywhere in the basement of her mother's house. Women of all ages swarmed around her. A few of the older ones, Joan's age and older, sat in a small group in a corner, somewhat separate from the festivities. They pretended to be jovial when anyone else talked to them or when they played party games, but Missy saw them clucking with disapproval more than once, nodding their heads together and whispering. *Who cares what those old cows think?* Missy thought. *They're just jealous.* And so was she. How she craved the spotlight that Vanessa had—so many women hovering around her, doing things for her, asking about her constantly. Vanessa talked about herself and the pregnancy at length, and no one seemed to grow bored of it. When the baby came, she would have a tiny version of herself.

When Missy daydreamed about having a baby of her own, she only imagined having a daughter, never a son. She would have someone to hold and play with, someone who would have to do whatever Missy told her to do. A baby, Missy believed, would be the only thing in the world that she could have that could never be taken away or repossessed, like Joan's new stereo had been the previous year. A baby could never belong to anyone else because the baby would *look* like her; it would be something *she* created.

As she walked the few blocks to Tanya's house, Missy thought of the colors she would choose for decorations if she ever had a baby shower. *Purple and gold? No, too much like a football team. Pink and blue? Boring and old-fashioned! Something women only did in old movies,* she mused. She wondered if Olivia Irwin would have a baby shower.

She knocked on the screen door to Tanya's house. It was a slightly more attractive version of her own house, without the two separate front doors since Tanya's house wasn't a duplex. The siding was freshly painted, and the tiny patch of lawn was neat and recently mowed.

"Well, hey, look who it is," Alex said after sidling up to the door.

Missy blushed and grinned at him through the screen. "You gonna to let me in or what?" she asked, smiling coyly.

"That depends," he answered, crossing his arms across his chest. "What's it worth to you?"

Missy considered this, still staring into his brooding gray eyes. She thought of the questions he'd asked her just a few weeks earlier and wondered, feeling both frightened and exhilarated, if she would soon have another chance to be alone with Alex. Maybe she could invite him over when Joan was at work, but she also didn't want Tanya or Carrington to find out. Despite all the scenes she'd imagined playing out between herself and Alex, Missy found herself tongue-tied. Tanya came bounding up to the screen door just then.

She shoved her brother playfully. "Stop harassing my friend, butthead," she told him, laughing.

Alex chuckled and walked away. Tanya opened the screen door, and Missy came inside gratefully, still blushing. Alex glanced over his shoulder at her as he headed to his bedroom. He held Missy's gaze for a long moment, a strange half smile on his face. The expression on Alex's face made her feel so many things: thrilled, flattered, amused, and more than a little bit nervous. She was a somewhat disappointed when he disappeared into his bedroom, but there was a part of her that was relieved, as well.

Chapter Eleven

"I think I met your mother once … several years ago," A. C. said awkwardly, calling up a vivid image of the rude young woman at Calvin's party.

Carrington's gaze was intent as she waited for A. C. to continue.

"But," A. C. paused, struggling to conceal her disgust, "I don't think she liked me very much," she concluded.

Carrington looked away, a warm pink blossoming across her cheeks. A. C. realized that Joan had probably told Carrington terrible things about the Brownes. She could just imagine the kind of filth that would come from Joan's lips. It wasn't Carrington's fault, she reminded herself. Still, she had to suppress a surge of resentment. *How dare anyone speak badly of Calvin! Least of all the likes Joan Coyle.* She took a large gulp from her glass of iced tea, hoping Carrington didn't see the anger glittering in her eyes.

"My mother doesn't like anyone," Carrington offered. "I doubt she even likes herself."

A. C. was filled with sympathy and guilt. Poor Carrington; it wasn't her fault at all. The waiter arrived, carrying food-laden plates, one in each hand.

"Your rosemary chicken and wild rice, ma'am," he said, carefully setting a plate in front of A. C. "And your sub sandwich with fries." He set Carrington's plate down and smiled. "Is there anything else?"

"No, thank you," they said at the exact same moment, smiling first at him and then at one another.

Carrington had a strange expression on her face. She seemed reluctant to eat. *Oh, the poor child,* A. C. thought as the realization hit her. *She's embarrassed.*

"Good Lord, am I starved!" A. C. exclaimed. "Let's dig in, shall we?" she asked, cutting into her chicken. "Your sub looks great!" she commented, nodding toward Carrington's plate. "I think I'll order that next time we come … um … sometime." A warm rush of color spread through her cheeks.

Carrington ate ravenously. The meal was mostly silent, except for the waiter checking on them a couple of times and A. C. asking if she could try Carrington's fries.

When the feast was over, they both leaned back in their chairs, satisfied.

"That was great," Carrington began. "Thank you so much, Mrs. Browne. Really, this was so nice."

A. C. smiled warmly at her.

"It was my pleasure. Truly. Now, do you think you have any room for dessert?"

Carrington threw up her hands in mock protest.

"Oh, no! No way, I am stuffed. I can't remember the last time I ate so much at once." She shut her mouth abruptly, realizing what she'd just said.

A. C. gazed at her with obvious sympathy, and Carrington looked away. She sucked noisily on her drink.

"I don't think I could eat another bite, either," A. C. said.

She was filled with such longing to touch Carrington, to embrace the girl, hold her close, and tell her that everything would be all right. "You don't have to be embarrassed," she wanted to say to her. Instead, she busied herself with counting out money for the check.

Carrington seemed to recover. She met A. C.'s eyes and managed a small smile. A. C. thought, not for the first time since they sat down in the restaurant, *She may have Joan's eyes, but those are my freckles and my hair color. This child must be Arnold's. She simply has to be.*

"I'm going to have to speak with your mother," she began, not surprised at the look of alarm on Carrington's bruised face.

It was obvious that the girl had been roughed up, no doubt by that God-awful Joan Coyle. The idea of it made A. C.'s jaws clench.

"My mother," Carrington repeated lamely.

The color drained from her face, and her freckles stood out like points on a map. Again, A. C. felt an almost overwhelming urge to cradle the girl.

"Well, it's really the only way," A. C. said gently. "I mean, at some point soon, very soon, I'll need to get in touch with my lawyer, who will be able to advise us, you and I, on how to proceed. There will be a test, I'm sure—some kind of blood test to determine if … well, if we're related." She paused for a moment. "But what needs to happen immediately is some kind of notice to your mother. She might be wondering this very minute where you are. As a mother myself, I can't bear the thought of making someone else worry about where their child might be and if she's okay."

"She's not worried about me," Carrington scoffed. "She didn't come home last night, but that's typical of her. She always has some boyfriend or another who she stays with overnight. She's left us alone for as long as a two days before. If she doesn't have to work this afternoon, she may not come home until tomorrow."

A. C. stared blindly at the thin teenage girl who was possibly her granddaughter. She hadn't heard much after Carrington said "us." *So, there must be another child in the house*, she thought, her chest tightening. Possibly Arnold's? *No, Carrington would have mentioned her brother or sister sooner if that was the case*, A. C. was certain.

"Is there another child at home, dear?" she asked, hoping that Carrington wouldn't hear the panic she was beginning to feel.

"I'm so sorry! I can't believe I didn't mention her before. Yes, yes, I have a younger sister. Missy. Well, Melissa, but she's always been called Missy. She's twelve. We're half sisters. Her dad left the state a long time ago, but he still writes. She looks like him. In fact, she and I don't look anything alike, really. People are usually surprised when they find out we have the same mom," Carrington said in one big rush.

A. C. sighed in relief. Still, the second child was going to complicate things, she realized. Joan Coyle obviously wasn't fit to care for one child, let alone two. But A. C. had no legal right to the second child. And, she realized guiltily, she only wanted Carrington.

"So, Missy is probably home right now?" A. C. asked, struggling to keep her voice neutral.

Carrington shook her head.

"I doubt it. Now that it's summer break, she'll be out most days. She spends a lot of time with her friends; she has a lot of them." Carrington's voice took on a hard edge.

A. C. felt a wave of pity for the girl. *Oh, my poor Carrington. She's probably never had a chance to make any close friends.*

"When do you think Missy will come home, dear?" she asked.

Carrington thought for a moment.

"It's hard to say, but I don't think until tomorrow, at least. Whenever she goes to her friends' houses, she almost always spends the night there. Sometimes even a couple of nights."

"And if your mother works this afternoon, will she come home beforehand? What time do you think she'll finish her shift?"

"If she has to work this afternoon, she might be home right now, just about to leave. She'll work until around six, and it's hard to say if she'll come home after that or not. Usually, I would say there is a good chance she wouldn't come home, but now that she's talking about getting an inheritance from my dad," she paused, blushing intensely, "it's possible she might come straight home after work and expect me to be there. She'll want to tell me what we're going to do and say."

Money, A. C., thought. *Money is the key. That's all Joan wants; that's all she ever wanted. I'll prove that Carrington is my granddaughter, and if I have to, I'll prove that Joan is clearly incapable of raising Carrington, or any child. But it may not come to that,* she reasoned silently, envisioning the look of pure greed on Joan's face. She sighed then, a sharp, almost painful release of air, closing her eyes as the breath rushed through her nose. *I'm basically going to have to buy my grandchild from this awful woman*, she thought. *And what about the other child?*

"Carrington, honey, would you feel okay about coming home with me for a short while? Just long enough to make some phone calls and talk a bit more so we can figure out exactly what to do. I know this is all so strange and so fast for both of us, but please," she paused, imploring Carrington with her radiant hazel eyes, "I'm asking you to trust me, dear. I know it's asking a lot, but I think the next few days, even the next few hours, may turn out to be very, very important."

She watched the child's face hopefully, hating how dramatic she sounded. It was true, though. Time was crucial. As Carrington herself had pointed out, Joan could already be looking for the girl and coming up with more vile schemes.

A look of relief swept over Carrington's face. The tightness in her lips and eyes ebbed away. She longed to hug Mrs. Browne, but she wouldn't dream of trying to, and certainly not somewhere public. And what if Mrs. Browne didn't want Carrington to touch her? That would be worse than anything, perhaps even worse than going home to Joan. Instead, Carrington blinked her eyes rapidly and took a deep breath of air.

"That would be fine with me. And thank you. Thank you so much."

A. C. reached across the table then—one swift, liquid motion—and gave Carrington's hand a firm squeeze. She was thrilled when the slender hand squeezed back.

Chapter Twelve

From the balcony attached to his study, Laurence watched Regina's Cadillac swerve sharply up the hill that led to their house. She screeched to a halt several feet away from the garage, narrowly avoiding a collision with Leo, the gardener who tended the grounds once a week. He was pushing a wheelbarrow full of fertilizer. Regina pounded her horn in short, barking blasts. Leo scurried out of the way, his straw hat fluttering off of his head and landing on the pile of manure.

"Dear God," Laurence muttered. "Why are you home?"

She was supposed to be gone for most of the afternoon. She'd left the house less than an hour earlier with plans to take A. C. out for brunch. Afterward, Regina would help her older sister organize her house. Personally, Laurence couldn't imagine why A. C. would consent to letting Regina have any voice in the way she kept her home. He assumed Regina had taken advantage of A. C.'s grief. Regina probably could have persuaded her older sister to set her house on fire, let alone tidy it up and pare down on some of her old things.

Laurence returned to his study with a sigh and settled at his desk. He wished he had decided to go golfing that morning. Regina's heavy shoes pounded up the stairwell. *Oh, boy,* he thought, suddenly feeling drained. *A. C. must have disagreed with Regina.* Laurence knew he was right as soon as Regina appeared in the study doorway, her expression more pinched and sour than usual.

"Hello, dear," he said mildly. "Everything all right? Did you cut your date short?"

"She is impossible!" Regina fumed. "Simply impossible. She is completely unreasonable. Her house is filthy, and she refuses to see the truth about anything!"

Regina traipsed across the parquet floor, dropped her handbag in one of the leather chairs facing Laurence's desk, and folded herself into the other with a heavy sigh.

"She just doesn't listen to anything I say," she continued. "Even when it's obvious that I'm right, she refuses to budge!"

Laurence leaned back in his seat, careful to keep his eyes focused on her. He had learned early on in their marriage that Regina didn't believe he was listening to her if his eyes weren't clearly trained on her. He cleared his throat.

"What happened? What did she say?"

"Well, first of all, she refuses to keep her house decent. It's a lovely house—a little on the small side for my taste—but it could be beautiful if she just put some effort into it! She could do a lot of entertaining there, but as it is, I would be embarrassed if anyone we knew saw it. Thank God I had the foresight to hire someone to clean up for the reception we had after Arnold's funeral."

What was the correct response? Laurence was never certain, even after thirty-five long years of marriage. Certainly, telling

Regina that she was an insufferable bitch was out of the question. He folded and unfolded his hands, elbows planted on the surface of his desk.

"Mmm," he finally offered, hoping Regina would continue her tirade so that he wouldn't immediately be forced to come up with right thing to say.

Regina didn't wait to find out if Laurence had more to say. "I don't know how she can stand to live the way she does. I'm not even talking about the way she keeps—or should I say, *doesn't* keep—her house." She paused, wrinkling her nose. "I mean, the way she spends so much time alone. After Cal died, she all but dropped out of sight at the club. She had a lot of friends there at one time, and they all looked up to Cal. She hardly returns their calls, doesn't join them for lunch, doesn't attend their children's weddings. Ugh! Very gauche behavior. Everyone at the club adored Cal!" She lowered her voice conspiratorially. "And they did so much for his career, if you ask me."

Laurence coughed into his fist to disguise a scoff. *Yes*, he thought, *those brownnosers at the club did about as much for Cal's career as you've done for my libido the past twenty-some years.* It would be pointless, he realized, to remind Regina that Cal and A. C. didn't join the Wyngate Country Club until a few years after Cal had been promoted to one of the senior management levels at Plasti-Corp. In fact, he suspected they joined mostly to quiet Regina's incessant pleas that they become members.

She sighed, and her gaze moved away from him, her eyes wandering around his study.

"Oh, Laurence," she breathed, as if it was an effort just to say his name, "you really ought to let me redecorate in here. It's starting to look so dated. Your desk looks like something from a library in the eighteen hundreds, for heaven's sake!"

Laurence gritted his teeth and closed his eyes for a moment. No. He would not let her change a single thing in his study. It was the one room in the house untouched by Regina's flashy taste and urgent desire to show off how much they could afford to spend. He shook his head.

"I like my study, Regina. No one spends time in here but me. I think it would be a waste of money to redecorate it."

Twin patches of crimson bloomed across her cheeks. One of the things Regina despised most in life, besides being reminded of her middle-class upbringing, was being turned down, by anyone, for any reason. She glared at him.

"It's not as if I'm suggesting that we gut your precious bookshelves and paint the walls fuchsia! I'm simply talking about updating this room a bit. What's wrong with that? We could get you a nice, sleek new desk, and maybe a few Tiffany lamps that will help soften the room a little." She looked around his study thoughtfully.

"I like my study the way it is," he repeated, beginning to sound impatient. "I don't see why I need to 'soften' anything in here. We don't use my study for entertaining. You certainly never set foot in here unless you want something."

"Well, perhaps I would come in here more often if I liked the way it looked," she huffed.

Oh, God, Laurence thought, *then maybe I'll paint the room in camouflage and hang a few nude pin-ups.*

"Regina," he began slowly, trying to regain some of his composure but failing, "I come in here to work on the weekends or to relax after I've been working all day. You spend your days at the club having lunch with your friends or out shopping, spending ungodly sums of money on this season's trends. Do you really want to spend your precious time with me, watching as I jot down ideas or sift through my newspaper? Would you like it if I invited myself everywhere you went? Do you want me to sit around with you and the girls at the club, dishing my two cents about Deidre's ungrateful children, Maggie's new Benz, or Virginia's latest trip to Europe? Do you want me to follow you around Saks commenting on what color lipstick suits you best?"

For the second time in one day, Regina was stunned. She stared at Laurence in disgust.

"How dare you speak to me that way! How dare you speak of my friends, our friends, like that! Trivializing my relationships with them and how I spend my time! For your information, Laurence, I just finished co-chairing the modern art museum's annual black tie benefit, which, I might remind you, your company agreed to sponsor. Your secretary hardly bothers to return my calls. It's like she's being instructed to ignore me." She glowered at him.

"I haven't forgotten, Regina," he snapped. "And Erin hasn't been ignoring you. We've all been working 'round the clock on four different acquisitions! Or did both Bloomingdale's and Macy's unveil new lines of high heels and wrinkle creams this week? Maybe you didn't notice I've hardly been home lately."

"You bastard!" she hissed, rising to her feet. "I can't believe I'm hearing this!" she cried.

Laurence looked somewhat shocked as if he, too, was surprised by his own words. He recovered his façade of calm and stared at Regina coolly.

"Oh, stop being so damned dramatic," he sneered. "Can we just talk about this some other time? I'm busy, Regina."

She glared at him.

"I suppose you've given absolutely no thought to our anniversary," she said, her voice shrill and accusing.

He leaned back in his seat and considered her with weary eyes.

"Do you really think now is the time to talk about that? Wouldn't it be better if we both cooled down for a bit and then discussed how we plan to celebrate thirty-five jubilant years of bliss?"

For the first time in years, he saw Regina's cool gaze dissolve and her eyes fill with tears. He felt a small twinge of joy.

"You know, Laurence, you can be so cruel sometimes. I feel like I don't even know you anymore!"

His jaw clenched and unclenched. He gripped the arms of his chair until the flesh across his knuckles was taut and white.

"What does that even mean, you don't know me anymore? You're not senile; I'm not senile. We've known one another for two thirds of our lives; of course you *know* me, Regina. For God's sake, if you want to speak to me, even if it's to charge into my study and babble on about the miserable hand life has dealt you, do you think it's possible to do it without borrowing lines from those mindless soap operas you watch? You're a grown woman with a college education, Regina. For God's sake," he said again, clearly disgusted.

She shook her head slowly, lips pursed.

"You smug son of a bitch. You were *nothing* when I met you. A text book scholarship case—a pitiful little whelp overfed on his own ego. You thought you were going to change the world. Ha! With what, Laurence? With your cheap suits and arrogant essays about leaving your mark on the business world? 'Restoration: Dignity and the Stock Market,'" she mocked him, lips turned up in a hateful little smile.

Laurence's cheeks burned. *You unbelievable bitch*, he thought.

"Reconciliation and integrity! 'Reconciliation: Integrity and the Stock Market!'" he spat.

"Oh, whatever!" she shot back. "Did it change the world, Laurence? Did any of your silly little papers make one damn bit of difference? Does anyone, outside of a handful of people, know your name?"

He chewed the insides of his cheeks, fighting the urge to call her the most obscene words he could imagine. There was a gaudy brass and crystal paperweight shaped like a sailboat on his desk, a Christmas present from Gloria. For a moment, Laurence imagined hurling it in Regina's direction, not to actually strike her, but to smash it into one of the walls, preferably above her head, and watch the horror, and possibly fear, on her face. He clenched his hands at his sides and finally rose from his seat.

"Oh, yes, my dear. Yes, there must be several hundred people across the country who know my name and address very well. Let's see: the credit offices at Macy's, Bloomingdale's, Saks," he ticked them off on his fingers as he went along, "MasterCard, Visa, American Express—all platinum, of course. Nothing but the best for my darling little wife. And how many spa memberships do you have now, love? Are you up to five now, or is it just four? I can never remember. You seem to be rushing out for an acid peel every Goddamn time I turn around! And they're doing wonders, honey, really. You have the turkey neck and crow's feet of a woman at least five years younger than you."

Regina gasped, and Laurence savored the look of pain on her face. She opened and closed her mouth a couple of times like a fish on the floorboards of a boat, trying to breathe. A couple of tears slid down her cheeks. Laurence suddenly felt a little bit frightened. He'd never spoken to Regina like this. Never. Not in the near forty year span of their entire relationship. How had this fight started? He hadn't woken up that morning planning to say horrid things to his wife. He couldn't honestly say that he liked her, but he really never wanted to hurt her. *If only she wasn't so damn grating and pushy*, he thought.

She sniffled loudly and seemed to regain some of her composure. When she spoke, her voice was strangely calm. It gave him a chill.

"You know, Laurence," she began, "you may have played your cards well and made a little bit of money, but deep down, you'll always be in the same pathetic class as your parents. Matthew Lithgow, a cobbler, how quaint and noble! And poor little Rose, a washer woman; and since she couldn't even do that very well, she had to change the diapers of other people's children on the side. I pity you, really." She shook her head and made the same clucking sound with her tongue that she made whenever she saw people panhandling. "I guess people really can't overcome upbringing, can they, dear?"

Her eyes, narrowed and unblinking, burrowed into him. At the mention of his mother, Laurence felt a painful stirring in his chest. For a moment, he thought he was going to be sick. He regretted having ravioli for lunch. He regretted staying home when he could have gone out golfing. But most of all, he regretted being married to the hardened, cruel stranger who stood before him. Of course, he had been just as nasty to her, he realized. What did it matter at this point? What did any of it matter?

Regina scowled at him for a moment longer before stalking out of his study.

"I wish I'd never married you," he said to her retreating back. She gave no indication that she heard him. Laurence didn't care.

He closed his eyes and rubbed his temples, sensing an impending migraine. He locked the door to his study, kicked off his loafers, and collapsed onto the sofa. His shoulders were tight and painful. *I can't believe she mentioned our anniversary,* he thought, feeling both glum and furious. *Who the hell thinks of something like that in the middle of a fight. Regina. Only Regina.*

Laurence never really understood his wife's obsession with status. Regina and her older sister weren't by any means born into poverty; their father was a mechanic who eventually bought and operated his own small chain of auto repair shops. He did quite well for his family. Regina's parents weren't college educated, but she and A. C. were. Their parents didn't have the nicest home they could have afforded, but that was only because they were saving for their daughters' educations and their own old age. Laurence could not comprehend the shame Regina seemed to carry about her family's history. He was proud of his own success, first in high school, then in college, and ultimately as co-founder of one of the city's most well-known and well-respected investment banking firms.

Growing up, his family wasn't nearly as well off as Regina's. Like Regina's mother, Laurence's mother stayed home to raise her children, but Laurence and his younger siblings didn't have the luxury of having their mother all to themselves; Rose Lithgow baby-sat neighborhood children and sometimes washed clothes to bring in extra money. She was a quiet woman, always with a faraway look in her watery blue eyes. Rose seemed to accept her station in life as a working-class housewife without any resistance or resentment. Her one luxury, her own private form of escape, was going to the movies once or twice a month. She even named her oldest son, Laurence, for her favorite actor, Laurence Olivier. Laurence's father, Matthew Lithgow, had been a cobbler, which was a dying profession even when Laurence was a boy.

Being the oldest of three children, Laurence was expected to earn a wage and contribute to the family finances as soon as he was old enough. Matthew didn't push his son into the shoe business because he knew there was no money it. They were barely scraping by on his salary and the money Rose brought in from baby-sitting and washing clothes. Instead, he encouraged his son to consider trade school. Maybe he could become an electrician, the older Lithgow often said.

Laurence had worked damn hard to get an education; he started working nights as a department store janitor while still in high school. He gave his parents a third of his wages, spent a few dollars here and there on himself, and saved most of it for college. In spite of his tight schedule, Laurence excelled in school. His grade point average was how he ultimately landed in college. He managed to win an academic scholarship to a state university. Laurence never let himself forget that without the scholarship, he never would have been able to afford college, not even with the savings from his job as a janitor.

His past was no secret, but over the years, if Regina overheard Laurence at cocktail parties talking about his childhood, she would admonish him when they came home. He decided early on in their marriage that silence was the best policy when dealing with Regina. Lately, though, it was becoming increasingly difficult to hold his tongue around her.

If his secretary or his golfing buddies were asked to describe Laurence, they would be forced to paint pictures of two separate men: Laurence Lithgow, an aggressive, successful investment banker with a shrewd mind and a dry wit, and Laurence Lithgow, the mostly silent, generally obedient husband of the forceful, social climbing Regina Lithgow. Laurence's closest friends didn't understand why he had remained by her side for so many years.

He couldn't say that he really understood it himself. Did he love his wife? Yes, he supposed that he did. They had been through so much together and had known one another for so long—since they were kids, basically. They'd gone to college together. It was nearly forty years that they'd known one another. She was the mother of his one and only child. She was his first lover. It was impossible not to feel some kind of familiarity-bred fondness for her. For the past several years, though, the resentment he felt toward Regina far outweighed the affection.

Regina wasn't nearly as attractive as she had once been, but he tried not to hold that against her. There were moments, especially on birthdays and anniversaries, when he felt obligated to reflect on his life, that Laurence realized he hardly resembled the dark-haired, lean, and handsome young man he once was. While Regina's curves had receded into hard angles on her body and the silky hair of her youth had become colorless and wiry, Laurence's once athletic frame drifted into soft shapelessness.

He'd developed a paunch around his waist that he kept well disguised with custom-made suits. When Regina nagged him about exercising more, he promptly reminded her that he golfed all the time, but secretly he knew that zipping around the course in his personal cart with friends and having caddies carry his clubs probably did very little for his body, especially considering he always enjoyed a hearty meal at the clubhouse after a game. His formerly dark brown hair, thick and full, had become as wispy as a newborn's hair, unevenly covering his scalp. He kept it short and plastered it to his head with the old-fashioned pomade that he remembered his father using. His cheekbones, once high and severe like his mother's, long ago seemed to melt into his face. There was a time in his life when Laurence looked in the mirror and saw a handsome man—maybe not handsome like Hollywood leading men, but good-looking enough. He no longer felt that way, but it was less important to him now than it had been when he was in his twenties and thirties. His looks had served their purpose, and now he no longer needed to rely on his appearance to establish himself or find opportunities. *Hell,* he sometimes thought, *who isn't good-looking when they're twenty-five?*

Regina had hardened, not only physically, but emotionally over the years. He never would have described her as gentle or sweet, but there was a time, during their first few years together, when Regina had been more relaxed, even charming. She'd been a dreamer, like he was. They met during his junior year of college, when she was a senior.

They sat next to one another in a business statistics class. Laurence admired Regina for being one of the few women in a higher-level business course. She was pretty, as well, even if her looks weren't the conventionally attractive features that usually appealed to Laurence.

He sometimes wondered why she picked him. She was popular at their school, stylish and poised. Her peers looked up to her. Regina pretended not to notice when Laurence pointed out how well-known and even envied she was, but he could tell she was terribly pleased by his observation.

Regina's grades slipped considerably after they started going steady. She barely passed the course, in spite of Laurence's attempts to tutor her in a subject that was dear to him. He was completely infatuated with Regina Carrington. It seemed clear to him that she was neglecting her grades because she was head over heels for him. Years later, though, Laurence would realize that this wasn't really the case. Regina had no intention of working in the business world after college. In fact, Laurence believed that she had no intention of working at all, at least not at a typical nine-to-five job. She took the business course to meet a future husband. *That's probably why she went to college at all*, he often mused. In college, she had a better chance of meeting a man with higher earning potential.

After Regina graduated, she continued living at home with her parents, all the while dropping not-so-subtle hints that it was high time Laurence proposed to her. He was a senior by then. The end of his life as a student was finally in sight, but he still had to spend long hours studying to maintain his grades. It wasn't easy juggling school, his part-time job, and his relationship with Regina. She wanted more and more from him the longer they were together. Regina only had eyes for the future, their future together as husband and wife.

A few months into Laurence's senior year of college, Regina's older sister, A. C., began dating Calvin Browne. Laurence took an immediate liking to Calvin. Regina called Calvin a cad behind his back. "He'll never marry her," she often remarked to Laurence. He wasn't sure why she thought this, unless it was simply hope that she would marry before her sister. Why was it so important to her to get married? he wondered. And what was wrong with A. C. getting married before her? A. C. was the older sister; it seemed natural that she would marry before Regina. Calvin was a great guy, and he would be a fool, Laurence often thought, if he didn't marry the gorgeous, intelligent, and vivacious A. C. He sometimes lamented that he had not met A. C. first, but there was no point in entertaining notions like that, so he seldom did.

When A. C. and Calvin began planning their wedding merely four months after they started dating, Regina was livid. She nearly broke up with Laurence then, and years later, he sometimes wondered if he should have let her walk out of his life. How dare he string her along for a whole year? she demanded to know. Calvin wanted to marry A. C. after only four months, so why hadn't Laurence proposed? She raged at him and even refused to see him or return his phone calls for a while. Laurence had no answer—at least, no answer that would satisfy her. It was not as if he and Regina hadn't discussed getting married. He'd told her months prior that he would propose to her when he could afford a proper engagement ring and a home for them. It would take some time, he'd said, and he asked her to be patient. He told her he loved her, and he meant it, but Regina's patience had a finite shelf life.

"He's just marrying her because she's pregnant, I bet," Regina said to Laurence many times in the weeks leading up to A. C.'s wedding. "I bet she'll be showing at her own wedding," she would whisper with a nasty little laugh. Laurence found Regina's behavior disturbing. It wasn't so much that she gossiped about her sister; most people he knew gossiped now and then about someone in their family. But Regina pretended to be completely supportive of the wedding, and she went out of her way to help A. C. with the plans and preparations. Regina made dozens of calls to florists, bakeries, and local bands. She spent hours shopping with A. C. and their mother for the wedding dress, and she addressed most of the invitations herself.

Two months before the wedding, A. C. announced that she'd asked her best friend from college to be her maid of honor. Regina flew into a rage. She threatened not to attend the wedding at all. She reminded her sister, in minute detail, of all the tasks she had done to help plan the wedding. She even threatened to tell everyone who was invited and everyone they had ever known that A. C. was pregnant. The result was a family meltdown. Her parents were appalled by Regina's tantrum and accusation. A. C. was devastated. The sisters didn't speak for over a month. After weeks of their mother's incessant pleas, Regina and A. C. had a lukewarm reconciliation just in time for the wedding, but the tension between them was palpable long after the wedding had come and gone.

Chapter Thirteen

Laurence removed himself from the leather couch only twice over the span of several hours; the first time was to draw the blinds, and the second was to pour himself a generous Scotch. He had no idea why he was flooded with so many memories. He really didn't want to think about anything, but his mind wandered erratically.

He thought of his own daughter, Gloria, who had recently turned twenty-nine. She was never a beauty, not even in her late teens and early twenties when most women, in Laurence's opinion, looked their best. Gloria looked very much like Regina, but she had Laurence's sharp, jutting cheekbones and his dark hair. On Rose, Laurence's mother, those dramatic cheeks had been fetching and alluring without overpowering the rest of her features. On Gloria, though, with her thin lips and pointy chin, the Lithgow cheek bones gave her a gaunt, starved look. Her eyes were the prettiest thing about her. They were gray, like Regina's, but somehow softer and larger. *Maybe Gloria would be more attractive if she smiled more often,* Laurence often thought. She'd always been a difficult child: fussy and sullen, refusing to give into Regina's demands, bossy and catty with the other girls at school.

Gloria, unlike Laurence, could afford to be nasty with other children. She'd been born rich, or at least comfortably well off, and Laurence had only amassed more and more wealth over the years. She attended the best private schools and the most exclusive summer camps, and had play dates with the wealthiest children in the county. Her playmates were the pampered offspring of Laurence and Regina's friends at the country club. That she came from a family of means, even if it was new money, meant that Gloria would never have to struggle the way Laurence had. This was a fact that he grieved. He'd spoiled the girl, he knew; or rather, he'd allowed Regina to spoil her. As with everything else where Laurence and Regina's relationship was concerned, Regina had immediately taken charge of Gloria's upbringing.

Laurence wanted to send Gloria to public school. He'd done the research, and the school in their district was a fine one. The money they'd save on tuition fees could later be spent on sending Gloria to the college of her choosing. Regina scoffed at this. "Why," she'd demanded, "would we send our daughter to a public school, where she'll be forced to associate with ... *less motivated* children, when we can afford to send her to the very best private school? Why would we deprive her of a solid foundation with the *right* kind of people?" He argued at first, but it was as futile as arguing with the sun about whether it should shine or not. And Laurence was just beginning to rise through the ranks of investment banking. While he worried about and doted on his young daughter as much as he could, Gloria's early years were spent mostly with Regina and nannies because Laurence was always at work.

As Gloria grew into a younger version of Regina, Laurence often wondered if it would have made a difference if he'd been around more often when she was a child. He tried to reassure himself that it wouldn't have made a difference at all. Gloria's personality was hardwired. *I could have been Mr. Mom and it wouldn't have changed a thing*, he sometimes told himself. For both mother and daughter, Laurence observed, life was about immediate gratification. Whatever Regina and Gloria wanted, they wanted it the very moment the idea was born in their heads.

Nearing thirty years of age, Gloria still behaved like a spoiled school girl. She lived in a condo that Gloria had given her as a college graduation present. Laurence wanted to give her something considerably less extravagant: a cruise to the Bahamas, maybe, or better yet, a small reliable car. But Gloria said they owed it to their child to see that she had a proper home. Regina originally hoped that Gloria would choose to live with them until she married, just as Regina had done so many years before, but the days of such arrangements were long past.

It took six years for Gloria to earn a bachelor's degree in art—six years from her nineteenth birthday, because she'd taken a year off after high school graduation to "find herself." Laurence rolled his eyes at the memory. She finally enrolled as a freshman a few months shy of her twentieth birthday, and then she failed out of school during her sophomore year. Gloria then took another year off, moping around the house, wearing all-black, ill-fitting clothes and scribbling melancholy poetry in a spiral notebook. She went through a string of oddball boyfriends around that time: "almost divorced" men who were ten or more years her senior; grubby, former military men who claimed disability status to keep from working full-time; and unemployed musicians. In fact, it was because of one such boyfriend that Gloria ultimately completed her degree at an out-of-state school. The university that had awarded Gloria her degree was over a thousand miles away from Roy, the thirty-two-year-old drummer who supplemented his career as a musician by occasionally working as an appliance salesman at Sears.

At first, Gloria resisted her parents' suggestions that she finish her degree, just as Laurence knew she would. She was, after all, her mother's girl. They even offered to let her do it through a community college, where the course load was less intense and she would still be able to live at home. Gloria didn't want to go to school. She wanted to backpack across Europe (on their dime, Laurence assumed, since she had never held a job in her life), staying in hostels and maybe learning to paint. She and Regina battled bitterly for months, sometimes not even speaking to one another for days at a time. And then Laurence had an idea. What Gloria needed, he told Regina privately, was independence, distance from her parents and everything that was old and familiar to her. She needed to see more of the country, to experience life as a young woman away from home for the first time. "It may even dissuade her from moving to Europe," he'd said, knowing that was the very thing Regina feared most. Going to an out-of-state college was the only way, he insisted, that Gloria would truly grow up and realize that she didn't need to shock her family by dating strange men. He knew it was the last point that would really sell Regina on the idea, and he'd been correct.

Only with a threat to completely cut her off financially did they manage to cajole her into going to school across the country. Laurence sold her car to make sure she understood that his threat wasn't an idle one. When fall came around, the three traveled to the university together. Laurence wanted to go only to ensure that Gloria actually made it to the dorm where she was assigned. If left to her own devices, he feared she would seek out the same kind of people she was running around with at home and once again blow off her studies. *What if,* he sometimes worried, *she fell in with the same kind of people as Arnold?* Regina, on the other hand, had a silly fantasy about getting Gloria settled into a dorm room and sharing a teary eyed mother-daughter moment when it was time for Laurence and Regina to leave.

Gloria was twenty-five when she finally graduated from college. Her parents continued to support her financially during her college years. She never so much as glanced at a bill for her tuition, and she withdrew money from her bank account for clothes, booze, cigarettes, art supplies, and dates whenever she felt like it. Regina's boasting about the prestigious school her daughter attended was somewhat subdued because Gloria was already two years behind. She was mostly just relieved that men like Roy, to her knowledge, were finally out of the picture.

In spite of all of her rebellion against her mother's plans for her, Gloria ended up exactly where Regina wanted her. She lived near them in the condo her parents had purchased for her in a trendy area of the city. She saw them a couple of times per month, more often when Regina had her way, and for the most part, she no longer dated anyone who Regina would call a "social dead end."

At one time, the neighborhood where Gloria lived had been a rundown area filled with old meat-packing warehouses and former sweat shops. Winos and prostitutes had dominated the neighborhood. They trolled the streets and squatted in the old buildings. It was theirs until a group of investment bankers took notice of this vastly unused, underdeveloped section of the city. It was a stone's throw, the investors noted, to the trendier area of downtown. It seemed like a natural progression to build up the old area and convert former warehouses into expensive lofts and high end nightclubs. And it had worked. The investment bankers made their money back in spades. Laurence was one of them.

Not only did Laurence own the building in which his daughter lived, he also owned the small art gallery she managed. She regularly introduced herself as the owner, but Laurence didn't mind. *What else would she do,* he often wondered, *if she didn't have the gallery?* He had even let her name it. After a couple of days deliberating, Gloria chose the moniker Lucinda's Lair for the gallery. "Why?" Laurence had asked. "Who is Lucinda?"

"That's the brilliance of it!" Gloria told him, delighted with herself. There was no Lucinda, so the gallery would always be shrouded in the mystery of a silent partner who was clearly too glamorous and too worldly to even visit her own business. The intrigue would draw artists and collectors in like bees to honey, she had insisted to her skeptical father. It would be a huge hit, Gloria had assured him. Strangely, she had been right, although Laurence still had doubts about the name. Lucinda's Lair was a chic, exclusive little hole in the wall that, so far, had raked in a considerable amount of profit.

Gloria managed the day-to-day operations, and she'd decided before the ink was even dry on the mortgage that *her* gallery would cater to a very specific group of artists and clientele. Regina, Laurence was not surprised, heartily approved of Gloria's vision of the gallery. Only the select individuals with the most refined artistic ideas should be a part of Gloria's gallery, Regina had said many times over the years. What she meant, Laurence knew, was that only the richest assholes in town could hang their homely, abstract paintings and display their dreary sculptures in *Gloria's* gallery. He supposed that as long as Gloria had something to do with her time, then he didn't have to worry so much that she might end up like her cousin, Arnold.

Chapter Fourteen

The afternoon sun blazed overhead as they walked to A. C.'s house. They went at a leisurely pace, not chatting much but comfortable in shared silence. Carrington was grateful that Mrs. Browne wasn't especially talkative; she found herself suddenly exhausted. There was just too much to think about, too many decisions to make. Where would she spend the night? She was genuinely afraid to go home, back to Joan, but how could she expect that Mrs. Browne would want a strange girl in her house? And even if she invited Carrington to spend the night, what then? Carrington wasn't entirely sure how she felt about staying overnight with Mrs. Browne, but then, hadn't that been the point of finding her? She struggled with these thoughts as they strolled along the wide, tree-lined streets in A. C.'s neighborhood.

They passed the park, Mastic Crossing, and Carrington knew they were halfway there. She gazed at each of the houses they passed. They were all so huge, with sprawling, manicured lawns, stone walkways, two, sometimes even three stories, and huge bay windows. She was painfully aware of her clothes, her shoes, even the purse she'd borrowed from Joan. What did she look like to the people who lived in these gorgeous houses? Were they watching her from their windows as she passed by, wondering, "Who is that shabby-looking girl and what is she doing here?"

Colorful flower beds adorned most of the yards, as well as decorative birdbaths and an occasional fountain. Carrington was so mesmerized by the neighborhood that she almost didn't notice when A. C. began to walk up the flagstone path to one of the houses. She paused for a moment at the edge of the lawn while A. C. continued walking. A. C. glanced back, seeing Carrington hesitate. She flashed a warm smile.

"It's all right, Carrington. This is my house. Please come in."

Carrington blushed and followed A. C. up the path.

Only on television and in magazines had she seen living rooms like the one in A. C.'s house. It was enormous and filled with overstuffed beige couches and blond wood tables. One of the extravagantly high walls was covered with framed photos. Some were black and white and appeared to be very old; others were in color and looked relatively recent. The floor was a rich, warm brown wood decorated with a large Persian rug in the center of the room and smaller matching rugs near each of the largest pieces of furniture. While A. C. put her sunglasses away and stowed her magazines and books in a magazine rack, Carrington tried to imagine living in a house like this one. She tried to envision herself curled up and reading on one of the fluffy couches, or coming home from school, unlocking the heavy front door, and kicking off her shoes in the entryway where she stood now. It was difficult to fathom. She could only picture Joan's face everywhere she looked; Joan, in her skin tight jeans and halter tops, pawing the furniture and wondering aloud about their cost, or eyeing the picture frames and speculating hatefully on what they might be worth. What would Joan do with a Persian rug? Brag to her friends at the bar about it? *What would I do with one?* Carrington wondered suddenly. *I have no more right to be here than Joan does.* The red in her cheeks deepened and spread to her ears. She was sweating profusely beneath Joan's blouse.

"Why don't we have something cold to drink?" A. C. asked.

Carrington nodded and followed A. C. into the kitchen gratefully, eager to escape her thoughts.

In the kitchen, A. C. poured glasses of iced green tea, and that reminded Carrington of the gift bag she'd been carrying all afternoon. She presented it shyly, sliding it across the kitchen table with a bashful smile.

"Well, what's this?" A. C. asked, clearly delighted.

"I just wanted to give you something ..." Carrington trailed off, unsure of what to say.

A. C. beamed at her and pulled the tissue paper gingerly from the gift bag. She peered inside at the two small bottles.

"Oh, this is lovely! And green tea, my favorite." She unscrewed the cap on the lotion bottled and brought it to her nose. "Mmm, this is wonderful! I used to have green tea lotion. When it ran out, I just kept forgetting to buy another. But I've never had green tea shampoo. You're a sweetheart, Carrington. You didn't have to do this, really." A. C. set down the lotion and focused on Carrington. "Do you know what a wonderful girl you are? Anyone would be blessed to have a young lady like you in their life."

Carrington was somewhat embarrassed but mostly overjoyed by A. C.'s reaction.

"You're just saying it's your favorite," she said with a small laugh, her cheeks a fiery shade of scarlet.

A. C. chuckled.

"Oh, no, that's not true at all! The only tea I drink is green tea. I've loved the fragrance for years now. You couldn't have chosen a nicer gift for me, dear, although you really didn't have to give me anything."

"I know," Carrington said. "But I wanted to." They smiled timidly across the table at one another.

It was so strange being in A. C.'s house. It was a lovely place, and A. C. seemed so kind, but Carrington still felt odd and incredulous about everything that had occurred. Just twenty-four hours ago, she knew nothing about her father or his side of the family, and now she was sitting at the kitchen table of the woman who could very well be her grandmother. Thinking about this, she began to feel dizzy, and the big lunch, heavy in her stomach, made her tired. She yawned behind one hand while A. C. refilled their glasses.

Carrington thought of Joan. Where was she right now? She glanced at the wall clock. It was two in the afternoon. If Joan had to work, she would be at the store by now. She probably would have come home and found the house empty. Carrington imagined Missy left the house soon after she woke up and showered. *I still have a few more hours,* she thought, *before Joan will be suspicious about why I'm not home.* The thought of facing Joan again made her fidget in her seat. A. C. eyed her with concern as she set the two glasses of tea down on the table.

They sipped their tea quietly, neither of them knowing quite what to say. A. C. glanced at her kitchen clock, hoping Carrington wouldn't see. She didn't want the girl to leave. She knew that at some point very soon she would have to contact the child's mother and her own lawyer, but not yet. A. C. only wanted to be near the lovely young lady sitting at her kitchen table. The more she studied the narrow, freckled face and the more she admired the girl's thick hair, identical in color to Arnold's and at one time her own, the more she was convinced that this girl was her blood.

"Try to relax, dear," she said to Carrington. "There's no hurry, and you don't have to be afraid. Let's just chat about whatever comes to mind, okay? No pressure." She reached across the table and gently patted Carrington's hand.

Carrington's eyes filled with tears when she met A. C.'s gaze. It all came rushing out then, like a monstrous surge of water from a busted dam. When Carrington later remembered that afternoon, she realized that she probably would not have been able to stop herself from sharing everything with A. C., every humiliating detail. She confided in her, with tears streaming down her face, about the times she begged Joan for a few dollars outside of Joan's favorite dive bars. She told A. C. how helpless she felt about Missy's problems in school and how worried she was that Missy would grow up and become just like Joan. A small eternity passed as she recounted the holidays she and Missy spent wondering when Joan would come home and hoping she would bring food when she did finally return. She wept as she talked about the endless parade of strange men in Joan's life.

Carrington never meant to sound so self-pitying. She hated the sound of her voice as she told A. C. about her life. She loathed the fat tears that slid down her cheeks and dotted her lap. She tried to choke them back, but it was a useless endeavor. Much to her relief, A. C. did not cluck piteously. She didn't say things like, "There, there, everything is going to be all right tomorrow; you'll see," or any of the other ridiculous things that Carrington felt adults said too often. She simply listened. She watched Carrington with obvious interest and concern, but her expression wasn't one of cheap pity.

When Carrington was finished, A. C. left the table just long enough to pour a glass of water and grab a handful of paper napkins. She was relieved to be away from Carrington's eyes, even if it was just for a few seconds. It wasn't because she didn't want to be near her; it was because she didn't want Carrington to see that her face was pale with rage, lips drawn into a tight line. *Joan Coyle. Disgusting, trashy Joan Coyle. All these years, she's been hurting this child, tormenting her. All these years, Carrington's had no one. My Arnold, he had a little girl, and he never even told us. How could he keep this from us?* A. C. bit her lower lip to keep from crying and returned to Carrington, handing her both the water and the napkins.

Carrington was clearly exhausted. She dabbed at her face and sipped her water, looking like a wilted flower. *This child needs to rest,* A. C. thought.

"You must be ready to fall over," A. C. said. "Why don't you lie down for a while? Close your eyes for a few minutes. I need to make a few phone calls, and while I'm taking care of that, you can relax. Sound okay?"

Carrington hesitated. It felt strange to have someone suggest she take a nap, but she was so tired. She felt like she could sleep sitting up in the kitchen chair.

She nodded in agreement. "Yes," she whispered. "Thank you."

A. C. smiled reassuringly and led her up the stairs to one of the guest rooms. It was just as lovely as the rest of the house, Carrington noted, wishing for the millionth time that she wasn't wearing scuffed sneakers and old jeans. She sat down on the pale blue and yellow quilt that covered the bed. It was so soft and thick beneath her hands.

"My mother made that," A. C. said quietly. "She gave it to me when Arnold was born."

"It's beautiful," Carrington murmured.

A. C. smiled. "Thank you. I think you'll be comfortable in here. Go ahead and rest. I'll check on you later. If you can't sleep or you need anything, please let me know, okay? Feel free to look around the house or help yourself to any books or a snack whenever you like. Now, get some rest, sweetheart." She gazed affectionately at Carrington from the doorway for a moment longer before closing the door behind her.

Carrington glanced around the room drowsily. She would have liked to explore the built-in bookshelf directly across from the bed. Along with scores of books, the shelves held old black and white photos in silver frames, including several that appeared to be from A. C.'s wedding. *Maybe later*, she thought, kicking off her shoes and lying back on the soft quilt. She pulled one of the pillows half over her face to block out the sunshine and was asleep within minutes.

Chapter Fifteen

When Carmen answered on the second ring, A. C. was surprised and relieved. Even though semi-retired, Carmen still frequently worked. When she wasn't working, she golfed or traveled. It was difficult to pin down Carmen Villareal, but in spite of her always full schedule, Carmen had flown in for Arnold's funeral and stayed with A. C. for a few nights.

"Honey, I was just thinking of you!" Carmen chirped brightly when A. C. greeted her.

"That's your standard line," said A. C., laughing. "You probably thought I was a man."

"Heck no, I just got rid of the last one. What do I want another one for right away?" Carmen answered without skipping a beat. "How are you feeling, love?" Her voice was more serious.

"Oh, I'm getting by," A. C. responded with a sigh. "I'm trying to stay busy. Sometimes it helps. How are you?"

"That's really good to hear, honey," Carmen said warmly. "I'm doing fine! Just broke up with Stanley, but he was such a dud. I should have done it a long time ago. Remember when he took me on that surprise Bahamas cruise a few months ago?"

A. C. thought for a moment.

"Oh, yes! You sent me that obscene postcard from Nassau," she recalled with a chuckle.

"Obscene, nothin'. Honey, you should have seen some of the postcards I *almost* sent you! Anyway, what I didn't tell you about that cruise was that it was Stanley's first—and not his last, mind you—attempt to get me to swing; and I don't mean the kind that involves Glenn Miller tunes."

A. C. gasped. "Did you do it?"

"Hell no!" Carmen exclaimed.

They both giggled. It was funny the way Carmen had always peppered her words with endearments like "honey" and "love." From anyone else, A. C. would have hated it, but when Carmen called her honey or sweetie, it was somehow comforting. It reminded her of when they were both young women away from home for the first time and sharing a dorm room in college. That seemed like a lifetime ago now. True, it was more than forty-odd years past. *Everything was so different then; our lives had yet to happen,* A. C. often mused when she thought of the early years of their friendship. *God, it's good to hear Carmen's voice*, she thought. *We need to get in touch more often. It seems like we only see one another when someone dies.*

Carmen's brother, her only sibling, had passed away a few years prior. He had had a massive heart attack and died in his own backyard where he was raking leaves. After his wife called Carmen, Carmen immediately called A. C. They cried on the phone together, and A. C. was on a plane within forty-eight hours. She stayed with Carmen for a while, helping her get through her kid brother's eulogy and burial. It brought back so many memories of Calvin's death. She and Carmen leaned on one another and sobbed as Manuel Villareal's casket was lowered into the earth.

Carmen seemed to read her mind.

"Please don't tell me you're calling with bad news," she said, her voice suddenly grave. "How are you really doing, honey?"

A. C. was moved by the genuine concern she heard in Carmen's voice. In her heart, Carmen was her sister in ways that Regina never would be.

"No bad news," she assured Carmen, "and I'm doing fairly well, although I had a bit of a blowout with Regina this afternoon. Honestly, though, I could use a little break from her. Isn't that terrible, saying that about my own sister? Well, Regina and I were never close. Anyway, I'm getting off track. I don't have bad news, but there's been … an interesting development," she said, unsure of how to tell her dearest friend about a possible grandchild.

"Oh, geez, A. C., you're not calling to ask for bail money, are you?" Carmen said with a chuckle. "What does 'interesting' mean? Tell me what's up already!"

A. C. grinned. Carmen would always be Carmen, and she loved her for it. She spent the better part of an hour telling her best friend everything. Carmen let out a low whistle. The normally chatty woman seemed at a loss for words. Her reaction worried A. C.

"Well, what do you think? What should I do? I need your advice as my lawyer, but I also need your advice as my best friend. Am I in over my head or what?" A. C. asked in frantic tone.

Carmen sensed her friend's anxiety.

"It's all right, A. C. This is going to be okay, I assure you," she said, her voice now the serious one she used with her clients. "So, the girl is there with you now?"

"She's here in the house, but not right here in the same room. Hopefully, she's sleeping by now. I told her she should rest for a while in the guest room; the poor little thing is exhausted. She was practically starving, too. I was tempted to buy her another plate of food, but it might have made her sick, and I can tell she's sensitive about accepting anything from anybody. Carrington has had to fight all her life. Joan Coyle has been hell on her," she said, clearly furious.

Oh, boy, Carmen thought, *A. C.'s already attached to this kid.* She sighed, dreading what she was about to tell her friend.

"You can't keep her overnight, A. C. She's a minor, and we don't know for certain that you two are blood relatives. Even if it turns out that you are her grandmother, right now you don't have custody of her."

There was a pause.

"I can't send her back to Joan, Carmen. I can't and I won't. You haven't seen the bruises on this child's face. You haven't seen how thin she is. Joan Coyle is a monster! I can't with good conscious send Carrington back there."

"You can't keep her with you, though. Not legally. I want to help you, A. C.; I want to help both you *and* Carrington. First we need to determine if she is indeed Arnold's child, and then we'll proceed from there. If you keep her away from her legal guardian, you'll be breaking the law. Joan will have that on her side. Worst case scenario, she could report you for kidnapping. Even if it turns out that Carrington is Arnold's daughter, with a charge of kidnapping against you, it could take months to get that cleared and prove that you're fit to raise her."

"What happens if I call the police right now to report Joan Coyle for child abuse?" A. C. asked.

Again Carmen sighed. It was unfair, she thought, that A. C., who could provide a safe and loving home to any child, might have to fight tooth and nail for the right to be a part of her own grandchild's life, assuming that Carrington was truly A. C.'s granddaughter.

"A unit would be sent to their home, the children most likely removed and placed in foster care, and Joan Coyle would be investigated. If the officers feel that either child appears to be injured or sickly, they'll be examined in a hospital. Once released from the hospital, they'll be placed with a foster family while Joan is arrested, investigated, and goes to court."

A. C. began to cry. Her tears were quiet, but Carmen knew she was weeping. She wanted to cry with her friend. It was all so unfair! But she would do whatever was within her power to make this work out in A. C.'s favor.

"I'm going to make a few calls, A. C. I can pull some strings and arrange for a paternity test at Mercy Hospital tomorrow afternoon. That's where … that's where Arnold was taken after he passed away, right?" She hated herself for asking, but it was necessary.

A. C. sniffed and dabbed her eyes with a paper napkin. *Arnold,* she thought. *My poor, foolish son.*

"Yes," she answered. "That's where his body was examined." She choked out the last word.

"It was recent enough that they may still have some blood or tissue samples," Carmen stated matter-of-factly. "At any rate, blood and cheek swabs will be taken from both you and Carrington, and even if the hospital doesn't have anything from Arnold, we can still determine any familial relationship based on the samples you and Carrington provide. Oh, damn!" Carmen exclaimed suddenly, startling A. C.

"What? What is it?" A. C. cried.

"I just realized that we'll need the consent of Carrington's legal guardian for any kind of medical procedure, even something as simple as a blood test."

Both women brooded silently for a few moments.

"Carmen, you mentioned that if we report Joan for suspected child abuse, her children may be taken to the hospital for examinations, right?" A. C. asked, sounding excited.

"Of course," Carmen answered. "And from what you've described of Carrington's injuries, A. C., maybe that's not such a bad idea. You've only seen Carrington's face. You commented that she's wearing a warm weather blouse and jeans. It's late May, for crying out loud. I have to wonder what the poor girl's body looks like."

A. C. cringed. She hadn't considered that. She swallowed hard, thinking of how painfully thin Carrington was. *Oh, that poor, sweet girl,* she thought, fighting back more tears.

"There's the other child to consider," Carmen continued. "Is it possible that she's also Arnold's daughter?"

"I don't think so," A. C. said. "Carrington says that Melissa, her younger sister, receives correspondence from her father on a semi-regular basis, and she also resembles him."

"It sounds unlikely that Melissa Coyle is related to you, but she's still a minor, and she shouldn't be in a home like the one you've described. She'll have to be removed from Joan Coyle's custody and placed into foster care. Even if I can get a judge to agree to let you have temporary custody of Carrington while Joan is investigated and awaits a hearing, are you prepared to accept the reality of Carrington's half-sister living with a foster family? Is Carrington prepared to deal with that?" Carmen asked.

A. C. began to feel dizzy. She was glad she was already sitting down.

"Well, of course I'm not prepared," she said. "I mean, I'm not really prepared for any of this." Her voice took on an edge of panic. "This morning I woke up thinking that the only family I have left in the world is a selfish battle ax of a sister and her daughter who was cut from the exact same cloth. Now I may have a granddaughter. A granddaughter! And she's this sweet, intelligent, respectful young lady who anyone would be thrilled to have as a grandchild." She was dangerously close to crying again. "I have to know, Carmen. I have to know for sure if Carrington is my granddaughter, and if she is, I want her to come and live with me."

"I'm not going to sugarcoat anything, A. C.," Carmen began. "Taking this on is probably going to be a very long, emotionally exhausting, and possibly expensive process. At this point, we know next to nothing about Joan Coyle. While I doubt it, we don't know if she has a lawyer on retainer. If she does, that will complicate things. Melissa Coyle is another complication. Even if she's not related to you, she's related to Carrington, and Carrington sounds like the kind of person who will worry about her younger sister." She paused for a moment. "A. C., what were you asking just a moment ago about the children being examined in a hospital?"

A. C.'s mind was momentarily blank. There was so much to consider, her head was swimming.

"Oh!" she cried out. "Yes! Well, I don't think it would hurt to have Carrington and her sister examined in a hospital. I haven't laid eyes on Melissa yet, but from what Carrington tells me, Joan hardly ever touches the youngest girl. Still, though, considering poor Carrington's face and what you said about … about her body, I think she *ought* to be examined by a physician. They both should. And during that time, Carrington and I could have our blood drawn for the paternity test. I want to start this process as soon as possible, Carmen, and I will spare no expense. Calvin did well for us over the years, both with his wages and his investments. He made sure I would be very comfortable as I grew older." She paused, remembering how they had planned to travel when he retired. Her hazel eyes filled with tears, but she quickly wiped them away and focused on her conversation with Carmen. "I will spare no expense," she said again. "I'll pay for the paternity testing, court fees, whatever it takes."

"Well, all right then. I should be able to fly in tomorrow or the morning after and meet you at the hospital to begin the DNA testing. Before you contact the police to report Joan for suspected child abuse, let me make a few calls. I'll see how much I can simplify this for us. I'll be in touch with you within the afternoon, so please try to stay home if you can. I advise you not to have any contact with Joan Coyle and not to keep Carrington at your home past her legal curfew." She sighed, knowing that A. C. was probably going to ignore the last part and invite Carrington to spend the night at her house. Not that she could exactly blame her. Carmen had a difficult time stomaching the idea of sending Carrington back into the violent hands of Joan Coyle.

"I'll keep the phone nearby," A. C. assured her. "Thank you so much, Carmen. I still can hardly believe this is all happening! It's like … it's like I have a second chance at being a mother." She began to weep again.

Carmen sighed and closed her eyes. *God, please let this kid turn out to be Arnold's,* she prayed silently. If Carrington wasn't A. C.'s granddaughter, she feared what the news might do to her closest friend.

"Anything for you, *amiga*," Carmen told her. "I'll do what I can. Remember what I said, and I'll be in touch soon."

They said their good-byes. A. C. stared at her furniture, the pictures on her walls, not really seeing any of them. She felt dazed. There was so much to do, and yet all she could do at the moment was wait to hear back from Carmen.

I'll keep busy, she decided, jumping to her feet and returning the phone to its cradle. *Even if it's just something mundane, I have to do something.*

She bustled around the kitchen, looking for a tablet to write on and a pen. A. C. tried to focus on writing a grocery list but found it nearly impossible to concentrate. *Well, then,* she thought as she stuffed the pad and paper back into a kitchen drawer, *maybe I'll just do some tidying. Carrington must think this place is a sty.* She busied herself downstairs, dusting, and plumping couch pillows. Every few minutes, she dropped whatever she was doing in a panic, terrified that she'd missed Carmen's call. She was alarmed by how rapidly her heart pounded in her chest. *My God, this is going to be the death of me,* A. C. thought, settling down on the chaise lounge in her living room. *How am I possibly going to get through this?* She leaned against the plush fabric and closed her eyes. The events of the day finally caught up with her. A. C. was exhausted. *Just for a minute,* she thought, *I need to rest just for a minute.*

Chapter Sixteen

Carmen took another sip of her cappuccino and stared into the wooded hills that surrounded her home. She stretched her sandaled feet and closed her eyes. After a few deep, cleansing breaths, she knew it was high time to start making phone calls. She had one hell of a task ahead of her, and she would do anything and everything she could to help her dearest friend. The most important thing, she thought, was to make certain that A. C. didn't land herself in hot water. What was the old saying? The road to hell is paved with good intentions. A. C. could easily find herself in trouble for simply trying to help a kid in need. Any situation involving minors was tricky, Carmen knew. With adults, things were more cut and dried, except in extreme cases. But when children were involved, well, it was a whole different playing field.

She'd been practicing law for nearly forty years and had intended to semi retire after her sixty-fifth birthday the previous year. Carmen found it difficult to stay away from her work. It was an addiction—her one vice, she often thought. She'd been unable to make two marriages work because she was a lifelong, unrelenting workaholic. But her work ethic had served her well in many other ways. From her third-floor master suite balcony, she surveyed the acres of land that stretched in all directions. The land and the sprawling, custom-built house and tennis court, all of it belonged solely to Carmen, and she had acquired it all on her own.

There were ways, Carmen knew, to circumvent the letter of the law. She was hoping to avoid the drawn-out scenario she'd described to A. C. It was quite possible that Carmen could get a judge to grant A. C. custody of her granddaughter, if the paternity test was positive, without an intense investigation and long trial. Most of that depended on Carrington's mother, Joan Coyle. If Carmen could get to Joan, talk to her in just the right way, there was at least a fair chance that Carrington might be able to move in with her grandmother without the trauma of a nasty custody battle. Carmen was always very straight with her clients, even if they happened to be her close friends, as was the case with A. C. Even if she had a hunch that she might be able to smooth the situation out better than they could imagine, she always made sure they were aware of the risks involved.

The bottom line in this case, Carmen knew, was money. A. C. had said as much herself. Joan Coyle was using her child as a bargaining chip to get cash. What she hadn't considered, it seemed, was A. C. and Carrington wanting a relationship. That could be problematic, depending on how angry Joan would be when she discovered that her daughter had gone behind her back. Still, though, Carmen was fairly confident that the dollar signs in Joan's greedy eyes would ultimately be the deciding factor.

Time would be a factor, too. The whole thing was very time sensitive. First, Carmen needed to establish that Carrington and

A. C. were, in fact, related. That would take a business week, maybe a little less, best case scenario. Carmen also needed time to do some homework on Joan Coyle. She was willing to bet that a woman as despicable as Joan probably had at least a handful of arrests to her name. If Joan tried to play hardball, having a criminal record would work against her and help Carmen's case. Digging up Joan's record, if any, wouldn't take long, but it still needed to be done as soon as possible. Carmen wanted to be heavily armed when she confronted Ms. Coyle. Even if Joan didn't have a criminal record, Carmen could probably threaten her with several counts of child abuse, as well as assault and battery based on what Carrington had been through in the past several hours.

Yes, time was crucial. Carmen grinned at the familiar rush that began in her chest and spread throughout her body. She could never give this up, she knew. She'd probably die behind her desk or in court. Carmen jotted down a list in her leather-bound notebook and then flipped open her phone to begin the first of many phone calls.

Chapter Seventeen

It was no surprise to Carmen to learn that Joan Coyle wasn't a stranger to the darker side of the law. She'd been arrested dozens of times: driving under the influence, possession of marijuana, and her most common offense, public intoxication. She'd never served more than a couple of weeks in jail, and she hadn't been arrested for over a decade. Carmen grimly realized that staying out of trouble for more than ten years could help Joan in court, if Joan chose to go that route. She was also disturbed by the fact that missing from Joan's lengthy list of charges were child abuse and neglect. It was obvious from what A. C. said that Joan Coyle employed violence and verbal abuse as everyday means of parenting. It wasn't impossible to prove that she was an abusive mother, but it would certainly help if there was some record of it. Carmen had high hopes, though, of devising a strategy that would be quick *and* successful for A. C. and Carrington. *Hopefully,* she thought as she jotted down notes, *they'll see as little of a courtroom as possible.*

There would be significant expenses for A. C., Carmen knew. Not that A. C. couldn't afford it; she was very well off, but Carmen still hated the idea of her best friend handing over money to such a cruel person.

Oh, well, she thought with a sigh. *If it buys her peace of mind and allows her custody of her grandchild, then so be it. Money well spent.* There was the little matter of proving Carrington was, indeed, A. C.'s grandchild, of course. *The blood test will probably be the least complicated task of the whole affair,* Carmen thought, *yet one of the most decisive.*

Setting up a paternity test was simple enough. Carmen made a call to the hospital where Arnold's body was taken after it was discovered in the motel room. She had friends there; she played golf with Maurice Lindt, the hospital administrator, whenever she was in town, and she exchanged e-mail and had lunch whenever she could with Ana Cortez, one of the hospital's senior pediatricians. She'd met them both in college. Other than A. C., Maurice and Ana were the only friends she'd had for more than a few years.

Maurice was a great bear of a man with short-cropped, salt and pepper hair and kind brown eyes. They'd dated briefly after college, but the relationship failed because she was busy with law school and he wanted to settle down and start a family. They had remained good friends over the years, though, and Maurice got a thrill out of teasing that Carmen was secretly, or not so secretly, still in love with him. She actually enjoyed egging him on about that. He was a huge flirt whenever he saw or heard from her.

"Well, hello, gorgeous," he cooed when he realized it was Carmen calling. "Just had to hear my voice, eh?" He chuckled.

She rolled her eyes but laughed.

"That's exactly it, Morrie." She was the only who called him by a nickname. "I was just sitting here idly with a bottle of merlot and my little black book, and I thought, 'Hmm, it's high time I started calling the few men I've ever loved and telling them every little thing about themselves that once made me all hot and bothered.'"

"What do you mean 'them'?" he huffed good-naturedly. "You mean I'm not the great love of your life? The one who got away? The one whose face you see when you wake up in the morning?"

Carmen laughed. "Oddly enough, Morrie, no, you're not. You know whose face I see first thing in the morning? Gilbert, my Pekingese."

Maurice chortled. "So, what's up, sex pot? If you're not calling to engage in illicit phone sex during my coffee break, then there must be something pressing." He laughed again.

Carmen sighed wistfully. Yes, some part of her heart would always belong to Maurice. But most of it belonged to her career and her independence. She launched into the tale she herself had only recently heard from A. C. She gave him the condensed version, focusing heavily on Carrington's plight at the hands of a horrendously abusive mother and the significant possibility that this child might be A. C.'s granddaughter. How soon, Carmen wanted to know, could they have the results of a paternity test.

Maurice was silent in thought for a few moments. His tone was serious when he finally spoke.

"Well, the main thing is getting the girl away from her mother," he said. "I mean, even if A. C. isn't the child's grandparent, the poor kid can't stay there anymore." He sounded sad.

"I know," Carmen responded. "And I'm going to do everything I can for her and for A. C. I really hope it turns out that A. C. *is*

Carrington's grandmother. This would be wonderful for both of them." She felt a lump form in her throat.

Maurice told her that he could authorize a rush order for the blood test, shortening the typical seven-business-day wait to three business days. Carmen told him she would be in town as soon as possible. He asked her to instruct A. C. and Carrington to be at the hospital in two days, and he would take care of the rest. She agreed and thanked him. Of course, he ended their conversation by telling her that if she really wanted to express her gratitude, she could go away with him on a weekend trip to Vegas. She laughed and agreed, but said she'd only go if he dressed up as a showgirl for her.

She had another cappuccino and became completely wired. It wasn't simply the caffeine, though. Carmen knew part of the rush was from working, and especially from starting a case that she hoped and prayed would help her best friend. She booked a next-day flight for herself. In a little over twenty-four hours, she'd be with A. C. and she would meet the young woman who might very well be A. C.'s granddaughter. She savored the last swallow of her coffee, inhaled the fresh perfume of the outdoors, and went inside to pack.

Chapter Eighteen

For the first time in a long time, Carrington's dreams were not nightmares. When she woke in the soft, comfortable bed in Mrs. Browne's house, she had only a vague impression of her dream: a sunny afternoon spent in a garden. She yawned sleepily and gazed around the bedroom. The shadows of the furniture on the hardwood floors appeared to have slanted considerably since she fell asleep. A few hours must have passed. Carrington sat up with alarm. She glanced anxiously around the room for a clock. Was Joan home? Was she looking for her?

She wondered if Mrs. Browne had contacted Joan, and if she had, what was said. She had such a difficult time imagining the two women occupying the same space. It was like having both day and night at the same time. Carrington couldn't decide which woman would eclipse the other.

She knew Joan was more than capable of putting on a performance of false benevolence, or at the very least, civility. She'd witnessed the charade many times, during the few school events Joan had ever willingly attended or those she was forced to attend. When Missy got into fights with other kids, Joan was required to go to the school to pick up her youngest daughter from the principal's office. She listened and nodded her head while the principal complained about Missy's attitude, and when it was her turn to speak, Joan blustered about giving her child a stern talking to and grounding her. It was sickening.

Missy was never punished by Joan, not really. Joan would threaten the girl and warn her to stay out of trouble, but that was the extent of it. In fact, Carrington was the one who would be punished. Not directly; Joan would never outright admit that she was hitting Carrington for something that Missy had done, but that's what would happen. The three of them would go home after Missy was suspended from school, Joan would nag Missy a little bit, and then she would start drinking. After three or so drinks, something about the house would anger her: the living room was dusty, the bath mat was gray with mildew—anything. All of it was Carrington's fault. Joan would berate her for hours on end, and the entire episode never failed to conclude with a slap across the face for Carrington, sometimes more than that, and several more drinks for Joan, usually consumed at one of her favorite bars. Missy was generally out of sight while Carrington was yelled at and smacked. She hid in their room or simply left the house entirely as soon as they came home, disappearing for hours without explanation. These were the nights when Carrington went to bed crying into a damp wash cloth, visions of leaving Joan's dark, little house for good lulling her into a fitful sleep.

Her mother, Carrington knew, would be wickedly angry when she found out that Carrington had sought Mrs. Browne on her own. She cringed at the thought of facing her. It would be terrible. Of course, if Mrs. Browne or, better yet, Mrs. Browne's lawyer made the first move to involve Joan, Joan would be forced as an older teen, Arnold was frequently doing something illegal in his room.

She had just raised her hand to tap on the door when the phone rang downstairs. She rushed down the staircase, nearly tripping on the last two steps.

"Hello, Carmen?" Her voice was urgent.

"You bet, kid," Carmen teased her.

A. C. sank into a chair and laughed. Somehow, Carmen always managed to make her smile.

Carmen explained what Maurice had said about the blood test, and told A. C. what she'd learned about Joan's history.

"Frankly," she said, "I'm surprised she hasn't done any time in prison. Poor Carrington," Carmen murmured.

A. C.'s breath caught in her throat. She nearly began crying, but she managed to hold in her tears.

"So, where do we go from here?" she asked.

Carmen let out a deep breath and closed her eyes. If she was a gambling woman, she would bet her life savings that the instructions she was about to give her dear friend would not be followed, not in the least.

"A. C., honey, I need you to not do anything rash. You have to be very, *very* careful about all of this," she warned. "If you keep Carrington with you, even if it's just overnight, Joan could cry kidnapping. You do *not* want any charges brought against you, especially one as serious as that. Not if you really want to help Carrington. You have to think about what's best for her, A. C. I know these things aren't fair, and sometimes it feels like the process is harder on the victim than it is on those who have done wrong, but if we want to win this, then we have to be smart about it."

There was silence as A. C. considered Carmen's words.

"All right," she said at last. "I will be careful, I promise you that, Carmen. Try not to worry."

Carmen sighed, hearing all that was unsaid in her friend's response.

"That's a tall order, *amiga*," she said.

They both laughed, a bit ruefully, and Carmen gave A. C. her flight information. She'd be in town very soon and would go with A. C. and Carrington to the hospital. Maurice had promised to set up an appointment for them.

"Is this really happening?" A. C. asked before they hung up.

"Yes, it really is," Carmen told her gently. "Are you sure you're ready for this?"

"Ready as I'll ever be, I guess. I'm still in shock, you know? Of all the things that could happen in my life, I never expected this. But … but it's like I've been offered this wonderful gift. I just want this so much it scares me. I don't think I can handle any more pain, Carmen. God, I hope this works out."

I hope so, too, honey, Carmen thought.

Chapter Twenty

There's no way in the world I'm letting Joan near Carrington. Not while there's breath in my lungs, A. C. thought as she hung up the phone. Carmen meant well, and probably knew best, but A. C. could not live with herself if she allowed Carrington to spend one more moment in her mother's presence. Who knew what a woman like Joan Coyle was capable of doing if she felt she'd been crossed? A. C. only had to look at the bruises that marred Carrington's face to imagine. No. Joan would never again lay a hand on Carrington.

She heard movement upstairs and was startled at first. She'd lived alone for so long that the sounds of someone else in the house were strange. It wasn't difficult to remember the days when she knew exactly what Calvin was doing, whether she could see him or not. The sounds of his life were as familiar to her as her own: his key in the front door, his coffee cup on the kitchen counter, the hum of his electric razor. The first few months after Calvin died were the worst, and not simply because her grief was at its rawest stage. She still expected to see him across the table every morning. When she was able to sleep at all, she often woke in the middle of the night, disoriented and distraught to find that he wasn't beside her. She had long ago adjusted to not hearing Arnold in the house. He'd left when he was so young and never came back to live with them. Adjusting to Arnold's absence in the house had been rough, but at least A. C. and Calvin had one another. Losing Calvin felt like losing everything: all of the big things that meant love and family to A. C., and all of the little things that comprised her everyday life.

What would it be like, A. C. wondered, to hear Carrington in the house each day? Was Carrington an early riser? Did she laugh out loud when she read, the way Calvin had? Did she slurp her soup the way Arnold used to, no matter how many times A. C. scolded him about it? Perhaps Carrington was a night owl. Maybe A. C. would have to remind her to get to bed on time and check on her to make sure she wasn't reading under the covers with a flashlight. Of course, kids probably didn't do that anymore. She imagined Carrington would have a computer. Maybe she would have to knock on her door late at night if she heard the tapping of the keys as Carrington stayed up late into the night, doing school work or chatting with friends. *I'm getting way head of myself,* A. C. thought, trying desperately to calm herself down. *I can't let myself imagine a life with this girl when I don't even know for sure she's Arnold's daughter.* Even as she thought it, though, the desire in her heart only increased. A. C. heard the water running in the guest bathroom and decided to busy herself in the kitchen, not wanting to make Carrington feel scrutinized when she came downstairs.

They were both sheepish. A. C. asked Carrington if she felt more rested; Carrington said she did, though she still looked tired. A. C. noticed that Carrington had refreshed her makeup.

It was obvious the girl wasn't used to wearing it; she'd applied it too heavily, and the thick foundation didn't match her skin. But it was also obvious that Carrington was trying to hide her face and not simply enhance it. Even though she now knew the truth about Joan's abusiveness, it was clear that Carrington wasn't ready to let A. C. see the results of Joan's most recent outburst. A. C. tried very hard not to shed any more tears, at least not in front of Carrington. She busied herself at a counter, making fruit salad and sandwiches for the two of them. She realized that time was becoming scarce. She knew she couldn't simply keep Carrington at her house forever without dealing with Joan Coyle. But she also knew she could not and would not let Carrington return to the monster that was her mother. If she had to bend or even break the law to do it, she would. Her own resolve frightened her a bit. She couldn't remember the last time she wanted something as much as she wanted Carrington to be safe and to be her granddaughter.

There were ways to buy time, even if it was just another day or two, and she would do whatever she had to do. She'd already decided that she would suggest that Carrington call her house and leave a message to say that she was spending the night at a friend's house. It didn't sound as if the poor child would be missed at all, unless Joan was looking for someone to shove around. Joan probably would be angry that Carrington wasn't home, but what did it matter at this point? Whatever Carrington did or didn't do, Joan would still be mean and vicious. A. C. thought she could manage to keep Carrington away from home for about two nights before Joan really began to question things. It sounded as if Joan may not even return home that evening. She didn't know or care much where her children were most of the time. *She doesn't deserve Carrington,* A. C. thought, not for the first time.

She set down two large plates on the table. Carrington smiled shyly up at her.

"I'm sorry; I should have offered to help," Carrington said. "I guess I'm just kind of in a daze."

"Don't worry, sweetheart. I understand," A. C. answered. "How about if you get us something to drink, and then let's dig in."

"Okay," Carrington agreed cheerfully, getting up from her chair.

They ate together in companionable silence, both of them worrying about time.

Chapter Twenty-one

A day later, A. C. picked up Carmen at the airport. Carmen fussed at her, saying it would have been no trouble to take a taxi to A. C.'s house, but neither of them would dream of not picking the other up personally when they visited.

A. C. wove her way to the front of the crowd near the security checkpoint. She glanced at her watch anxiously. She was on time, and according to all of the Arrival screens in the airport, so was Carmen's plane. A surge of passengers came around a corridor. The crowd around A. C. buzzed with anticipation. A middle-aged woman standing next to her began weeping into a crumpled piece of tissue, and a young man near her was on a cell phone, making dinner reservations. A. C. squinted and caught a glimpse of Carmen behind a swell of suit-clad men. Even after three hours of air travel and an hour layover, Carmen still looked fresh and lovely. She walked with a confident gait through the airport terminal. She wore a simple summer dress in a shade of pale pink, and a matching lightweight sweater hung from her shoulders. Her creamy brown complexion seemed to glow next to the fabric. Like A. C., Carmen had stopped coloring her hair several years prior. It was mostly gray. She usually kept it pulled back in a long, silver ponytail, but A. C. noted that it was several inches shorter this time and flowing freely around Carmen's oval-shaped face. The gray against her light brown flesh made her dark eyes seem larger and brighter than usual.

A. C. gave Carmen an enthusiastic wave as the passengers began spilling into the greeting area. Carmen squealed like a school girl and rushed into A. C. outstretched arms. A. C. noted with familiar amusement that several of the men in the crowd took notice of Carmen, letting their gazes linger admiringly on her.

"Oh, look at you!" A. C. exclaimed, throwing her arms around her best friend. "You look gorgeous! I swear, you stopped aging at forty."

"Tell that to my breasts," Carmen answered with a laugh, not caring who heard what she said.

A. C. snickered. "You are so bad!"

"And you love it," Carmen shot back.

They beamed at one another through a few tears and linked arms as they walked to the baggage carousel.

It wasn't until they were settled in the car that A. C. told Carmen that Carrington was still at her house.

"What?" Carmen gasped. "You've kept her with you all this time? A. C., I told you not to do that! Oh, God," she groaned.

"It hasn't been that long!" A. C. cried. "I couldn't let her go back to that awful woman, Carmen, no way."

"Where does her mother think she is?" Carmen asked.

"Spending the night at a friend's house," A. C. answered in a quiet voice.

"If she stays at your house again tonight you will have kept her away from her legal guardian for *two days*!" Carmen was clearly annoyed.

"What else was I supposed to do?" A. C. asked, her tone rigid with anxiety.

"Contact the authorities. At least take her to the hospital and have the abuse documented. I told you about the appointment Maurice set up for Carrington tomorrow afternoon! A. C., do you realize you've broken the law? Joan Coyle could have a field day with this!"

A single tear slid down A. C.'s cheek, and Carmen instantly regretted the exasperation in her voice.

"We'll make it okay, honey," she soothed. "I know. I understand, and for what it's worth, I agree. No child should have to return to the waiting hands of an abusive parent. We just need to try to be as rational as possible and remember that every decision right now is crucial for Carrington's well-being."

She squeezed A. C.'s hand, and they both felt somewhat calmer. *I'll fix this somehow,* Carmen thought.

Carmen's resolve to help her dearest friend was only cemented when she finally came face-to-face with the mystery girl known as Carrington. She fell in love with her almost immediately. And after she overcame her initial shyness, it was clear that Carrington liked Carmen, as well.

Over the next couple of days, Carmen worked her magic. That's the way it appeared to A. C. and Carrington. Privately, Carmen called in every favor she was ever owed. She spent hours on the phone, explaining, negotiating, and demanding. The first thing she had to do was buy A. C. time. The worst possible thing that could happen would be if A. C. suddenly found herself with a criminal record for keeping a minor away from her custodial parent. It took some hard dealing and a number of heated phone calls to Joan Coyle herself, but Carmen was able to swing it. *The mouth on that woman,* Carmen thought more than once after speaking with Joan. *She'd make a sailor run crying home to mommy.* Once Joan realized that she was actually going to receive a considerable chunk of money, she was quite willing to work something out about custody of Carrington. It was disgusting the way Joan had no qualms about using her daughter as a bargaining chip. Carmen repeatedly had to remind herself that the bottom line was to help A. C. and Carrington. There were moments she would have preferred being dropped into a live volcano over talking to Joan Coyle.

With Maurice Lindt's help, the blood work was expedited and proved that Carrington was indeed Arnold's daughter. She cried with A. C. and Carrington when it was confirmed that they were related by blood. The three celebrated the news with dinner at one of Carmen's favorite restaurants, an upscale place that specialized in fondue. They were excited and chatty, but behind each of their smiles was the anxiety about what was to come. Proving that Carrington and A. C. were related was only the beginning of the battle.

A few days later, the paperwork was ready. It was time, at last, for Carmen to meet and confer with Carrington's natural mother in person.

Chapter Twenty-two

The lunch rush had been over for a couple hours, so Carmen and Joan had no trouble spotting one another in the diner. At any rate, Carmen recognized Joan the moment she saw her. Carrington had been extremely detailed in her description of her mother, right down to her high-heeled boots, bleached hair with dark roots showing at her scalp, and thick makeup.

Joan pulled a package of cigarettes out of her red faux leather purse and slid a cigarette out of the pack. She was just about to light up when a tired-looking waitress shuffled over to their table.

"You can't smoke in here," she informed Joan tonelessly.

Joan glared first at the waitress and then at Carmen. She looked as if she might argue, but she finally stuffed her lighter back in her bag, although the package of cigarettes remained on the table.

Carmen asked for iced tea; Joan ordered coffee. When the waitress asked if they needed separate checks, Joan remained silent.

"I'll take care of it," Carmen finally said. *God, what a piece of work,* she thought, staring across the table at Joan.

"I want to thank you for meeting me this afternoon," Carmen told Joan, keeping her voice low and even.

"Did I have a choice?" Joan sneered. She drummed her long fingernails against the tabletop. They clicked noisily next to her cigarette pack.

Carmen suppressed a scowl and ignored Joan's question.

"I'll cut to the chase, Ms. Coyle," she said. "My client sympathizes with how difficult it's been for you, as a single parent, to raise Carrington for the past fourteen-plus years. She's very sorry that she wasn't able to assist during that time, and she's prepared to recompense you, granted that she becomes Carrington's legal guardian. This isn't anything we haven't discussed over the phone for the past several days, but I want to go over everything while you sign the paperwork. Are you ready to discuss this further with me?"

Joan didn't blink. "How much?" she asked.

Caught off guard, Carmen had to pause. "I beg your pardon?" she asked, though she knew full well what Joan was asking.

Again, she could scarcely believe how quickly this woman seemed willing to trade her parental rights for cash.

"I said, how much?" Joan repeated. "How much is Arnie's mama willing to shell out?"

"We've discussed this part of the case already, Ms. Coyle. We settled on an amount some time ago."

"You just said we're here to do it all in person," Joan snapped. "I wanna make sure I ain't gettin' a raw deal. You better show it to me in black and white or I will change my mind and walk out right this minute," she hissed, glaring into Carmen's eyes.

Carmen fought to keep her expression impassive. She unzipped the binder that sat next to her in the booth and removed the packet of documents. She turned to one page in particular and slid the stack of papers across the table.

"Pfft," Joan dismissed after a quick glance at the paperwork. "That's ridiculous! I should have nearly fifty thousand dollars comin' to me. And that only covers Carrie's life up until now. What about the next four years 'til she's not a minor anymore?" she demanded.

"Carrington won't be in your custody for the remainder of her legal childhood; therefore, raising her will cost you nothing," Carmen answered coolly. "And, Ms. Coyle, I will remind you that you did agree to this amount in our past conversations."

Joan was momentarily silenced, her lips a severe red line. Her long, lacquered fingernails drummed faster than ever on the table.

"You're so sure I won't get to keep her, huh?" she hissed. "I'm her mother. I gave birth to that kid. She's *mine*."

In nearly four decades of law, Carmen had met plenty of callous, cold-hearted people. None of them gave her quite the same chill that Joan Coyle gave her. She cleared her throat and didn't let her eyes stray from Joan's intense gaze.

"Physically bearing a child doesn't make one a fit parent," she told Joan. "Even if you try to make this difficult, Ms. Coyle, Carrington will *not* be returned to your custody."

"Difficult," Joan repeated, her lips curling around the word as if she wanted to spit. "You have no idea how difficult I can make this, lady."

Carmen didn't answer for a moment.

"Mrs. Browne and I are both prepared to make certain that Carrington receives the best possible care in a healthy and loving environment. Your home is not it, nor has it ever been, such an environment, Ms. Coyle. I have serious doubts that it ever will be, and I am prepared to prove that in court."

She let this sink in and took some satisfaction that Joan abruptly stopped tapping the table with her nails.

Then she added calmly, "And please note, if you choose to take this matter to court, you will be charged with child abuse and neglect. I've seen Carrington's injuries myself," there was a note of anger in her voice that she couldn't quite restrain, "and you would be lucky if you received only a few months in county jail."

Joan clenched her hands into fists and glowered at Carmen. "Spankin' a kid ain't against the law," she finally growled.

Carmen glared back. "Spanking a child is not against the law; beating a child with enough force to cause injury, however, is illegal. The abuse Carrington has suffered at your hands has been documented, Ms. Coyle. We have pictures of her injuries and her testimony."

"And, of course, you believe every word that comes out of her mouth, right?" Joan drawled nastily. "Of course, she's above lyin'." She shook her head at Carmen, lips pursed.

"I'm not going to sit here and debate your daughter's integrity with you, Ms. Coyle," Carmen said. "Do you want to accept the settlement that's been offered or not?"

Joan sniffed. "I *still* think I'm entitled to more." Her voice had taken on a whiney tone.

Carmen knew then that she'd won.

"Then you're choosing to hire your own attorney and take this issue to court?" she asked, knowing full well what Joan's answer would be.

"I didn't say that, did I?" Joan barked.

Carmen simply kept her eyes level with Joan's and waited. It was a struggle to keep a small smile off of her lips.

"How do I know I'm really gonna get the money?" Joan demanded. "I could say yes but get screwed over. I wouldn't put it past Arnie's mom. Or you."

"I'm prepared to give you a cashier's check for the full amount. We could go to your bank right now and deposit it," Carmen answered calmly.

"And that's it?" Joan was incredulous.

"First, you'll sign several documents to relinquish any and all parental rights where Carrington is concerned. Then you'll get the money. It's that simple."

"Do I get to see her again? Carrie?"

Carmen was surprised at the sudden wistful sound in Joan's voice, but even if Joan started sobbing, she wouldn't feel an ounce of sympathy for the woman. Joan Coyle was a brute—a crass, cruel slob of a woman who had terrorized her daughter for years. Once again, Carmen struggled to maintain her cool and not tell Joan Coyle exactly what she thought of her.

"Well," she began, making her voice as even as possible, "that will be up to Carrington and her grandmother, Mrs. Browne. If Carrington wishes to contact you, she may do so, but ultimately, the extent of your relationship with her will be determined by what Mrs. Browne thinks is best for Carrington." *And I hope she won't let her see your sorry ass at all,* she thought.

Joan nodded. "Okay," she said. "All right."

"Okay?" Carmen questioned. "I need you to be more specific, Ms. Coyle. Are you agreeing to the terms I've offered?"

Joan's eyes blazed, and her lips twitched before she spoke. She was clearly livid.

"Yes," she hissed. "I agree. I accept the damn deal. Now show me where to sign, and I want my Goddamn money today!" She was practically shouting.

Carmen flinched and looked around the near-empty diner, embarrassed.

"Please calm yourself, Ms. Coyle. There is a considerable amount of paperwork that we need to go through in order to complete this …" For the first time since their meeting began, she struggled for the right word. "Transaction" seemed too cold, but for Joan Coyle, that's exactly what it was. She was selling her child. Carmen simply left her statement trail off, once again chilled by Joan's hateful eyes.

She explained each page in the thick file she'd brought. Even with Joan impatiently rushing her through it, the process still took well over an hour. They ended up ordering sandwiches from the haggard waitress, who seemed eager to get them out of the booth.

After Joan signed the last paper and Carmen paid their tab, Carmen offered Joan a ride to the credit union. Joan accepted and sat in silence as Carmen drove the short distance. She eyed everything in the car, including Carmen, with contempt.

At the credit union, she insisted that Carmen accompany her into the building and wait while the check was deposited. She still didn't seem to believe that she would soon have thirty thousand dollars in her bank account. Carmen quietly went along with it, reminding herself that dealing with Joan would soon be over, and most important, A. C. and Carrington could finally be together without worrying about Joan interfering. She also reasoned that Joan was least likely to cause a scene if she simply stayed with the greedy woman long enough for Joan to see the four zeroes on her bank receipt. She waited near the lobby chairs while Joan stood in line, the cashier's check fluttering in her shaky hands. Per credit union policy, the teller called A. C.'s bank to ensure that a check of such proportion was duly authorized. Joan was clearly impatient with this. She tapped her long fingernails along the counter as she had in the diner. Carmen rolled her eyes. *Ignorant fool,* she thought. *Carrington is going to be so much better off without you.*

Her mind wandered to Carrington's younger sister, Melissa. Carmen closed her eyes as a wave of pity washed over her. There was no kind grandmother wanting to take her in and change her life. Carmen hoped that Carrington would stay in touch with her younger sister. Of course, it was quite possible, likely even, that Melissa would be bitter and resentful toward Carrington for many years to come. She would be envious, Carmen imagined. What child wouldn't be? Suddenly, Carrington would have everything a girl could want, and Melissa would be stuck with Joan, a cruel, drunk mess of a human being. Social workers, Carmen knew from experience, were extremely overworked. It would be almost impossible to get Melissa on their radar. Melissa didn't have the same kind of scars that Carrington had, the ones that showed on the outside. And it was doubtful the younger girl would say anything against her mother. Melissa Coyle possessed a strange and fierce kind of loyalty where her mother was involved.

Carmen meandered toward a quiet corner of the lobby and pulled her cell phone out of her purse. She pressed the speed dial button for A. C.'s phone number and was not one bit surprised when her best friend answered after only one ring.

"Well?" A. C. asked breathlessly before even saying hello.

Carmen couldn't help but grin. "She signed the papers! Joan agreed to every one of our terms. We're at her credit union right now, depositing the check. She's yours, my love. Carrington is officially your girl now. I'm on my way to file the paperwork, but the hardest part of this is behind us now."

A. C. began to cry then, and even though Carmen knew they were tears of joy and relief, it was all she could do not to burst into tears too, right there in the lobby of the bank.

"Congratulations, honey," she told A. C. "I'm so thrilled for you and Carrington! Listen, we're about to wrap up here, so I'll say adios for now. I just wanted to give you the good news as soon as I could. I'll see you in a little while, okay? As soon as we finish up, I'll come right over. I want to take you and your lovely granddaughter out for a celebration dinner!"

"That would be wonderful, Carmen. Thank you so much," A. C. managed to answer through her tears. "I have to tell Carrington the good news; she's been pacing around the house like a nervous cat all day. Love you and see you soon!"

They said good-bye, and Carmen slipped the phone back into her purse. She glanced over at Joan in time to see the teller count out what appeared to be an enormous amount of cash into Joan's outstretched palm. *Stupid, stupid, stupid,* though Carmen, shaking her head. *What a waste.*

She lingered, wondering reluctantly if she should offer Joan another ride in the rental car. Joan finally finished at the counter and walked away, distracted as she gazed down at the thick wad of bills in her hand before stuffing them into her purse. She glanced up at Carmen and looked as if she might say something. Carmen waited, bracing herself for a nasty remark. To her surprise, Joan said nothing. Just a slight nod, and then she turned on her stiletto heels and strolled out of the bank.

Part II

Chapter Twenty-three

For the first few weeks, A. C. was terrified that Joan was going to show up at the house one day and take Carrington away. To her great relief, Joan didn't try to contact them at all. A. C. wasn't sure what to expect, and even though Carmen reassured her that Joan no longer had any legal say in Carrington's life, she worried that Joan might harass them: either to get more money or just to give them grief, or both. Two and a half months had passed since A. C. and Carrington first met in Mastic Crossing, and it had been six weeks since Joan signed the papers that made A. C. Carrington's legal guardian.

The change A. C. saw in Carrington was remarkable. She'd known from the very first time they met that Carrington was an intelligent, well-spoken child. There was no question of that. As time passed, Carrington became better able articulate how she felt and what she wanted. The first week after Carrington moved into her house was the hardest. Carrington was so jumpy and hardly slept at all. She walked around the house as close to the walls as possible. It was a test of will for A. C. to hold in her tears each time she saw the fear and anxiety in her granddaughter's face. *My God,* she thought so many times, *what has that wretched woman done to you?*

She knew that there was something Carrington was holding back. She saw it on her face when they sat down to meals, and she sensed it during the pauses in their conversations. As much as A. C. longed for Carrington to confide in her, she knew she shouldn't push. Carrington had grown up in a home where she was never safe. The one person who was supposed to care for her and protect her had been the person who had tormented her for years. It made A. C. sick to her stomach to imagine all of the horrible things Carrington had seen and experienced in her young life because of Joan Coyle. She realized that pressing her granddaughter would only hinder Carrington's progress. She did not have to wait long, as it turned out.

One evening during dinner, Carrington timidly admitted that she was interested in calling Joan. It was all A. C. could do to remain calm. Her gut reaction was to tell Carrington it was a bad idea and to disconnect their phone service for a while, just in case. Of course, she realized even as she thought it that she was being irrational. There was a stab of envy, too. She might have legal documents that rightfully declared that Carrington was, for all intents and purposes, now her child, but Joan Coyle had given birth to the girl and had raised her for over fourteen years. In many ways, A. C. and Carrington were still strangers to one another, even though they were related by blood and had developed a strong, warm rapport from the very beginning. Joan, on the other hand, had been there when Carrington first started talking and walking; she'd seen the child sprout from a freckled toddler into a tall and beautiful young lady. Even if she was a hateful drunk who probably didn't remember half of her daughter's childhood, she'd still been there. She was there during all those first times, and A. C. was not. And it stung.

Against better judgment, A. C. told Carrington is was okay if she wanted to call Joan. In fact, she told her granddaughter with a deep sigh, it was certainly okay and well within Carrington's rights if she kept in touch with both Joan and Missy. Any visits with Joan would have to be supervised at first—this was A. C.'s rule, not a court-ordered one—but she would allow visitation if that's what Carrington wanted. She was far less reluctant about Carrington maintaining a relationship with her younger sister than with her natural mother. Missy posed little threat in A. C.'s mind. She wasn't the one who made Carrington's life hell all those years, and she wasn't someone Carrington saw as a role model. In many ways, A. C. felt deeply sorry for Melissa Coyle. Even though Carmen managed to arrange it so that Missy would be checked on once per month by a social worker, the girl still had to live with Joan.

It was a miracle, A. C. had marveled more than once, that Carrington had turned out as well as she had after being in Joan's charge for so long. A surge of pride often followed this thought. *She's my girl; Carrington and Browne blood runs in her veins.*

Carrington told her grandmother that she wasn't entirely sure what she wanted as far as her relationships with Joan and Missy were concerned. She only knew that even though she was happier in A. C.'s house than she'd ever been in her life, it felt like there was a hole, a void.

Privately, A. C. had called Carmen in tears about this. Carmen, as always, was sympathetic. She listened to A. C.'s insecurities and anxiety, and gently suggested a family counselor. At first, A. C. was reluctant. She would never quite be able to shrug off the attitude she'd been raised with toward mental healthcare, no matter what she had accomplished in Dr. Meyer's office. But the more she considered it, the more sense it made. As fond as she already was of Carrington, it was strange and difficult to get used to having her in the house full time. *How much harder it must be for Carrington*, she thought. Maybe it wasn't such a terrible thing that Carrington wanted to call her mother and sister. Why wouldn't the girl, on some level, long for familiarity? Later, Carmen called back with Dr. Margaret Burke's phone number and a hearty recommendation from Maurice Lindt.

Dr. Burke, or Margaret as she encouraged her clients to call her, was a licensed psychiatrist who specialized in family counseling. At first, Carrington had been skeptical, but A. C. soon realized the child was just frightened. And why shouldn't she be? In a matter of weeks, she'd discovered that her father, whom she had never met, died of a drug overdose, and she was moved out of her abusive mother's home and into the home of her deceased father's mother, which was an entirely different environment from the one she'd known all her life. Carrington's uneasiness was completely understandable, Margaret repeatedly assured both Carrington and A. C. It would probably take years, Margaret said, before she felt truly at peace with herself and at home in her new surroundings. So, Carrington began to see Margaret twice a month: one private session and one joint session with A. C.

A. C. had a chat with Margaret about Carrington calling Joan. She said she'd already told Carrington that it would be okay to contact both Joan and Melissa, but now she regretted it. Margaret thought it would be fine, but gravely warned A. C. that Joan might be especially hostile to Carrington. She would be bitter and jealous, Margaret told her. She reminded A. C. that now it was up to her to make the parental decisions in Carrington's life. If A. C. thought Carrington was ready to talk to Joan after everything that had happened, Margaret said, it was her decision to make.

A. C. shared with Carrington some of her exchange with Margaret. She certainly didn't tell her granddaughter how jealous she felt at the thought of Carrington and Joan spending time together or the very real fear she had that Joan would go out of her way to be cruel. Carrington absorbed her grandmother's words without much comment, and for a few days, the subject was dropped. Later in the week, while they worked in the garden together, Carrington quietly informed her grandmother that she would call her mother later that day. A. C.'s stomach plummeted, but she managed to nod and assure Carrington that that was fine.

She went out later, on the pretense of grocery shopping, but they both knew that it was her way of trying to give Carrington privacy. How she longed to stay home and sit with her granddaughter while she made what must have been a terrifying phone call. She admitted to herself that part of this urge also stemmed from the envy that was hard to shake, simple curiosity, and a deeply rooted instinct to protect Carrington from Joan. But Carrington was not a little girl. A. C. left the house to let Carrington have her phone call, all the while wondering if she was doing the right thing.

Chapter Twenty-four

Carrington was relieved when the manager of the store informed her that Joan wasn't there at the moment but would start her shift later in the day. Of course, this also meant that the knot of dread would lay heavy in her stomach that much longer. She sucked on two chalky antacid tablets while she thought of what she should do. Eventually, Carrington decided to call her mother's house. She'd originally decided to call her at work because she figured Joan would be forced to be more civil at work than she would be at home.

With shaky fingers, she dialed her old phone number. After three rings, Missy answered.

"Hello? Alex?" Missy sounded anxious yet pleased.

"Um, hi, Missy," Carrington said. "How are you?"

Missy sighed. "Oh," she said. "It's you." She made no attempt to mask her disappointment.

"How are you?" Carrington asked again.

There was a long pause, and Carrington thought maybe Missy had set the phone down and gone to find Joan.

"Oh, I'm just swell," Missy said finally, her voice thick with sarcasm. "And how are you, Princess Carrington?"

Carrington bit her lower lip. *Please don't do this,* she begged silently.

She faked a laugh. "Oh, c'mon, Missy. Don't be like that. How are things going? What have you been up to?" She hesitated, her stomach more jumpy than ever. "How's Mom?"

Missy sighed.

"Mom's … fine. I don't know; she's Mom." There was an edge in her voice that betrayed her ambivalent answer.

"I tried calling the store," Carrington said. "They said she doesn't start work until later. Is she home now?"

Missy barked a harsh, angry laugh.

"Why the hell would she be here?" she asked. "When did she ever stay home just 'cause she has to work? Anyway, she might not work there much longer. She's even talking about moving. I'll have my own room and my own bathroom." Missy was smug.

"Move?" Carrington cried. "Where? When?"

"Don't sound so surprised," Missy snapped. "You don't live here anymore, remember? *You ran away*. Why should we tell you every little thing we do or talk about?"

Carrington winced. "I didn't run away, Missy. I didn't do anything wrong." She wished desperately she could think of something else to say, something that didn't sound so weak and would make sense to her younger sister.

"Whatever," Missy said in a bored voice. "Anyway, Mom's been looking into buying another house and renting out both sides of this one. She's out looking at a house now with what's-his-face … Abel."

Carrington shuddered.

"Ugh, Abel? You guys are going to live with Abel?"

She hadn't meant to sound so harsh. She couldn't ever remember her mother having a boyfriend who didn't cause her to wrinkle her nose in distaste. Abel was no exception.

"I don't know; maybe," Missy said. "So what? What do you care?" Missy demanded.

"Missy, I *do* care," Carrington insisted.

Missy snorted. "Right," she said. "Anyway, I don't see why it's any of your business anymore. You don't live here and you're not going to, so butt out, okay? God!"

There was a brief pause, and then Carrington heard a loud click. For several seconds, she refused to accept that her sister hung up on her. She said hello several times and almost cried when the recorded voice came on the line suggesting that she hang up and try dialing again. *Fine,* she thought with grim determination. *Fine. So Missy isn't ready to talk to me. I'm still calling Joan. I'm not scared. There is nothing she can do to me now.*

Carrington watched the clock restlessly. She tried reading, watching television, and flipping through the magazines on the coffee table, but she couldn't concentrate on anything. She forced herself to eat some fig bars and drink a glass of milk because the pediatrician A. C. had taken her to decided that she was too thin. The food felt like a lump of clay in her throat, but she forced it down. Finally, it was time to call Joan at the thrift store. Carrington had to wipe the sweat from her palms.

She was put on hold for about a minute, though it felt much longer. The synthetic hold music was annoying; it distracted her while she tried desperately to decide what to say. *God,* Carrington thought, *I should have thought of what I wanted to say* before *I called.* She was wiping her palms on her shorts for a second time when a familiar gruff voice came on the line.

"Yeah," said Joan. She erupted into a dry, rattling cough. "Who is this?"

She sounds worse than ever, Carrington thought. She found that her throat was suddenly tight, her mouth dry and sticky. She thought of all the times she'd been afraid to come home from school. She remembered how mortified she'd been that Joan might actually attend a parent-teacher conference and yet how crushed she was that she never had—not once, not in eight years of school, nine if she counted kindergarten. The only time Joan ever went to school for either of her daughters was when the school nurse insisted that the child was too sick to stay or when Missy got into trouble and either her teachers or the principal insisted that a meeting was required.

"Hello?" Joan grumbled impatiently. "Anyone there?"

Carrington cleared her throat.

"Hi, Mom," she said.

"Missy?" Joan asked, sounding confused.

"No, Mom, it's me. It's Carrington."

It was Joan's turn to pause. Carrington knew her mother hadn't disconnected because she could still hear the sounds of the store in the background: the chatter of customers, the ding of the cash registers. It sounded like a busy day. It would be a good excuse, Carrington thought, for either of them to end the call.

"Hey," Joan said finally. "What's up?"

"Nothing. I just … I just wanted to say hi, see how you're doing. I called the house earlier, but Missy said you were out. So, how … how have things been?"

Joan scoffed. "You're callin' me at work for chit-chat?" Her voice took on an all-too-familiar tone. "What do you really want, Carrie? Your rich granny decide she doesn't want you around anymore, is that it?"

Carrington sucked in a deep breath of air. She felt like she'd been slapped. Why had she decided to call Joan at all? She closed her eyes, willing the tears not to fall.

"I didn't call to bother you," she said in a high-pitched voice that she hardly recognized as her own. "I really just wanted to say hello and ask how you're doing. Nothing's wrong, I'm fine." She began to prattle on nervously, not entirely conscious of what was going to come out of her mouth next. "I'm starting school in a few weeks. I'm thinking of joining the student counsel, and—"

"I can't believe your Goddamn nerve," Joan growled. "You called me up at my fuckin' job to brag to me about your snotty-ass little school and tell me how your life is nothin' but roses since you left my house? Well, that's just fuckin' wonderful, *Carrie*," she drawled out the nickname she knew her daughter hated. "But some of us don't have a rich bitch fairytale grandma to make everything magically better! So if you didn't call to apologize or tell me something important, then I need to go."

Carrington clamped her lips shut, bracing herself for the slap that Joan would never again be able to deliver. Her chest began to burn; the fire spread up her throat and into a deep flush across her cheeks. *Apologize!*

Carrington forced her voice into a calm, neutral tone. "I *didn't* call to apologize," she said evenly, proud of herself even though her hands were shaking. "I called for just what I said: to say hello and ask how you're doing. It's not unheard of, you know, for family members to do that. It's actually pretty normal, in fact. But I don't want to bother you. If you want to reach me, you know where I am. Good-bye …" The word "mother" caught in her throat.

She didn't slam the phone down, although she wanted to. She eyed it warily for several seconds, expecting Joan to call back and unleash a stream of curse words into the receiver. The phone didn't ring, and Carrington's heart did a somersault. She wiped her tears on the back of one hand.

Why am I crying? she demanded of herself. *What did I expect?*

Chapter Twenty-five

Dear diary, she wrote and then crossed it out, blushing at how melodramatic it sounded. *Margaret suggested that I start keeping a journal. She said it would help me process my new surroundings and get to know myself better. I'm not entirely sure what that means. I mean, sure I know what each of those words means individually, and I basically understand what she's talking about, but the past couple of months have just been so … I don't know, chaotic? Stressful and scary and wonderful all at once.* Carrington smiled and underlined the word "wonderful" twice.

I've only talked to my … to Joan once since I moved out, and it was awful. I know I shouldn't be surprised that she behaved like that. What did I expect? I don't know. I've only talked to Missy once, too, but I don't know how much that conversation counts since she hung up on me. Wow, that hurt. Way more than I thought it would. It's not like Missy and I have ever been close, but we're sisters. I mean, we'll always have that bond … won't we? It feels like she hates me. Margaret says that she probably misses me and is envious, but she doesn't think Missy hates me. Margaret doesn't know Missy.

I can't really say that I miss my sister, but I do think about her a lot, and I wonder what will happen to us. Will we ever be able to talk? What's Missy going to be like in a few years? Will we even want to stay in touch when we're older? Mrs. Browne … Gran says that …

She paused and frowned. The term "Gran" wasn't coming naturally yet, not even in writing. A. C. had told her that she could use the term when she was ready to use it, but so far, it stuck in Carrington's mouth. It was strange to continue calling her Mrs. Browne. A. C. was, in fact, Carrington's biological grandmother. A. C. told Carrington that when she was a girl, she'd called each of her grandmothers Nana. Nana seemed childish to Carrington. A. C. suggested Gran simply because she liked the sound of it. Grandmother was too dowdy and formal, she said. Carrington had promised to try to call A. C. Gran. So far, she had mostly avoided calling her grandmother by any title.

Gran says that I should give myself and Missy time to adjust to everything that's happened. She said we may be able to relate more when we're a little older, but she shut up right away when I asked about her own younger sister, Regina. I wasn't trying to be snotty, and thank God she didn't take it that way. I know she's told her sister about me and everything that happened, but I still haven't met her yet. Sometimes I wonder—I feel stupid even writing it here, where I am the only one who will see it—but I wonder if Gran is a little embarrassed of me, of how I found her and the way I grew up and everything. Could I really blame her if she was?

I'm terrified at just the thought of meeting Aunt Regina, Uncle Laurence, and their daughter, Gloria. I have the weirdest impression that of the three of them, Gran really only likes Uncle Laurence. I'm sure I'm wrong. She will only say of Aunt Regina and Gloria that they are "preoccupied with things that, at the end of the day, don't make a bit of difference." I have no idea what she means by that, and it seems to be a sore subject, so I'm not going to bug her about it. As scared and nervous as I am about meeting them, I'm also dying of curiosity! Gran's weird comments only make it worse. I feel like a girl detective whose mysteries are based on finding out what's wrong with each dysfunctional family member. Ha ha. Seriously, though, what is so awful about them?

Chapter Twenty-six

"No, no, too blue, too cutesy, and just ugh, no," snapped Gloria Lithgow to her assistant, Dirk. She scowled at the five canvases spread across the huge work table in her office. "Honestly, do these people think I'm kidding? These are pathetic! And clowns," she groaned, glaring at the fourth canvas, which featured a variety of colorful circus clowns offering bouquets of lollipops to rosy-cheeked children. "Who the hell wants to see clowns? When was the last time you even heard of the circus being in town?" She didn't wait for Dirk to answer, she rarely did. "Unless they're fucking and or killing each other in graphic detail, clowns will never hang on the walls of Lucinda's Lair! Send these back. Or hell, just call the *artists* responsible for these atrocities and have them pick up their precious little paintings. Why should we waste money on postage?" Gloria waved dismissively at the motley collection of pictures and stalked back to her desk. "Oh, and can you get me a latte, Dirk? Not too much sugar this time; I'm trying to cut back. Thanks!"

Maybe you should cut back on breathing, bitch, Dirk thought with a grimace. He sighed and stacked the paintings neatly in the center of the table. He dreaded calling the artists. In all the months he'd worked for Gloria, he felt like the only thing he ever did was call hopeful artists to turn down their work, fetch Gloria's lattes, and sometimes, when she felt like it, have sex with her.

That was mostly why Dirk had taken the job as her personal assistant in the first place. Not so much to be Gloria's occasional lover, but because she, with the last name Lithgow and all the money and influence attached to that name, represented a lifestyle that he'd always coveted. He'd worked his way through school living on student loans. He finally had his degree. After all the years of hard work and sacrifice, Dirk found that his teachers, every last one of them and even his own mother, had lied to him.

Education had opened few doors for him. What could he do with his bachelor's degree in liberal arts? He could accept an entry-level position, answering phones and making coffee, making slave wages and barely scraping by. He could try temping and hope it developed into something permanent and lucrative. He'd done both for more than six months each, over a year of his life wasted. Then he met Gloria—a chance meeting at another art gallery. She was there scouting artists and looking to maybe score a couple lines of coke and company for the night. He was there because a co-worker at the temp agency had given him her ticket to the private showing, she having landed a last minute date. Dirk went mostly because the ticket said there was going to be a free buffet and open bar at the showing. It was four days until pay day, and he was sick of instant noodles and peanut butter on stale bread.

At the showing, he stuffed his face with miniature Swedish meatballs and chocolate dipped cannoli. While he was sipping his third complementary glass of flat champagne, he found himself appraising the same painting as Gloria. Dirk didn't know then who she was. He only knew that a well-dressed, rather thin, and almost attractive woman was checking him out as much, if not more, than she was checking out the painting.

"It's lurid, isn't it?" he intoned without meeting her eyes. He would never normally use a term like "lurid," but at the time, he thought it sounded clever.

Gloria kept her gaze on him when she answered, "Oh, yes, absolutely. Are you a collector?"

He blushed and imagined hanging one of the overpriced, oversized canvases in his dark little apartment.

He shook his head. "No, just … shopping around."

He finally met her gaze. Her eyes were her best feature: gray-blue and piercing. Or maybe it was her high cheek bones, although they were so sharp they overpowered the rest of her face. He smiled at her, and she smiled back.

She launched into a monologue then, about her gallery, about how difficult it was to find talent, especially local talent.

"I can't very well have a gallery that only displays only *my own* paintings," she declared with a laugh, fingering the delicate diamond necklace draped around her throat.

Dirk knew even then that Gloria would be thrilled at the idea of a gallery that exclusively sold her artwork.

She invited him over to her studio for a drink and a look at her art collection, both her own paintings and the paintings of young hopefuls who wanted their work hung and sold in Lucinda's Lair. He accepted, and before they departed, Gloria hurriedly scribbled out a check to the gallery owner for an obscene amount of money, choosing three of the paintings from the show, one of which was the one she and Dirk had been viewing at the same time.

"I can resell these for an enormous profit," she bragged to him under her breath as they left the gallery.

It was when she wrote out the check, and he saw all those zeroes without a decimal point to separate them into an imaginable sum, that he recognized her. Gloria Lithgow, daughter of Laurence Lithgow, founder and head of Lithgow-Masterson Enterprises, although now just Lithgow, since old man Masterson had died some years back. Because he fantasized about what it would be like not to worry about making his rent payment or being able to shop for clothes whenever and wherever he wished, one of Dirk's guilty pleasures was to read the society columns in a handful of local newspapers. He knew their names, their faces: the wealthy elite of the city. He hated and idolized them for their debutante balls, art auctions, and black tie benefits that really seemed to benefit only themselves.

He'd seen Gloria Lithgow in the newspaper a few times, standing in between her parents. Laurence Lithgow was kind of a shapeless man; the only things striking about him were his intelligent eyes and somewhat feminine face. It was obvious that he'd passed on his cheekbones to his daughter. Regina Lithgow was basically an older version of Gloria: the same haughty smile, wide mouth, and sinewy body. Maybe she had been more attractive than her daughter when she was a young woman, but Regina Lithgow had not aged well. The Lithgow fortune wasn't the only money in the family, Dirk knew. Sometimes, the Browne family was mentioned in the columns, but very seldom were there pictures. A. C. Browne, sister of Regina, had married Calvin Browne, once vice president of the lucrative plastic manufacturing company

Plasti-Corp. The Browne fortune seemed to be significantly less than that of the Lithgow family, but it was still considerable.

It was that evening at the art show, the one he had only attended for the free food and booze, that Dirk found his ticket to the life he had always dreamed about and always known that he *deserved.* Going to college was nothing, almost a waste of time, except that it gave him some leverage over his peers without college degrees. Still, he knew of former high school classmates who were now earning almost twice what he could earn with trades like plumbing or auto mechanics, or they had simply held onto their high school jobs long enough to move up the ladder.

If he could have, he would have stuck with modeling, which he did steadily through his childhood. His mother, Carole Godfrey, had recognized early on that her son was a truly gorgeous little boy. He grew up to be a beautiful man, with wavy brown hair, naturally tan skin, wide green eyes, a perfect complexion, full lips, and a deep set of dimples that showed even when he wasn't smiling. The calls for modeling jobs stopped early in high school, though, because Dirk stopped growing. His body filled out somewhat, and he diligently jogged four times per week and worked out with free weights, but he grew no taller than five feet seven inches. That was barely tall enough to be a professional female model, let alone a male one. By seventeen, Dirk was no longer the dewy-faced man-child who had once graced the covers of JC Penney catalogues and Footlocker ads; he had a near constant five o'clock shadow and a strong, square jaw line. He was still an impressively handsome man, but not what modeling agencies wanted.

Dirk was self-conscious of his height, but he tried never to mention it. He sought shoes that gave him at least two inches, but it was hard to come by thick and high-soled shoes for men that didn't look like a throwback to the disco era. Cowboy boots were useful, as long as they were snake, eel, or alligator skin. He would never dream of wearing vinyl, no matter how overworked his credit card was, and it was. He'd barely scraped by in college with his a handful of small grants and several student loans. Paying off his loans was constantly in the back of Dirk's mind. He was three years out of college now, with no end to his debt in sight, although working for Gloria was, financially at least, a definite step above the entry level positions he'd worked shortly after graduating from college.

Sure, it was still grunt work. He answered her phones, made her appointments, even picked up her dry cleaning, and went to the deli salad bar for her on the rare day that she actually ate lunch. But Gloria paid him nearly twice as much as what he earned at his old jobs. He was salaried, of course, which at first had seemed like a great deal. She'd cheerfully explained to him when she offered him the job that even if she sent him home early or he had the day off because of a holiday, he would still receive the same amount of pay. Of course, Gloria never sent him home early, even when there was absolutely nothing to do in the gallery. And holidays? They couldn't take holidays off, she insisted; that's when the working schleps who could afford to buy art often browsed the galleries.

Dirk's plate was full under Gloria's supervision. If she suddenly decided that the ceiling of Lucinda's Lair should be blood red, it was Dirk's job to see that it happened as soon as possible. He didn't actually do the labor himself, but he hired the contractors and oversaw their work. If Gloria called him in the middle of the night, craving physical companionship for a few hours and a container of spicy noodles from the twenty-four hour Thai place across the street from her condo, Dirk had better show up on her doorstep no less than two hours later, showered, enthusiastic, and laden with food and condoms. Once, when he had the flu, he'd ignored her middle-of-the-night phone call. She'd been livid and had locked him out of the gallery for two days, refusing his phone calls until he'd sent her so many bouquets of roses that Lucinda's Lair looked more like a flower shop than an art gallery. Even after she claimed she had forgiven him, she'd been lukewarm to him for weeks and warned him that he was back only on a trial basis.

Dirk hated Gloria. He loathed and resented her. And he wanted nothing more than to marry her. There was no other way, short of buying a winning lottery ticket, that he could become rich in his lifetime. Hell, he thought, even if he ever did win the lottery, the newfound money still wouldn't buy him the status of being a Lithgow.

He mused bitterly sometimes that if he was a woman and Gloria was a man, he would, at some point in their relationship, find himself accidentally-on-purpose pregnant. It wouldn't be worth it, though, to try to get Gloria pregnant. He'd considered it. He could forget to use a condom some night, but even if he succeeded in knocking her up, he knew Gloria wouldn't hesitate to have an abortion. She'd had two in college, she once confided in him. She didn't want children, at least not for a long, long time. She even joked that if she wasn't married by the time she turned thirty-five, she would have herself "spayed."

Dirk had yet to think of a way to get Gloria to seriously consider him as a potential husband, but for the past two years, he'd been nothing more than her well-paid servant. Sometimes he was hopeful that she was finally going to profess her undying love for him, like the rare occasion when she asked him to escort her to a function at her parents' country club. *It's her way of introducing me to her crowd and letting them get used to me,* he told himself.

But on those nights when he found himself stuffed into a rented tuxedo and surrounded by wealthy assholes, Dirk was nothing more than what Gloria had asked him to be: her escort. She held onto his arm and engaged in conversation with dozens of people as if he was nothing more than mink stole draped around her shoulders. Maybe, he allowed himself to think from time to time, that's all he was to her: decoration.

Gloria's mother, Regina, treated him with indifferent disdain and an underlying air of suspicion. She sometimes asked probing, embarrassing questions about his parents, and he lied his ass off to her. His father was dead, he told her, having died young in a boating accident, and his mother suffered from Parkinson's and slight dementia, and lived out of state with her sister, who, Dirk hinted, was well-off. It was possible that Dirk's father was dead, but he wouldn't know. He'd never met the man, and his mother was tight-lipped about the subject. The only truth he gave to Regina Lithgow or anyone else who asked about his mother was that she did, indeed, live out of state. But she suffered no illness. Carole Godfrey was alive and well. She lived on her pension as a retired teacher and an occasional check from Dirk. He felt like he owed her, but he didn't enjoy spending time with her. She reminded him too much of the lean years of his childhood, when his school clothes came from thrift stores and they survived on potatoes and ground beef. For holidays, he sent her cards, flowers, and fanciful gifts that he knew she would never use: a gold-plated fountain pen, an imported silk scarf, a collection of tea from around the world. It comforted him somehow, buying his real mother the things that his imaginary mother would have.

Gloria didn't seem to care much at all about his pedigree. She accepted the well-rehearsed stories about his family without question, mostly interested in complaining about her own parents or talking about the gallery. And she was as selfish a lover as she was a confidant. Dirk knew she'd grown up feeling no need to compete in life or pine for things she couldn't afford, and this sense of entitlement followed Gloria into the bedroom. She'd lie there, almost as a spectator, while Dirk pleasured her. Her body, at least, was sexier than her face and her attitude. She had pale, smooth skin, like the marble floors of her parents' country club, and a firm body with larger than average breasts. Dirk couldn't quite tell if her breasts were natural or implants, but what did it matter? He often pointed out to her that because their sexual relationship was so blissful (a lie on his part, but he was sure Gloria would never doubt him) why not take the next step? She seemed amused by the idea of their living together, but quickly shot it down, saying that her parents, her mother especially, would give her hell about such an arrangement. She never outright said so, but Dirk knew that her parents financed their daughter's high-priced lifestyle as long as she played by their rules. She was a kept woman, much the way she kept him.

As much as Dirk fantasized about making Gloria his wife, he had a difficult time envisioning what it would actually be like to be married to her. Would they live in her condo, which was cluttered with new clothes, furniture, and art that she constantly bought? Would she still expect him to do things like schedule the gallery's showings and go out for her lattes? Surely not. They would move into a house, and he would make certain that both of their names appeared on the deed. He would refuse to sign a prenuptial agreement. Maybe he would work, maybe not, although he suspected he would go through the motions. It would be nice to stay at home, go to the gym, lounge at bookstores, and go where he wanted when he wanted, but he knew that if he didn't have his own job, Gloria would expect him to spend his days at the gallery. He would have a home office, he often thought, where he would try his hand at day trading and maybe buying and selling property. It would be paramount for them to have at least one child. Even if they eventually divorced, he would always have a link to her life, and to her money. Also, an heir might force her mother to treat him like more than just hired help.

Being married to Gloria would be much more palatable, Dirk knew, if he didn't have to spend as much time with her as he was forced to as her assistant. Some days, he was barely able to make it through their hours together in Lucinda's Lair without telling her she was the most obnoxious, uppity bitch he'd ever met. Sometimes, to keep his cool, he pretended he was on a catwalk in Milan, being ogled by hundreds of people. He wore a cool smirk on his face and spoke as little as possible. His daydreams about being an international supermodel helped somewhat, but he was always relieved when Gloria left for the day.

Dirk felt he had been biding his time for long enough. He couldn't tolerate existing the way he did much longer. He wasn't entirely sure what he would do, but he knew that he had to make his move soon.

Chapter Twenty-seven

The mailbox was stuffed, mostly with junk and other things Missy didn't care about: pizza restaurant coupons, credit card offers, and plenty of bills. It looked like several days worth of mail. Joan clearly hadn't been home any more than Missy had. Missy had not spent the night in her own bed for three days, and there had been no word from Joan. After the first night, Missy came home briefly to grab a few clothes, and at the last minute, she scribbled out a quick note for her mother and left it under a magnet on the refrigerator. *I'm at Tanya's. Love, Missy.* Not that Joan would care, Missy thought. Her mother was cool that way. She knew some of her friends envied the amount of freedom she had.

Of course, she never told her friends about the scary nights when Joan didn't come home at all, or worse, when she brought a weird guy home with her, both of them so drunk they staggered around the house, half dressed and groping at one another. Once, one of the guys, a heavy man with a scraggly beard and cowboy boots, had wandered into Missy and Carrington's room. Their bedroom light was off, but Missy could see more of him than she cared to see because of the light in the hallway. He'd been shirtless, and his jeans were unbuttoned all the way and drooped on his waist. She'd caught a glimpse of the thick hair that protruded from the top of his boxer shorts. He seemed to smile at her beneath his patchy facial hair. "You have the wrong room," Carrington had informed him in a loud, firm voice. Missy was startled, and so was Joan's catch of the night, it seemed. He took a half step back but still watched Missy and Carrington in their beds. Finally, Joan wandered out of the bathroom, wearing only her bra and panties, and dragged him to her bedroom. Missy had to listen to the sounds of her mother and the ugly, strange man having sex, but at least he wasn't in her bedroom. She'd been surprised by her sister that night. She wasn't sure what she would have said if he'd come any closer, and she certainly hadn't expected Carrington to speak up. The two girls never discussed it, but from then on, whenever Joan went out, they closed the door when they went to bed and sometimes shoved their dresser in front of it.

Missy wondered if Carrington still went to the library. *I guess not now that she has money to spend,* Missy thought with a snort. *It's totally unfair!* She'd actually hoped for a glimpse of the mysterious woman who had whisked her sister out of her life. "The rich old bitch," as Joan referred to A. C. Browne. Joan had not revealed much about this woman, but from what Missy could piece together, A. C. Browne was a stuck up, mean, and wealthy woman. She'd given Joan a lot of money to get Carrington to come and live with her. Missy wondered if Carrington realized this. *Probably so,* she thought. *They probably planned it together,* she fumed.

She dumped the entire pile of mail on the coffee table and wouldn't have looked at it again if the familiar, small, neat letters spelling out her name hadn't caught her attention. The envelope was powder blue, and this time, her father had included a return address. Missy held the envelope in trembling hands, staring hard at his name and address, half fearing that it would disappear if she looked at it for too long. He was out of state, but not so far away. It was addressed to her, Melissa Coyle, as all of the cards he sent were, but this time, she'd found it before Joan did.

Now she might have her own plan. She hoped so, at least. Then Carrington and her stupid, rich grandma could kiss her ass. Joan, too. Missy's stomach fluttered as she tore open the envelope with her father's handwriting on it. Inside was a simple card, just like all the others he sent. But this time, he'd written more than "Love, Dad" or "Take care, honey" inside. Missy cried as she read his words.

My dearest Melissa,

How are you, sweetheart? I wonder that each and every day. I am ashamed of myself as I write this. All these years, and I have never been able to say what you deserve to hear, and I have never been able to be a true father to you. I've tried many times to call you, but your mother doesn't want me to bother you. I don't know. Maybe she's right. I don't have any excuse for being a deadbeat dad all these years. I thought this time I would try writing what I'd like to say. I'm not great with words, but I want to give this a shot. I don't even know how to put into words how sorry I am. I hope someday you will forgive me. I probably don't deserve a chance to get to know you, but that is what I am asking for. Since you are nearly grown up, I think it is time for me to completely honest. The truth, Melissa, is that I am an alcoholic. I have been sober for one year, nine months, three weeks, and two days. On your thirteenth birthday, I will mark two years of sobriety. I never thought I could do it. You're the reason I finally got my life together, honey. I just hope it's not too late for us to get to know one another. I know I can't make up for all the years I have been absent from your life. I can't go back in time and make better decisions, as much as I wish that I could. I can try to be there for you now, though. For the past year and a half, I have been working in a nursing home as a certified nurse's aide. I went to school for my certification a few months after I quit drinking. I have a two-bedroom apartment in a pretty nice neighborhood. There is a middle school two blocks away, and I see kids walking to school all the time. Every time I see a girl who is about your age, I think of you, Melissa. And I feel like a bum for not being a part of your life. For a while after I stopped drinking, I thought it might be better for you if I didn't bother you. I don't know if I'm making a mistake by writing this. I would never want to hurt you or make your life any harder. But I had to take a chance. I'm so sorry for my mistakes, honey. I want us to know one another, and I want to be a father to you. I have vacation time saved that I would like to use soon, and I know you must be on summer vacation from school now. I'd like to come and see you. I thought about coming for your birthday, but I don't want to wait that long. I realize now as I am getting older how precious time is. Again, I'm sorry I haven't been any kind of a real father to you all these years. I wouldn't blame you or your mother if you told me to leave you alone. I am enclosing my cell and home phone numbers and my address. I pray that you will choose to use them, but if not, I understand. I love you, my darling. I hope your mother and your big sister Carrie are doing okay. Please tell them both hi from me. Carrie was a sweet kid; I'm sure she's been a good older sister to you. I hope to hear from you soon, honey.

Your dad,
Gary Ruiz

Missy read her father's letter five times. The edges of the card began to curl because her hands started to sweat. He'd enclosed an old picture. She stared in shock at the tattered photograph. She was a chubby toddler wearing a pink plastic cowboy hat and perched on her father's lap. She remembered that hat. It had been Carrington's, but Missy had made such a fuss about it that Joan took it from her oldest daughter and gave it to Missy. In the picture, Joan and Gary sat on a lumpy, blue couch, and Gary had his arms around Missy. A kindergarten-aged Carrington stood off to one side, pouting slightly. *God, she thought she was too good for us even back then,* Missy thought, anger flushing her cheeks. She couldn't believe how much younger her mother looked. Joan must have been in her late twenties then, Missy reasoned. It wasn't that Joan looked younger than she really was in the picture; it was that she looked so much older now. She wondered if Gary looked old and tired now, too.

Her father was slender in the picture, with raven black hair that brushed his shoulders and a thin moustache. He was laughing. She could see that she had his smile. *He's handsome,* she thought. *My dad is handsome.* Joan had only a handful of pictures of Gary, and she kept them stuffed in her room where it was hard for Missy to get to them. She'd thrown so many of them out over the years. Once, Missy had fished in the garbage can to rescue a picture of her father and Joan drinking shots at a bar that was decorated with twinkling holiday lights and tinsel, but Joan found the picture. She'd slapped Missy across the face and burned the picture with a cigarette lighter right in front of her. It was one of the few times Missy could remember her mother actually laying hands on her instead of Carrington. Missy never told Carrington about because she didn't want her older sister to think they had anything in common.

She slid the picture Gary had mailed into her back pocket. She knew that she shouldn't let Joan find out about the letter, but she was so engrossed in reading it again and again, she didn't notice Joan coming through the unlocked door.

"Hey, stranger," Joan greeted. "Whacha doin'?" she asked casually, barely glancing at Missy.

She made her way into the kitchen and poured herself a rum and coke.

Missy began to panic. It was too late to run to her room and hide the letter. She shuffled the thin piece of stationery and envelope underneath the rest of the mail.

"Hey, Mom," she answered. "Nothin' much. Just got home from Tanya's. I may go back over there later."

Joan returned to the living room, full glass in hand.

"You stay away from them Guzman boys," she said with a chuckle. "They're gettin' more handsome every day. I sure wouldn't kick that older one out of bed."

Missy cringed. "Mom!" she squealed, genuinely embarrassed.

The thought of her mother and Michael Guzman anywhere near a bed together made her stomach do somersaults.

Joan laughed again and chugged from her drink. She set it down on the coffee table and looked at Missy as if seeing her for the first time.

"Why are you upset?" she asked.

Missy wished she'd had time to wash her face before Joan came home. She tried to sound and look as nonchalant as possible.

"I'm not upset."

"You look like you been cryin'."

"I haven't been crying. I'm fine. I guess I'm just tired." She added a yawn for effect.

"Hmph," Joan responded. She eyed Missy skeptically and took another swig from her drink. "Hey, is that the mail? Give it here." She held out her hand.

Missy hesitated. She knew she couldn't stall her mother. There was no way she could hide Gary's letter. She sighed in defeat and handed the stack of paper to Joan.

Joan sifted through the pile without comment, tossing coupons and bills on the coffee table unopened. Missy held her breath. Finally, Joan came to the opened letter from Gary. She stared hard at the envelope for several seconds, a frown settling onto her face.

"When did this come?" she demanded.

"I just saw it here when I got home," Missy's voice was barely audible.

"You opened it?" Joan glared at Missy.

"Well, I thought … I thought since it was addressed to me—"

"Don't get smart with me, Missy!" Joan interrupted sharply.

"I'm not!" Missy cried. "I was just curious and I was going to give it to you when you got home."

It took most of her will power to meet her mother's eyes.

"Yeah, I bet!" Joan said. "That why it was on the bottom of the pile, huh?"

She began to read the letter and didn't press Missy for a response. Occasionally, she snorted dismissively. She looked in the envelope to see if there was more.

"He send anything else?" Joan asked, eyes narrowed to green slits.

"Just that," Missy answered.

"Are you sure, Missy?"

"Yes. I promise, that's all there was."

"Hmph," Joan said again. She folded up the letter and stuffed it back in the envelope. "Well, sounds like your dad is just as full of shit as he always was."

"He put his address and phone number in there. He wants me to call him," Missy squeaked.

"I ain't blind, Missy. I saw what he wrote!" Joan snapped. "I bet you just can't wait to call him, right? You think he's some great guy who's going to treat you like a princess. I got news for you, kiddo; your dad always has been and always will be nothin' but a lyin' sack of shit!"

Missy felt a cold knot of fear form in her stomach. *I want my dad,* she thought, fighting back her tears.

"Maybe he's nice," she managed to say.

"Ha!" Joan cried. "Maybe he's nice!" She mocked Missy in a high-pitched voice. "Yeah, your dad's a nice, great ol' guy, and I'm the queen of England!"

She stood abruptly, and Missy flinched. Joan squashed the envelope into a wad and jammed it in her pocket.

"You better not ever even think of hiding mail from me, girl," she hissed. "Now get the hell out of my face before I kick your ass!"

Missy fled to her room and forced herself to close the door gently instead of slamming it as hard as she could. How she longed to bang the door shut! She knew it would be unwise to push her mother, though. Joan was already dangerously angry. She'd seen that look and heard that tone many times before, but it was usually focused on Carrington. Missy felt a stab of sadness thinking of her older sister. She fought the feeling off and punched her mattress several times, crying soundlessly.

I hate everyone! she thought as her fists slammed violently into her unmade bed. She thought of her mother's face, greasy with makeup and frowning. *I hate you most of all,* Missy thought. *I wish you would just die.*

Chapter Twenty-eight

The maid took carefully measured steps toward the breakfast table. She barely managed not to teeter under the weight of the tray. Her starched uniform made soft swishing sounds as she laid the silver coffee pot, sugar bowl, cream pitcher, two dainty, bone china cups, and two elaborate fruit plates before Regina and Laurence.

"Thank you, Sonja," Regina said tonelessly without looking up from the morning newspaper.

Laurence smiled his thanks at the young woman. She seemed to appreciate the eye contact. He felt sorry for the people his wife hired, not because they were underpaid—he made sure they received fair wages—but because they had to deal primarily with Regina.

Distracted, Regina didn't really read anything in her section of the newspaper. She flipped the pages idly, pausing now and then to take an extra glimpse at advertisements. Laurence stirred one spoonful of sugar into his steaming hot coffee and sipped it with pleasure. It was the same way his father liked his coffee:

no cream and one small pinch of sugar. He sifted through the business section of the newspaper, making mental notes and plans for things to do and people to call at work the next day.

Regina looked up at him.

"Imagine, just imagine," she said, sounding exasperated.

He knew before she said anything specific what she was going to complain about. It was all she could think about ever since A. C. broke the news that Arnold had fathered a child who was now permanently in A. C.'s custody. Much to Regina's chagrin, A. C. was thrilled about it.

He looked up from the NASDAQ.

"What, dear?" he asked, humoring her.

"Can you believe it?" she cried. "A. C. has a grandchild! A nearly grown one, at that. Who knows—what if Arnold had other children? A. C. could have a whole litter of ragamuffins searching for her, just biding their time until they get to move into granny's big house."

She set her coffee cup down forcefully, making a big drop slosh onto the tablecloth.

Laurence cringed at "litter" and "ragamuffin." *You have no class, Regina,* he thought. *Never have, never will.*

"Come on now, dear," he tried to comfort her. "That's highly unlikely. The fact that A. C.'s discovered this girl after so long is, in itself, a rarity. I really doubt there is a group of other children fathered by Arnold just waiting in the wings. Arnold made his own life hard for himself; I imagine he had few friends and fewer lovers." He paused, not sure he believed his own words. "It's a fluke that he fathered one child. Don't worry," he told Regina, staring intently at her. When she didn't meet his eyes, he said it again. "Don't worry!" he insisted. "It's going to be all right. What is the worst that could come of this?" He instantly regretted his question.

Regina wasted no time. "I'll tell you what the worst that could come of this is!" she snapped. "A. C., in her weak state of mind, lets this little hoodlum wreck her house and swindle her out of every cent she has! This child will ruin A. C.'s reputation, as if it hasn't already been completely dragged through the mud after everything Arnold did." She paused, lips curling in distaste. "And now this. A child born out of wedlock, born to a lowlife mother and raised in a slum. This child is a bad seed; how could she not be?" she demanded. "A. C. is a fool. She'll never be the same, not after burying her husband and her only child. It's not her fault, really." She softened slightly. "She needs to be taken care of; she needs someone to keep track of her affairs so she doesn't make a huge mistake like the one she just made!"

Laurence clenched his teeth and suppressed an eye roll. He closed his eyes for a long moment, trying desperately to calm himself. After their huge fight a few weeks prior, he was resolved to salvage his marriage and make his relationship with Regina, at the very least, civil. She didn't make it easy, though. It was the least expensive of his options. He'd still been poor when they married and had no idea he would become so financially successful. At the time, it had never occurred to him to make Regina sign a prenuptial agreement. Lately, hardly a day went by that he didn't mentally kick himself for this lack of foresight.

"A. C. has a lawyer," he reminded her gently. "She's going to be fine. Your sister's no fool; you know that. She's suffered more than anyone on this earth deserves to suffer, but the past hasn't rendered her incompetent. She's going to be fine," he said again, firmly this time.

Regina shot him a disgusted look. Laurence let his gaze wander back to the newspaper. He should have known better than to mention Carmen Villareal, even if not by name. Regina loathed Carmen. She had immediately disliked Carmen when A. C., as a freshman in college, brought her over for Thanksgiving dinner. Regina hadn't planned on having to share her older sister with an outsider. She had been looking forward to A. C.'s visit for months, and when A. C. showed up with Carmen, Regina was livid. The fact that her parents took a near instant shine to Carmen only firmed her resolve to find fault in her older sister's new friend. In the beginning, Carmen made a genuine effort to befriend Regina. She showed interest in the younger girl's life, asking her about school and boys, admiring her taste in clothes. It soon became apparent, though, that Regina would not be won over by A. C.'s charming friend. Eventually, Carmen stopped focusing on Regina and simply treated her with polite indifference. Of course, Regina complained about this to her parents and her own friends, describing her sister's best friend as an "ice maiden with the fakest smile anyone's ever seen." Years later, when A. C. asked Carmen to be her maid of honor, all pretenses of Regina being even remotely civil to Carmen went out the window. Over the months, then the years, Regina's hostility toward A. C.'s best friend faded into the occasional thinly veiled barb. Overall, she seemed to pretend that Carmen Villareal did not exist.

"Let's not even get into that," Regina huffed. "My sister has made the dire mistake of choosing an attorney based solely on friendship, with no regard to the attorney's competence. She trusts Carmen *too* much, if you ask me."

Laurence forced himself to maintain a neutral expression. He'd always been fond of Carmen. In fact, he developed a crush on her when they met for the first time, but by then, he was all but married to Regina. Laurence admired Carmen Villareal. He found her witty and exciting. Her ambition was attractive, too. She'd built her law practice and her reputation from the ground up, much as he had painstakingly developed his own career. He marveled at her. When she was in town visiting A. C., he sometimes found excuses to drop by and say hello. He tried to imagine being married to a woman like Carmen, someone who seemed to sparkle wherever she went, someone whose smile and laughter were contagious, someone who could verbally disembowel even the most well-prepped and stubborn witness. Of course, he realized that it wasn't a perfect world. Clearly, Carmen had made her own sacrifices, and not even she could have the best of both worlds. She'd been married twice, and both marriages, it seemed, had been destined to wither away because Carmen always put her career first. In this way, he supposed, she was selfish. But Laurence respected her even more for it.

He decided to change tack. No more talking about Carmen, even indirectly.

"So, when do we get to meet the new young lady in A. C.'s life?" Laurence asked, trying to sound light and happy.

Regina responded with a sigh and pecked at her breakfast. She looked older and more tired this morning than she had in a while. For a brief moment, Laurence felt a flicker of concern. In her thin face, he caught a glimpse of both his past and his future. He remembered the spunky, stylish girl he had fallen in love with, and then he envisioned a much older Regina, cheeks hollow, mouth turned down at the corners. Why? Why was Regina always so unhappy? Had he been a bad husband? Laurence knew he wasn't the most affectionate or attentive man in the world. It just didn't come naturally to him. But he had loved her dearly once, and in his own way, he believed, he'd shown her how much he loved her. Regina, for whatever reason, was immovable. None of life's major events touched or changed her the way they did others—not marriage, and not motherhood. He knew she cared a great deal about image, though. God forbid any of her friends at the country club think anything was wrong in Regina's life. *Maybe,* Laurence mused sadly, *Regina is, and always will be, shallow as a fucking puddle.*

"I don't know," she admitted. "A. C.'s being vague about it; you know how she is. I told her maybe she should bring the child with her to brunch at the club one morning. I mean, my God, you'd think she wasn't a member and hasn't known these people for decades, the way she stays away," she complained.

I wish I could stay the hell away from them, too, Laurence thought. He just nodded and sipped his coffee.

"I'm actually glad that she turned that idea down, though," Regina continued. "This child was raised in an entirely … *different* atmosphere. Taking her to the club, well, that just has disaster written all over it! At least I offered, though," she congratulated herself.

Laurence just stared at her. *Who are you?* he wondered. He forced himself to speak, knowing that it would be worse if he just sat silently and brooded. They would end up having another explosive fight if he allowed himself to stew in his feelings.

"I have an idea!" He felt like he was hearing another man do an impression of his voice. "Why don't we have a dinner here at the house? We could have it catered. We can just invite a few of our closest friends. Maybe Carrington can bring a little friend, someone her age, to help her feel a little more comfortable around a bunch of strangers."

Regina pursed her lips in distaste.

"Well, maybe she doesn't need to bring a friend," Laurence said quickly. "But why don't we make a nice little event of it? We haven't had a party at the house in ages; you know everyone loves your parties, honey."

Again, Laurence had the strangest sensation that he was listening to another man make plans with his voice. Or maybe it was the voice of the real Laurence and he was just along for the ride. Maybe *he* was the imposter.

Regina prodded her fruit with her fork, forehead furrowed in thought. She allowed a small smile at his compliment.

"Well, I do know all the best caterers and florists," she admitted.

"Of course you do, darling," Laurence said. "The benefit at the museum last month was brilliant! Everyone in the office is still talking about it," he lied.

It was, in fact, a pleasant party, but it was also unremarkable. The people who worked for Laurence were accustomed to such events; there were a handful of these parties every season. It was always the same group of women planning them, the same queen bee wives. They seemed to rotate the titles they gave themselves, but what difference did it make, Laurence wondered, whether Regina was Madame chairperson or chair of the decorating committee? Whatever her title, every couple of months he still found himself stuffed into a tuxedo, sitting at a table surrounded by expensively dressed couples, clapping mechanically after the guest speakers made their pitch, and donating a hefty check to whatever cause was most fashionable at the moment. Laurence found it all incredibly dull, but Regina seemed to thrive on these things. She was always a little deflated for a couple of days following one of the parties she coordinated. That is, until the next big cause found its way onto her radar.

Her eyes took on a familiar glow; he could already see the plans for an overly lavish dinner party forming in her mind. It would keep her busy for weeks. Laurence could play golf as often as he liked on the weekends. He returned to the business section with a private little smile on his lips.

Chapter Twenty-nine

A. C. set the phone down and rubbed her temples with the tips of her fingers. She had just spent nearly an hour on the phone with her sister. There was a dull but steady ache building behind her eyes. Why did Regina always have to make things so complicated? She couldn't simply agree to come over and meet Carrington at A. C.'s house for a simple lunch or dinner. No, she insisted on making a huge deal out of it. A. C. knew that Carrington was going to be uncomfortable with Regina's plans for a party in Carrington's honor. She was uncomfortable with it herself. She didn't understand her sister's apparent need to turn as many of life's events as possible into expensive, showy affairs. Regina had always been like this, even when they were children, and it never ceased to aggravate A. C.

Carrington had come a long way in the short while they'd been living together and seeing a family counselor, but A. C. knew she was still quite vulnerable. Carrington was nervous enough about meeting the rest of the family; a party, especially one of Regina's gaudy bashes, would be hard on her. A. C.

didn't entirely understand Regina's motives. She knew Regina didn't approve of Carrington moving in with her. Regina had not been blunt enough to say that she didn't like it, but A. C. knew her sister well enough to predict how she would react. Regina used the same cool, condescending tone whenever she disliked anything. She asked leading questions and alluded to dire outcomes. Regina's words and deeds rarely matched. She was offering, insisting really, to host an elaborate party for A. C.'s newly discovered granddaughter, but she continuously implied that A. C. was making a huge mistake by becoming so involved in the young girl's life. It was infuriating.

A. C. wasn't entirely sure why she put up with her sister at all. Some sense of familial guilt and loneliness, she guessed. Had Leslie Carrington lived to see A. C. and Regina age into their sixties, it would have broken her heart to see her children become estranged. Without Cal or Arnold, Regina and Gloria were the only blood relatives A. C. had. But now she had Carrington. Was it at all possible, she wondered, for Carrington to fit in with Regina and the rest of the family? She didn't care if Regina ever gave Carrington her bourgeois seal of approval, but she supposed that it would make life so much easier if Regina did eventually relent and accept Carrington as a member of the family.

A. C. poured herself a glass of iced green tea and swallowed two aspirin. Really, she was amazed that she'd been able to keep Regina at bay for this long. As soon as Regina heard of Carrington's existence, she'd been clamoring for information. A. C. hadn't committed to Regina's party plans, but she knew she would probably end up agreeing to it. Carrington would have to meet the rest of the family eventually. If having a party would make Regina just a little bit easier to tolerate, then why not?

A. C. would see to it that Carrington would meet her great aunt and uncle before the party. It would be way too hard on Carrington if the night of the party was the very first time the poor child had to meet her entire extended family. She decided to let Carrington choose; they could have Regina and Laurence over to the house for lunch or meet them at a restaurant. Both options had their pros and cons. Carrington might feel most comfortable in the house, a place she had grown to love and that she associated with A. C. and a feeling of protection. On the other hand, meeting Regina and Laurence in a restaurant might be easier because there wouldn't be the forced intimacy of having strangers in her living space.

Regina and Laurence had been in A. C.'s house hundreds of times over the years, but it was never their home. It was now the home she shared with Carrington, and that felt so *right*. She loved coming downstairs and finding Carrington sitting cross-legged on the sofa and reading. She loved passing by the bedroom that now belonged to Carrington and seeing the girl lying across her bed, scribbling in her journal. She looked forward to the meals they made and cleaned up together. It was amazing how well they clicked with one another. A. C. felt years younger. The changes she'd seen in Carrington were astounding. It made her chest swell with pride that Carrington was so comfortable around her. Several times over the past few weeks, she had tears in her eyes when she saw that the cautious, wounded expression had all but disappeared from Carrington's face.

A small part of A. C. was relieved when Joan and Missy were so nasty to Carrington on the phone. She hated herself for it, and yet it was a feeling she could not deny. It wasn't that she wanted to see her granddaughter hurt; quite the contrary. All Joan Coyle had ever brought into Carrington's life was pain. A. C. had a bad feeling about letting Carrington contact her mother, but she knew she shouldn't try to stop her. Their own relationship was still so new, after all. Carrington would want something—an idea, a reminder of her past. It was only natural. A. C. felt it was important that people never lost sight their personal history; history would keep a person focused on the future and remind her to enjoy the present. A. C. hoped that when Carrington was grown up, she would look back with tenderness at the time she spent with her grandmother. A. C. also hoped to live to a ripe, old age so that she could watch her granddaughter's life unfold.

Her headache began to dissipate. She would agree to Regina's party only if Regina promised to keep it very small: Laurence, Gloria and a guest (if she was dating; A. C. never knew what her niece was up to), and only a handful of their closest friends. That was it. She would insist that Regina and Laurence have lunch with them several days before the party so they could meet Carrington without any spectators. Lunch and the party would be hard enough on Carrington; there was no need to turn it into a circus. If Regina didn't agree, then she wouldn't get to throw her party; that was that.

A small smile spread on A. C.'s lips. The best part would be taking Carrington shopping for a party dress. They'd already gone shopping for everyday clothes, but so far, there had been no reason for Carrington to have any formal wear. Shopping for a few blouses, jeans, and shoes had been hard enough on them both, so at the time, A. C. didn't want to push the issue of a party dress or two. She didn't much care for parties herself.

That first shopping trip had been difficult; Carrington was obviously ashamed of the clothes she'd brought with her from Joan's house, and she was embarrassed to let her grandmother buy anything for her. A. C. didn't dare remind her that she was now Carrington's legal guardian and therefore responsible for making sure the girl was properly clothed. It would have come out wrong, no matter how delicately she tried to phrase it. The fact was, it made A. C. feel more fulfilled and purposeful than she'd felt in years to buy clothing for her granddaughter. They'd been through so much in such a short time together, though, that she realized that trying to explain this would only add to the intense muddle of feelings they were both dealing with. Why make it any more awkward than it already was? So, she'd been casual about it. She presented the shopping trip as a fun way to spend an afternoon. It would be a women's afternoon out, A. C. told Carrington. She knew that Carrington hated the clothes she had, so the first stop they made was to a huge department store where Carrington could immediately get a completely new outfit to change into. Carrington had tears in her eyes when she saw herself in brand-new clothes that fit and flattered her slender frame perfectly—not Joan's hand-me-downs or leftovers from the thrift store, but things that were just for her. In spite of the rocky beginning, eventually they both had a wonderful time shopping together. A. C. also bought a few things for herself, which she hadn't done in ages.

Taking Carrington out to get a party dress, A. C. hoped, would be much more relaxed than their first shopping trip had been. A. C. would give her granddaughter a taste of the finer things in life. She would buy Carrington a dress fit for a princess. Let Regina have her garish display of wealth. Carrington would be the very picture of elegance and style; A. C. would see to it.

Chapter Thirty

Gloria didn't need to answer the door when Dirk arrived. He had his own set of keys. He could hear the television blaring even before he unlocked the door. Gloria often left her TV on all day. Dirk had the impression it somehow eased the loneliness that she would never admit to feeling.

She was sipping from a wine glass when he let himself inside. She wore a silk kimono nightgown and sported streaks of mascara on her face. Her sharply pointed nose was red and raw looking. When she looked up at him from where she slumped on the couch, Gloria burst into a fresh bout of tears. Dirk almost felt sorry for her. He'd never seen Gloria look so miserable.

He fetched a box of aloe-coated tissue from the master bathroom and joined her on the couch. Gently, he pulled the wine glass from her hand, set it on the coffee table, and began to dab at her ruined face.

"What is it, sweetie?" he cooed softly.

She didn't answer immediately. She closed her eyes, tears still sliding down her face.

"Oh, Dirk," she said at last, voice trembling. "The worst has happened. The absolute worst!"

She buried her face into his chest and began to sob as uncontrollably as Dirk had ever seen anyone cry. He was shocked and somewhat frightened. What would the "worst" mean to Gloria? Her father had died? Or simply decided to stop funding the gallery? Had Gloria just discovered that she had a horrible, incurable disease? And if so, was it something that could be sexually transmitted? He began to feel mildly alarmed.

"What's happened, honey?" he murmured into her hair. She smelled of cigarettes, sweat, and the obscenely expensive shampoo she used.

She leaned away from him slightly.

"My mother called. A child's been discovered; apparently my loser cousin had a kid he never bothered to tell anyone about—a girl. My Aunt A. C. has actually adopted the kid! Can you believe it? Oh, God, Dirk, this is the most terrible thing that's ever happened to me!"

He was relieved that she'd once again pressed her face in his chest so she wouldn't see the confused look on his face. Questions swam through his mind. How old was this child? Considering that Gloria's dead cousin was ten years her senior, it was possible that his kid was legally an adult. How, Dirk wondered, would this affect Gloria's inheritance?

"What do you mean, sweetie?" He tried to sound as gentle as possible.

Gloria sobbed into his two hundred dollar shirt. It didn't matter. He'd charge it to the business account without notifying her; he did it all the time.

"I mean," she wailed, "there's someone new in the family. Some kind of … long lost relative. It's absurd. My Aunt A. C. is apparently head over heels for the kid." She drenched him with snot and tears.

Kid. Dirk was thoughtful. So, the girl couldn't be more than what, sixteen, seventeen? He ran his fingers through Gloria's dark, wavy hair.

"Have you met her yet?" he asked, his tone soft.

She glared up at him briefly. "No, you idiot. That's just it!"

Dirk suppressed the urge to shove her away. He braced himself, waiting patiently for her outpouring. He didn't have to wait long.

"Mother's planning a party for her, almost like a debutante ball!" Gloria blubbered. "I just can't believe it. My cousin Arnold was a total loser! He never did anything right in his life! Now suddenly there's this kid, this apparently gorgeous girl. And, what, I'm just supposed to embrace her with open arms? As if I haven't been the one who's been here all these years! And what did I get for it? A second-rate degree from a college my parents chose? An art gallery that my dad controls? Constant check-ins from my bitch mother? What, does it matter, Dirk? What does it all fucking matter?"

You have no idea, Dirk thought as he caressed Gloria's back.

"So, your mom is planning a big bash for her?" Dirk asked lamely, already knowing the answer and anticipating Gloria's snide response. "I mean, it's in the works?"

"Are you fucking deaf?" Gloria snapped.

Once again, Dirk forced himself not to push her away.

He instead cooed, "Oh, my poor darling," several times into the nest of her sweaty, mousse-encrusted waves.

Gloria wept for several more minutes, and strangely, Dirk felt himself growing hard inside his Dockers. It was an odd sensation.

He'd had sex with Gloria many times; that wasn't anything new. But actually *wanting* her was an unexpected sensation.

"I think I'm going to puke," Gloria slurred into his shoulder.

He dutifully followed her into the bathroom, where he held her hair back as she wretched into the toilet. Dirk was amused, in spite of the smell. *What would your mother think of you now, you stupid bitch?* But he said nothing, except for murmuring sympathetic sounds every few seconds. If Gloria noticed, she didn't say so, and she didn't thank him. In fact, when she had emptied her stomach, she slapped his hands away and stumbled over to the sink.

"I want a Perrier," she mumbled as she splashed water onto her cheeks.

Dirk stood near her like a guard faithfully protecting his charge.

"Dirk!" Gloria snapped.

He rushed out of the bathroom, loathing her more and more with each step. *Fucking cunt,* he seethed. *I hope you die from alcohol poisoning.* But even as he poured her seltzer water over ice into a genuine crystal goblet, he knew he didn't want Gloria to die. Not until she married him, of course. Sans pre-nup.

A genuine smile spread across his face. He knew exactly what to say to comfort her and exactly what to suggest that would make everything right in her world. It was so simple, so obvious. He scurried back to her, careful not spill any of the iced Perrier. She was just stumbling out of the bathroom.

"About damn time," she snapped, snatching the glass from him.

Dirk ignored this and followed her back into the living room. Gloria lapped sloppily from her mineral water, alternately holding the frosty glass to her forehead and drinking from it.

"So," he began cautiously, "tell me about this would-be cousin of yours."

Gloria groaned and slurped loudly.

"There's not much I can say," she croaked, her voice hoarse. "I only know that my idiot, junkie cousin Arnold fathered a kid with some white trash woman, and suddenly this kid has shown up in Aunt A. C.'s life. It's obvious, though," Gloria snapped, "that she's angling for attention and an inheritance. And my feeble-minded old aunt is ripe for the picking. No doubt this little girl smells money," Gloria said, setting her empty glass on the coffee table.

"Well, it's not like your dad's going to write her into his will overnight," Dirk said.

"Oh, Dirk," Gloria said with a sigh. "You don't get it. Daddy has, like, a hard-on for poor people. I can't tell you how many times he's tried to tell me how rough he had it when he was a kid. It's so stupid. It's like he has no clue what he's become. You have *no* idea how hard a time he gave me about starting up Lucinda's Lair! As if *my gallery* hasn't done wonders for the family," she huffed indignantly.

Dirk blinked several times to keep from rolling his eyes and exhaled through gritted teeth. Sometimes he couldn't help but wonder if Gloria believed the bullshit she spouted. Was she truly that oblivious?

"All right," he said. "So a blood test proved that your cousin Arnold actually had a kid with this woman. Gloria," he paused, not sure if he dared to say it, "your mother barely accepts the things *you* do; what in the hell makes you think she's going to welcome this kid with open arms?" He sucked in a deep breath of air.

For a long moment, Gloria was silent. She looked not exactly at him, but through him. It was completely unnerving. Dirk thought for sure she was going to throw him out. To his shock, she began to nod.

"Well, maybe … maybe you're right," she said finally.

"Of course I am," he announced, suddenly feeling bold. "But maybe you shouldn't absolutely count on your parents', especially your dad's, loyalty."

"I know, I know!" Gloria began to cry again.

Dirk couldn't help grinning. This was working out much better than he could have hoped.

"And that's just it, sweetie," he murmured, lightly stroking her hair. "I don't think it's so much that she grew up poor. It's that she's blood—to you and your mother, at least." It was tripe and he knew it, but he couldn't stop for some reason. "Your father's a good man; he'd do anything for your mother and you," he added quickly. "Because you're blood. *His* blood. Just imagine," he said in a near whisper, "how excited he would be to have his name carried on."

Gloria stiffened beneath his touch. Dirk broke out into a cold sweat. He'd gone too far. But, to his surprise and immeasurable relief, Gloria looked tenderly up at him, the tears continuing to spill from her eyes.

"You're right," she said. "You're absolutely fucking right. Daddy would flip if his name was carried on. Of course, what he's always really wanted is a son. Mother is way too old to have another child … but I'm not. And I know she must be so jealous that Aunt A. C. has a grandkid and she doesn't. She can't stand it when Aunt A. C. has anything before her."

Finally, Dirk thought. *Yes, yes, this is what I've been waiting for.*

"An heir, Gloria. That's what your father wants. That's what he's wanted for ages. And if you had a child, your mother would have everything your aunt has and more. Think … just *think* of how grateful they would be to you."

She wept into his chest. "I know," she whispered, her voice hoarse. "I know. You don't know … you don't know how many times … how much she fucking pesters me about getting married and having a family. You have no idea how much of that garbage I had to hear from her when I was a kid!" She went on for a while, mostly repeating herself.

Dirk barely listened as she prattled on about her oh-so-sad childhood. He was tired of the sound of her voice and her laughable tale of woe. Mostly to shut her up, he nuzzled her neck, sucking and licking her smooth flesh. He felt his penis bulge against his zipper.

"I can give you that heir, my darling."

For the first time since he'd known her, Gloria was speechless. She didn't disagree, and that, Dirk thought, was most important. She didn't pull away from him as he removed her kimono and unzipped his pants. She didn't flinch or utter a single word of resistance as he entered her. Of course, she didn't necessarily seem to enjoy the sex, but she never really did, as far as Dirk could tell. He often wondered why she wanted to have sex with him at all. Having sex with Gloria was one of two things: an act that Gloria observed with aloof amusement, or something angry and vicious that left marks on Dirk's flesh for days afterwards.

This time she was mostly mute, but he didn't sense her usual cold detachment. She moaned a few times, and he was relieved when she wrapped her arms around his shoulders. Clearly, she wanted him, too. Perhaps she just wanted to be held. But cuddling didn't occur to Dirk as he fucked Gloria. He never thought of their sex as making love. In fact, rarely, if ever, had Dirk thought of any of his sexual encounters in such a manner. Oh, sure, he would certainly call it love if pressed by the woman whose bed he was sharing. But those were just words, a means to an end. Like fucking Gloria.

He panted onto her shoulder after finishing. Usually she pushed him away as soon as it was over, but this time she clung to him. There was something desperate and strange about it.

She started to speak, but still feeling bold, Dirk shushed her. He pressed a finger to her lips and caressed them. It worked. He was stunned by the swift transfer of power that had just occurred. It was like a trap door or a silent alarm had been activated. Dirk saw Gloria with new eyes. Yes, she was still an obnoxious, self-absorbed bitch, but she was no longer the one calling the shots. There was something frail and needy about her, and it was a need that only he could fulfill. Who else would put up with her? Who else had put up with her for so long? No one but Dirk. Even her own family barely seemed to tolerate her. And now, it was finally time for his generous reward. Not the over-inflated salary he'd received for the past couple of years. No, he could have found that elsewhere, Dirk told himself. It was finally his day, his turn, his chance. It was finally time for Gloria to pay him back for everything he'd done for her and the countless humiliations he'd suffered at her manicured hands.

Dirk knew from experience that Gloria's strings were much easier to pull if they were well lubed with alcohol. So, that's what he would do. He would keep her boozed up for as long as it took. Not that Gloria needed any assistance in staying intoxicated for days on end. But Dirk would make sure she was drunk enough to need him and too drunk to refuse him. If he could also provide the occasional tablet of Ecstasy, Valium, or Xanax, so much the better. He had a couple of acquaintances who sold small amounts of pills. And when she became pregnant, it would be simple enough to wean her off all of that stuff. Gloria was a pain in the ass, but if having a child would mean cementing her role as the center of her father's world, she would do it and she would do what was best for the baby, Dirk told himself.

A child, he thought. *My child.* But visions of baby's first Christmas, learning to walk, and the first day of kindergarten did not stream through his mind. Dirk imagined a closet full of tailored suits and a couple of customized, enormous sport utility vehicles with personalized license plates, dining in the very best restaurants and going first class any time he traveled, which would be often. If Gloria had his child—no, *when* Gloria had his child—he would be forever linked to the Lithgow family. She couldn't just fire him from the gallery and erase him from her life.

Gloria began to snore lightly. She looked haggard and small, like a sickly, young girl. Dirk gazed at her with something akin to affection and imagined what he might name a yacht.

Chapter Thirty-one

Laurence balked at the price of Regina's gown, and it had been years, decades perhaps, since he, personally, kept track of what she spent. After he reached a certain income bracket, he tried to act as if the obscene amounts of money that Regina spent didn't matter very much, but mostly he just couldn't stomach her extravagance. It made him physically ill when he remembered his mother on her arthritic knees, scrubbing away at kitchen linoleum, yet his own wife hired someone to take care of even the simplest tasks at home. Sometimes he thought it was a wonder that Regina hadn't entirely squandered away his earnings and landed herself, Laurence, and Gloria on the streets. He was careful, though. Regina knew he made a lot of money, but not exactly how much. It wasn't that she was stupid or incapable; she had a degree in business and could have been near the top in her class if she had applied herself. It was simply that, Laurence observed, the money and security made her lazy. Lazy yet ever more demanding. So, for years, he'd been successfully able to conceal his exact worth from Regina.

Eventually, an accountant was hired to keep track of the household expenses, including the gobs of cash Regina parted with on an almost daily basis. While Laurence was silently appalled by how his wife spent their money, he feigned nonchalance. What did he care if she spent over a hundred dollars on lunch and nearly one thousand at a spa in a single afternoon? Some of his investments earned that in interest alone during the span of a few days. But, for reasons even he didn't fully understand, he took interest in the party Regina was planning for Carrington. He'd intended for it to be something to distract his wife, but begrudgingly, he found himself involved in everything from the menu, to the guests, to what Regina would wear.

She had hired a dressmaker to create a custom gown, and said gown was atrocious, like most of the things Regina chose. Despite all her efforts to the contrary, Regina could not buy taste. It had nothing to do with her working-class background. Laurence only had to look at A. C. to know this. Compared to her friends at the Wyngate Country Club who had been wealthy all their lives, Regina's childhood was modest at best, perhaps even downright Dickensian by her country club friends' standards. Perhaps that was why Regina was bound and determined to prove to the world that she could easily spend just as much on one dress as any of her country club friends.

Considering Regina's conservative taste in clothing, the dress she hired Lola from Paris (which was how Regina always referred to the dressmaker) to design and create sported a savagely low neckline. The only thing that shielded Regina's jutting collar bone from the rest of the world was a sheer, off-white crumb catcher. The gown was nearly floor length, but it had a long slit up the left side. Laurence was surprised; Regina usually criticized revealing dresses by saying they belonged on cheap women who spent time in slimy bars. Fashion train wreck or not, Regina's dress was certainly not cheap—at least, not monetarily. It occurred to Laurence more than once that he probably could have purchased a number of the slimy bars of Regina's imaginings and every drop of booze in them for roughly the cost of her party dress. The color was a strange blend of burgundy and milky white; its hue was created with thousands of sequins, half of them genuine chips of mother-of-pearl and the other half ordinary maroon sequins. Each shiny little circle was securely fastened with translucent silk thread.

The high heels Lola from Paris dyed to match Regina's dress drew another ungodly sum of money from their bank account. Lola made it sound like a rare favor when she explained how she attached a handful of sequins to each outrageously high heeled shoe. Regina flushed with pride when she tried on the dress for Laurence. He felt embarrassed for her. The sea of resentment that roiled precariously between them threatened to overwhelm him there in Lola's little boutique, where one had to have an appointment to consult with the famous Lola from Paris. On Gloria, Laurence would have found the one-of-a-kind dress gaudy and tacky. On Regina, it was pathetic. She was trying too hard, as she always did, but this particular dress seemed to be a painful culmination of all the decades she had clawed and schemed to not only to blend into what she believed to be the upper crust of society, but to exemplify it.

Laurence suspected that Lola from Paris fudged here and there on the expenses of creating Regina's gown, but he would never dream of making such an accusation. What Regina wanted, Regina would have, just as it had been for decades. He despised her for it, but he despised himself even more. Sometimes, as he washed up before going to bed, he spat used mouthwash at his reflection in the mirror. He'd been doing it for years. It didn't make any sense, and Laurence would never admit it to anyone. But on occasion, the sight of his own face so enraged him that he could not contain his disgust.

Still, he went along with whatever Regina desired for the upcoming party. She spent more on catering than he'd spent for his first car. The cost for the food would have fed several dozen people, let alone a party of eight. Besides Regina, Laurence, Gloria, Gloria's friend/assistant Dirk, A. C., and Carrington, Regina had invited her closest friend, Deidre, and Deirdre's husband, Samson. Compared to the galas Regina regularly organized, it was miniscule, yet Laurence actually felt nervous about this particular event. Why? He had nothing to lose (besides several thousand dollars), and nothing, really, to gain. But he had absorbed a great deal of Regina's anxiety about the whole affair.

Outwardly, Regina made a lot of noise about this being something that would benefit Carrington Coyle, an unfortunate girl who'd stumbled upon a "decent" (Regina's phrase) pedigree and a chance at a better life. But Laurence had known Regina for the better part of forty years. This party had as little to do with A. C.'s recently discovered grandchild as it had to do with the first human being on the moon. This event was utterly and entirely about Regina. This party was yet another one of Regina's attempts to prove to her friends, to Gloria, to Laurence, to A. C., and to herself that she could be an accepting, gracious, and charming woman. Fine, Laurence thought over the weeks that Regina spent poring over the party's details. Fine. If that's what it took to keep her satisfied and occupied for a while, then the cost didn't matter much. But deep within his chest, in the place where his overworked, unkempt mother dwelled, he knew otherwise. The party would be a disaster. Laurence was as sure of this as he was that his daughter would ask him for an "advance" around the first of every month.

Lately, Gloria complained that business was slow and the art world was becoming stagnant. No one appreciated avant-garde art anymore, Gloria said. Laurence knew this was wholly untrue—not so much that no one appreciated the strange and meritless artwork that Gloria peddled without shame, but that Lucinda's Lair was unable to earn a buck. The gallery earned a fair sum, even by his standards. What Gloria did with the profit, though, was the mystery.

Sure, some of it was obvious. She shopped the way her mother did. Why wouldn't she? Regina was her lifelong example. But there should have been something left each month from what the gallery earned. Laurence wondered, as he often did, if he should have his accountant audit Gloria's expenses. Would it be worth the feud? There were some things, many things, about her lifestyle that he didn't need an accountant to determine were unnecessary. Her personal assistant was the ultimate example.

Why, exactly, did Gloria need a personal assistant? How did Dirk assist Gloria? The possible answers to this question made Laurence blanch on more than one occasion. While Gloria did keep Dirk busy with the day-to-day handling of the gallery, Laurence still thought that Gloria didn't need an assistant any more than Regina needed another pair of shoes. Not only that, but if Gloria insisted on having someone at her beck and call, Laurence wished that he could have chosen the person himself. He would have been very careful, very deliberate in his choosing, and never, not in a billion years, would he have chosen Dirk Godfrey.

The young man was a gold digger. Laurence was convinced of this the first time he met Dirk. Personally, Laurence could care less about pedigree. He certainly hadn't come from a well-to-do background. In fact, he admired people who had to strive to overcome hardship. He noted, though, that Dirk was very dodgy about the subject of his background. Gloria didn't seem to notice or care, but Laurence realized this was because she didn't consider her relationship with Dirk serious. At first, Regina had been quite suspicious of Dirk, but when she realized that Gloria had no intention of marrying the rather short but strikingly handsome man, she backed off somewhat. Her recent conversations with Gloria were spent dropping not-so-subtle hints to Gloria about eligible men, usually the sons and nephews of friends from the country club. Gloria paid her mother's suggestions no mind. It was an ongoing cycle, one that usually resulted in a throbbing headache for Laurence and a few days of silence between Regina and Gloria.

Initially, Dirk had tried like mad to get on Laurence's good side. To Dirk, this meant kissing Laurence's ass whenever they were in the same room together. He behaved like an adoring, drooling fan might behave in the presence of a favorite actor. He laughed too hard if Laurence made a quip. He openly admired everything about the Lithgow family: their various properties, the artwork that adorned their home, Laurence's suits, the country club they belonged to. It appeared that Dirk worshipped anything and everything about the Lithgow family. Laurence found it pathetic. He might have felt sorry for Dirk if he didn't find the young man's blind devotion so transparent. Seeing the way Gloria treated Dirk was enough to inspire pity in just about anyone. She dragged him around country club gatherings as if he was an expensive little rat dog in a designer carrying case. She looked at him sharply if he talked too much, and had absolutely no qualms about interrupting him. She sometimes made jokes at his expense, but mostly, Gloria ignored Dirk. Worst of all, Laurence thought, was that Dirk took it all. He allowed Gloria to put him on display, ridicule him, and overlook him without ever standing up for himself. He showed up faithfully at Lucinda's Lair for work, even on the days when Gloria herself didn't make an appearance (although this was rare; one of the few things Gloria ever seemed genuinely enthusiastic about was the gallery). He presented her at the country club whenever Regina threatened that if Gloria didn't find a date, she would find one for her. He did her grunt work, whatever it was (not that Gloria did any real work that Laurence could discern), and he cleaned up the messes in her life, both literally and figuratively.

Dirk's loyalty was not cheap, though. Laurence knew the young man received a rather generous salary for working as Gloria's lackey. Laurence was certainly in favor of employees receiving fair wages, but he wasn't entirely clear on how much genuine work Dirk actually performed; and whatever it was, he was certain that it wasn't worth what Gloria paid him. His obvious lust for the Lithgow money could be twofold, Laurence had considered more than once. Who wouldn't want to come into a lot of money without having to do much for it? But perhaps Dirk's greed was also fueled by necessity. It wouldn't surprise Laurence one bit if he learned that Dirk was in debt up to his calculating green eyes and saw Gloria as not only an easy ticket to the world of the upper crust, but as a way to avoid bankruptcy. The question was, how far would Dirk go?

Clearly, Gloria had managed to hold him off for a couple of years already. She seemed no more attached to Dirk Godfrey now than she had been the day she first introduced him to her parents as her personal assistant. She was no kinder to him than she was to the Lithgow family maid or gardener. But Dirk's behavior had definitely changed, Laurence observed. The young man seemed increasingly desperate. The more Laurence considered it, the more he was convinced that Dirk was in some kind of trouble, financial or otherwise. The walls were closing in, and Dirk was realizing that he had to do something and do it fast. Laurence decided he would have to do something, as well. He had to protect his assets, both his daughter and his money. In the weeks before Regina's party for Carrington, Laurence hired a private detective to unearth as much as possible about Dirk Godfrey.

Chapter Thirty-two

They had lunch at the same restaurant where they ate the first afternoon they met. It was a gorgeous day, extremely hot, but beautiful nonetheless. A. C. gave it to Carrington plainly. Regina insisted on having a dinner for Carrington. It would be a dressy event, but it wasn't a huge deal. There wouldn't be a lot of people there, A. C. reassured her, just the family and one or two of Regina's closest friends. At that, she had to suppress an eye roll. *Regina's friends*, she scoffed inwardly. *Nothing but a pack of pretentious, face-lifted gossips who do nothing but complain.*

Carrington listened quietly, her face solemn and contemplative. She had grown less anxious over the past several weeks, but A. C. could see the panic in her eyes. Though Carrington had never said so to her grandmother, A. C. knew that the girl was ashamed of growing up poor. So many times she'd longed to comfort Carrington and reassure her that there was absolutely no shame in not having much in the way of possessions. Having money didn't make anyone smarter or nicer. It couldn't guarantee good health and a long life. *If that was true,* she thought sadly, *my Cal and Arnold would still be here.* But for now, she held her tongue on this subject. They would talk about it when Carrington chose to openly express her feelings on the issues of privilege and poverty. A. C. feared it would be too uncomfortable and too painful for Carrington to talk about it she was ready.

Of course, she had to do something to prepare Carrington for being in Regina's house, and certainly, for simply being in Regina's presence. If every corner of Regina's house screamed that its occupants had gobs of cash, Regina's appearance, even while she slept, did it tenfold. She once proudly told A. C. that she spent a few thousand dollars buying new pajamas. She went into vivid detail explaining how she divided them by the seasons. It was one of the most boring conversations A. C. could remember having with her sister, but then, the majority of her conversations with Regina were dull and one-sided. They consisted mostly of Regina demonstrating how wealthy she was, either by simply declaring it (as with her nightgown story) or showing it, flaunting a brand-new pair of Jimmy Choos while last week's pair were already collecting dust in her custom shoe closet.

For all of Regina's criticism that A. C.'s long hair was unbecoming of a woman in her sixties, Regina behaved like a spoiled child where her money was concerned. It was sickening, A. C. often thought. She suspected that Laurence found Regina's behavior obnoxious, too. If he didn't have something to occupy him, like a newspaper, a faraway expression came over his face whenever Regina opened her mouth. A. C. couldn't imagine staying in a miserable marriage for so long. Still, she envied that Regina was able to go to sleep every night next to her husband. A. C. would give every cent she had to spend one more night with Calvin. She doubted her sister shared such sentiments about her own husband.

Carrington chewed her food slowly, her brow furrowed in thought.

"So, I'll need a dress," she said at last. "For the dinner party."

"That right, dear," A. C. said cheerfully. "Let's make this fun. After lunch we can walk around the mall, and you can try a few things on. I'll even try something on; it's been ages since I went clothes shopping. I didn't have anyone to go with until now." She beamed at her granddaughter and was relieved when the girl seemed to relax a little.

"The place settings and silverware … I'm worried that I won't know which ones to use." Carrington was embarrassed to admit.

"Oh, it's not difficult," A. C. reassured her. "I'll show you when we get home. You'll pick it up like *that*." She snapped her fingers and smiled again. "You're going to be fine, kiddo. This party is just Regina's way of welcoming you to the family. I admit my sister isn't always easy to get along with," again she had to force herself not to make a face, "but she means well, and she really wants to meet you. And I think you're really going to like Uncle Laurence. He's quiet, but he's very, very kind, and he reads all the time, just like you. It'll be a nice evening; you'll see."

She could tell Carrington was still nervous about the whole thing. A. C. was worried, too, but she wouldn't dream of burdening Carrington with her own fears about Regina's plans. It would only feed Carrington's anxiety.

After eating, they walked leisurely through the mall, which was crowded with lunchtime shoppers and kids on summer vacation. A. C. asked Carrington what her dream dress would look like, but that proved to be a bad idea. Carrington stammered that she'd never owned any kind of dressy clothes before. The dresses she had when she lived with Joan were just old jean skirts that used to belong to other people. A. C. could have kicked herself. How could she be so insensitive? Of course Carrington had never owned a party dress. They were both quiet and tense for several minutes. To break the ice, A. C. suggested they test perfume in one of the larger department stores. Carrington seemed relieved by the idea.

They had a wonderful time. Carrington was drawn more to the floral-based fragrances while A. C. preferred the perfumes that smelled of spice and citrus. Of course, they agreed that the green tea fragrance was the best of the lot. A. C. was trying to convince her granddaughter that it was really no trouble if Carrington wanted a green tea bath and eau de toilette set, when Carrington gasped. A. C. followed her granddaughter's stunned gaze over to the shoe department. Carrington stared open-mouthed at a group of four kids; two boys and two girls stood laughing around a display of high-heeled sandals. One of the boys pretended to try one on, and the group became so loud that the saleswoman glared at them and asked them in an icy tone if they needed any assistance. The kids quieted down after that and shuffled over to the spinning racks of costume jewelry directly across from the perfume section. The cashier in that section eyed them suspiciously but said nothing. He went through the motions of sorting gift boxes and untangling necklaces, but he was watching the kids the entire time.

The boys appeared to be around Carrington's age, the girls a bit younger. A. C. thought there was something vaguely familiar about one of the girls, a tall, extremely thin brunette with a tan complexion and a low-cut tank top. The girl wore a slash of red lipstick that didn't complement her skin color at all. It made her lips look like a clown's mouth. Her dark eyes were ringed with heavy black eyeliner. She obviously wanted to appear tough and older than she was, but she mostly just looked self-conscious. Then it came to A. C. She'd seen the picture that Carrington had in her wallet, and though it was an outdated photo, there was no mistaking the sinewy, brash girl.

"Isn't that your sister?" she asked in a hushed tone, praying she didn't sound accusatory.

Carrington nodded mutely. She seemed unable to speak for several seconds. A. C. was about to suggest that they look around another store or even another mall.

"She looks horrible," Carrington whispered.

A. C. looked again at Melissa. She wanted to argue with her granddaughter, but she knew it would be a lie. The child did look awful. Almost like a child actress playing a teen prostitute in a made-for-TV movie. Melissa and her three companions began to make their way in the opposite direction, toward the sporting goods department.

"Do you want to say hello to her?" A. C. asked.

"I don't know," Carrington answered. "I mean, kind of, yes. I guess I miss her, even though I know she probably hates me. But I'm … I'm afraid, Gran." Her voice quivered, and A. C. longed to hold the child. She restrained herself, though.

They watched the group of kids saunter away, laughing loudly and receiving more than a few dirty looks both from customers and employees.

"She'd probably be flattered if you made the effort, dear," A. C. tried to sound hopeful. "But being afraid is perfectly okay and natural. I would be afraid, too. Families are so complicated, aren't they? In theory, we should be closer to our blood relatives than to anyone else, but sometimes that just doesn't happen, for whatever reason."

She thought of Regina and her eyes filled with tears. She was annoyed with herself for her reaction, even though she'd just finished telling her granddaughter that there was nothing wrong with being upset. She disguised a sniffle by clearing her throat.

"Do you want me to go with you?" she asked.

"Oh, no," Carrington answered quickly.

She immediately felt guilty. *Gran's going to think I'm ashamed of her,* she thought. Nothing could be further from the truth. She hated to admit, even to herself, that she was ashamed of Melissa, ashamed of what Melissa represented. Carrington's own past was still so fresh, so raw, like a deep wound that had only just begun to heal. There was no way Melissa would respond kindly to her. She'd been clear enough on the phone. Carrington could imagine how much nastier her younger sister would be in person. But then, Carrington would have the element of surprise on her side. Missy certainly wasn't expecting to bump into her older sister at the mall or anywhere else. But being with her friends was a mark against Carrington. Their presence would only fuel Melissa's tough façade.

"I don't think she's going to be very happy to see me," Carrington admitted to her grandmother after a few seconds. *That's putting it mildly,* she thought sadly. "I doubt she'll be very nice to me, let alone … well …" Carrington trailed off awkwardly.

A. C. held her granddaughter's gaze for a moment longer. She understood better than Carrington might have imagined. She managed a reassuring smile.

"I'm going to wander up to the third floor; I think that's where they keep the dressy stuff for old ladies," she said with a chuckle. "You go ahead and take your time, dear. Look around here some more or say hello to your sister—whatever you'd like to do. Why don't you meet me upstairs in a little while? But don't feel rushed. Take all the time you need, okay?"

Carrington felt an overwhelming rush of affection for her grandmother. She longed to hug her, but she was too keyed up after seeing Melissa. Instead, she returned the smile and nodded. She watched A. C. get on the escalator and waited until her grandmother was out of sight to decide what to do. She could no longer see or hear her sister from where she stood at the perfume counter. *Missy might already be gone,* she thought, feeling guilty for the twinge of hope she felt.

She thought of her grandmother browsing around for what A. C. called "*Golden Girls* dresses." Carrington couldn't suppress a smile. Couldn't her grandmother see herself the way she saw her? *She shouldn't be shopping in the mature collection,* Carrington thought. A. C. was a youthful woman. She could easily pass for fifteen years younger than she really was. The one give away about her true age, though, was the sorrow she carried around in her eyes. They were a lovely, rich shade of hazel, but the pain that A. C. had endured in her life was evident in them, even when she smiled. *Pain,* Carrington observed, *ages a person.* Briefly, Carrington wondered what it was like to lose both a spouse and a child. It was a difficult thing to ponder. After witnessing years' worth of her mother's drunken, volatile relationships with men, it was hard to imagine a happy relationship. She realized with a bit of a start what an incredibly strong woman her grandmother was. *I'm ready to cry like a baby and hide just because Missy walked by,* she chided herself. *I'm going to face her.* Her nerves steeled as much as they could be, she strode through the cosmetic and shoe departments to see if she could find Melissa.

Chapter Thirty-three

Missy sat on the couch and leaned back, eyes closed. She pictured her sister and cringed. *Maybe I should have talked to her, just for a little while,* she thought. Seeing Carrington at the mall had taken her by surprise, to say the least. Missy was there with Tanya, Tanya's brother Alex, and Alex's friend, Efren.

Both Alex and Efren would start high school after summer break. Missy and Tanya were going into middle school, the sixth grade. She'd been thrilled when Alex and Efren had agreed to go with her and Tanya to the mall. She silently congratulated herself for wearing lots of makeup and putting extra tissue in her bra. She knew Alex liked her; she just needed to make sure she had his attention. Efren wasn't cute like Alex was. He was kind of fat and short, and he had bad acne, but he was funny. He kept them laughing on the bus ride to the mall, making fun of the old people who rode the bus and mimicking the sound of passing gas whenever someone sat down. The bus driver and several of the other passengers gave them dirty looks, but they just kept talking and laughing. Missy loved the secure feeling she had when she was with a group of friends. Nothing could touch her; no one could get to her.

She learned that afternoon, though, that it wasn't true. Her friends hadn't been able to keep her stomach from feeling like it was going to climb up her throat and out of her mouth when Carrington called her name. Missy had recognized her sister's voice immediately. For a moment, right before she whirled around to face Carrington, she had to clench her teeth and think of something boring to keep from crying. She missed Carrington, she realized with a shock. She actually missed her. Not that she would ever admit it out loud to anyone, least of all Carrington. Instead, she'd looked at her older sister coolly, with as much nonchalance as she could muster.

It must have worked. Carrington opened her mouth to speak, but nothing except for a timid "Hi" came out.

Carrington blushed bright red, and Missy felt her own cheeks burning. Tanya, Alex, and Efren watched them curiously, standing a few steps away and whispering.

Missy just nodded at her sister, and muttered, "Hey."

There had been a long, awkward pause then, Carrington and Missy eyeing each other shyly and Missy's friends exchanging furtive glances.

It was Tanya who finally broke the silence. "The bus is coming, Missy," she reminded her friend.

"Oh, yeah," Missy said, relieved to look away from Carrington's eyes. "I gotta go," she said to her sister. "Bye."

With that, she turned and teetered away unsteadily on the cheap pair of high heels that belonged to her mother. Again, Missy had to fill her mind with images and thoughts that were either bland or mildly pleasant. *Don't cry; do* not *cry,* she commanded herself, angry at her rebelling emotions. She half expected Carrington to follow her or at least call out to her, but she didn't. Missy forced herself not to look back to see if her older sister watched her walk away. She couldn't decide if she was more relieved or more disappointed that Carrington didn't try to stop her.

She was quiet on the bus ride home, in spite of Efren's best efforts at making her laugh. Thankfully, no one mentioned her sister. Tanya knew that Carrington had moved out of Joan's house, and Missy assumed that Tanya had told her family. None of the Guzmans had questioned her about it, and she was grateful for this. It was tough to explain, and she didn't entirely understand it herself.

It was strange to think that Carrington suddenly had a brand-new family, and they apparently had a lot of money. It angered Missy. Who did Carrington think she was, pretending that she belonged with a bunch of rich snobs? Who did she think she was fooling? And most infuriating of all, why was Carrington the one who got to leave? She was such a teacher's pet, too. Missy hated that about her older sister. She hated that Carrington had never received less than a B in school. She loathed that her teachers never failed to comment on what an intelligent, well-mannered older sister she had. They always said it as if they were shocked that Missy could possibly be related to anyone so smart. She knew they were disappointed that she wasn't a clone of Carrington.

It was true: she had a hard time keeping up in class, but it was mostly because she didn't care to pay attention. Sometimes Missy actually followed along with what the teachers said and the information made sense to her. But she only did that if she was really bored. She could usually manage to get the attention of one of her classmates, preferably a boy. Missy noticed that she had less girls as friends the older she became—but she'd been close with Tanya forever, ever since early elementary school. They had been two of the most popular girls, and for whatever reason, they clicked rather than rivaled. It didn't hurt that Missy found both of Tanya's older brothers exceptionally cute.

Missy had been what Carrington called "boy crazy" for as long as she could remember. Carrington was such a nerd! She acted like an old woman more than a teenager. Missy couldn't wait to be a teenager. Her thirteenth birthday was only two months away. She couldn't believe that Carrington had already wasted her first teen year, and now most of her second year, studying and being alone most of the time, though Missy couldn't imagine why anyone would want to hang out with her sister. Carrington was a bore. She would rather read than watch a movie. She never wanted to go to the mall. One time, out of a combination of boredom and curiosity, Missy followed her older sister on a Saturday afternoon. She hoped her sister was sneaking off to meet a boy (mostly because then Missy would have something to hold over her head) or at least hang out at the mall. But no; dumb old Carrington just went to the library, of all places. The library on a Saturday afternoon! Could anything be lamer? Missy didn't think so. Later, she wanted to make fun of her sister, but that would have meant admitting that she'd followed her. She didn't want Carrington thinking she gave a damn.

No, she decided. *I won't ever forgive her for leaving me here.* She wiped her eyes with the back of one hand and grabbed her backpack with the other. She was spending another night at Tanya's house and had only come home for a change of clothes.

Chapter Thirty-four

The muscular, dark-haired man shrugged out of his green smock with a weary sigh. Another shift at the nursing home was finally over. He balled up the smock and shoved it into his backpack. In another zipped compartment of his backpack, he kept his cell phone. He paused before he turned the phone on, long enough for a brief, silent prayer. He stared at the phone's screen for several seconds after turning it on. No messages, no new calls. He sighed again.

"Good night, Gary," said Kristen, one of the night shift nurses' aides. She had just arrived and was stowing her lunch in the employee refrigerator. If Gary hadn't been so focused on his phone, he might have noticed the admiring glance she gave him.

He barely made eye contact with her.

"Hey, Kristen. How are you? Oh, Mr. Dickerson is asking for his grandmother again."

Kristen trained her gaze on Gary, but he was preoccupied with changing out of his thick-soled work shoes into a pair of sneakers.

"Oh, yeah?" she asked. "Poor guy. I'll see if I can get a few extra minutes with him. A story usually calms him down."

Mr. Dickerson was one of the many patients at Angels of Rest nursing home where both Gary and Kristen worked as nurses' aides. Mr. Dickerson suffered severe dementia and often thought Kristen, a woman young enough to be his granddaughter, was his grandmother. He would cry and carry on, demanding a bedtime story, sometimes even when it was the middle of the day. Kristen was one of the few nurses' aides who could calm him down.

Gary slid on his backpack and finally turned to Kristen to wave good-bye. *She looks different,* he thought, trying to figure out exactly what it was. It had only been two days since he last saw her, so he knew it couldn't be that she lost or gained weight. *More makeup? Less? No. Her hair!* There were golden streaks in her chestnut brown hair. He tried to decide if he liked it or not. She looked at him expectantly, a small smile turning up the corners of her mouth.

"Kristen, your hair looks great!" Gary said at last.

She beamed at him. "Thank you," she responded in a shy voice.

Yes, he decided. *Her face looks more open now. And her eyes … the blond streaks bring out her eyes more.* Kristen had very pretty blue eyes. Gary had always thought so but figured it would seem too forward to say so.

"You just have it done?" he asked, immediately regretting his question.

He'd seen her just two days previous. *Of course she just had it done, you idiot,* he chided himself. He felt a blush spread to his cheeks.

Kristen didn't seem to mind.

"Yeah," she said proudly. "Do you really like it? I kind of let the hair dresser talk me into it. She's such a saleswoman! I'm not sure if I like it yet." She raked her hand self-consciously through her long bangs.

Gary gave her a reassuring nod. "It looks really, really good."

They smiled at one another in awkward silence for a few seconds.

"Well, uh … I guess I better check on Mr. Dickerson," said Kristen.

"Yeah, I should get home. I've got stuff to do … laundry, grocery shopping, yadda-yadda," said Gary with a chuckle.

"The swinging life of a bachelor, huh?" Kristen teased him.

He laughed. "Yup, it's just one big party after another for me."

"Um, listen, Gary, if you're not busy tomorrow night, I have the night off, and I was wondering if you'd like to maybe meet downtown for dinner and drinks?"

The smile faded from Gary's tan face. His lips twitched.

"Well, Kristen, I would like to, it's just, I, um …"

Kristen blushed and looked at the floor for a few seconds.

"Oh, no big deal," she said when she finally met Gary's eyes again. "I know it's short notice; I just thought I'd throw it out there. I know you're in a hurry to get home, and I've got tons to do around here, so I'll get out of your way now."

She ducked her head and made a beeline for the door.

"Wait!" Gary said. "I'd love to hang out with you tomorrow night, Kristen. It's just that … well, I don't drink. It seems like every time I tell someone that, they back off like I've just said I have rabies or something," he said with a nervous laugh.

She grinned at him. "So, no drinks, then. No problem! I'm not a big drinker myself. I just figure it's something to do."

"Oh, there's plenty to do without drinking," he said, returning her smile. He felt his face fill with heat and color once again. "I didn't mean, y'know … oh, geez. This just gets harder and harder the older you get, doesn't it?"

They grinned at one another.

"How about dinner tomorrow and then maybe a movie, or we could get some ice cream?" Kristen suggested.

"Sounds great," he agreed. "Pick you up at six?"

She nodded, still smiling. "I'll call you tomorrow to give you directions to my apartment."

Another aide came into lounge then for her dinner break, so Gary and Kristen said a quick good-bye, each of them with a secretive smile on their lips.

Gary Ruiz shielded his dark brown eyes with sporty sunglasses and walked across the parking lot. He thought of Kristen and found himself smiling. *Well, that was unexpected,* he thought as he climbed into his truck. He tossed his backpack in the passenger seat and started the commute home. He tapped his fingers impatiently at a red light and changed the radio station twice. *Maybe I shouldn't have agreed to go out tomorrow,* he told himself. *If Kristen only knew about my past, she wouldn't want anything to do with me. She'd be better off if she just told me to go to hell.* He caught a glimpse of his unhappy expression in the rearview mirror. He let his foot off the break and merged into traffic.

"Damn it," Gary muttered. He hated when he started having doubts and putting himself down. More and more lately, he'd been able to catch himself doing it and stop the so-called "stinking thinking" before it got really bad, but it was still a struggle. He thought back to how stupid he thought the whole thing was at first—recovery—especially the jargon he heard at AA meetings, phrases like "stinking thinking" and "let go and let God." Recovery had scared the hell out of him in the beginning, and he masked his fear with sarcastic comments and put-downs.

The people at the AA meetings he attended never judged him or turned him away. They seemed to understand how Gary felt. Initially, this made Gary even more suspicious of them. "This is nothing but a weird cult," Gary had yelled at the group more than once in the beginning. "You're all full of crap! You give me nothing but the same stupid little cutesy phrases that don't make any sense. What do any of you know about what I'm going through?" But they did know. One by one, Gary listened to their stories and was astonished to learn how much he had in common with a group of strangers.

For the first time in his adult life, he had a group of friends who spent time together without ever drinking a single drop of alcohol. There was a time for Gary when this was unthinkable. What was the point of getting together with his buddies if they weren't going to get drunk and raise hell? That's the way he'd lived for so long. It was the way his parents had lived. The lifestyle was ingrained in him from childhood. There was never a Ruiz family gathering that didn't involve copious amounts of booze, which everyone from his grandparents to his teenage cousins gulped down.

It had been strange at first, getting together with people socially and not drinking. They all seemed a little stiff and uncomfortable in the beginning, but eventually they were able to relax and even laugh at themselves. Sometimes the laughter masked pain or the shame they all still felt for the way they had once lived, but they were happier now. They had lost so much because of their drinking. That was something Gary and his friends all had in common. He went bowling with his friends once a week. An outsider might think they were an odd mix of men. They came from all walks of life. Among them was a retired cab driver, a former minister, a computer programmer, a construction worker, and of course, Gary, a certified nurses' aide. Their ages and races were as diverse as their careers. There were plenty more people in the AA meetings he attended, but his bowling buddies were his closest friends.

Dating was an entirely different story, one that seemed nearly forgotten and dusty from disuse. Even when Gary noticed a good-looking woman, he wouldn't dream of approaching her. *What have I got to offer anyone? Why would any woman in her right mind want to go out with me?* he often thought, despite the frequent reminders he had from AA not to knock himself down like this. Gary liked and appreciated himself so much more sober than when he was drinking, but he still didn't think he'd make a very good boyfriend, let alone husband. He tried not to think about women very much, although it was difficult.

A couple of times, Gary had dated women he met through AA, but he soon decided this wasn't a good idea. One of two things happened: either they spent their time together basically having a mini meeting and discussing only their struggles with alcohol and how they were each striving to stay sober or, as in two cases, the woman relapsed and nearly took Gary down with her. It had been a while since he'd dated anyone at all, and now he wasn't sure that it was a good idea to jump back into things by going out with someone at work. But he didn't want to let Kristen down. He liked her, and she was attractive and sweet. *And yes,* he realized, *I'm lonely.*

There was also the fantasy he sometimes entertained that he would meet and marry a caring, wholesome woman, and eventually Melissa would come to live with them, and his life would be complete. His wife would be a perfect mother to Melissa, and after a while, Melissa would grow to love them both. Gary felt foolish when he had these thoughts; he knew how naïve he was being, but he couldn't help it. More than anything, he wanted to know his daughter, and his biggest regret in life was that he'd already missed so much of her life. *But that's going to change,* he told himself. *I'm going to be a real father to her. If only she'll let me.*

Chapter Thirty-five

For the fourth time in an hour, Laurence read the contents of the file folder on his desk, his jaw clenched. It was the report from his private investigator on Gloria's dubious assistant, Dirk Godfrey. To say that the young man was a liar would be a mild assessment. His mother wasn't ill or wealthy, he was no stranger to the inside of a jail cell, and his name wasn't even Dirk. It was Darren, Darren Cecil Godfrey. Laurence could see why Dirk had not simply gone by his middle name like so many people chose to do. The fact that he chose not to go by his birth name was of little consequence. Laurence knew many people who had changed or shortened their names. But for Darren Godfrey, he suspected the name change was mostly an attempt to conceal his past. It was clear to Laurence that he had been correct about his daughter's friend all along, but he derived no pleasure in being proven right.

Telling Gloria would be a nightmare. She wouldn't believe her father; she might even accuse him of fabricating the investigator's findings. The girl simply couldn't stand to not get her way. Laurence realized that, despite being nearly thirty years old, his daughter would probably always be a girl emotionally, just like her mother. The best route would be to confront Dirk. He might even try to make a deal with him, if the threat of being exposed failed. After all, it was obvious that money was what Mr. Godfrey sought.

Darren Cecil Godfrey's first arrest had been in his mid teens, for breaking and entering. He served only a few days in a juvenile detention center and fulfilled the rest of his sentence doing community service. He did not graduate high school, but instead dropped out during his junior year and tested for his GED. He worked on and off at various fast food restaurants for about a year and was arrested once again, this time for underage drinking. He served over a week in county jail and afterwards attended two months of a state-run substance abuse program. Dirk managed to stay out of trouble for a while and even enrolled in college. His mother, Carole, borrowed from her retirement account to help finance his education. Dirk also managed to acquire an occasional grant for underprivileged students. What his mother and grants couldn't cover, he paid for in student loans. He squeaked by in college and barely graduated. He was making minimum payments on his student loans. His mother lived modestly several miles away, and he rarely saw her. Dirk had managed to stay out of legal trouble, but it seemed that every other aspect of his life was a mess.

Besides Gloria, Dirk was involved with at least two other women. Laurence didn't know where he found the time. He knew Gloria kept him on a short leash, but somehow, Dirk made time to play the field. Of course, Laurence had never heard Gloria refer to Godfrey as anything more than her assistant or her friend, so he realized that exposing this part of Godfrey's life wouldn't be the most damning, although Gloria had never been one to enjoy sharing her toys. Finding out she wasn't the center of Godfrey's universe would be a blow to her ego, if nothing else.

The finding that troubled Laurence the most was Darren Godfrey's friendship with Jessie Krueger. Jessie Krueger was a known and convicted drug dealer, having served a handful of one- and two-year sentences throughout his nearly forty years of life. The investigator's report contained no solid evidence that Darren Godfrey was buying drugs from Jessie Krueger, but Laurence could not imagine a reason for their friendship otherwise. Darren Godfrey was a social-climbing fraud whose biggest goal in life was to appear in the newspaper's Society column; there was no way he would risk the façade he'd spent years crafting unless there was something in it for him. He was either buying or dealing drugs, and considering he never had more than a few hundred dollars saved up, Laurence figured he probably wasn't selling. He sat upright in his chair, a cold sweat making him loosen his collar. *Unless he is using the gallery as a front.*

For years, Laurence had wondered how Lucinda's Lair managed to turn a profit. The art Gloria bought and sold was atrocious at best. Laurence had attended some of the showings she regularly held, and they seemed to be little more than expensively catered parties where Gloria's pretentious friends gossiped viciously about one another while simultaneously sucking up to Gloria. Laurence had the impression that they toned their behavior down a little when he was around, so he could only imagine what the parties were like when he was not in attendance.

He took a drink from his glass of Scotch and stared hard at the photos of Jessie Krueger. The private investigator had included one of Jessie's many mug shots and a recent picture of Jessie and Dirk having coffee together. Did Jessie look familiar? Yes, yes he did. Laurence closed his eyes and concentrated. Where had he seen this vile man before? Was he simply imaging this because he was so upset? Jessie Krueger had a very bland look about him; perhaps this was carefully cultivated. He was a career criminal; of course he wouldn't want to attract attention. He had short-cropped, dark hair; a thin beard that failed to conceal his weak chin; and small, close-set eyes. His build and height were average. The only thing outstanding about Jessie's appearance was the tattoo on his right forearm reading "Leeann" in vine-like letters. It was an ugly thing, crooked, faded, and crudely crafted, probably in a prison cell.

Laurence opened his eyes and gasped. He remembered. He'd seen Jessie at one of Gloria's shows just a few months ago. He noticed Jessie's tattoo when Jessie rolled up his sleeves and took it upon himself to haul another case of champagne out of the caterer's van. Jessie was clearly drunk, but so was everyone else. No one except the waitstaff and Laurence really noticed him. Gloria didn't seem to care that Jessie was helping himself to a bottle of champagne, but then, why should she? She hadn't paid for any of it. Laurence managed to track down Gloria's dutiful assistant, who was busy flirting with a giddy trio of women, one of whom was the featured artist that evening. Laurence pulled him aside and pointed out Jessie, simply saying, "He needs to leave. Now." Dirk had seemed thrilled at the prospect of doing something for Laurence. *Of course,* Laurence thought now, *brownie points with the old man.* He kept his eye on Godfrey only long enough to ensure that he actually approached the overly enthusiastic champagne drinker and had a few words with him. At that point, Laurence helped himself to the open bar and took a bathroom break, and when he returned, the man with the tattoo was gone and Dirk gave him a rather dramatic nod from across the room.

"What a fool I've been," Laurence said aloud in his study. "What a damn fool."

Chapter Thirty-six

Dirk couldn't remember a time when Gloria had been more annoying. After the night at her condo when he told her that she should produce an heir for the Lithgow family, he was sure he faced an uphill battle. She would sober up and the next day she would be her usual bitchy, self-absorbed self. This much was true, but to his surprise and initially his delight, her focus had been altered. She no longer envisioned herself as Gloria Lithgow, art connoisseur and woman in charge. She was still in charge, no doubt about that, but she now saw herself as a soon-to-be bride and much adored center of her parents' world once she produced a grandchild for them. She never used the words "wife" or "mother." She only talked at length about how her parents would worship her when she, for once in any of their lives, did something they would appreciate.

"Mother will finally get off my ass about being married, and Daddy will be so pleased that I'm continuing the Lithgow name," Gloria said more than once to Dirk.

When she wasn't fantasizing aloud about the attention and affection her parents would soon shower upon her, Gloria was planning her wedding. She never called it *our* wedding; it was always *my* wedding. Dirk had yet to ask her to marry him, but he supposed a formal proposal mattered little. He didn't love her, and she didn't love him. They never said as much to one another. They weren't crass enough to admit to each other that the marriage was one of convenience and status, but neither would they pretend that it was about romance.

During the few moments each day when Dirk was honest with himself, he realized that Gloria's father had never indicated that he gave a damn about having a grandchild. Why Gloria latched onto the idea that she would become something of a heroine in her father's eyes if she reproduced was beyond Dirk; but he didn't allow himself to question it too much. After all, his plan was coming together. Whether or not Laurence Lithgow wanted to be a grandfather was moot. The important thing was that if and when Gloria had Dirk's child, he would forever be linked to the Lithgow family. Marrying Gloria first would be extremely helpful in this endeavor, he knew. Regina Lithgow was stodgy enough that an illegitimate grandchild would make her even colder to Dirk than she was now.

He knew that she didn't consider him good enough for Gloria. He expected the announcement of their engagement to be met with a lukewarm response, at best. But Regina would not forbid it. Oh, no; she quite wanted her daughter and only child, nearly a spinster now at twenty-nine with no husband in sight, tucked safe within the bonds of matrimony—safe from gossip. Dirk was well aware that Regina's circle of friends was a band of spiteful old vultures. Regina wanted desperately to keep her life as far away from the rumor mill as possible. It wasn't the scrutiny she minded. She just wanted to be known, but only for her triumphs: her top-earning husband, her jewels, her custom-made gowns, her professionally decorated home, her parties catered by gourmet chefs, and any other way she could dream up to display her wealth and alleged good taste. Gloria had made Regina's goal of being la crème de la crème nearly impossible her entire life. But if Gloria was married in a suitably lavish ceremony, and if she had a child soon after becoming married, Regina would not only feel immune to being verbally dissected by her friends, she would, in fact, feel superior. Dirk knew that some of her friends were just as desperate as Regina was for their offspring to marry and produce little heirs and heiresses.

Dirk was not especially surprised when he received a phone call from Laurence's secretary informing him that Mr. Lithgow wanted a private meeting. He was not afraid, but he was a bit wary. Obviously, Gloria must have told her father that she wanted to marry Dirk, and the old man probably wanted to get Dirk alone to deliver his own meek version of the "if you hurt my daughter, I'll hurt you" speech. More likely, he wanted to dance around the subject of a prenuptial agreement. Dirk wouldn't put it past Laurence Lithgow to have the paperwork ready to sign. He continuously reminded himself that although socially Laurence was wimp, when it came to business, he was as sharp and able as they came.

If Laurence was more outgoing, more likable, Dirk might have looked up to him. As it was, Dirk was mostly disgusted by Laurence. He saw Laurence's life as something of a waste. The man had more money than he knew what to do with, yet he hardly traveled and spent most of his down time on the putting green. It was a damn shame. And why he remained married to Gloria's shrew of a mother was yet another annoying mystery.

Dirk shrugged off thoughts about the adage that to know what one's wife would look and be like in middle age, one only had to look at his mother-in-law.

Gloria would soften with age, he hoped, especially if she had a child. At any rate, the child would divert her enough that he wouldn't be expected to keep her entertained constantly. Sometimes Dirk swore Gloria was the dullest person he'd ever met. It wasn't that she was stupid exactly, but left to her own devices, she just couldn't figure out what to do with herself. She also couldn't go more than a few minutes without blathering on and on about something Dirk found inane. It was like she thought of the world as her personal stage. She required near constant attention.

Dirk decided to dress up for his meeting with Laurence. At the gallery, he usually wore a button-up shirt and dress slacks, but for meeting Laurence, he donned a full suit, and his best one at that. He took extra time making sure the knot in his Armani tie was perfectly even, and he spent nearly an hour styling his hair. Before he left his condo, he practiced the most charming yet casual smile he could muster. He wanted to seem pleased to see Laurence, but he knew the old man would immediately be on guard if he thought Dirk was schmoozing.

"It's all yours, kid," Dirk said with a grin to his reflection.

Though still a bit nervous, he was in a good mood as he drove to Laurence's office. He whistled along with the radio and checked his hair at every stoplight. He couldn't remember when he'd looked so handsome. Of course, the same thought occurred to him more than a couple of times per week.

Dirk made sure he arrived early at Laurence's office. No doubt the old man considered everything about this meeting a test for Dirk, including his punctuality. Dirk caught a glimpse of himself in one of the polished walls in the lobby. He paused long enough to straighten his already straight tie and admire himself. His stomach finally began to settle. *This is going to be a piece of cake,* he thought, a confident smile spreading across his face.

He greeted Laurence's secretary, Erin, cordially, and she asked him to take a seat. She was a portly, attractive woman in her late thirties, sporting a trendy blond bob and black wire-rimmed eyeglasses. She seemed unimpressed by him, but Dirk paid her no mind. She was a nobody. Soon enough, he would be able to issue orders to someone just like this petty woman. He smiled smugly and flipped through an investment magazine.

"Mr. Lithgow will see you now," Erin announced after a few minutes. She looked directly into his eyes without smiling or making any expression at all.

Dirk was annoyed. Who did this woman think she was? She probably made Laurence's coffee each morning and called in his lunch reservations. Dirk could have her doing the same things for him in a few months. He pursed his lips and glowered at her.

"Mr. Godfrey, I said Mr. Lithgow will see you know," she said, somewhat louder and with a note of disdain in her voice.

Dirk took his time setting the magazine down, standing up, and smoothing down his jacket and pants. He met her indifferent eyes with a cool smile.

"Thanks. And I'd like a cup of coffee, Irma," he said, knowing full well her name was Erin.

She didn't blanch at his obviously deliberate mistake.

"There's a Starbucks across the street, Mr. Godfrey. I'm sure they'll still be open when Mr. Lithgow is finished with you."

Dirk gritted his teeth and glared at her for another moment but couldn't think of anything to say to her. He made a mental note to notify Laurence that his help was insubordinate and downright rude. The nerve this foolish woman had! He all but stomped down the hallway to Laurence's office.

Laurence sat at his large desk and was flipping slowly through a thick file when Dirk entered the room. Dirk had seen Laurence's office a couple of times before, only when Gloria wanted his company when she went to wheedle something out of her father. Each time he saw it, Dirk was impressed by the sheer enormity of the room. This visit was no different. He marveled at the high-backed leather chair Laurence sat in comfortably, *Like a king*, Dirk thought. Slightly less grand chairs flanked the opposite side of the Danish teak desk. A leather sofa and glass coffee table sat unused on the other side of the room. The walls were adorned with expensively framed prints of famous impressionist paintings—nothing that Gloria had any interest in, of course. One of the four built-in bookshelves housed a collection of golf trophies and family photos. The outward-facing wall of Laurence's office was all tinted glass. His view from the eighteenth floor was spectacular.

Dirk imagined sitting behind Laurence's desk, feet propped up, hands behind his head, watching the sun set over the rest of the city. But as usual, pathetic Laurence Lithgow seemed oblivious to his stunning surroundings. In fact, he appeared to be oblivious to Dirk's arrival. He continued leafing through the contents of the folder while Dirk stood with increasing agitation just inside the doorway.

Dirk cleared his throat.

"Good afternoon, Mr. Lithgow," he said, trying his best to sound pleasant.

Laurence looked up from the file and met Dirk's gaze. He did not smile. There was a strange expression on his face, a knowing look mixed with … with what? Dirk could not quite decipher Laurence's face. Whatever it was, though, it was clear that Laurence was not overjoyed to see him.

"Mr. Lithgow, I was so glad when your secretary called me for a meeting with you. I've really been wanting to talk to you about—"

"Sit down, Darren," Laurence interrupted sharply.

Oh, fuck, thought Dirk, the color draining from his face as he lowered himself into one of the chairs across from Laurence. He glanced again at the folder that Laurence had been so engrossed in only seconds earlier and recognized some of the papers. Arrest records, photographs, school transcripts, all his. A cold sheen of sweat appeared on his face.

Laurence followed Dirk's eyes to the papers on his desk.

"These look familiar, do they?" he asked coolly.

"I'm … I'm sure there's been some kind of misunderstanding," Dirk stammered. "I can explain about my name. I've just never much cared for Darren, and Dirk is a nickname I gave myself. It's no big deal, really, Mr. Lithgow. And as for … as for …"

"As for your history of criminal activity and somewhat extensive relations with ex convicts?" Laurence supplied.

Dirk attempted the smile that usually smoothed things over and charmed even the most uptight people. Laurence was completely unmoved. He did not let his eyes stray from Dirk's face.

"I admit, I made some mistakes as a kid," Dirk tried to sound apologetic. "I started hanging out with the wrong crowd and doing stupid things out of boredom. But that's all way behind me, Mr. Lithgow, I swear it! I haven't had any legal trouble in a very, very long time. I honestly wasn't aware that anyone I know now has a criminal history," he lied. "I would never knowingly consort with anyone like that." His green eyes were round and earnest.

"I know you don't like me, Mr. Godfrey," Laurence began, leaning forward slightly in his chair. "But of all the qualities about me you hold in contempt, is stupidity truly among them?"

Dirk squirmed in his chair, wishing with everything in him that he could be somewhere else, somewhere as far away from this office as possible.

"Of course not, Mr. Lithgow! I've never thought anything but the best of you and your family! I admire you very much, sir, and I adore Gloria. In fact—"

"In fact, you're a sniveling, two-bit con artist who has been scheming since day one to woo my daughter into marriage so you can help yourself to her bank account. Darren Cecil Godfrey, you are the most transparent, amoral climber I've ever met, and believe me, that's saying a lot."

For once, Dirk was stunned into silence. Laurence took advantage of this.

"Here's what's going to happen," he said. "You are going to remove yourself from my daughter's life. You will not work for her, you will not see her socially, you will not *accidentally* bump into her anywhere. You will not call her or write to her. Do you understand what I'm saying, Mr. Godfrey?"

Dirk was still too rattled to speak, but he found himself grinding his teeth together furiously. After another few seconds of silence, he found his voice.

"Now, listen here, Mr. Lithgow," he began, somewhat shakily. "Gloria is a grown woman, and I'm an adult as well. We both have every right to be together, and frankly, even though the nature of our relationship is none of your business, the fact is, *sir*," he sneered, "we care for one another very much. I was

Gloria's assistant, I became her friend, and now it has grown into much more than that. We don't need your permission to do anything, Mr. Lithgow. I have to say, I am hurt and disgusted. I never pegged you as someone who would look down on me because I don't come from a wealthy background." He tried to affect a wounded tone.

Laurence stared at the young man before him.

"You know, Mr. Godfrey," he began, "you'll never win an Academy Award or a Tony, but you just might have a future in dinner theatre." He took some pleasure in the unguarded expression of shock and offense on Dirk's face. "Where you have absolutely no future, however, is in my daughter's life. I've made no mystery of my own humble beginnings, so the idea that I would keep you away from my family over a lack of wealth and status is ridiculous, but you can think whatever you like about my decision. Speaking of family, does your mother know that you tell people she's unwell and dependent on a well-to-do sister? A sister who doesn't actually exist, of course." Once again, Laurence felt a mean-spirited little stab of joy at Dirk's expression.

"My mother," Dirk repeated stupidly. "You don't understand. My mother … she and I, we …" he faltered and lowered his gaze as if the right thing to say was printed on his sweaty hands.

"I thought as much," Laurence scoffed. "You're a cheat and a liar, *Dirk*," he sneered. "And you're not very good at either, it seems. Your games and arrogance have caught up with you. You'll waste no more of my time, nor will you jeopardize my daughter any longer. You have forty-eight hours to remove any of your personal effects from Lucinda's Lair, and as of this very moment, your relationship with Gloria is over. You will not answer her calls or communicate with her in any way. In fact, I've arranged for Gloria to be out of town for the next couple of days, and I, personally, will inform her of what's happened when she returns."

Dirk stared open-mouthed at Laurence, his face twisted into an expression of disbelief and rage.

"You can't ... you can't do this," he stammered. "You just can't tell me that I suddenly have to give up my career and the woman *I love*," he emphasized, "because my past offends your delicate sensibilities. That's not the way things work, Mr. Lithgow. This isn't the old west, in case you hadn't noticed," he hissed. "You can't round up a posse and run me out of town."

"You're as predictable as you are cocky and dishonest, Mr. Godfrey," Laurence said, staring the younger man squarely in the eyes. "Do you expect me to suddenly change my mind because of your little outburst? I knew you wouldn't go quietly. You would never have the sense to do that. As I've already established, Darren, I've done my homework on you. A spotty past as a teenager is one thing, but your underhanded exploits continue to this very day."

Laurence paused and flipped through the folder on his desk until he had one of the several photographs of Darren and Jessie Krueger together. He shoved it across the desk.

"If the police searched your apartment today, Mr. Godfrey, would your charm be enough to keep you out of prison?"

Dirk stared glumly at the photograph.

"The police have no right or reason to search my apartment. This isn't a game of Clue, Mr. Lithgow. Having more money than intelligence does not make you a god, *sir*."

Laurence glowered at Dirk.

"Are you saying, then, that you are going to gamble with your freedom? Do you really want to test me? Do you truly believe, Darren, that this photograph is the only damning piece of evidence I have against you?"

Actually, it was. Gloria would undoubtedly be upset to learn that Dirk had lied about his past and his name, but the information Laurence had attained was not enough to do much of anything in a courtroom. He could expose Darren Godfrey's dishonesty to Gloria and to the community in which Darren had worked so hard and so long to ingratiate himself, but Laurence could not have the man arrested. He held his breath and prayed Darren Cecil Godfrey would not be able to call his bluff.

Dirk stared across the desk at Laurence. He gripped the arms of his chair, squeezing them the way he would have liked to squeeze Laurence's pale, fleshy throat.

"You can't prove anything," he snapped, feeling as he said it that he had lost.

Laurence did not move his eyes away from Dirk's. His thin lips curved into something resembling a smile.

"Get out," he said. "Get out of this building and out of my daughter's life. If you choose to be a fool about this, Mr. Godfrey, your life will become a million times more difficult than you ever thought it could be."

Dirk didn't move.

"Dragging my name through the mud means nothing, Laurence. But do you really want to put your daughter through that? Do you really want to expose your wife, *and her friends*, to the skeletons you claim you've found in my closet?"

He raised one eyebrow and cocked his head to the side, waiting for an answer.

Laurence was not unprepared. He'd actually expected Darren Godfrey to hint at a pay off much sooner in their conversation. The mention of Regina and her cronies managed to rattle him somewhat. Though Laurence had no doubt that he had the upper hand, the young man could still make things ugly for everyone in the Lithgow family.

"My wife's peace of mind is important to me, yes," Laurence admitted.

"How important?" Dirk asked with a predatory smile.

"Important enough," Laurence answered.

He grabbed one of the gold-plated pens from the display set on his desk and jotted down a figure on a sheet of paper. He slid the paper across the desk to Dirk.

Dirk looked at the figure, scowled, grabbed one of the other pens, and scribbled down another figure, adding two digits. He shoved the paper back to Laurence. Laurence scoffed at Dirk's demand. They continued this for a few minutes before finally reaching an agreement. The sum was less than Laurence was ultimately willing to pay, though he certainly didn't let on as much. He made out the check to Darren Cecil Godfrey and was mildly pleased to see Dirk frown at this.

Before Laurence handed over the check, he made Dirk sign a letter of resignation he'd dictated to Erin in the days past. The letter also stated that Dirk would not have any future contact with Gloria, professional or otherwise. Laurence called Erin into his office to witness the signing. She brought with her two cups of coffee, one for Laurence and one for herself. She smirked at Dirk as she set the cups down on the table and took a long sip from her own cup. Dirk glared at her for a long moment, lips twitching to withhold all of the filthy, hateful words he wanted to scream. Finally, he signed the letter, his shoulders sagging in defeat. He shoved the check deep into one of his pockets and stalked out of the office without another word to either of them.

Chapter Thirty-seven

Joan blotted a generous amount of liquid foundation onto her fingers and rubbed it over her face, spending extra time on the bluish-gray patches beneath her eyes. Lately, the dark half moons were a constant presence on her face, no matter how much she slept or how much makeup she used. She dusted bright peach rouge onto her cheek bones, eyeing her reflection critically. *I look damn old,* she thought with dismay. She tried to shrug off the feeling and instead concentrated on following the contour of her eyes with black liquid eyeliner. Her hand trembled, and the liner made a thick streak across her glittery blue eye shadow.

"God damn it!" Joan swore, throwing down the wand of eyeliner.

Teeth and fists clenched, she sat as still as she could for a few seconds, taking deep breaths and trying to force herself into a state of calm. Lately, nothing she did felt right. *She* didn't feel right. She was tired all the time, and she noticed that if she so much as bumped her arm against a doorframe, she'd have a nasty-looking bruise that would last for days. A few times in the past several weeks, she'd woken up with a bloody nose. One rare morning when Missy was home, she had meekly asked if Abel was hitting Joan. It was one of the few times in recent memory that Joan could recall being on the verge of tears. Of course, she didn't let Missy see that. She'd scoffed at her youngest daughter's concern and told her to stop bugging her with stupid questions. Missy didn't dare press the issue. Joan couldn't explain her bloody noses. She wasn't a coke head. For one, she couldn't afford it; for another, it was just too intense. She'd tried it a few times, but the overwhelming rush of energy and the heightened awareness of every single sensation was the exact opposite of what she sought. *Maybe it's just allergies,* she told herself lamely.

Not only did her body seem to look and feel twice its age, but Joan couldn't remember the last time she was able to think clearly for more than a few minutes at a time. Gin or rum used to help settle her nerves and guide her through day-to-day decisions, but even drinking hardly helped anymore. She'd gleefully quit her job at the thrift store several weeks after receiving the check from Arnie's mom, but she soon found that she actually missed the place. She missed having people she could brag to, and she missed having an audience for her bar stories. She was bored all day. Missy was hardly ever home, which suited her fine, but being alone in the house was somehow suffocating. Abel worked during the day and usually just wanted to stay home, drink, and have sex after his shift ended. Sometimes Joan found herself in one of her favorite bars by eleven in the morning. She'd wake up, shower and dress in a hurry, or sometimes just refresh her makeup and change her clothes, and rush to Fensen's Lounge or the Red Knight Tavern. She preferred Fensen's because the drinks were stronger there, but Red Knight was good too because there were always more men than women there.

With a weary sigh, she licked a swatch of tissue and rubbed away most of the smudged eyeliner from her lids. She took a gulp from the bottle of rum that she kept in the top drawer of her dresser. Warmth spread through her chest, and she began to feel a little better. She brushed darker eye shadow, a shade of plum, across her eyelids to cover the smeared eyeliner that remained. *There,* she thought, *I look as good as I always have.* It wasn't true, but what did it matter? She had another drink of rum and applied a fresh coat of merlot-colored gloss to her lips. She gave her reflection what she thought of as her come hither look, the one she used when she met a new man who she wanted to get to know better.

It was only one in the afternoon. Missy had spent the previous night at a friend's house and would stay for another night, Joan assumed. Abel would be at work for another four hours, at least. She thought of Abel's proposal and had to steady her stomach with another swig from the bottle. He wanted to get married and buy a house with her. He also wanted to have his name added to the deed of her duplex. They would rent out both sides while living comfortably in their new home, he'd said. An involuntary grimace crossed her features. He'd suggested it a week before as they lay in his bed. It certainly wasn't the romantic proposal she envisioned as a kid, but then Abel wasn't exactly her dream guy. Joan knew that she wasn't in love with him and doubted she ever would be. She sometimes wondered if she could love anybody. Abel never said he loved her, but he treated her well and he was decent to Missy, too. He didn't leer at Missy the way some of Joan's boyfriends had or sneak her drinks when he thought Joan wouldn't notice. Abel would have been good to Carrie, too, if she hadn't skipped out to live with Arnie's mom.

Damn ungrateful little shit, Joan thought, her mouth curling into a snarl. *She always thought she was better than me. I'm the one who put up with her ass all these years! I'm the one who raised her, not that snobby old bitch!* For a moment, all Joan could see was A. C. Browne's face, the judgment in her eyes that night, so many years ago, when Arnie took Joan to his parents' party. *She never liked me, never gave me a chance. Thought I was trash before he even introduced me,* Joan fumed. She took another drink of rum.

The house was too quiet. She had no idea when Missy would be home. In the back of her mind, there was a small voice, a murmur really, that told her she should be more aware of what was going on in her youngest daughter's life. The whisper of guilt sometimes unleashed a flood of scenarios in her imagination: Missy in a car with a group of older boys; Missy getting high on whatever was handy. She doused her worries into silence, polishing off her rum in one long, burning swallow. It would be better if Missy spent another night or, hell, the rest of the week with her friends. Joan couldn't remember the last time she'd gone grocery shopping, but Missy looked fine, so clearly she was getting her meals somewhere. It was better when Missy wasn't at home too much. There was no doubt in her mind that her youngest child was her favorite, but that didn't mean the girl was above grating on her nerves.

When she allowed herself to have such thoughts, Joan was unsure why she'd ever had children. Neither pregnancy had been intentional. To some extent, her first pregnancy was, but that was only because Joan knew that Arnie's family had money. At the time, she'd hoped that a pregnancy would force him to marry her. How wrong she had been. Arnie seemed vaguely proud when Joan broke the news to him, but not at all enthusiastic. She might as well have congratulated him for always scoring the best pot.

Arnold never suggested that he and Joan should marry, and she realized that he never would have mentioned the word "marriage" if she hadn't broached the subject. He gave her excuses at first: he didn't have a good enough job to take care of a family or he thought they were too young to settle down. Eventually, he started avoiding her. The two deadbeat guys he shared an apartment with were obviously lying when Joan tried to reach Arnie on the phone. They stammered their way through hollow explanations of his whereabouts. She tried to track him down at the warehouse where he was employed, but a couple months into her pregnancy, he apparently lost his job and didn't bother to tell her when and where he found a new one. It was only when she showed up at his apartment, her belly so swollen that she could no longer see her feet, that Joan and Arnie finally had it out about their baby.

At first, he accused her of trying to fool him. He insisted that the child she was carrying couldn't be his. She was nothing but a cheap whore looking to trick someone into supporting her, he'd raged at full volume from the doorway of his apartment. There was no way he could be sure that it was his baby, he said repeatedly. Joan was equally vicious. She informed Arnie that the only thing about him that worked as it should was in his pants, and she would gladly submit to a paternity test. Her eagerness about a blood test was what quieted him. He finally allowed her to waddle through the door. He asked her if she wanted a hit from his bong. She declined, collapsed onto one of the saggy beanbags in his living room, and lit up a cigarette. They eyed one another warily for a long time before either of them spoke again.

Arnold broke the silence by saying that he never wanted to get married—not to Joan, not to anyone. He'd help as best he could with the kid, he said, but he wasn't going to play the role of dad and husband. There were so many things that Joan wanted to say to him. If she hadn't been so weary and unable to rise from her seat without help, she would have crossed the room and belted him across his unshaven face. She thought of threatening to sue him or telling his parents about the baby. She thought of turning him into the cops for drug use, but quickly decided against it.

Those moments in Arnie's dingy living room made Joan realize that getting what she ultimately wanted would take far more time, thought, and effort than an unplanned pregnancy. She basically let him off the hook, though she still threatened to tell both the police and his parents about everything. She dropped the subject of marriage altogether. Joan realized that she'd be better off without Arnie. She knew that if they tried anything long term, she would be the one to carry him. He was a bum, pure and simple. Arnold Browne had nothing to offer except the occasional spot of cash that he begged off his rich parents and regular access to a variety of drugs.

The threats were effective. For months after their confrontation, Arnie gave her several hundred dollars a month. He saw the baby, even held her a couple of times, but it was clear that he was uneasy around a child, even one that obviously resembled him. The only thing he ever showed any interest in was the baby's name. She would be named Carrington, Arnold demanded. Joan protested at first, saying it was a ridiculous name for a little girl. She liked the name Amanda. She had visions of a smaller version of herself that she would call Mandy, a little girl who would both fear and respect her mother. But he was strangely insistent. His daughter would be named Carrington, and that was the end of the discussion. Joan relented. The extra wad of cash that he handed over played no small part in Joan finally agreeing to name the child Carrington. But with the middle name, Joan had her say. Plus, Carrington shared Joan's last name. Carrington Amanda Coyle came squalling into the world on May 3 at 2:17 in the morning.

Even though having Carrington eventually paid off, it had taken way too long, and Joan hadn't received nearly as much as she felt she should have. Thirty grand was not at all worth what her oldest daughter had put her through for nearly fifteen years, including a difficult pregnancy. It wasn't worth the years of knowing she was being watched and judged by a sullen, snotty little girl.

Joan sneered at her reflection, thinking of how easily she'd given into the rich bitch's lawyer. She should have held out for more money.

She flipped through her closet. It was jammed with clothes, shoes, and purses. Even if Abel wasn't a prize, he had a good idea about getting a new place to live. Her house felt more and more cramped every day. She hated the duplex. Everywhere she looked, she saw either her father or Carrington. They'd both betrayed her; they'd both left her before she was ready for them to leave.

She had to admit to herself, though, that her father's death was somewhat a relief. He was a surly drunk, but mostly he just wanted to be left alone. He seldom raised his hand to her and thankfully never tried any of the nasty business Joan had heard all about from the few female friends she'd had over the years. Mostly, Douglas Coyle was just a cold, hardened man who had no patience for a child. He worked as often as he could. Joan couldn't remember going hungry as a child. She didn't have especially nice things, but she had enough. It was almost as if her father knew he would die young, or perhaps he simply wanted to. He paid off his house as quickly as he could and left it in Joan's name, along with a modest sum from an insurance company.

Joan felt her eyes well with tears. She wanted to scream in anger. *Only dumb asses cry over ancient history,* she thought. *Get a hold of yourself, damn it.* She yanked a sparkly, violet mini dress from the closet and randomly chose a pair of black patent leather high-heeled shoes.

Joan pulled the dress over her head and was at first pleased to find that it hung loose on her. Throughout her thirties, she had battled her weight, and it seemed like a mostly losing battle. She could never quite get rid of the roll of fat that circled her waist and hips, no matter how little she ate. In fact, concern over her weight was partly why she steered clear of beer. It was bloating, and her stomach felt much heavier after a few beers than it did after a few shots. Shots also took her to that fuzzy, nearly numb place much faster than beer could.

She surveyed herself in the full-length mirror that hung from her bedroom door, sighing at how saggy her breasts looked. *Like week old balloons,* she thought sadly. The bones in her shoulders showed; her wrists and ankles reminded her of twigs. She didn't remember losing any weight or going to any pains to lose it, but the evidence stared back at her from the mirror. She couldn't remember, exactly, the last time she'd worn the shimmering purple dress, but she'd filled it out then. She'd had cleavage and hips. Now her body was shriveled and yellowish, a shadow of what it once was. What had happened to her body in just a few months? She thought suddenly of how thin and frail her father had been just before he died.

Joan wrenched the dress off and kicked it under her bed. She browsed through her crowded closet for a few more minutes and finally chose a tight, stretchy, red T-shirt. It had been much too small when she brought it home from the thrift store several months prior. Of course, she put on her push-up bra first. She never left the house without her push-up bra. She coupled the T-shirt with a short black skirt and high-heeled, leather sandals. She glanced admiringly at the sandals. They were brand-new and cost more than she cared to admit, but hell, cashing the check from Arnie's mom had been reason to celebrate. The sandals had clear heels, and the straps glittered with multi-colored rhinestones. The heels were so high that she was forced to basically stand on her toes, which made her legs flex and her back side jut out. Joan fluffed her hair, a look of near satisfaction settling on her face. She almost looked like her former self.

She left a terse message on Abel's answering machine to meet her at Fensen's after he got off work. She doubted Missy would come home for the evening, but at the last minute, she left a twenty on her youngest daughter's bed. *What the hell,* she thought, leaving another twenty. There was plenty of cash in her purse.

Chapter Thirty-eight

Joan steadied herself against the graffiti-covered bathroom stall and fell onto the toilet. She leaned forward and clutched her abdomen. There was an awful pain in her gut, worse than anything she had ever experienced, including labor pains. After a couple of tries, she managed to yank down her pantyhose. She was glad she'd decided to wear underwear that night, because her soaked panties were the only thing that had, so far, kept the blood from flowing down her legs.

"What the hell?" she slurred angrily, wadding up some toilet paper.

It wasn't time for her period. She did her best to soak up the blood, and then she realized with horror that it wasn't coming from the area of her body that she originally thought it was. She reached for more toilet paper and tried not to cry. Joan hated crying. It was weakness, pure and simple.

She had to decide what to do. The six gin and tonics she'd had since arriving at Fensen's two hours earlier made her head feel impossibly heavy. She wished she could curl up in her own bed. But the flow of blood wasn't slowing down. She had seen bleeding like this before. When her father became sick, he often woke up bleeding. Joan had been terrified the first time she saw blood on his sheets. She thought he'd murdered someone. But Doug had told her it was nothing, that she ought to mind her own damn business and leave him be. So she had. He died a couple of months later of complications related to cirrhosis of the liver.

Joan forced thoughts of her father as far away as possible. Her panties stuffed full of toilet tissue, she stood on shaky legs and teetered out of the bathroom. She saw Abel waiting for her at the bar and nearly broke down into tears. For once, she was genuinely glad to see him. She leaned against a wall and raised one unsteady hand in greeting. At first, Abel didn't notice anything was wrong. He flashed a grin and toasted his beer bottle to her. The pounding din of the bar—the voices, the music—everything rushed together in Joan's head as she collapsed on the grimy carpet just outside of the restroom.

Chapter Thirty-nine

"You simply cannot drink as much as you have for as long as you have and not expect your health to be affected." Dr. Murphy's tone was weary but not unkind. The diagnosis was grave. She stood near the foot of the hospital bed and looked solemnly into Joan's face. "The damage to your liver is extensive, Ms. Coyle. If you continue drinking like this … actually, continuing to drink *at all* will cause severe hemorrhaging."

"Yeah, I always said you drink like a cowboy, Joan," Abel said and chuckled.

Dr. Murphy shot him a look of disgust.

"Shut up, Abel," Joan said quietly without looking at him.

"This is no laughing matter," Dr. Murphy told them both. "You have cirrhosis of the liver, Ms. Coyle. It is a very serious condition. Right now, you have approximately 30 percent liver function, perhaps a bit less. There's no way to reverse the damage, but with a proper diet, a good regimen of light physical activity, perhaps some medication, and *absolutely no drinking*," she paused and gave both of them an especially stern look, "we can hopefully prevent further damage and minimize complications."

"What do you mean 'we'?" Joan sneered. "*You* don't have to do nothin'," she snapped at Dr. Murphy. "I'm the one who's just supposed to change my life overnight, like magic! Like it's just so damn easy! And anyway, I have bad arthritis. I can't do aerobics or any of that stuff."

Dr. Murphy sighed. "I'm only trying to inform you and help you make healthy choices, Ms. Coyle." The pager on the waistband of her blue scrubs buzzed. "I'm sorry; you'll have to excuse me now. I'll be back to check on you before you're discharged, and there will be a nurse around if you need anything. I'll make sure you have some literature about dealing with cirrhosis."

Dr. Murphy gave Joan one final imploring look and rushed out of the room.

Joan glared at the doorway for several seconds after Dr. Murphy left. She closed her eyes and sighed.

"Aw, what does she know, babe?" Abel said without enthusiasm. "Doctors don't know everything. You could always get a second opinion or something." He patted her on the shoulder clumsily.

Joan jerked away from his touch.

"Will you get your hands off me?" It was a demand, not a request. "Always touching! You're too damn touchy-feely, Abel. Makes me sick."

She glared at him.

Abel pulled his hands away and swallowed hard. He looked confused.

"I was just trying to make you feel better," he said sheepishly.

"Then leave me the hell alone!" she barked. "You're gettin' on my damn nerves. I need to think right now, and I don't need you all over me, tryin' to act like you give a shit." Abel began to protest, but Joan cut him off. "We've never been a real couple, Abel; you know that. Don't you? Jesus, I can't believe you thought we would get married!" she scoffed. Abel's face turned a shade of deep red. "I ain't in love with you, and I know you don't love me, not like that. You gonna take care of me now, Abel? Now that I'm sick? You gonna look after Missy and make sure she goes to school and does okay in life? You gonna take care of the house and make sure she has what she needs? Shit, you can't even take care of yourself! You live in a dump, you drink every damn night, and you got no idea how to raise a kid."

Her green eyes blazed with rage and tears.

A strange expression came over Abel's face. It was one Joan had never seen on him before.

"I think that doctor was right sayin' you drink too damn much, Joan," he said. "Ruined your head. You're havin' delusions that you're mother of the year. Your oldest girl ran away from you as soon as she got the chance, and can you honestly say you even know where Missy is right at this minute? Don't tell me nothin' about raisin' kids, Joan. Maybe I don't know nothin' about bein' a family man, but at least I'm not a drunk, fake bitch who uses her kids to get pity and buys booze with her welfare checks!"

Abel's chest and cheeks puffed out as he finished. He looked a bit shocked at his own words, but it was clear he wasn't going to take them back or apologize.

Joan glared at him through her tears, disgusted both at the sight of Abel and the pain she knew was evident on her face.

"I never been on welfare, you asshole, and I never will be! My kids are my business! You been nothin' but a pain in my ass since we met. Look at you; who do you think you are, Abel? You're nothin' but a slob, and I don't know why I wasted my time on your ugly ass. You better—"

"Well, then it's a good thing you don't have a whole lotta time left, huh?" Abel snapped.

Joan gasped. Abel stared hard at her for a few more seconds, his face sweaty and flushed. Finally, he turned away and strode out of the hospital room. Joan watched the doorway, certain he would come rushing in at any moment to beg for her forgiveness. A minute passed, then two minutes. She kept glancing at the clock across from her bed.

After five minutes, she began to cry in a way that she hadn't allowed herself to since her father died. Great, heaving sobs shook her entire body. Joan felt weaker and more frightened than she had ever felt in her life. She thought of Missy and wondered briefly what would happen to her youngest child if she died. But Missy was only a fleeting thought. *This isn't fair,* Joan thought miserably. *This isn't fucking fair. I never had anything in my life that really made me happy, and now some asshole in a white coat says I don't have much time left. What have I done to deserve this?*

The notion of not drinking anymore was remote and alien. The doctor may as well have told her that she should have all of her limbs removed. Why? Why did she have to quit drinking? Joan didn't think she drank too much. It was just the way things were. Life was hard. She needed something to help her cope. Especially lately … what with Carrie running away from home like a little coward, and Missy becoming more and more distant. Who did Joan have now? Abel was worthless. Even if he hadn't walked out on her, she couldn't imagine she would have stayed with him much longer.

What would she do now? She closed her eyes and tried to will unconsciousness to take her, but sleep would not come. Not without a drink. *This is ridiculous,* Joan thought angrily. Come what may, Missy would be okay. Joan had learned to take care of herself when she was just a kid; it was obvious that Missy already knew how to get by. She was hardly ever home and seemed to be doing just fine. *What does any of it matter?* Joan thought. *It's my damn life. I'm the one who's running out of time.*

She cried for a while longer, sniffling loudly and blowing her nose into the corner of her bed sheet. She told the nurse on duty she was in terrible pain—not completely untrue—and was relieved when they allowed her a small dose of pain medication. It made her drowsy, and Joan was finally able to sleep.

Chapter Forty

Later today, I will meet my Aunt Regina and Uncle Laurence. Their daughter, Gloria, my father's first cousin, won't be coming. I can tell the subject of cousin Gloria makes Gran uncomfortable. I get the impression she isn't thrilled about the way Gloria lives, but she won't outright say so. All I know about Gloria is that she has an art gallery and Gran worries that she has too much of a "party lifestyle." It's weird to think of these people as my aunt, uncle, and cousin. I've never had any family. Well, of course there's always been Joan and then Missy, but that's all. No grandparents to visit on the weekends, no aunts, uncles, or cousins coming over for Thanksgiving.

For a while, Missy's dad lived with us. Even though I never really considered him family, he was actually nicer to me than Joan ever was. Maybe that's why I couldn't put him in the same category as my mom. I don't remember him all that well, but what I do remember isn't bad. Of course, even though he never hit us, Gary didn't exactly qualify for Father of the Year. He could never be relied on for anything; even Mom used to say so. After he left, he did next to nothing to stay in touch with Missy. I can see why he wouldn't want to be a part of Joan's life or mine, but his own daughter? It's almost worse that he sends the occasional card and money order. It's embarrassing. Poor Missy. She's always so proud when she gets those stupid cards in the mail. If only Mom would let her open them herself for once. But that's Joan. Whatever's in her house is hers, including her children and anything they have.

Even though I've only been with Gran for a few short months, when I look back at the years I lived in Joan's house, I can hardly believe I made it. There were times I thought she might kill me, not necessarily because she wanted me dead but because she would go into a rage, and I was the first thing she saw. Funny how she never laid a hand on Missy. Well, not funny exactly. Gran hates when I say things like that. I don't mean to upset her. Sometimes I have to say things like that or I feel like I'm going to burst. I can't believe how angry I've been lately. I have never been so angry in all of my life. I had a dream the other night that I was back in the house with Joan and she came at me, reeking of the bar and ready to smack the hell out of me. I had a weapon in my hand. I don't even know what it was … the leg of a chair or something else blunt and large. When she came at me, I let her have it. I cracked her hard across the chest and just kept whacking and whacking, even after she stopped moving and was sprawled out on the floor, all bloody and disgusting. I just kept wailing on her. I was so happy in my dream. I felt powerful for once. It scares me. Am I like Joan? If I ever had a child, would I abuse it? And just look at my biological father. What does that say about me? I'm his child. Am I going to become a drug addict and die before I'm even forty years old?

I just read over what I've written and it doesn't make much sense. I started out talking about how nervous I am about meeting Gran's family, and now I'm wondering if I am destined to become a loser. My mind is all over the place lately. The therapist tells me this is normal, considering what I've been through. Honestly, nothing seems normal lately. What is normal?

Thank God Carmen is here. Having her around makes me feel a little less nervous. She hasn't said so, but I can tell Carmen doesn't like Regina. Gran says those two never got along, something about Regina being jealous that Carmen was the maid of honor in Gran's wedding. Gran has said more than once, "If there's one thing my sister is good at, it's holding a grudge." But then she usually shuts up and seems embarrassed to have said something like that. It's weird and kind of alarming to hear things like that. What if I do or say something that upsets Regina? Will she hate me forever? I'm worried that she won't like me at all and she'll convince Gran to send me away. I know that's a really unlikely and childish thought, but still.

Carrington paused, pen still pressed against the page, but nothing more came. She felt there was more she should write, but she didn't have much time. Aunt Regina and Uncle Laurence were supposed to arrive at noon, and it was already ten thirty. Gran had told her so many times not to worry, everything would be fine, but Carrington could tell her grandmother was anxious, as well. *How could this not be a huge deal for everyone?* Carrington wondered.

She, A. C., and Carmen had been cooking for two days in preparation for this day. A. C. remarked a few times that maybe Regina had the right idea about having everything from baby showers to wakes catered, but she still seemed to have a good time showing her granddaughter how to use various appliances in the kitchen and passing on old recipes that she hadn't used for ages. Carrington caught on quickly. Soon, she was handling all of the utensils and gadgets with ease.

Carmen was enjoying herself. She'd grown genuinely fond of Carrington, and it was a novelty to do so much cooking and bustling around the house. She hardly ever took time for such things in her own home—not because she didn't want to or didn't care, but mostly because she was too busy, either with work, despite her semi retirement, or travel, or friends, or a little of everything. Seeing how well Carrington and A. C. complemented one another made her a bit wistful, though. She wondered what it would have been like if she'd had children of her own and eventually grandchildren. She guessed this was the next best thing. For her entire adult life, A. C. had been more like a sister to her than simply a friend.

They didn't voice it specifically, but both A. C. and Carmen were dreading Regina's presence. They didn't so much mind Laurence. Carmen felt a bit sorry for him, being married to such a hateful woman for so long, but at the same time, she resented his weakness. He didn't *have* to stay with Regina. Even if his excuse was that he was staying in an obviously unhappy marriage for his child's sake, Gloria had long since grown up (at least physically) and flown the nest. There was a brief period, very brief, when Carmen thought she and Laurence might make a good match. She had envied Regina, if only for a moment. When it came to his business, Laurence was shrewd and ambitious. Carmen hardly needed to someone to take care of her; it wasn't a meal ticket she sought. She identified with his drive: his overriding desire—his *need*—to be the best, to win.

Professionally, he had accomplished this, even if his personal life was a train wreck. Not that Carmen should be so quick to point any fingers, she sometimes reminded herself. She only had to think of her own two failed marriages to remember that her life wasn't exactly rife with examples of healthy romantic entanglements. *But at least I won't just stay on a sinking ship and drown,* she thought, comforted somewhat.

There was so much food! They made chicken curry finger sandwiches, beef Wellington, Caesar salad, and, for dessert, A. C.'s mother's key lime pie. Carrington thought the beef Wellington was the hardest to make. It wasn't easy getting the dough just right. It took a few tries, but by the end of their stint in the kitchen, she had all but taken over prepping the meat. A. C. was impressed.

"Have you ever considered studying to be a chef?" she asked her granddaughter.

Carrington blushed. She'd been used to doing all of the food preparation when she lived in Joan's house, but it was never anything fancy or complicated. Most of the time, they ate soup and sandwiches. She still felt strange about receiving compliments, even when they were from Gran. Secretly, she thought she was doing a fine job, too, and was thrilled that both Gran and Carmen noticed. It was the first time in a long time Carrington could remember feeling genuinely proud of herself.

Carrington went through the clothes in her closet, all things that A. C. had bought for her when she moved in. A. C. said she should wear whatever she felt like for the lunch with Aunt Regina and Uncle Laurence. It was a difficult decision. As much as Carrington was dreading the fancy dinner party, at least deciding what to wear had been easy; not that she had a clue about dressy clothes, but at least she had a vague notion of the type of clothes that ought to be worn. The gown that A. C. had helped her choose for the dinner party was breathtaking. Carrington was both thrilled and terrified at the prospect of wearing it. As she often had in the days since it had come back from the department store's alteration shop, she unzipped the heavy garment bag just to gaze at the gorgeous dress. But there was little time for that now. She gently pushed the dress bag to the back of her closet and finally settled on a pale green polo shirt, a soft khaki skirt, and coffee-colored, ballerina-style slippers.

Sometimes she still couldn't believe that all of the things in the closet were hers and hers alone—things that had been purchased both because they fit her well and because she liked them. Never once had Joan asked for Carrington's opinion about the clothes she made her wear. Most of the time, the clothes just appeared without notice. Carrington would come home from school to find a plastic bag on her bed stuffed with old T-shirts, faded jeans, and a couple pairs of sneakers. Most of the clothes fit well enough. Things that were too small were given to Missy, if Missy wanted them, which she usually didn't. When Missy needed clothes, Joan took her youngest daughter to the thrift store where she worked and let Missy pick out what she wanted. With her employee discount taken off the already low prices, Joan paid next to nothing for what her daughters wore. Carrington knew that deep down, Missy was ashamed that every item of clothing she had was secondhand, but at least Missy got to pick her own outfits.

Also new was her hairstyle. Carrington pulled on her clothes and ran a brush through her now layered hair. It was still fairly long but framed her face instead of just hanging in one great, reddish-brown sheet. She thought the new style made her look older than fourteen. A. C. loved it and said it was very sophisticated.

It was still somewhat strange not feeling embarrassed of her clothes. What an exhilarating yet bizarre sensation it had been the first time A. C. took her shopping. A. C. had been prepared to simply stand back and let Carrington browse and choose whatever she liked. Carrington was shocked and flustered when A. C. gave her free reign to choose her own clothes. *What a disaster I was,* Carrington thought with a wry chuckle. Thank

God her grandmother was a patient woman. She'd never met anyone so kind.

In spite of her grandmother's obvious reservations about having her sister over for lunch, Carrington found some comfort in thinking that anyone related to A. C. had to be nice. How could anyone who had the same blood in her veins as A. C. not be a basically good and kind-hearted person? Maybe Regina was tough on the outside and uncompromising, but surely she was like her older sister in some ways, Carrington hoped. *Right, just like I have so much in common with Missy,* she thought. She pushed the thought out of her mind and finished getting dressed, fully aware that her hands were trembling.

Chapter Forty-one

Carrington nearly jumped when the doorbell finally rang. She was in the living room, making sure that everything was in its place: not a mote of dust on the hardwood floor, not a single picture frame askew, and not a sagging pillow on the sofa. Everything was perfect. She smoothed down her already neat hair once again and glanced at herself in the hallway mirror. Her cheeks were a bit flushed, but otherwise she looked well enough. She glanced doubtfully down at her polo shirt. Perhaps it was too casual. The doorbell chimed again.

A. C. rushed into the living room from the kitchen. She smelled of curry and looked gorgeous. She wore a salmon-colored cotton blouse with pearly buttons, slim-fitting beige slacks, and dark brown, open-toed sandals. She looked comfortable yet elegant. Carrington was thrilled that Gran had worn her hair down. She could hardly believe her grandmother was nearing her seventies. Just a touch of makeup gave A. C. a fresh, sunny look. A. C. flashed a big confident smile at Carrington and gave her a quick reassuring hug on her way to answer the door.

"Did I just hear the doorbell?" Carmen's voice called from the kitchen. She was putting the finishing touches on lunch.

"Yes!" A. C. and Carrington answered in unison.

"I'll be right out," Carmen answered in a cheerful, sing-song tone.

A. C. swung the heavy door open, and there stood Regina and Laurence. Carrington stood timidly behind her grandmother and surveyed the two strangers. Despite being a handful of years younger than her sister, Regina appeared much older than A. C. She wore a scowl on her face that seemed to have caused permanent lines around her pursed lips and narrowed eyes. Her hair was a stark white cap of curls, stiff with hairspray. Carrington thought briefly of the chapters in her history text books devoted to the white, powdered wigs politicians once wore. Regina, like her sister, wore a minimal amount of makeup, but the colors were all wrong for her, making it appear that she was wearing far too much of it. Carrington thought of Joan and stifled a shudder. Regina's thin lips were a cruel slash of plum, and her eyes were dark pebbles beneath a layer of mascara. Carrington could see, though, that Regina had probably once been a very pretty woman before the years had hardened her. She had the grace and the bone structure of a dancer, but even when her face contorted into something that was supposed to be a smile, she appeared deeply unhappy.

Laurence looked subdued and bored behind his wife. He smiled blandly at A. C. He was a doughy-looking man, reminding Carrington of a clay sculpture that had yet to be set and glazed. She imagined his pale flesh felt like putty. He had sparse, dark hair that was shiny with some kind of oil, a wide face, and kind eyes. His eyes were the nicest thing about him, Carrington decided immediately, feeling guilty for appraising his looks. Like Regina, Laurence gave her the impression that he had once been rather attractive, but time had not been kind to him. He held himself stiffly. He had broad shoulders that suggested a once athletic build, but from the chest down, he was round and soft. They were both overdressed. *Or maybe we're underdressed,* Carrington thought miserably.

Regina wore a silk, navy blue blouse buttoned up to her throat and charcoal gray slacks, both too warm and too formal. Leather loafers adorned her feet, still stiff with newness, and a matching handbag hung from one wrist. A small cluster of diamonds and sapphires glittered from each ear lobe. Carrington tried not to stare at Regina's wedding band. The diamonds were enormous, certainly much wider than Regina's bony finger. It looked absurd. Laurence's clothes were only slightly less formal than his wife's but still a bit much for what was supposed to be a casual summer lunch at his sister-in-law's house.

He's dressed, A. C. recognized immediately, *for an afternoon on the golf course. Regina probably had to drag him away from his clubs,* she thought with a small sigh. *Of course, if I had to choose between an afternoon with Regina and an afternoon swatting at little plastic balls with metal rods, well …* she didn't allow herself to finish the thought. She smiled graciously at them.

"Regina, Laurence," she greeted them, giving each a peck on the cheek. "Please come in. This," she said, putting her arms on Carrington's shoulders, "is Carrington. Carrington, this is my sister and her husband, your Aunt Regina and Uncle Laurence."

Regina's thin lips smiled, but her eyes did not. She held out one cool, slender hand, which Carrington reached for shyly. It was the briefest of handshakes.

"Well, hello, Carrington," she said in a stiffer than usual voice. "At last we meet the mystery granddaughter." It sounded like an accusation.

Laurence, at least, gave Carrington what appeared to be a genuine smile, and he pumped her hand with enthusiasm.

"You look so much like your grandmother," he told her. "It's wonderful to finally meet you."

I guess I shouldn't have expected more from Regina, damn it. Thank God for Laurence, A. C. thought, the corners of her mouth twitching as she tried to keep the smile plastered on her face.

Carrington smiled at both Regina and Laurence and tried to maintain eye contact.

"Thank you so much," she said, instantly feeling foolish. "I'm really glad to meet you both, too … Aunt Regina and Uncle Laurence." The words tumbled awkwardly from her lips like a half-remembered speech.

"Hello, you two! My, it's been some time, hasn't it?" Carmen sailed into the room in a cloud of turquoise linen and Chanel No. 5.

She wore just the right amount of lipstick and blush, and a small platinum charm sparkled from her throat. She looked enchanting. Laurence's shoulders stiffened visibly. He drew his hand away from Carrington's and gulped. Regina pursed her lips and glared at Carmen with undisguised repugnance.

"Carmen," she said, "I didn't expect to see you today." Her words were cold and clipped.

Laurence swallowed again, his face flushing. A. C. almost giggled. *No fool like an old fool,* she thought.

"Well … hello, Carmen. How nice to see you again. You look … you look, lovely," he faltered when Regina looked up at him sharply. "That is, you all look so nice. It's my lucky day; I get to have lunch with a group of beautiful women," he finished with a forced chuckle, his face a shade of pink.

I am such an idiot, he thought, wishing he could pour himself a Scotch and spend the afternoon alone in his study. Seeing Carmen was always a jarring experience for Laurence. He had been smitten with her since the very first time they met. There was something electrifying about Carmen. She walked into a room and charged it with energy. When she looked at him, he felt as if he was the only person in the world. No one else had ever managed to make Laurence feel that, and yet he knew it wasn't because Carmen wanted him. It was just her way, her intense focus that could either make someone feel as if he was standing before a benevolent goddess who wanted only to reward his good deeds, or as if he was bound and gagged before a firing squad. After so many years and so many different occasions, this never changed. Each time Laurence met Carmen's eyes, the feelings were there, always as strong as every time before. They were feelings of scrutiny and, on some level, of understanding.

He wondered, more often than he cared to admit to himself, if they had met under different circumstances, what would their relationship be? Carmen Villareal was sharp, hardworking, and disciplined. She was also stylish, funny, and incredibly pretty. Even if he'd met her while they were both single, he had a difficult time imagining that an amazing woman like Carmen would be interested in him romantically. Still, that didn't stop Laurence's stomach from doing somersaults whenever they were in the same room together.

They all stood in the living room for too long a time, sort of smiling and waiting for each other to speak. A. C. smiled pleasantly at Regina, willing herself to conjure up feelings of love and gratitude for her sister. Regina, however, was too preoccupied appraising Carrington. She looked her up and down, at times pursing her lips or squinting. Carrington glanced nervously around the room, not quite meeting anyone's eyes. She tugged self-consciously on the bottom of her shirt. Laurence kept a steady gaze at the wall of photographs. There wasn't any picture in particular that held his interest; it was just a diversion to keep his eyes from landing and staying on Carmen, who finally took the lead.

"You two are in for a treat," she said to Regina and Laurence with a smile. "We've been cooking up a storm for days, and our Carrington here shows a real knack for the culinary arts."

Carrington couldn't help but grin and blush. It wasn't so much the compliment, but it made her feel warm and safe to hear Carmen call her "our Carrington."

"Yes, why don't we move into the dining room?" A. C. said, annoyed by how high and nervous her voice sounded.

Regina sighed. "You all have been cooking?" she asked doubtfully. "You didn't hire a caterer?"

A. C. ears began to burn. She was glad she'd worn her hair down so no one would see them become red. *I will not let her get to me; I will not let her get to me,* she repeated silently in her head several times.

She tried to laugh. "Well, that takes all the fun out of having a party," she said.

Regina sniffed loudly but said nothing. They all followed A. C. into the dining room, where the table was set with a colorful collection of dishes. They were new. She had not wanted Carrington to feel as if she had no say about their home, so A. C. had asked Carrington to choose a new set of dishes. Carrington had been touched and flattered. She chose a cheerful yellow and pale blue set. A. C. thought they were lovely. She never would have chosen such a bright set herself, but lately she found herself drawn to more colorful things. Shopping with Carrington reminded her so much of the early years of her marriage. Calvin had always appreciated color. He even tried to incorporate something bright into his work attire, usually an eye-catching tie or kerchief for his breast pocket. A. C. felt as if Carrington had reawakened that part of her life. She only wished that Calvin had lived long enough to meet his beautiful granddaughter. A. C. knew he would have adored her.

The food was spread out on a dark wood buffet table, which stood against one wall. A. C. couldn't help but smile. They'd done a wonderful job; she didn't mind acknowledging this to herself. Everything looked delicious and inviting. She met Carmen's gaze and smiled gratefully. It was hard to remember a time when Carmen hadn't been there for her. She couldn't have asked for a better friend. Carmen gave her a broad, warm smile that made her feel a little less nervous.

"What's this?" Regina asked, poking at a chicken curry salad sandwich with a pair of serving tongs. "Egg salad?"

For God's sake, A. C. thought. But she simply smiled and responded, "It's chicken curry salad, dear. Try it; it's wonderful. Carmen chose the recipe."

Regina looked repulsed, as if she'd just found a hair on her plate.

"Hmph," she said, dropping the serving tongs and moving on to the beef Wellington.

"Everything looks and smells incredible," Laurence said, helping himself to four of the finger sandwiches that had so offended Regina. He ignored the glare she shot at him.

He must be immune to her, thought Carmen. *He'd probably be shocked if she actually smiled at him,* she mused sadly. She suddenly wondered if they had separate bedrooms. She couldn't imagine them ever lying next to one another, let alone making love. It was a wonder they had produced one child. Carmen felt herself blush. Why should she care whether Laurence slept next to the block of ice that was his wife? She grabbed a plate and headed for the buffet table.

A. C. sat at the head of the dining table, with Carmen and Carrington on one side and Regina and Laurence on the other. Carrington was relieved that she wasn't directly across from Regina. She wouldn't be able to eat if that cold gaze was piercing into her the whole while. She knew Regina was watching her, but since she wasn't immediately in front of her, Carrington wouldn't have to look into her aunt's stony eyes for the whole meal. Laurence, on the other hand, was considerably more pleasant. She didn't feel like she had to be on guard with him.

"So, for the dinner party," Regina began, poking at the food on her plate as she spoke, "I've hired Buffalo Nickel Catering. You remember, A. C., Janice Nickel's boy, Peter, owns it. God, I wish Gloria would give him a call; they would be great for each other." At this, Laurence rolled his eyes, but Regina didn't notice. "They did the bridal shower we went to last year at the club. You were so fond of the crab cakes, so they're going to serve them at the party next week." She looked very pleased with herself.

A. C. had only a vague memory of attending a bridal shower with Regina the previous year. There had been nothing remarkable about it. She had probably just told Regina she liked the crab cakes because Regina had pressed her to talk. *It feels like I'm always trying to figure out what to say to Regina,* A. C. realized with a sinking feeling. She had a sudden urge to invite everyone except her sister out for lunch. *Let her stay here and talk about her stupid catered parties until the end of time,* she thought angrily.

Laurence was watching A. C. closely. He recognized the look on her face. He knew it was the same expression he used to wear when dealing with Regina, before he learned to simply tune her out and only pretend to listen.

"So, Carrington, I hear you're about to start high school in a few weeks," he said.

He didn't care if his voice rang with false cheer or that Regina was looking at him as if she wanted his head on a pike. It would be worse if he didn't try to stop A. C. from blowing up at her sister.

Carrington gave him a small smile. "That's right," she said.

Regina trained a cool gaze on Carrington.

"Where are you going to school, dear?" she asked.

"Morgan Public," Carrington answered.

"Morgan Public?" Regina repeated. Her face was blank for a moment. "Oh, yes! I know of that school. A. C., why haven't you enrolled her in Keaton Day Academy? It's only a little farther away than Morgan, and it's a *private* school, the best in the state, actually. Gloria went there."

A. C. somehow managed to keep from rolling her eyes, though it was a struggle. *Yes, and look what an accomplished young woman she turned out to be,* she thought, feeling a stab of guilt. When Gloria was born, A. C. had imagined that Gloria could be the daughter she never had. For months, even the first few years of Gloria's life, she tried to be close with the child. It soon became apparent, though, that Gloria was just like her mother. She was a younger, even more demanding version of Regina, and whether Regina realized it or not, her parenting only seemed to make Gloria's spoiled, impetuous behavior worse.

"Actually," Regina continued, "now that I really consider it, you're smart to enroll her in Morgan, A. C. You've been going to public school all your life, I assume?"

Regina's eyes were once again on Carrington.

"Yes, I have," Carrington managed.

"I thought so," Regina told Carrington. She turned back to A. C. "She'd be way behind the children at Keaton. Most of them have been in private schools all of their lives; some of them have even attended boarding school abroad! Why, just the other day, my good friend, Deirdre—you know her, A. C. There was the big scandal last year when her daughter nearly married that *waiter.*" She wrinkled her nose in disgust. "Anyway, she

was telling me about her nephew, Kenneth; he's a senior this year at Keaton. He said—"

"Carrington has had terrific grades all of her life," A. C. interrupted, her voice sharp. "Her test scores place her in the top 5 percent for her age, state wide. Morgan is a great school. Over 90 percent of their graduates go onto college, and—"

"Yes, but which colleges?" Regina broke in, apparently unfazed. "Community colleges? State schools?"

She made a clucking sound with her tongue and looked at Carrington the way she might look at a sick puppy.

Carrington looked stricken. A. C. gritted her teeth and tried to figure out what she should say. She couldn't just sit by idly and let Regina embarrass Carrington. Why did Regina have to act like this? What had Carrington, who was basically still a child, ever done to Regina? But A. C. knew that the problem was Regina's, not Carrington's. Regina would never stop being petty and spiteful. *This is ridiculous,* A. C. thought. *I should have never agreed to this lunch, let alone Regina's party.*

"Your aunt is right," Carmen piped up, just as A. C. was about to speak. "You better watch out for all those nasty public schools and dreadful state-run colleges. You keep going to those and you're going to wind up a real loser like me, or like your uncle Laurence, or worse yet …" she had an exaggerated cringe on her face, "like your awful, creepy grandmother!" Carmen concluded in a stage whisper that sounded like an announcement on a loud speaker.

Carmen grinned at A. C. There was a moment of stunned silence, and then everyone except Regina laughed. A. C. couldn't remember the last time she'd seen Laurence look amused. *The poor man,* she thought sadly. Regina sat stiff and erect as a marble column in her high-backed chair.

"Well," she said. "I was only trying to convey the importance of an education to Carrington."

She shot a look at Carmen and turned her attention to the untouched food on her plate.

"You know, Carrington," Laurence began cheerfully, completely ignoring his wife, "your grandfather attended a state college. It was before we knew one another, but I know the school he went to well. It's a fine university. I thought of going there myself, but I ended up getting a scholarship to another school. Plus, I had to work, and the college I attended was closer to my job."

"Really, Laurence," Regina chided with a small snort, "no one wants to hear about that. It's ancient history! And rather dull history. Now, I've decided that for the party—"

"Where did you work, Laurence?" Carmen asked with genuine interest. "I worked summers in a drugstore and a dress shop my junior and senior years. By then, Manuel, my brother, was in college, too, and it was so hard for my folks to make ends meet! I hated taking their money for tuition every semester. The drugstore and dress shop gigs didn't pay a whole lot, but they helped."

Laurence was pleased by her interest. "Well, during my freshman year, I worked for a florist, but unfortunately the business ended up folding. The following three years, I worked as a file clerk for a company that printed text books. It was somewhat boring work, but the pay was decent for back then, and I really couldn't have afforded college otherwise."

"Speaking of boring," Regina snapped, alternating her glare between Laurence and Carmen. "No one wants to hear hard-knock stories from ye olden days."

"Actually," A. C. began coolly, "I think it's fascinating what Carmen and Laurence went through to get an education. Calvin worked his way through school as well, and I firmly believe it made him a stronger person. I've never known any other person with Cal's work ethic," she finished proudly, eyes glistening with tears.

"Cal was one of a kind, that's for sure," Carmen said, smiling gently at her best friend.

No one said anything for a moment as A. C. regained her composure. Carrington felt increasing awe and affection for Carmen. She had liked her from the first moment they met, and it was obvious to her why her grandmother loved Carmen like a sister. Laurence seemed like a nice man, if a bit stuffy. Carrington wondered what his life had been like when he was her age. By his own admission, his family didn't have much material wise. Why did Regina act like it was so silly and meaningless to have worked through college?

Carrington glanced at her grandmother. A. C. was smiling once again, but her eyes were still sad. *Poor Gran,* Carrington thought. *She wanted everything to be so nice.* Carrington glanced at Regina, who, much to her relief, wasn't looking her way. The woman had an unnerving stare. Looking into Regina's eyes reminded Carrington of looking into Joan's eyes. They were both hateful, bitter women, but they suddenly seemed much less threatening than they had seemed just a short while ago, even as recently as the night before. Carrington realized something as she sat across the table from her grandmother's sister. *I am not afraid anymore,* she thought. *Not of Regina, not even of Joan.* She sat up a bit straighter in her seat.

"Have you given much thought to what you'd like to study when you're in college, Carrington?" Laurence asked.

Carrington liked that he said "when" and not "if." She smiled at him.

"Some thought," she said. "It's hard to say right now, though, since I'm just starting my first year of high school. But I kind of like the idea of becoming a librarian or maybe a teacher."

A. C. beamed with pride. Laurence smiled, as well.

"You know, I think those are two of the most important and yet underappreciated professions," he said. "My mother always wanted to be a teacher." He sounded wistful. "She was wonderful with children; everyone thought so. But her family couldn't afford to send her to school. A shame, really. But enough of the sob stories. Your grandmother worked as a school teacher. Did you know that?"

"Oh, yes," Carmen said. "A. C., you were a wonderful teacher! Did you ever consider going back to teaching? The kids always adored your grandmother," Carmen said to Carrington. "She was tough with them, but fair. And fun! You should have seen her fire up a classroom!" Carmen boasted to everyone at the table.

"She didn't *have* to work," Regina sounded defensive. "Calvin did very well for his family. I don't really understand why you ever wanted to be a teacher at all, A. C.," Regina said rather icily to her sister. "Such a tedious profession. So much labor and so few rewards."

"Gran showed me some pictures," Carrington answered Laurence. "I bet she was a great teacher." She smiled at her grandmother.

They ate a few bites, and no one said much of anything. A. C. wished she had never agreed to the lunch at all. Regina was not very subtle about eyeing Carrington across the table, scrutinizing every little thing she did. To her credit, Carrington pretended not to notice. She ate as much as she could and kept a pleasant expression on her face. *You're one tough kid,* A. C. thought, feeling very sad.

"So, what's this I hear about the huge bash you're having for our young Carrington? And why is it that I'm never invited to these big, society affairs?" Carmen teased Laurence.

Regina set her fork down with a loud clatter and glowered first at Carmen and then at Laurence. A. C. fought the urge to grimace. She knew Carmen and Regina couldn't stand each another, but she wished that once, just once, they could keep from picking on one another.

For a moment, Laurence seemed alarmed. He gave Regina a sideways glance, trying to gage her reaction. No doubt that whatever he said would be the wrong answer. What did it matter anymore? There was a long pause, and just as Regina was about to answer for him, he flashed a rare grin at Carmen.

"As if you're ever home long enough to accept an invitation," he responded playfully. "You're the one always jetting off from one exotic hot spot to the next! You make our little get-togethers look like Tupperware parties."

"Actually," Regina annunciated slowly, the way she did when she was especially angry, "the dinner is going to be a quiet affair—you know, *family* and *close* friends only."

Carmen looked directly at Regina and smiled, but it wasn't a friendly gesture. A. C. knew that smile, and she almost felt sorry for Regina. She cleared her throat loudly, hoping to get Carmen's attention. No such luck.

"Oh, pooh," Carmen said. "Well, you're right, of course, Regina. I was only the maid of honor at A. C.'s wedding! It's not like I've given her a kidney or something. I wouldn't want to infringe on such an intimate gathering."

A strange shade of salmon bloomed across Regina's spiky features. Laurence tried unsuccessfully to hide a smirk behind his water glass.

Oh, Lord, thought A. C. *Here we go.*

"And I still remember how amazing you were in that gauzy peach bride's maid dress, Carmen," Laurence said with a wistful sigh. "At the reception, you taught me the rumba. Do you remember that? Your shoes were black with scuff marks from mine by the time the night was—"

"That," Regina interrupted sharply, "was a very long time ago."

She glared at Laurence and Carmen for several seconds without blinking. The flush in her cheeks darkened until she was the same shade as a near ripe tomato.

"I do remember those lovely gowns," Regina said, "and yes, Carmen did look well in her dress. As I recall, though, it was a bit more expensive than the other dresses because the hips had to be let out quite a bit." Regina gazed at Carmen, eyebrows arched and a haughty smirk on her lips.

Carrington leaned forward in her seat, following the repartee like a tennis match. She tried her best to look impassive and calm, but she sensed the explosion coming. She just wasn't sure who would be the one to erupt.

Carmen smiled with tight lips at Regina.

"You have a good memory, Regina. My dress was a little bit more expensive, and *expansive*," she laughed, "than the other bride's maid dresses. I've always had a hard time getting just the right size for my hips." She patted her side noisily. "But then, these hips are, in part, what make me such a good dancer and an effective teacher. Isn't that right, Laurence?" she purred.

"Now, children," A. C. chided, "please try to behave." Though A. C. was smiling, Carrington could sense the warning behind it.

Carrington's cheeks were pink with excitement. She couldn't help but enjoy the needling Carmen was giving Regina and her near immunity to Regina's snipes. She thought of Regina's party and felt a flash of panic. Was this a taste of what it would be like? People eyeing one another to see who was wearing what, casually dropping references to what things cost, and exchanging the latest and most vicious gossip about the rest of their friends? Carrington shivered.

Regina took a small sip of water. A. C. saw the tremor in her hand as she raised the crystal to her lips. She knew her younger sister only trembled when she was angry. A. C. bit her lower lip, bracing herself for what was to come. *I'd better do something,* she thought.

A. C. raised her own glass.

"I would like to propose a toast," she began cheerfully. "To my lovely granddaughter and to all of you." She took a moment to smile at each of them, starting with Carrington. "You all are my family. I love each of you dearly, and I am just so thrilled that we can all be together."

She raised her glass high and waited for the others to join her. One by one, they did.

"Hear, hear!" said Carmen heartily.

Laurence clinked his glass with A. C., Carmen, Carrington, and eventually with Regina, although she barely moved her glass toward anyone. They had to reach across the table to touch their glasses to her glass.

Poor Regina, A. C. thought sadly. *She'll never be a happy woman. She has so much, and yet she'll never, ever see it. And she can't stand to see anyone else happy.*

No one said anything for a few awkward moments, and then Carmen and Carrington volunteered to clear away the lunch dishes. Laurence excused himself to the restroom.

A. C. tried to smile at her sister. She held out her silver pastry slicer.

"I made key lime pie for dessert. Mother's recipe," A. C. said to her sister. "Will you help me slice it and serve it?"

Regina sighed. "I don't know why you won't hire someone, A. C. You're not getting any younger, you know." A. C. flinched, but Regina didn't seem to notice or to care. "And why shouldn't you have someone to help you around the house? I mean, especially now. You wouldn't even have to pay for a full service maid. Carrington can take care of the simpler things; I'm sure she's used to that kind of thing by the looks of her and all that you've told me. But you could have someone like my Sonja come in a couple times a week for the larger tasks. And when you decide to entertain, I have a list knee high of fabulous caterers!" She began to sound somewhat excited again at the mention of a party.

A. C. just stared at her sister as if seeing an exotic, somewhat frightening creature from a distant planet.

"By the looks of her and all that I've told you," she echoed Regina's words slowly. Her voice sounded tinny and strange, as if coming from a hidden speaker. A dull throb began behind her eyes.

Regina smiled blandly and blinked several times.

"What?" she asked. She was still thinking of all of the caterers she knew. "Did I tell you who took over the Bon-bon Appétit shop after Carl sold it? You'll never guess! Remember that Moroccan gentleman Laurence did business with a couple of years ago, the one with the really young wife? Well, the wife's sister—"

"Regina," A. C. interrupted, setting down the stack of dessert plates. "What did you just say about Carrington?"

"Hmm?" Regina asked without looking up from the pie.

The slices she made with A. C.'s silver pie cutter were perfectly even. Regina finished the last slice with a small nod of satisfaction, clearly pleased with herself.

"What about Carrington?" she asked, finally looking up at A. C.

"I said, what did you say about Carrington? What did you mean, about the way she looks and what I've told you about her?" A. C.'s words were clipped and high-pitched.

Regina seemed genuinely confused. "The way she looks?" she asked, reaching for the stack of dessert plates. "What about the way she looks?"

"Regina, don't you dare blow me off! Set down those damn plates and look at me when I'm speaking to you!" A. C. was livid.

Regina pulled her hand slowly away from the plates and looked at her sister in surprise.

"A. C., what on earth is the matter with you?"

A. C. was quiet for a moment as she glared at Regina. *Oh, where do I begin?* she thought. *This charade has gone on far too long.*

"Are you suggesting," A. C. began slowly, barely able to get the words out, "that I use my granddaughter as a servant?"

Regina stared at her, open mouthed, for a moment before laughing nervously.

"Well, of course I'm not!" She raised one hand to her throat and began to fiddle with her necklace. "I only meant—"

"You only meant," A. C. sneered. "You only meant," she repeated with a slight tremble in her voice. She was angrier than she had been in a long time. "Regina, your very presence makes me ill. And my God, though it pains me to say that, it's the truth. We're sisters; so what? That is an accident of nature; it happened by chance. But we can never be friends, Regina. Never!"

Regina gasped. "A. C., what's gotten into you? I never meant that Carrington would be your servant! What a ridiculous thought! It's so ludicrous, it's embarrassing!"

A. C. shook her head. "Is that all you care about? What people will think? How something might embarrass you?"

"Stop twisting my words around! It's like you're deliberately misunderstanding me! Laurence and I came all the way over here for your little tea party, and you're behaving like a big baby! You're so ungrateful! I don't have to throw a dinner party for your illegitimate, orphan Annie granddaughter, you know!"

A. C. stared in horror at her sister. Regina seemed somewhat stunned by her own words. She swallowed hard and lowered her voice.

"I didn't mean … you have to admit, A. C., this is all rather shocking and bizarre."

She glanced around the room as if the furniture or wallpaper might inspire a way to explain what she meant.

"I think," A. C. began, having regained her composure enough to speak without clenching her teeth, "what I find most shocking and bizarre is that I am a reasonably intelligent woman in my sixties, and this is the first time in my life I am admitting to myself that my sister is, always has been, and always will be, a phony, hateful wretch of a person who will never truly care about anything other than what the Joneses think!"

"How dare you speak to me like that!" Regina cried. "How *dare* you! After all I've done for you! You have no clue how hard I've worked to keep an ounce of dignity associated with our family name! I can't hide how or why Arnold died, but at least I've kept people from giving you hell about it! And now this: a long lost child who stepped out of the pages of *Oliver Twist*. Wonderful. And worst of all, you're happy about it! You didn't have to take her in! You could have just established a trust fund and let it be! Don't you know how ashamed Mother and Daddy would be over this, A. C.? Maybe I should just let everyone say and do what they will, if this is the thanks I get!"

A. C. could not stop the tears that began to roll down her cheeks, but she did wipe them away. She thought of Arnold and choked back a sob.

"I may not 'have a clue,' as you so graciously phrased it, about playing the pathetic, juvenile games you and your country club cronies play. But I do know that you have a knack, Regina, a real talent, for fabricating elaborate, expensive disguises to conceal real life issues, the same issues that you and many of your so-called friends have experienced, with your lives like houses made of cards!"

The tears, hot and angry, would not stop coming. She wiped them away with the back of one hand, but other than that, she did her best to keep her hands pinned to her sides. She found that they had transformed into claws as Regina spoke. A. C. was suddenly relieved that it was Regina who had the dessert knife nearby and not herself. She wanted desperately to lash out physically. The fury that burned in her chest was nearly more than she could bear.

Regina's face burned bright red.

"Who are you to throw around a word like 'pathetic'? You've been a hermit and a doddering old crackpot since Cal passed away! Now suddenly you have a playmate, some strange kid your drug-addled son fathered. Your life is a trashy talk show! I don't care what you think you know and don't know; there is no way Mother and Daddy would not be ashamed of this!" she charged, her voice filling the large room.

"No one can speak for the dead, it's true. But they were kind, fair people, your parents," Laurence's quiet voice came from the doorway across the room, startling both women. He slowly made his way toward them. "Hugh and Leslie Carrington had good hearts, and neither was overly concerned with money or status. I don't know what they would say about any of our lives," he continued, "but I, Regina, your husband of thirty-five years and the father of your child, *I* am deeply and unequivocally ashamed of *you*. I suspect that your parents, God rest their souls, would feel the same way about the way you've been treating your sister and those she loves."

He stood before her, tall and upright, his shoulders squared in determination and his eyes boring into Regina's eyes. Regina blinked away her tears, her face registering shock. Laurence's gaze was unwavering, both in its persistence and anger. Regina wiped her face savagely with one hand, smearing her makeup.

"Who are you to speak for my parents?" she demanded of Laurence. "You hardly knew them!"

"I think he's absolutely right, and what's more, I think you know it," came Carmen's voice from behind A. C.

Once again, A. C. and Regina were shaken. All eyes turned to Carmen. She put one arm around A. C.'s shoulders. "I asked Carrington to wait in her room," she said in a reassuring tone to her friend. A. C. gave Carmen a grateful hug.

"I am sick of you interfering with my family!" Regina snarled at Carmen. "Ever since you wormed your way into my sister's life, you've been nothing but a nuisance! Just because you don't have a life of your own, that doesn't give you the right to live vicariously through our lives!"

Carmen couldn't help it; she snorted. "I hardly think, Regina, that your sister would have allowed me to be a part of her life for the past forty-some, nearly fifty years if she didn't want me to be."

There was so much more she would have said if it was just she and Regina in the room. How she longed say that Regina had no clue what being a sister or a friend really meant. She would have relished informing Regina, in no uncertain terms, that taste and dignity could not be purchased in an exclusive boutique. Love and loyalty were not handed out at five-star spas like Egyptian cotton towels. But she would not say anything else that would bring more grief to her dearest friend. She placed one hand on A. C.'s back.

Carmen and Regina glared at one another. Finally, A. C. spoke.

"Laurence, I apologize for how this afternoon has gone. I appreciate that you came here to meet my granddaughter and have lunch with us. I think, though, that it would be best for everyone if you and Regina left." Her voice was quiet but firm.

"Don't think for one damned second, A. C., that if you kick me out of this house, I will ever throw a party for you or for Carrington!" Regina huffed, nostrils flaring wildly.

"And don't think that I will ever again even consider attending one of your pretentious little name-dropping gossip orgies," A. C. told her, voice still level.

Regina looked stricken. Laurence silently cheered. *You tell her, A. C.!* He thought.

"I understand completely," Laurence said to A. C. in an apologetic tone. "It's time to leave," he told Regina in a much cooler voice.

Regina was not ready to leave. "What is this?" she demanded. "Have you all lost your minds? How has my life become an episode of a soap opera all of a sudden? How dare all of you gang up on me like this! What have I ever done to be treated this way? I've done nothing but work my fingers to the bone planning the most elegant party for you, A. C., and you think you can speak to me as if, as if …" she began to sputter. "As if I'm a cheap lowlife like your son was and your granddaughter is!"

Carmen stepped in between the sisters just in time. A. C. swung hard, her hand slicing the space just in front of Regina's reddened face.

"Get out! Get out of my house! Get out of my life! And stay the hell out of both!" A. C. spat, struggling behind Carmen. "It seems to me, *sister*," she sneered, "this is the second time in the past few months that I've told you to butt out, and this time, you had better damn well heed my words. I wouldn't subject

Carrington to one more moment of your company if my life depended on it!"

Laurence followed Carmen's lead and moved so he was just in front of Regina. He felt strangely elated, and he wondered if Carmen wasn't there, would he have bothered to get in between Regina and A. C.? He honestly wasn't sure. He would have loved to see Regina receive a much deserved wallop across the face. He shook his head, forcing himself to focus on what needed to be done. Carmen was depending on his help.

Laurence took a firm grip on his wife's arm and steered her toward the kitchen door.

"We're leaving," he informed her flatly. "Now. We're grabbing our things and we're leaving. Let's not let this get any uglier than it already is. If you have a sliver of self-respect left in you, Regina, then you will come home with me. Now," he said again, in a loud voice when Regina tried to pull away from his grip.

He sighed with relief when they made it through both the kitchen and living room without running across Carrington. *Smart kid,* he thought ruefully. He was also relieved that Carmen and A. C. did not attempt to follow them. The whole while he grabbed his things and Regina's, Regina was weeping and muttering hysterically about how ungrateful everyone was and how terribly ashamed she was of them all. Laurence rolled his eyes more than once and grabbed her arm again, basically dragging her to the doorway. He glanced back, hoping to see Carmen's face, but she must have remained in the dining room with A. C. *Of course,* he thought. *She's a good friend. A better one than I have ever known or been.*

Laurence sighed and half walked, half carried Regina to their car. She had mostly given up struggling but seemed unwilling to move much at all. He glanced at her face once before depositing her in the car, but went out of his way not to look at her again during the trip home. She was a pathetic, sniveling mess with streaks of mascara tracking her face and a garish ring of lipstick that had worked its way around the outside of her lips. Laurence made no mention of the box of tissues in the glove compartment. She knew they were there, he reasoned. He couldn't bring himself to speak to her. He was relieved when he heard the click of the gold pill box she carried around in her purse. *Take a damn Valium,* he thought. *Take a hundred of them.* Save for Regina's occasional half coherent, angry utterance, they rode in silence back to their house.

Chapter Forty-two

As soon as the lunch dishes were stacked neatly on the counter, Carmen suggested, in a kind but firm tone, that Carrington should wait in her bedroom. She knew what was coming. The less Carrington heard out of Regina's hateful mouth, the better.

Of course, Carrington hadn't stayed away long. It wasn't that she was eager to disobey anyone, certainly not someone she admired and respected like Carmen. But how could she resist? The morbid fascination and curiosity were too much to keep her in her room. The inevitable explosion began building the moment Regina and Laurence arrived; Carrington had sensed it immediately. She knew her very existence played a huge part in it, and it was clear that Carmen's presence that afternoon was also a major source of anger and frustration to Regina. Worse, Laurence seemed genuinely happy to see Carmen.

She stayed in her room only for a minute or so. It took some deep breathing, but Carrington finally worked up the nerve to tiptoe down the stairs and make her way into the kitchen. She could hear their voices, shrill and angry, from behind the dining room door. The first thing she heard clearly was Regina accusing Carmen of interfering in their lives. She had the distinct impression that she'd missed most of the fight. Maybe that was for the best. It was clear from the near hysterical anger in her grandmother's voice that Regina must have said some truly awful things. Then she heard Regina say that Arnold and Carrington were cheap lowlifes. Her mouth fell open in pained shock, and tears filled her eyes. She felt for a moment like she was back in the duplex, facing a drunk and furious Joan, but Regina's words stung more than anything Joan could have said to her.

Regina's outburst was followed by the sounds of a scuffle. Carrington wondered briefly if she should call the police. The voices from the dining room were choked with emotion. Nothing much of what they said was clear after that. Carrington was crying too hard to focus on what was happening in the next room. She darted out of the kitchen when she heard Laurence announce that he and Regina were leaving. She rushed through the kitchen's main doorway and managed to make it halfway up the stairs and out of sight before they were in the living room.

Carrington locked herself in a bathroom and glared at her reflection in the mirror while tears streamed down her face. *It's my fault; it's all my fault! If it wasn't for me, Gran could be close with her sister. I'm a cheap lowlife just like Regina said.* In the back of Carrington's mind, there was a small voice that told her this wasn't true. Someone as kindhearted and unpretentious as A. C. could never be close with Regina. This was obvious from everything Carrington had seen and heard during the time she'd been living with her grandmother.

She managed to calm herself somewhat, and after she was certain that Laurence and Regina were gone, Carrington joined her grandmother and Carmen in the dining room. They wept together for a few moments, the way they had when the blood tests confirmed that A. C. and Carrington were related, but this time their tears were not joyful or relieved.

A. C. apologized profusely to her granddaughter for Regina's behavior. Carrington and Carmen both insisted it wasn't A. C.'s fault. Together, the three cleaned up the remnants of the afternoon.

Chapter Forty-three

I'm dying, she thought. *I'm gonna die soon.* The words lingered in her thoughts each and every day since being released from the hospital. They floated in her mind, bobbing along and clinking together like the ice cubes that swirled around in her drink. Joan flicked ashes from her cigarette and set it down to take a sip from the rum and Coke that hadn't left her side all day. She polished off the drink in one long gulp and reached for the pitcher of rum. Since being discharged from the hospital, she had been watering down her drinks. There were two large plastic pitchers in her refrigerator. She dumped her rum in one, her gin in the other, and filled the empty bottles with water that she added to the pitchers. Joan hated the weakened drinks but figured they would give her a little more time to carry out her plans.

Even as she was in her hospital bed, she knew she couldn't just wait around for the inevitable the way her dad had. *If I have to die, I'm going to die when I say so, God damn it,* she thought. She raised her drink in a silent toast to her father and took a healthy gulp. *Severe hemorrhaging, my hide!* she thought, draining the glass. *That fool doctor doesn't know a thing.* Sure, she'd had some bleeding and her back and sides were now in constant pain, but she was still alive. She would decide when it was time to go. That power was in her hands.

The gun wasn't hard to find. It was where it had been for years, in the bottom of Douglas Coyle's foot locker. She only had to rummage for a few seconds before her hand brushed against the cool steel. It was beneath a pile of her dad's shirts. Joan set the gun gently beside her. She lifted one of the faded shirts from the foot locker and held it to her face, inhaling as deeply as she could. Just one more time, Joan desperately wanted a scent of her father, but only smelled dust and the rotting, wooden interior of the old locker. She sighed in defeat and tossed the tattered shirt aside. After a few more moments of rifling around in the locker and pulling out old shoes and yellowed newspapers, Joan finally located the box of bullets.

She snapped open the chamber and loaded the bullets the way her father had shown her decades before. One night, he'd been in a downright cheerful mood, and before he passed out, he taught his daughter to load a gun. Together, they shot at beer cans in the backyard. It was the best time Joan could remember having with her father. Her eyes watered at the memory of it.

"I'll be seeing you soon, Dad," she whispered.

Everything was set. Gary was on his way. Missy would be fine; she'd have someone there for her. *I don't need to worry about Carrie,* Joan thought with a flare of contempt.

She glanced at the clock next to her bed. It was nearly three o'clock in the afternoon. Gary was supposed to arrive sometime after three. It was a four-hour drive, he said, as long as he didn't run into traffic. He had no idea what Joan had in mind. He only knew that for the first time since he'd left, she was allowing him to see Missy. He didn't know he'd be taking his daughter home with him for good.

Joan thought of Missy and felt a twinge of guilt. She had given Missy a wad of money to go to the mall for the afternoon, and she'd asked her daughter to bring home a pizza for dinner. She rarely asked anything of Missy. The girl had been surprised and happily agreed to bring home dinner when she saw the cash in her mother's hand. She knew that giving Missy a task, especially if a nice profit was involved, would ensure that she would actually do what Joan wanted her to do. Tonight was important. She could not risk Missy deciding to ride the bus around aimlessly or crashing at her friend Tanya's house for two nights in a row.

Joan told Missy she was inviting Abel over for the night. She'd hinted that Abel wanted to talk to them both about something important. No doubt, Missy thought Abel was going to propose to her mother or Joan and Abel would at least announce they were moving in together. The truth was that Joan hadn't seen Abel since she left the hospital. He'd called her twice, and she avoided him both times. He had not called back again, and she found she really didn't care much. She knew, though, that of all her boyfriends throughout the years, Missy had liked Abel best. Perhaps it was more realistic to say that she minded him the least. All of that no longer mattered, though.

She'd lied to Gary, as well. She told him she thought it would be best if he met them at the mall, a public, neutral space where hopefully they would all feel more at ease. Gary believed that Joan would be there with Missy and they would all share a meal together in the food court. It was true; he would meet Missy at the mall, though Missy had no idea about it. Neither of them knew that as they became reacquainted after some ten years, Joan would be ending her life. She supposed that eventually Gary would take Missy home, and she hoped he would have the sense to go in the house by himself. Surely, he'd be bright enough to piece together that something was wrong when he learned that Joan wasn't at the mall. For all she knew, they could be meeting this very minute, each realizing that Joan had misled them. She would have to be quick.

Joan felt guilty, not just for lying to her youngest daughter, but also because she knew the shock her death would cause. It was a lot for a girl to handle, she knew from experience. At least she'd been an adult when her own father died—a young adult, but an adult nonetheless. Missy had Gary, though. That's what made this okay. She didn't need Joan anymore. Even if Joan let nature take its course, she would probably never live to see Missy graduate from high school. At least she could go out with some dignity and spare Missy the hell that she had experienced seeing her father decay and shut down before her eyes. *I'm doin' her a favor,* Joan thought. *She'll know that when she's grown.*

Joan took the loaded gun back to her bed. She frowned at the watered-down rum. *What the hell does it matter at this point?* she thought. She rolled her aching body out of bed once more and searched her dresser drawers with shaking hands until she found two bottles: one of gin, which contained perhaps a third of its original contents, and one of vodka, which held less than that. Joan drained the vodka bottle and tossed it aside, taking the gin with her to bed.

She eased into the pile of musty pillows on her bed, laying the bottle of gin next to the gun. From beneath one of the pillows, she pulled out the old envelope of photographs. There they were, Joan's parents, so young and happy. What had they been like as a couple? How different would things have been if Maria had not died before Joan had a chance to know her? She stared hard at their fresh, smiling faces. For a moment, Missy's face flickered over the image of Maria's face. It was true; Missy did resemble her grandmother.

"She's a good kid, Mom," Joan whispered to the picture of her mother. "She's pretty like you were. And she's tough as nails. I wish she coulda known you. I wish … I wish I coulda known you." Joan began to cry, and nothing, not a healthy swig from the bottle of gin and not a stream of venomous curse words directed at her own crying, could stop the flow of tears. She curled into a fetal position in the center of her bed, crying even harder than she had cried in the hospital.

Chapter Forty-four

Missy was reluctant to go. Normally, she would have jumped at the opportunity to bum around the mall with a few bucks in her pocket. Something in her mother's face, her eyes especially, made her linger. Joan looked unwell. Her face was strangely yellow, even with plenty of makeup, and her eyes were sunken in like those of a much older woman. Missy blamed Carrington. *How could she hurt Mom like this?* Missy wondered as she took the bills from her mother's trembling fingers. *I hate her. I will never forgive her. Never.* She stuffed the money in her pocket. Joan had been much more generous with money ever since Carrington left.

"Go on, Missy. Go get a pizza. Keep the change." Joan flashed a rare smile at her youngest daughter. "Get goin', kid," she urged when Missy hesitated. "Bring back the pizza in a couple hours, after me an' Abel have a chance to talk. Okay?"

Despite the strange color of her skin and the deep lines in her face, her green eyes burned as intensely as ever into Missy's eyes. Missy felt the familiar rush of fear she associated with her mother.

"Okay," she agreed, turning to leave. "Bye, Mom," she called over her shoulder.

At the mall, Missy was restless. Nothing appealed to her. She bought a pair of earrings and a tube of glittery lip gloss, but that didn't help. Usually, shopping improved her mood, but not this time. She paused to consider the display of mini dresses in a department store window.

"You know your mom isn't gonna let you out of the house in that," came a teasing voice from behind her.

Missy whirled around, already blushing and grinning.

"As if I care what my mom says!" she taunted back, smiling broadly at Alex Guzman.

"What are you …" they began to ask at the same time. They both laughed.

"You first," Alex said, still grinning.

Missy shrugged, wondering if her hair looked cute. She'd not used the hair dryer that morning and now regretted it.

"Just hangin' out," she said.

"Are you here with anybody?" Alex asked.

"Nope. You?"

"My brother and his friend Brian are at RadioShack. Michael got his driver's license yesterday, and Mom and Dad let him take the car out. I told them I'd go with to make sure he doesn't do anything stupid."

Alex and Missy laughed together. God, he was handsome! His thick, dark hair curled naturally at the tips, and his face was so smooth. Missy wondered what it would be like to kiss his full lips. She had to look away for a moment, afraid he would know what was on her mind.

"Michael wants to take the car out on the highway; then I think we'll grab some Taco Bell. You wanna come?" Alex sounded hopeful.

Missy snapped her gaze back to Alex's face. Was he asking her out on a date? She guessed it was kind of a date, even though two other people would be around. She felt more nervous than ever and wished Tanya was going, too. She'd never talked much to Michael Guzman. What if he didn't want a twelve-year-old tagging along with them?

"Are you sure your brother and his friend won't mind?" she asked.

"Nah, it's cool," Alex reassured her.

Missy grinned at Alex and began to relax a little. Over Alex's shoulder, she noticed a man lingering a few feet behind them. He made eye contact with her and didn't look away. Missy became annoyed and uneasy. Why was this creepy guy staring at her? The man looked nervous.

Alex sensed that he no longer had Missy's complete attention.

"What's wrong?" he asked. "What is it?"

"That guy over there," Missy whispered. "He's staring at us."

She glanced toward the strange man, alarmed and angry to see that he was approaching them.

Alex tensed up, too. It was clear to Missy that Alex didn't know the man either. She was suddenly filled with fiery indignation. Who the hell did this weirdo think he was? They weren't doing anything wrong! She cocked her chin up and glared at the stranger. He had a jittery smile on his face. There was something familiar about him. He seemed kind of old … not really old like some of her teachers, but at least as old as her mother.

"Melissa?" the man asked timidly.

Missy became frightened. Alex seemed fearful, as well. How could this guy know her name? Was he one of her mom's old boyfriends? Missy had the sensation that she'd seen him recently. There was something in his face, something pleading and hopeful, that filled her both with sadness and rage. She had a strong urge to and run away from both Alex and the strange man.

Instead, she stared him squarely in his dark eyes.

"Yeah?" she asked, trying to sound as tough as possible.

"It's me, Melissa," the man said. "I'm Gary Ruiz. I'm, well … I'm your dad."

Alex stared open-mouthed at the man. Missy swallowed hard and blinked several times. The color drained from her face.

"I think I should go. Michael's waiting for me." Alex was the first to speak.

"Alex, wait," Missy said. "I want to go with you guys."

She was suddenly terrified of being left alone with this stranger who claimed to be her father.

"Melissa, I need to speak with you," the man said. "Can we sit down and talk? Where is your mother?"

"I really have to go now," Alex insisted, looking every bit as distressed as Missy felt.

Missy watched miserably as he retreated and blended into the mall crowd. He looked back at her only once, a combination of curiosity and alarm on his face. *Oh, God,* Missy thought. *He's going to tell Tanya and Efren and everybody about this!*

She turned to face the stranger who claimed to be her father, confusion and anger twisting her features.

"Melissa, where is your mother?" the man asked again.

"Who *are* you?" Missy snapped. "How can you just come up to me and say you're my dad? Why should I believe you? I don't know you! I don't know you at all!"

Her voice trembled and she hated herself for it.

She recognized him. Yes, the man who stood before her was the same man in the picture he'd sent to her recently. He was at least a decade older than he'd been in the picture, and his tired face seemed to reflect every single moment that had passed. She could barely believe that, if she wanted to, she could reach out and touch the man who apparently was her father. She'd imagined this moment so many times in her life. None of the scenarios she envisioned were at all like what was happening.

"Honey, please," Gary tried to sound calm and reassuring. "I know how strange and frightening this must be for you. It's hard for me, too. There's so much I want to say to both you and your mother. Should we go find her? Do you think she's waiting for us in the food court?"

He glanced around anxiously.

"Mom's not here," Missy stated flatly. "Why would she be? I still don't get why you're here. Are you like, some kind of stalker or something?"

Gary ignored the stalker comment.

"What do you mean, your mother's not here? Did she drop you off? Is she coming back to pick you up in a little while? Didn't she tell you that we were all supposed to meet tonight to talk?"

His string of questions annoyed Missy. Was he lying? She started intently up at him.

"I don't believe you," she said, though it wasn't true.

She did believe him, but admitting that meant she would have to consider why her mother would lie to both of them and orchestrate their meeting at the mall.

"Melissa, can't we talk? Please? That's all I'm asking for, a few minutes of your time. We can talk here, out in the open. I'm not asking you to go anywhere with me. We can just find a bench and talk. Please," he said again.

She considered him through narrowed eyes. She hated the way her name sounded when he said it. And didn't he know that everyone called her Missy? She loathed that she had his dimples and his eyes.

She gave him a shrug. "Fine."

Gary seemed relieved and found a table in a deserted corner of the food court. After a moment's hesitation, Missy took a seat across from her father.

"So," he said, gazing at her with wet-looking eyes. "So here we are." Gary cleared his throat.

Missy said nothing but rolled her eyes. This guy seemed stupid. *What a dumb thing to say,* she thought. *I could have been hanging out with Alex.* She sighed.

"Is that kid your boyfriend?" Gary asked, as if reading her mind.

He jerked his head toward the direction Alex had walked.

Startled and embarrassed, Missy looked away.

"No," she finally answered. "What do you care?"

Gary winced.

"I care, Melissa. I care very much. He seems a little … old for you."

Missy glared at him.

"I said he's *not* my boyfriend! Not that it's any of your business. And stop calling me Melissa! Everyone calls me Missy."

"Okay, then, Missy," he said, nodding. "I'll try to remember that."

He attempted a smile.

"What are you doing here?" Missy demanded, relieved to ask a question of her own.

"I came here to meet with you and your mother," Gary answered simply. "Where is your mother?" he asked again.

"She's at home," Missy told him as if it was the most obvious answer in the world. "And I still don't see why she would tell you to meet us here."

She folded her arms across her chest and stared at him defiantly.

"Are you sure she's at home?"

She let out an exasperated sigh. Was this man slow?

"Yes, I'm sure. God!"

He considered her with a weary gaze.

"You hungry?" he asked.

Missy hated to admit it, but she was. "I guess," she answered with a shrug.

"Let's grab a bite then," Gary said, trying to sound cheerful. "You like pizza?"

Missy remembered that Joan had requested a pizza.

"Mom wants me to bring a pizza home," she said quietly, more to herself than to Gary.

The worried look returned to his face.

"I think we should call her, at least."

Missy met his eyes. "Okay," she agreed.

Her stomach began to churn. She watched his face closely while he dialed the number. He tried three times, his eyes more and more anxious with each call. He shook his head.

"There's no answer. I think maybe I should check on your mother."

"She probably just went out or something," Missy offered. "Her boyfriend was supposed to come over, anyway. Nothing's wrong." She tried to sound firm.

There was a small part of her that hoped the mention of Joan's boyfriend would hurt him. If he was bothered by it, it didn't show in his face. Missy sighed in defeat.

"Even so," Gary said, "it wouldn't hurt if we just went over there and made sure she's okay."

"I'm not going anywhere with you!" Missy snapped.

"Well, I'm not leaving you here by yourself." Gary was suddenly impatient. "But I need to find out what's going on with your mother. I think I should call the police and have them meet us at her house."

The police? Missy felt like she was going to be sick.

"This is stupid!" she huffed. "Mom's going to be so mad if you do that. She either went out or just doesn't want to answer the phone. I don't see why you're making such a big deal out of this."

Gary was already on the phone with the local police department. He outlined the situation to them.

"All right. Okay. Yes. Thank you," he said before hanging up. "They're sending an officer to meet us here and follow us to your mother's house," he told Missy grimly. "If you don't want to ride with me, you can ride with the police officer."

His words echoed in her head.

"Let's wait outside by the main entrance," Gary said before she had a chance to respond.

Missy followed him wordlessly. She didn't quite believe anything he'd said until she saw the black and white police cruiser arrive. When given her options by the stern young police officer, Missy chose to ride with Gary.

Chapter Forty-five

Bleary eyed from just waking, A. C. pulled on her robe and rushed to the phone. She was filled with panic and dread even before her hand found the receiver in the faintly lit room. Sunlight was just beginning to peep through the curtains. She knew it could not have been much later than six in the morning. She also knew that no one ever called with good or even random news very early in the day or very late at night.

"Hello?" she greeted, her voice full of caution and still groggy.

"Hello, Mrs. Browne?" a male voice answered back.

"Yes, this is Mrs. Browne. Who's calling? Do you know it's not even seven in the morning yet?"

She didn't mean to be so cranky, but she was suddenly overwhelmed by worry and fatigue. She sat down in the plush easy chair next to the phone table and wished she was still beneath the warm covers on her bed.

"Yes, ma'am, I know. I'm really sorry to disturb you so early. I've been waiting all evening to call you. It was so late last night when we finished dealing with the police and the hospital. And Melissa was so upset that I just couldn't stand to leave her alone until she went to sleep."

The night the policeman came to tell her about Arnold flashed in her mind.

"What is this all about? You haven't yet told me who you are," said A. C., her voice straining with anxiety.

"Of course, of course. I'm sorry for that," the man apologized. He sounded sad and tired. "My name is Gary Ruiz. I'm Melissa Coyle's father. Melissa is your granddaughter Carrie's little sister."

"Oh! Melissa! Of course. I haven't met her, Mr. Ruiz, but I know Carrington cares for her younger sister very much. What's happened? Is Melissa okay?"

"Please call me Gary," he said. "Melissa is … well, she's fine. I mean she's physically fine. Finally got her to go to sleep, poor thing. The thing is, Mrs. Browne … well …" he trailed off uncomfortably.

"Yes?" A. C. coaxed in a gentle tone. "And please, call me A. C."

"Joan, Melissa and Carrington's mother," he was careful to use Carrington's proper name, "she's gone. I mean, she passed away. It happened last night."

"My, God!" A. C. cried. "Was there an accident?"

Gary sighed heavily.

"No, I'm afraid not. It wasn't an accident. Joan had a gun, and she … she," his voice cracked, and A. C.'s chest began to ache as Gary swallowed a sob. "Joan took her own life. She shot herself in the house where she and Melissa lived."

A. C. closed her eyes.

"Did Melissa find her mother that way?" she asked in a near whisper.

"No, no. Thank God, she didn't," Gary answered quickly. "The police found her. You see, I met Melissa yesterday at the mall. I was under the impression that I'd be meeting Melissa and Joan there to talk. I haven't seen Melissa in years, and I want very much to be a part of her life." There was shame and anger in his voice. "I've been trying for some time to get in touch with Melissa, but Joan was resistant, to say the least. Anyway, I found Melissa at the mall alone. Well, unsupervised, at any rate; she was chatting with some kid." There was a note of disapproval in his tone. "Anyway," he cleared his throat and continued, "we talked, and it soon became clear that Joan had deceived us both. She instructed Melissa to go to the mall and bring home something for dinner. She told me that I'd be meeting the two of them at the mall for dinner. When I realized that she lied to us, I knew something was wrong. Believe me, Melissa wasn't thrilled to see me or speak with me right away, but I did learn that Joan hasn't been well for some time now. Melissa didn't know exactly what was wrong with her mother, but she knew that Joan was sick—I mean, physically."

A. C. felt nauseous.

"Was Joan terminally ill?" she asked.

"I think so, yes," Gary said. "She was an alcoholic. Looking back, I honestly believe she was an alcoholic even when we were a couple. I'm a recovering alcoholic." Once again, shame crept into his voice. "Even if she wasn't terminally ill, I imagine so many years of hard drinking had taken a toll on her state of mind."

"Yes, it's a terrible disease," A. C. said, Arnold's face clear in her mind. She wiped away a tear. "How strong you are, Mr.

Ruiz—excuse me, Gary—to be in recovery. That is no small feat. I'm glad Melissa has you."

Gary paused, embarrassed by her kindness.

"How … how is Carrington doing?" he asked.

"Carrington is wonderful," A. C. answered, her voice thick with affection. "She's the kindest, most intelligent child I have ever known. She's not awake yet. Oh, how I hate to break this news to her. She's been through so much. And I'm so sorry for what Melissa has gone through, as well."

"I know," Gary lamented. "I'm really sorry, myself. The girls have been through so much. I just wish I had been more involved in both their lives. I wish I could take back the last several years. Maybe none of this would have happened! Maybe Joan might have even … I don't know," he trailed off miserably.

"You mustn't think that way, Gary," A. C. said. "You could have stayed and watched Joan every minute of the day, but that doesn't mean she wouldn't have continued drinking or that she wouldn't have sought to end her own life. If someone had watched you every minute, do you think you would have done things differently? Would being watched or scolded by someone have had an impact on your impulses and your decisions?"

He was startled by the bluntness of the questions. Once again, there was a silence.

"I'm sorry," A. C. said. "Maybe I shouldn't have said that. I didn't mean to sound as if I was judging you, Gary. It's just, well, my late son, Arnold, was an alcoholic and a drug addict. His father and I spent years blaming ourselves and analyzing every moment of his childhood, trying to figure out what we did to cause or trigger his addiction. After Cal, Arnold's father, died, I continued to hate myself, thinking I'd somehow broken Arnold and made him into an alcoholic and drug addict. It simply isn't true. I think there must be some part of you that knows that. You've had your own journey to recovery. Oh, listen to me." A. C. laughed uncomfortably. "Rambling on and on. I'm sorry. I guess I'm still partially asleep and of course shocked to hear about Joan," she finished with a sigh.

"You're right," Gary said quietly. "It wouldn't have made any difference. Hell, having children to look after didn't make a difference to Joan. I just feel so guilty for leaving them. I hope I'm not too late to make a difference in Melissa's life. My God, this poor girl. In one single day, she's lost her mother and found her father. It would be too much for most adults to deal with, and she's only twelve years old. I don't know how we're going to do it, me and Melissa, but I'm going to do right by her, I swear."

The determination in his voice was genuine.

"I know you will," A. C. said gently. "And I think it would be great for both Carrington and Melissa if they had a relationship with one another. We can't force it, of course; we can't make them close, but we can encourage them, and we can make sure they always have a way to be in touch with one another. I know Carrington wants to be a part of Melissa's life, Gary. And I know she'll want to help Melissa deal with their mother's death. Please let me know how I can help. You can call me anytime, anytime at all."

"Thank you so much," Gary said. "I'm so grateful that Carrington is in good hands. She's a great kid, always has been. I agree with you; I hope the girls will always keep one another in mind, and I'll do what I can to help them stay in touch." He sighed heavily. "I should go. I want to check on Melissa. The hospital is keeping her overnight for observation. She became hysterical when she was told about her mother. The doctor said Melissa is slightly undernourished, but overall—I mean physically, at least—she's okay. I'm going to sit with her until she wakes up. I'll be in touch, Mrs. Browne—I mean, A. C."

"You're a good father, Gary," A. C. told him. "Please give Melissa our best wishes and let us know how she's doing."

Gary promised he would call again soon. They said goodbye, and A. C. hung up the phone. She heard the sound of running water upstairs. Carrington was awake. *Oh, Carrington,* she thought. Her vision blurred with tears and she wiped them away. *You're a survivor, sweetheart. And I will be with you every step of the way.*

Epilogue

I survived my first year of high school! Carrington scribbled in her journal. She made a mental note that there were only a few blank pages left. She was looking forward to using the pale blue, leather-bound journal Carmen had given her as a birthday gift.

I'm in the top 5 percent of my class. I feel sort of bad for writing that, like I'm being cocky, but Gran says I should be proud. She tells me she's proud of me all the time. I usually make a dumb joke about it, but I know she means it, and I love her so much for saying it. I can't take a break from studying, though. One of my goals this summer is to get my driver's permit. I can't believe I'm going to be behind the wheel soon! I don't think Gran can believe it, either. She jokes that an old woman is probably the best teacher for a teenage driver. I know Gran will be seventy in a few years, but I wouldn't guess that if I didn't know her. She's the most energetic person I know. She would put half the girls in my gym class to shame. I love that she's been getting out more. She says having me around makes her feel young again, but I think Carmen has a lot to do with it, too.

Carmen's the best! Carrington blushed at her unbridled joy but continued writing.

I hope I have a friend like Carmen one day. Really, if it wasn't for Carmen, I probably wouldn't be living with Gran right now. Maybe I would be, but it would have been so much harder. I might even have been sent to a foster home or something first. She is the most amazing woman I have ever met. Besides Gran, of course. Carrington smiled to herself.

She paused and the smile faded from her face.

Next week it will be a year since Joan's funeral. It wasn't much of a funeral. Gran, Carmen, and I were there. And Gary. Missy refused to go. Well, that's not entirely true. She waited in Gary's truck. She refused to actually go to the grave site. Joan was cremated, so it's not like Missy was afraid to see the body. The ashes were in a plain wooden box. The cemetery had their own minister, I guess for all the people who die without any arrangements already made. It was kind of weird. He said a couple of generic prayers and then he asked if anyone wanted to say anything, but none of us did. I didn't cry, not at the funeral. I did later, though. A lot. I wasn't crying because I was sad, though. Not really. I was mostly just angry. Then I felt numb for a couple months. Lately, whenever I think about Joan, I am angry again. I am more than angry; I am furious. I hate her for the way she treated me when I lived with her, and I hate her for dying the way she did. She never gave me a chance to ask her anything or tell her anything. I don't know what I would have said, but it's just not fair. And what about Melissa? She shut us both out. Margaret wants me to forgive Joan, she says for my own sake, but I'm not ready. Maybe someday. I'm not there yet, though. Carrington sighed heavily and turned the page.

Melissa's improving. Little by little, I guess. She's doing a lot better in school. Gary is so good to her, but I don't know if she realizes it yet. She went from having no rules at all to actually having structure. Of course, she hated his guts for like, the first three or four months she lived with him. She even ran away twice. Poor Gary was frantic. Both times, she went to her friend Tanya Guzman's house. And both times, thank God, Mr. and Mrs. Guzman called both Gary and Gran. Considering Gary's apartment is a few hours away, it was no small thing for him to come and get her. The man should be sainted!

It was only a couple months ago that Melissa and I finally spoke for the first time since Joan died. I couldn't believe it when she called. At first, I panicked. I thought maybe something bad happened. Why else would she call me? It was awkward, and I have no doubt that she probably called because both Gary and her therapist kept telling her to, but the point is that she called me. Neither of us really knew what to say. It wasn't a long talk. I think it took most of her courage just to dial, so I tried my best to keep the conversation going. I asked her about school and about the city where she and Gary live. I think she was relieved that I didn't bring up Joan. I was surprised when she told me she wanted to be called Melissa. I never thought she cared about her name. Maybe she didn't care before. Maybe it's too painful to be called by the name that Joan used to call her. I can't really do anything other than speculate. I sort of hope that at some point we'll talk about Joan and everything that happened. I wonder if Melissa has Joan's old pictures. I didn't take anything from the house after Joan died. Gary asked me if I wanted anything, but I was just too shocked to think about it. Gran says Gary packed up whatever seemed important and it's in storage. She says Gary is a wonderful person. I agree. The four of us are getting together for the Fourth of July weekend. We're meeting kind of halfway between where we live, at a Six Flags amusement park. This will be the first time I'll see Melissa and Gary since the funeral. I'm nervous and excited.

About a month ago we received an invitation for a big party that Gran's sister, Regina, is having. Gran was angry when she saw it. She actually said she'd rather be bound, gagged, and tossed into a bonfire than go to one of Regina's parties. Sometimes she talks about when they were kids, and it sounds like Regina has always been the same. Poor Gran. She says she'll never be close with her sister. They exchanged Christmas cards, but that's the only communication they've had since last year. I can't imagine two sisters being any different than Gran and Regina. Laurence seems like a nice man. Gran says he's changed a lot over the years. Regina has drained the life out of him, she says. I've still never met their daughter, Gloria. Carmen heard from some mutual acquaintances that Gloria has been in and out of drug rehab over the past few months and her father closed her art gallery. Gran says Gloria is a troubled young woman. She doesn't talk about any of them very much.

Tonight we're going to the tapas restaurant that opened last winter. I love that place! Gran says she wants to celebrate my successful freshman year in high school. I'm sure it doesn't hurt that she and the owner of the place, Mr. Garcia, flirt like crazy. She totally denies it, but it's obvious they like one another. I think he looks just like Rossano Brazzi. Gran says I'm being silly, but she blushed about four different shades of red when I said that he's really handsome and nice. We're flying out to see Carmen in a couple of weeks. I can't wait until we're all together so we can both tease Gran about Mr. Garcia.

Well, I guess I'll close for now and get ready for our dinner out. I wonder if I can get Gran to wear that sundress I convinced her to buy a few weeks ago. No matter what she wears, she'll look great. She always does.

I used to dread the end of the school year, but this year, I'm so excited for the summer to begin.

Printed in the United States
138414LV00001B/1/P

9 781440 123139

STRENGTH *from inspiring* STORIES

Confrontation at Chicago State
The Day Granddad Died
The American Major and the Iraqi Colonel
A Daughter's Last Request
Five Veterans Meet in Heaven

David Leatherberry

Stories that reveal truth need to be passed on to the next generation. That is why David's narratives will strengthen the faith of my seven wonderful children. I am convinced the stories can do the same for your children.

Strength from Inspiring Stories has deepened my desire to impact the lives of others for all eternity.

Darryl Morton, truck driver, Strafford, Missouri

I have known David for 52 years since the time he was a seminarian. His consistent walk with the Lord Jesus Christ has always inspired my own walk with God. I was aware of some of the events in the stories as they were taking place. The stories David has skillfully penned will strengthen you as they have me.

Jack Smith, retired US Postal employee, Rockford, Illinois

I have known David and Julie since 1984 and have heard him tell many of these stories in person. David is a gifted descriptive writer whose word pictures draw the reader right into each story where you feel every emotion embodied in the characters. These stories touch the depth of the heart cry of the human spirit.

Donna Krstulovich, Ph. D., Intercultural Studies

We first met David at Intervarsity Christian Fellowship while attending Evangel College (now Evangel University). Through the years we have been inspired by David and his wife Julie's unwavering commitment to the Lord Jesus Christ and to their calling to minister, with great love, both at home and abroad.

Strength from Inspiring Stories reflects that commitment and love. The individuals in this wonderful collection, though facing painful difficulties, are led to experience true joy and hope. These compelling stories will touch your heart.

Jim and Gwen Davidson, served more than 20 years as school teachers, reside in Dallas, Texas

David and I have been the closest of friends since he was nine and I was twelve. His true life stories and created stories reflect a lifetime of rich experiences which flow out of his in-depth relationships with people and his close walk with God. You will be fascinated as you see the unseen hand of God orchestrating circumstances and events due to His love. These inspiring stories will enrich your own life.

Dr. Noel Caldwell, served as Chairman of Engineering and Technology, Midlands Technical College, Colombia, S.C.

As a mere ten-year-old boy, I met David when he visited my church. Coming in contact with David's real and enduring relationship with a loving God led me to desire the same, even now as a young man. When you read these pages of David's life and his heart, you'll gain entrance to a beloved friendship of man and God that will touch your soul and inspire you in your own walk with God.

Levi DeVries, student, University of Nebraska, Omaha

These stories beautifully demonstrate that you are never too young to learn or never too old to believe. When honest seekers read these stories, they may be surprised to discover answers to some of their own thoughtful questions.

David and I graduated together in 1960 from Howland High School. Our warm friendship continues to the present.

Ronald Belak, served for 37 years as a high school math teacher, resides in Howland, Ohio

David's stories will inspire you to live for God and share the hope we have in Christ. Life with Christ is meaningful and worth it all.

Elish Tram, administrative assistant to AGWM Regional Director for Asia Pacific, Springfield, Missouri

STRENGTH
from
INSPIRING STORIES

David Leatherberry

ENHEARTEN BOOKS

Strength from Inspiring Stories
By David Leatherberry

Edited by Carol Nichols

Printed in the United States of America
ISBN: 978-1-880689-38-7

Published by Enhearten Books, Springfield, Missouri

Cover Design and Interior Layout by Jimmie Frantz

Dedicated
to
Violette and Ray Miller

My sister Violette and her husband Ray have been great anchors in my life. For 25 years they cared for my mother so I could serve overseas. Their faith and fervent prayer life have always inspired me. Violette served as a faithful elementary school teacher who went early every morning to pray over the desk of each student before the students arrived. Ray faithfully served 19 years as a highly respected chaplain for the San Bernardino Police Department.

Acknowledgements

I learned a long time ago that no man is an island and what he may accomplish by the grace of God is often due to the assistance of others whom the Lord sent to help or to encourage.

My heart is full of gratitude for the following persons:

Carol Nichols, who patiently worked with me as she skillfully edited one story at a time. Her insights brought the book to a higher level.

Rollene Storms, who meticulously proofread the manuscript while at the same time making valuable suggestions that greatly improved the book.

Jeannie Royer, a proofreader who has a keen eye like an eagle. She caught the little errors that most readers would not notice.

James Carlton, my wonderful neighbor, who is a gifted artist. His sketches truly enhanced the book.

Jimmie Frantz, who beautifully designed the cover and did the interior layout of the book.

H. A. Baker, my great uncle, who was an incredible pioneer missionary to China 1919-50, especially to the Kado people in the Yunnan Province of southwest China. He was a prolific writer. His life has always been a great example for my life. His writings have inspired me to write for the benefit of others.

Most of all, I am indebted to my wife Julie, the love and joy of my life, who patiently walked with me through the many drafts of the manuscript giving very valuable advice. I will love her forever.

INTRODUCTION

On life's journey we face unexpected challenges. At such times a word of encouragement can strengthen us. When I've had my moments of discouragement, God has often placed the right book in my hands at just the right time. I am grateful to the writers who took time to pen their stories. The purpose of the short stories I have written is to strengthen you on your life's journey.

Eleven of these stories are true and drawn from my life. Nine are created from my heart based on what others have shared with me from their experiences, as well as my own experiences and observations. With Julie, my wife of fifty-five years, I have had the privilege of living among many people in different lands and cultures. It was a great joy to live among the Afghans, to teach in colleges throughout Eastern Europe, and to minister in Russia to the veterans of the Soviet/Afghan War. Six of the stories are in settings that reflect the Russian culture.

It is my dream when you and I reach home at the end of our life's journeys, I will have the honor of meeting you. Until then, may these narratives I have penned strengthen you on your way.

David Leatherberry

Contents

An Encouraging Message

TRUE STORIES FROM MY LIFE

THE LITTLE BOY AND HIS GIFT

Autumn brought great excitement as I entered the first grade in Bristolville, Ohio. When the big yellow bus stopped at our house that first day, its flashing lights seemed to blink, *Hurry ... hurry*. After I said goodbye to my two-year-old sister, Violette, my older sister, Eloise, took my hand and helped me cross the road. We made our way around the bus's shiny front bumper and up the big stairs. Walking down the black rubber aisle, we sat down on one of the smooth seats. I tightly held the new treasures I had brought with me for my first day of school. I was proud of my new lunch box. It was decorated with a cowboy picture. I had a brand-new pencil and an orange box of crayons.

I wiggled to sit up as tall as possible so I could see out the window. After the bus driver closed the doors, the bus began to move. *At last*, I thought, *I'm going to school.*

The days passed quickly. Soon the falling snow of winter replaced the beautiful falling leaves of autumn. Coloring pictures for my mom and learning the ABC's competed with snowball fights for excitement that year.

Almost before I knew what was happening, the aroma of fresh-baked cookies and the sound of carols filled our home, announcing Christmas was fast approaching. Childish anticipation over the soon-to-be received presents mounted with each passing day.

What will I get this year? I wondered as I looked at the growing mound of brightly wrapped gifts under the tall, beautifully decorated tree.

Though it seemed as if Christmas morning would never arrive, it finally did. Eloise, Violette, and I jumped out of bed and raced for the gifts. I soon had each one that was marked "Davey" in front of me. Pushing aside the smaller packages, I unwrapped the biggest one first. It was the most beautiful toy car I had ever seen—a shiny white convertible with real mirrors, white sidewall tires, and a red interior. When I'd spin the wheels and let it go, it would race across the floor with the sound of a smooth whir-r-r. Though I liked my other gifts, none compared with my new car.

On the first day back in school following our Christmas vacation, my teacher, Mrs. Brown, asked us to tell what we had received for Christmas. Immediately I raised my hand as high as I could. I wanted to tell about all the wonderful gifts I had received, but I especially wanted to talk about my car. However, Mrs. Brown decided to go around the room row by row so I had to wait my turn.

In the first row next to the window, about the fourth seat back, sat a boy named Albert. When it was his turn, Mrs. Brown said, "Albert, what did you receive for Christmas?" When Albert didn't say anything, Mrs. Brown asked him again.

Finally, holding up a single row, 10-cent box of crayons, he haltingly answered, "This box of crayons."

"And what else did you get for Christmas?" Mrs. Brown asked.

"That's all," Albert said. His face turned red.

I thought about the many toys I had received and the great times I had had playing with them. Thinking about Albert's single gift, I lost my enthusiasm to talk about all the things I had received. In fact, I was relieved when my turn was over.

Throughout the day all I could think about was Albert. He usually came to school in the same shabby clothes that always needed to be washed and pressed. He had one droopy eyelid, and often his face needed washing. I particularly noticed his dirty ears because my mother always checked mine to be sure they were clean. *His mother must not check his,* I often thought. Albert wasn't as smart as most of the kids in our class, so the other children would play tricks on him and make fun of him.

That night, after kneeling by my bed and saying my prayers with my mom, I snuggled down in the warm covers but I couldn't sleep. Once again I recalled Albert's unsmiling face and the box of crayons. I began talking to Jesus, "Jesus, what about Albert? He doesn't have much. Jesus, what are You going to do about Albert?"

A reply quickly came to my mind: *David, what are you going to do about Albert?*

Me? What can I do? I thought. Then an idea suddenly sprang into my mind. I knew what I could do; I could give Albert one of my toys. That would make Jesus and Albert both happy.

I reviewed my new toys one by one, finally selecting a small plastic cowboy mounted on a horse. "Jesus," I said, "I'm going to give Albert one of my cowboy toys."

As I waited under the covers for a commendation, there was nothing but silence. Finally a question came.

Why not give your best toy?

My very best? I knew exactly which one He was referring to—my super-duper, white convertible.

How can I part with that? I thought. I loved playing with that car. It was my dream car and I handled it with special care. Then I considered all I had and all Albert did not have. I could imagine how excited he would be to have such a car. Finally I said, "Okay, Jesus, I'll give my best toy to Albert."

I knew I'd better talk with my mother about my decision since I would need her permission to give it away, so I slipped out of bed and quietly walked into the living room. My mother was sitting in a big overstuffed chair. As I entered the room, she looked up, surprised to see me.

"Mommy," I said, "I have been talking with Jesus and He wants me to give my best toy to Albert." Then I told my mother about Albert and what had happened that day at school. When I finished, Mother said, "You know, Davey, if you give your best toy to Albert, a week or two from now you cannot ask for it back and we can't replace it. So, Davey, go back and talk with Jesus again and make sure this is what He is saying to you."

"Okay, Mom," I said. I went back into my room, pulled the covers up over me, kept my eyes wide open, and said, "Jesus, Mom said I should talk with You again about Albert and make sure You said I should give my best toy to him."

You should, came the answer.

"Thanks!" I told Him, and I jumped out of bed and ran out to the living room.

"Mom," I said, "I'm sure Jesus wants me to give it. Please can I give my car to Albert?"

Mom replied, "Sure, Son, you can. I'll help you get it ready in the morning."

My mother had dedicated me to God even before I was born, and she prayed for me continually. If she was ever surprised by what I said about my conversations with God, she wisely kept her thoughts to herself. This allowed me to develop a natural and close relationship with God.

The next morning I awoke full of anticipation. Though giving away my car pained me somewhat, thinking about how I would surprise Albert brought excitement to my heart. Mom found a green cardboard tomato box with a handle in the middle, and my car fit into it perfectly.

On the way to school I thought about how and when I would give the car to Albert. I decided it would be best to wait until right before school was out that day. I knew Albert could easily be tricked, and I was concerned that someone would cheat him out of the car if I gave it to him any earlier. It would be hard to wait all day, but on the other hand I could still look at it and play with it at recess times. Throughout the day, everyone admired my shiny car.

The bell that rang five minutes before the dismissal bell warned us it was time to get our coats and line up. I picked up my box and took one long, last look at my beautiful car. Then I walked over to Albert.

"Albert," I said, "I have a gift for you. I want you to have my car."

Albert looked at me in disbelief.

"Here, please take it. It's yours," I said, trying to hand it to him. Still he would not reach out his hand to take it. Instead he backed away and turned sideways, eyeing the car.

"It's really yours, Albert," I said again. I wanted him to know I wasn't pulling a mean trick on him. Carefully he reached for the handle, half expecting me to jerk it back. When he had it in both hands, he didn't know what to say, but a beautiful grin broke across his face.

The children who were nearby heard me and began talking with each other.

"David's giving his car to Albert," one said. They gathered around, looking at the shiny car in Albert's hands.

Pretty, well-dressed Karen said, "David, why didn't you give me your car?"

Why does she, who has so much, want Albert's gift?" I thought. Her attitude upset me.

Frightened that someone might try to take the car from him, I stood close to Albert.

When the teacher appeared and asked why we hadn't lined up, someone said to her, "David gave his fancy car to Albert."

She looked at the box Albert was holding. After pausing for a moment, she then looked at me and asked, "David, did you give your car to Albert?"

"Yes, Mrs. Brown," I replied.

"Did your mother give you permission to give your car away?"

"Yes, Mrs. Brown."

"Are you sure?" she persisted.

I felt desperate. I knew she suspected I was not telling the truth, so with all the sincerity I could muster

I said, "Yes, Mrs. Brown. I asked my mother and she said I could give it to Albert."

"Okay," she said slowly. I knew she still had her doubts, and I was relieved that she let Albert keep the car.

We put on our coats and stood in line, waiting for our bus numbers to be called. When I heard "Number One," I bolted out the door. Then I stopped and looked back. Albert was standing there clutching his new treasure with bright eyes and a wide smile.

Suddenly I felt a deep happiness welling up inside of me and I began to choke up. I pressed my lips hard together and blinked. I hadn't known that giving could make me so happy. I thanked Jesus and whispered, "Albert is happy, Jesus. I'm glad I gave him my car." Going down the concrete steps of the school, I prayed, "Jesus, please don't let anyone take that car away from Albert."

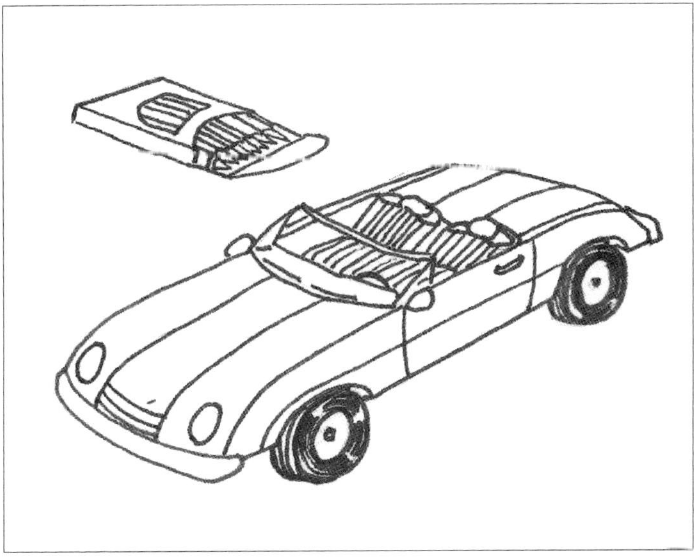

The Happy First Grader

I was a happy first grader. As long as I could remember I had anticipated the joy of entering first grade. Finally, the time came, and each morning I bounced out of bed, looking forward to another delightful day at school. Now I could learn to read and write and enjoy recess with the other children.

But one day a strange thing happened. I found myself in a corner surrounded by six big third graders. They were giants! I looked up into their faces. They had their fists raised, determined to give me a beating. My heart began to pound rapidly as panic closed in. There was no way out. No escape route.

Feeling sick but trying to act brave, I raised my feeble fists. Fear gripped me. Suddenly a thought came to me. I dropped my fists and looked straight into the eyes of my Goliaths. Slowly I said, "I want you to know something before you hit me." I then shouted with all my might, "God is with me!" Peace filled my heart and I no longer cared if they beat me. To my utter astonishment all six giants suddenly turned and fled down the hall. I stood looking up in awe of God. He had delivered me!

Years later while living in Kandahar, Afghanistan, when the fanatical Taliban were in power, I never forgot what I experienced as a happy first grader when I faced my Goliaths.

ONE STEP SHORT

It was 1959, my senior year at Howland High in Howland, Ohio. With great anticipation I had waited for this school year to begin. This year would be different from all the others, I reminded myself continually. I could just feel it in my bones.

I had attended the Youth for Christ conference in Winona Lake, Indiana, the summer before. I became excited as I listened intently to other high school kids telling how Christ had helped them to make positive contributions to their school life. Their testimonies inspired me to believe that I, David Leatherberry, could somehow serve Christ in my school as well. Though my other school years had been mediocre, God had given me a sense of expectancy about this one.

Maybe if I did something well, people would listen to me, I reasoned. Then my testimony for Christ would have punch.

In all my school years, I had never been outstanding in anything. My grades were not above average no matter how hard I tried. I was never in band, and I often wondered why I was in choir; I could hardly carry a tune. Athletic teams usually cut me during tryouts because I was not physically gifted either.

Every child strives to be important in his parents' eyes, and I was no different. My dad believed the way to make a child good was by continual correction. After all, a compliment might spoil a youngster. He had grown up under this type of treatment, so that was the treatment I received. All through grade school and beyond I desperately tried to do something—anything—well, just so I could please my father.

How excited I was when I tried out and made the seventh-grade basketball team. Though I was only on the third string, I was on the team! *Finally,* I thought, *I will have a chance to make my dad proud.*

Knowing I would play little or not at all in a real game, I started trying to talk Dad into coming to a practice. After much coaxing, he finally agreed.

On the appointed Saturday morning, we drove to the gym in silence. I could hardly contain my excitement. *Dad is going to see me play,* I thought happily.

During the practice I raced up and down the court as though it were the most important game of the season. I worked harder than I'd ever worked before. I didn't care if it was just practice; my dad and a few other parents were in the bleachers. I had an audience to play for and I was going to make the most of this opportunity. I leaped for every loose ball and rebound. Though I didn't score much, I hustled and did my part.

After practice I couldn't wait to see Dad. I showered quickly and ran out to our car. I was a skinny seventh grader with wet hair and a happy heart, waiting for a word—any word—of commendation. Even a little show of pride or satisfaction for hard effort would suffice ... but none came.

The silence grew deafening. When I could stand it no longer, I looked over at Dad with a tentative smile on my face and asked, "What did you think?"

As I waited for an answer, my heartbeats measured the long seconds of silence that followed my outburst. But Dad just kept looking straight ahead.

After what seemed to be an eternity, he finally cleared his throat and said, "Well, those other guys were really good. What was your problem?"

Crushed, I hung my head. I could feel tears forming. Turning toward the window, I quickly flipped them away. As I bit my trembling lip, I decided I would never ask my dad such a question again. Yet I never stopped trying to live up to what I imagined he wanted me to be.

Those feelings followed me into my last year of high school. Somehow, though, I knew that final year was one of great promise. I believed strongly something good was going to take place.

The big news at the beginning of my senior year was that a student teacher from the former year, George Landis, had been hired to teach English and to be the new track coach. Howland hadn't had a track team for several years.

When I first saw Coach Landis, I was encouraged. He wasn't big, probably only 5'9" or 5'10", but he had a sinewy, athletic build. He had been a high school football and track star.

It wasn't long before everyone at school liked Coach. The girls at Howland swooned over his handsome olive skin and curly black hair, and the guys were impressed by how well he could run hurdles and dashes.

Long before the track season began, word was out among the students that anybody who tried out would make the team. There would be no cuts. To lose your sweat suit, the symbol of being on the team, you would have to quit. With a heart full of excitement and great anticipation, I signed up for the team. Maybe, I reasoned, I could somehow be a testimony for the Lord.

The team was made up of many upperclassmen like myself—those with little or no previous experience in track or any other organized sport. Though the other coaches laughed at the looks of the team, Coach Landis stuck to his promise and no one was cut.

After our first meeting, I stopped Coach and asked to be excused from Thursday practice.

"The Youth for Christ Club meets Thursday after school," I said. "But I will do the workout routine afterward by myself if it's okay."

"Fine," he said, without hesitation.

Just like that? Maybe it doesn't matter because he doesn't expect much from me anyway, I thought.

That first week of track, I walked quickly from my Thursday afternoon Youth for Christ meeting toward the locker room to change clothes. The other team members had finished their workouts and were getting ready to leave. As I approached the gym, Coach was standing by the open door of his car. He looked over the top of the car and studied me intently.

I felt awkward under his gaze. I wondered how he really felt about my doing Thursday workouts alone. Perhaps he would think I wasn't as committed to the team as I should be, that I'd take it easy. Or maybe he really didn't notice me that much. Perhaps it didn't make any difference what third-stringers did.

After a long pause, Coach smiled and said, "Hi, David. How are you?"

Nervously I answered, "Oh, I'm fine, Coach. Just on my way to do my workouts. I had a Youth for Christ meeting this afternoon. I'll be sure to do all my workouts."

"Oh, I know you will," Coach said. "No problem."

Then he paused again, giving me his full attention. It was as if I was the only person in the world—me, of all people.

Finally he said, "David, you're doing just fine, you know, just fine. You're going to make a good 880 man. Don't worry, okay?"

"Okay," I answered casually, trying not to show how thrilled I was at the impact of his words. *He believes in me,* I thought as I watched him slip into the seat of his car and drive away.

The chilly March air and a cold light rain hit my face as I worked out that afternoon. But with each lap I felt uplifted. As I ran around the track, my thoughts also raced: *Coach Landis actually remembers my name. He is not upset with me. He understands about YFC. He actually thinks I can be a good 880 man.*

As the steady thump of my track shoes rang in my ears, I prayed, "Lord, help me to be a winner for You, Coach, and the team."

Somehow, I just knew I would make the 15 points I needed to letter. I had no doubts whatsoever. I would be a winner.

As I continued running that day, I realized I'd forgotten to thank Coach Landis for his encouraging words. But somehow I had the feeling it wasn't necessary.

It didn't take too many practices before I felt comfortable as part of the team. The coach's smile always put me at ease, yet his soft brown eyes, which seemed to light up when he grinned, could be penetrating as well. Coach Landis was a Catholic with a strong belief in God. He had our respect, for he never used foul language or anger to either intimidate or motivate us.

Because two other 880 men were more talented, I ran third string. For me, it was always a minor miracle to cross the finish line. Years later I learned why running was so difficult. I had bronchiectasis in my left lung, a weakness I apparently had since birth.

It was always the wind sprints that got to me. That's when you run hard for 220 yards, jog briefly, and then sprint another 220 yards. Long-distance runners, those who ran the 880 and up, were expected to complete this routine six times. I would run hard until I was in pain, gasping for air. After a brief time to recover, I'd do it again. One of my worst problems was I ran like a duck—my feet turned out instead of in or straight. Though Coach and other team members tried to teach me to redirect my feet, I couldn't.

Every time I ran, I prayed for Coach and for every member of the team. Sometimes I jogged with Big Jim Nycum, our shot-putter. We called him Big Jim because he was 225 pounds of solid muscle. Jim was also a basketball star. He was quite a contrast to my 6-foot, 132-pound frame.

"Jim," I'd say, "if you died today, would you be ready to go to Heaven?"

I knew I had better be ready to go if Jim was in a bad mood, because he could have put me out of this world in one fell swoop. Usually, though, he would just laugh and say, "Preach it to me, Davey. Preach it to me."[2]

The track season progressed reasonably well. Participating on the team was a great effort for me, and I didn't make much progress. Yet, I enjoyed every minute of it. I was part of the team.

One April afternoon Coach Landis reminded us that Ursuline, a constant powerhouse school in our area, would be our next opponent. We also knew Ursuline was the school where Coach Landis as a student had set a record in low hurdles. We wanted to do especially well.

On the day of the meet, our enthusiastic, patched-up team met the veterans head-on. Throughout the meet, the score was close.

Coach Landis drew us into a huddle. "We're dead even with them," he said. "Our last two events, the pole vault and the 880, will make the difference. Do your best!"

The vaulters started their last pole-bending thrusts into the air about the same time we were getting ready for the 880. To relieve my tension I walked past the empty stands and glanced at the vaulters.

"Come on, man!" I shouted to Jim Frazier who stood facing the bar with his pole in his hand. He gave me a thumbs-up sign.

I liked to run the 880. It was my race. I just knew I could place and help our team win. Although I had never placed higher than fifth in any race, my goal was to place fourth in this one because that was the last spot that was awarded a point.

Dave Wise, who would later do great things at Kent State University in track, had just finished first in the mile. He came over to encourage me. Our team enjoyed special unity—a spirit inspired by the attitude of our coach, who treated everybody equally.

This race was important for the team, the coach, me, and, I felt, for Christ too. I desperately wanted to contribute. I walked around shaking my hands and then, one at a time, my legs. I bent over, stretched, stood up, and paced some more.

When a voice called, "880, line up," I walked to the line, suddenly conscious of my spindly legs and shortness of breath. The starter snapped shut his pistol. I took three breaths, breathing as deeply as I could, and bent over once more to stretch.

"On your mark." I stepped to the line on the inside lane. "Get set." Coach's words were in my mind: *We're even. Do your best.*

Crack! The shot was fired; the race began.

Three runners had sprinted to the front by the end of the first turn. The rest of us were running together in a pack. Everyone's position was maintained for the first lap. Shortly into the second lap, my lungs began to burn, but I was feeling pretty good and had a nice rhythm going. Two runners in our group started to fade slightly on the backstretch and continued to do so throughout the race.

As the last turn came into view, I was breathing heavily and a weakness began to creep down my legs. When we started the kick, there were three runners ahead of me I would never catch, one close behind me, and two others who trailed far back. It didn't take much calculating to know I only needed to stay in front of that one runner for less than 10 yards to make fourth place. Just one man for 10 yards. I could do it.

Landis' voice was in my ears. "Run hard! When your legs are screaming stop, that's when you turn it on!"

I strained with all my might, ignoring the sweat that stung my eyes and the fire that burned my lungs. Fourth place was within my grasp. I could feel it in the rhythm of my steps and the smooth pump of my arms.

This is it! This is it! I am flying, I thought.

Just then the runner behind me was suddenly shoulder-to-shoulder with me. We had about seven paces to go.

No! He won't do it! I determined in my mind. But even as I increased my effort, so did he. Step for step he matched me in perfect rhythm. *I can do it!* I kept telling myself. *Just a little more.* I gasped for air, clenched my teeth, and tightened my fists for one final assault on the finish line. I strained my whole body and stretched every muscle to the limit as I forced my toe to the line and flung my exhausted body across it.

Yet all of my last-second efforts were to no avail. I failed. I lost by one step and my team lost the meet by one point. I was one step short.

Dejection, like the black of midnight, blanketed me.

Though Coach Landis should have been disappointed, he didn't seem to be. He wasn't even upset by my inadequacy and failure, for he knew I had given all I had.

As he laid his hand on my shoulder, I exclaimed, "Oh, Coach, I wanted this for the team!"

"It's all right, David," he said.

Though I knew in my heart he meant it, I could not be consoled. *Oh, God, I prayed about this race and I did it for you. Why couldn't I make at least fourth place?*

My dreams vanished. I wasn't a winner. I was a fifth place finisher.

In May, a few weeks before graduation, I was struggling as usual during a Saturday workout. I ran as hard as possible until I got so physically sick I left the field to vomit. Afterward I walked away from the track about 30 yards and sat on a hay bale. I wanted to be alone, but Coach Landis came over and sat down beside me.

Looking directly at me, he said, "David, I want you to know that some guys don't have the physical bodies for this, even though they give it all they've got. I know you try your best. In fact, I wish everyone I coach had the same kind of spirit you have. I want you to be aware that I know you are giving it everything and that's all a man can do."

Though his comments made me feel better, each time I lost an event the 15 points it took to letter got more and more improbable, and the big letter "H" for Howland slipped further and further away from my grasp. It wasn't long before I knew it was impossible for me to letter. I didn't have one single point, and the way things were going I probably wouldn't earn any during the remainder of the season. Yet Coach continued to encourage me.

Finally, the day arrived for the county championship meet. We blew out every team. Our score reached 78 points; our nearest competitor had less than half that number. What a proud day for our school. Coach Landis's no-cut team became county champions. In fact, we were the only sports team in our school to have a winning season that year.

How happy and proud I was to be part of the team. Though I hadn't contributed points, I had added spirit, encouragement, and an example of hard work. The year-end awards assembly was always a highlight at school, but I looked forward to this year's event more than usual. Finally I was a team member—a member of a championship team no less. More than 700 students filled the bleachers and gym floor that morning. How excited I was as Coach Landis summoned our entire track team to the front. The principal presented Coach Landis with the big, gold championship trophy amid thunderous applause, whistles, and shouts. Cheerleaders waving orange and black pom poms yelled, "That's our team!" The deafening roar in the gym sounded beautiful to me.

With a hearty handshake and his familiar smile, Coach Landis walked down the line and presented a small trophy to each team member. Receiving my own trophy that day was one of the brightest spots of my high school experience.

The coveted "H" letters were then presented to Dave Wise, Big Jim Nycum, Jim Frazier, and several others. Though disappointed I had not lettered, I was thankful just to stand up there with those guys.

It was quiet for a few seconds, then Coach Landis said, "Now, will David Leatherberry ..."

The sound reverberated from the cement block walls and stunned me. Shock would not allow my ears to receive this.

A mistake, a cruel mistake! I thought.

Speechless and unsure, I didn't move until the guy next to me slapped me on the back and insisted I walk over to Coach Landis. Since I was on the end, I had to walk by every team member. They all knew I had not earned one single point, let alone the 15 required to letter.

What will they think? I wondered.

But as I walked past them, my embarrassment gave way to joy. The team members were smiling and they all shook my hand or patted me on the back, saying things like: "Hey, man, that's terrific." "Great!" "Congratulations!" Coach, in the manner I had come to expect, talked directly to me as he shook my hand. Offering me the big orange "H", he said, "I want you to know, David, I'm not just giving this to you. You earned it. Congratulations, you lettered!"

Later I learned Coach Landis had great difficulty getting the necessary approval from the athletic department for my special letter. Somehow in the end he convinced them a third-stringer had given as much as he possibly could, and even though he hadn't earned a single point he had given enough to earn a letter.

How deeply I treasured that letter and trophy. Every time I looked at them they reminded me of the lessons I learned from Coach and from running on the team.

I'll always be thankful for Coach George Landis.[3] He knew I was not track material but he gave me an opportunity to be part of a team when anyone else would have cut me. In his eyes my efforts were superior even when my performance was not. From a coach who was more interested in molding a young man's character than in winning a meet, I learned not to quit—even when it was painful to keep going.

After being on the Howland High track team, I thought about God's no-cut team. My Life Coach never takes anyone's sweat suit either. To get off His team, you have to quit. I purposed in my heart never to quit, but to letter for God with my life. It used to bother me I wasn't a gifted individual, but I decided God had made me the way I am for a purpose. Since He accepts me as I am, so do I. When I stopped comparing myself to others, I found a new freedom.

THE CHALLENGE

"David, you're a product of your environment. If you were born in the middle of an Islamic country, you would be a Muslim. You would believe that Islam is the only way to God."

These words flowed smoothly out of the mouth of Travis[1] who sat across from me in my small dorm room. Travis enjoyed stopping by from time to time to needle me about my Christian faith. He was a brilliant, agnostic freshman who lived down the hall.

Travis was a skinny fellow with a black mustache who wore wire rimmed glasses. I had to work at liking Travis. I had never met anyone so arrogant. He delighted in making my life miserable as he attempted to dismantle my Christian faith.

I sat quietly as I pondered Travis's statement. What he said seemed to make sense. I said nothing. Travis grinned.

"David, how do you know the Bible is true?" I opened my Bible and read 2 Peter 1:20, 21 as proof it is true. Travis smiled, "David, is a book true because it says it's true? Isn't that circular reasoning?"

"Travis, if you would accept the Bible by faith you would see that it is true."

Travis laughed, "Muslims also say if I would accept their Holy Qur'an by faith, I would see the light and realize it is true. Sorry, but I'm not into blind faith. Well, I have to go and study for an exam tomorrow. I'll see you later."

After Travis departed I leaned back in my chair very frustrated. No one had ever challenged my faith as Travis did. In high school I was well respected by my fellow students and teachers. They appreciated my sincerity as I tried to live out my Christian faith. Now here I was a sophomore in a Christian college being hammered by Travis.

Two days later Travis again appeared in my doorway. "Please come in Travis. I'm glad to see you." But in my heart I wasn't so sure that I was. I reached in my desk drawer, pulled out a Hershey bar, and handed it to Travis.

"Thanks David, that's my favorite chocolate."

"Be careful Travis. It might cause you to put on too much weight." We both laughed.

"David, I have a question to ask you. If God is all powerful and all loving as you say He is, why doesn't He stop all the evil in the world: the bombing of babies, the raping of innocent women, the horrible wars that take the lives of innocent civilians, the violent murders that constantly take place in our big cities? Do I need say more? That doesn't sound like a loving, compassionate God if He has the power to stop all evil in the world but doesn't do it."

"Travis, I will have to think about your question," I responded.

"Well, let me ask you another question to ponder. Do you believe the multitudes of people who die having never heard the Gospel of Christ are all going to hell? If so, do you believe that is just?"

"Travis, before I can answer your questions, I must think about them."

"Please do. Do yourself a favor and don't let yourself be trapped by those who tell you, 'Don't let your mind get in the way. Just believe with your heart.' That's foolishness. Be willing to free yourself from such faulty thinking.

"May I be honest with you, David, and tell you what really bugs me about those who claim to be born again Christians? They are so narrow-minded, have tunnel vision and are intolerant of those who have different worldviews. David, you do not want to be like that. You need to honestly face the realities of the real world."

Silently I looked across my brown study desk at Travis. Finally, while trying not to show the stress I was feeling I said, "Travis, you certainly have given me a lot to think about."

He smiled broadly wrinkling his nose. "Well, I am headed for the library. Let me know the next time you have a Hershey bar handy and I'll relieve you of that burden." We both laughed.

After Travis left my room, again I felt extremely frustrated. I decided to walk to a nearby park to get fresh air and to think things over. I found a lonely faded green bench under a large oak tree surrounded by flowers. For several minutes I just sat there trying to clear my mind. Then I began to think about all that Travis had said. I had to admit his logic sounded very good and I certainly did not know how to answer his skeptical, thought-provoking questions.

To be intellectually honest I could not dismiss his questions even though he was the epitome of arrogance and loved to make my life miserable. I decided I would not become an anti-intellectual who somehow blindly held onto his faith. But I also decided I was not about to throw away my Christian faith until I thoroughly checked everything out.

Perhaps there were sufficient answers to Travis's questions, but I just did not know what they were. Perhaps there was a solid objective basis for the Christian's subjective experience he claimed to have with God, but I was not aware of it. I concluded if what I believed was true it could stand the test of hard, honest, intellectual questioning. If it could not stand that test, then it was not worth believing.

For nearly a year I constantly and diligently researched and studied this whole matter. I was determined to find out the truth no matter where it led. In time I discovered there are sufficient answers to the hardest skeptical questions. There is solid objective evidence upon which the Christian faith is based. Realizing this caused me throughout my life to passionately pursue Christ with all my heart and to follow Him wherever He desired to lead me.

I am very grateful for the challenge by Travis. He caused me to know why I believe what I believe and the basis for that belief. I learned how to love, respect and engage skeptics, agnostics and atheists. Thank you, Travis.

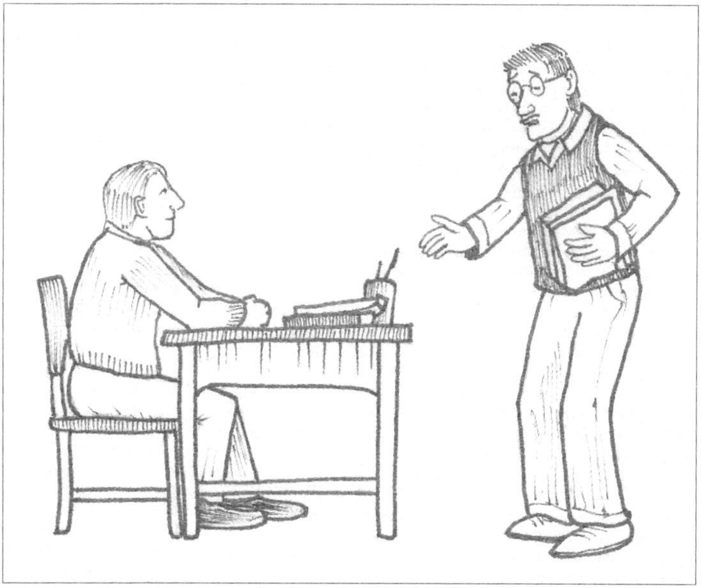

CONFRONTATION AT CHICAGO STATE

"Mike, you're a big phony," Betsy said in a sarcastic voice. "You're always talking about that Jesus stuff." You see, Mike's life had been transformed by Christ and he could not stop sharing with other students at Chicago State University about what Jesus had done in his life.

Mike responded with a smile, "Betsy, I challenge you to come with me this Thursday night to Pastor Dave's Bible study in his home and check out for yourself whether or not what I'm saying is true."

So there she was Thursday night in my home. She sat quietly as she watched the other students sing, pray and study the Bible with me and my wife Julie. A few months before Julie and I had started a church from zero in the summer of 1971 in Lansing, Illinois. We met on Sundays in an elementary school gymnasium. A number of young people had encountered the living Christ and their lives had been changed.

Betsy left the meeting with a copy of the New Testament in her hands which I had given her. She returned week after week. Finally she became convinced that Jesus was the Savior and committed her life to Him. Her new life in Christ changed her. She was no longer a worldly girl with a sharp tongue living for herself. Her values changed and she became a loving, caring person.

One day Betsy came to see Julie and me. She was taking a philosophy class. Her middle-aged, silver-tongued professor felt that his calling in life was to make everyone an atheist. When he noticed the change in Betsy and realized she had become a follower of Jesus, he began to ridicule her in class day after day. As a new Christian, Betsy did not know how to deal with him.

I said, "Betsy, please ask your professor to invite me to his class to give a lecture on the validity of Christianity." Betsy did so and the professor was delighted to invite me. I did not know he enjoyed devouring nice, polite pastors.

The date was set for my presentation. I thoroughly prepared my lecture and a 16-page set of apologetic notes to give to each student. The notes included well-documented evidence for the historical validity of the four Gospels, quotes from the famous Oxford/Cambridge professor C.S. Lewis as well as materials about the problem of evil, etc. I felt well prepared.

The day finally arrived for me to give my apologetic lecture. It was a cold but sunny afternoon as Mike and I drove to Chicago State University on the south side of Chicago. When I entered the classroom, I immediately sensed the hostility. Professor Jackson[1] coldly greeted me. With a condescending attitude he introduced me to the class. About five minutes into my lecture a few students began to snicker as the professor, who sat at the side of the class where he could see everyone, egged them on with his can-you-believe-that glances. At times students mockingly laughed and shook their heads.

Now and then I paused to give time for the students to ask questions. Arrogantly they acted as if they knew everything and I knew nothing. It was a very, very long frustrating hour that I thought would never end. Finally, it did. Professor Jackson gleefully stood and invited me to return the next day to give another lecture. I accepted, knowing he felt he had caught a mouse in a trap and would have more fun.

Mike and I left the room and walked down a long hallway headed for an outside door. About halfway down the corridor a well-built athletic student from the class ran up to me. "Hey, man, you're not really coming back tomorrow are you? If you thought it was bad today wait till you get here tomorrow."

I replied, "Oh, I will be back tomorrow. That's for sure." I knew I'd be back, but I sounded more confident than how I really felt.

Once in the car Mike said, "Pastor Dave, you were not nearly as good as you usually are when you present such a lecture."

"I know, Mike, I know. And I used all my big guns today. I have no idea what I'm going to do tomorrow."

Late that afternoon several young people from our church joined Mike, Julie and me to pray about the challenge I would face the next day. After they left I continued to pray. In fact, most of the night I walked the floor pouring out my heart to God as I prayed in tongues, that supernatural prayer language from the Holy Spirit, because I did not know what else to pray in English.

At five o'clock in the morning the Holy Spirit showed me what I was to say and do. Mike arrived at my house early because the class that day began at eight o'clock. I said, "Mike, please drive. I need to keep praying." On that cold January morning, Mike silently drove as snowflakes rapidly fell on the windshield and the wipers dispelled them.

We entered the classroom and took a seat. Professor Jackson rudely ignored me as the students were abuzz talking with each other. Within a few minutes the professor went to the lectern, looked over the class and said, "This guy from yesterday is back. Let's see if he has anything to say." As I went forward the professor took the same seat as the day before from where he could see all the students.

When I stepped behind the lectern the power of the Holy Spirit came upon me. At the same time the power of the Holy Spirit came upon the students. They did not laugh. They did not snicker. It was as if they were glued to their seats. There was no movement. As he did the day before, the professor attempted to egg them on to mock me, but it did not work. The students just sat silently looking at me.

I said, "Yesterday you told me you could not know anything. Do you think we have sufficient evidence that you are in this classroom today? Do you think we have sufficient evidence that you are going to die someday? What do you think?

"Yesterday you told me you were intellectually honest. If that is true you will say, 'God, I do not know if you are there or not. But if you are there, I want to know it. I don't know if that skinny guy up there knows what he's talking about or not. But if what he says about Jesus being the Savior is true, I want to know it.'"

I briefly told about Nicky Cruz, perhaps the most violent teenage gang member in New York City whose life had been completely transformed by Christ.

Then I turned to Professor Jackson and pointed at him. I said, "Sir, you are not intellectually honest. Yesterday after I left the classroom you said, 'He is a dumb clown. He doesn't know anything.' Now if I am a dumb clown and I don't know anything, why did you invite me back today? Sir, you are not intellectually honest, and I don't play this game according to your rules."

I turned to the class and said, "I'm taking no questions. If you would like to speak with me after class, I will be down in the cafeteria."

I looked again at the professor, "Sir, the class is yours." You could have heard a pin drop as I walked across the room, picked up my winter coat and briefcase and walked out with Mike following me. Halfway down the hall I leaned against the wall and took a deep breath.

I thought I would collapse. I could not believe what I had just done, for I am a soft-spoken person.

Meanwhile back in the classroom the professor got up and perhaps for the first time in his life was all befuddled. Finally he said to the class, "Do I ever call anyone a dumb clown?"

A student in the back of the room spoke up, "Yes, you do that."

Dr. Jackson asked, "What should I do?"

Betsy, seated in the middle of the class, said, "Repent!"

Another student said, "The guy said he would be down in the cafeteria if we wanted to talk with him. So let's go talk with him." The whole class stood and started for the cafeteria. The professor followed meekly behind.

I just got seated in the dining hall still trying to recover when I looked up and saw the whole class of nearly twenty-five students coming my way. They politely sat around Mike and me. The atmosphere had completely changed.

I said to the students, "Please ask any question you would like. God is not afraid of honest skeptical questions." So they sincerely asked questions for more than an hour. Other students in the cafeteria came over and joined the conversation. The professor sat quietly to one side and did not enter into the discussion.

When the students finally had to leave, they were kind and gracious with their comments. Who would have believed they were the same hostile young people I had met the day before!

On the drive home my heart was overflowing with joy for what the Holy Spirit miraculously had done. I learned a very vital lesson I vowed never to forget. I knew my Christian apologetics, but I had failed to fully prepare myself spiritually, for I did not realize what kind of spiritual forces I was about to confront.

THE QUARTER

I felt honored and humbled at the same time. I was invited to give a one-hour Christian apologetic lecture at the North Central Chi Alpha regional SALT[1] conference to be held in Ogden, Iowa, December 30, 1974-January 4, 1975. More than 100 university students from the Midwest would attend. It was the first time I had received such an invitation. It was exciting to me because I would have an opportunity to present the rationale for Christianity and the claims of Christ to a number of skeptical students who would be there with Christian friends.

One day as I was praying and preparing for the lecture, a strange thought entered my mind. It seemed like a command: "Halfway through your lecture you are to stop, reach into your pocket, pull out a quarter, flip it high into the air, carefully watch it fall to the floor, and then continue your lecture as if nothing had happened."

What a ridiculous idea, I thought as I quickly pushed it out of my mind. A few days later while in prayer the same absurd idea occurred. Again I forced the disturbing impression out of my mind.

One week before I was to speak at the conference while on my knees in prayer, the same distressing idea came again to me. I said, "Lord are you trying to tell me something or is this a product of my mind?"

"It's Me," came the answer.

"Okay," I responded, "I will obey and take the risk. But I want you to know I don't like looking foolish before all those students while I am defending the faith."

The second morning of the conference I was graciously introduced. I hoped the young people did not notice my nervousness. The lecture was going especially well when halfway through I stopped, put my hand in my pocket, pulled out a quarter, flipped it high into the air and carefully watched it fall to the floor. Then I continued my lecture as though nothing had happened, ignoring the puzzled look on the faces of the students.

Finally I concluded my address and sat down, wondering what flipping the quarter was all about. Looking up I saw two young women making their way towards me. One was slender and smiling with her arm around her dark-haired weeping friend. When they reached me, I gently asked, "How can I help you?" It took a few moments for the crying student to regain her composure.

Through tears she said, "While you were speaking I said, 'God, if you are really there, have the guest speaker do something completely out of the ordinary that has absolutely nothing to do with his lecture.' When you flipped the coin, I knew God was real."

Wiping her tears, her voice broke as she said, "I want to surrender my life to Christ." Together we prayed.

That night as I closed my eyes I whispered to God, "Lord, may I always be willing to take a risk for You and to look foolish when that is part of Your unknown but incredible plan."

THE DAY GRANDDAD DIED

While growing up, it was always fun to go to Grandma and Granddad Bedlion's house. I could walk right in without knocking and announce, "Grandma, it's David," and know I would be welcomed without hesitation.

"Well hi, Davey," she'd say. "Are you hungry?" seeing I had already opened the fridge and was checking it out. Grandma always gave me free access to the refrigerator. It was pure pleasure to choose one or more hidden treasures within: homemade pudding, a cold chicken leg, fresh green onions, tasty dill pickles, strawberry ice cream, and a can of ginger ale. My big snacks between meals never seemed to dampen my hunger at mealtime.

Slender and a little taller than Granddad, Grandma was a lovely mother of eight. The wrinkles in her face seemed to be a fitting part of her beauty. She enjoyed sewing and I'll always remember the green flannel cowboy shirt she made especially for me. Every time I was with Grandma I felt completely at ease. I knew she loved me. I never had to worry about her scolding me when I made a mistake.

It was also delightful to be around Granddad. He was an ideal storyteller. Many of the stories came from his boyhood; tales from the days when at the age of 12 he began working alongside his father in the coal mines of southern Ohio because his family was so very poor. Granddad was 5 feet 8 inches, and very muscular with square shoulders due to his work in a steel mill in Warren, Ohio. His full head of silver-gray hair accented his rugged gentle face. Granddad's warm smile put people at ease. Granddad liked to fish and hunt. Often he took me with him to fish from the shores of Mosquito Lake. He sang little ditties and told me humorous stories that made me laugh. Those sun-filled, happy days of my childhood made pleasant memories.

At the age of seven I began to sincerely pray for Granddad. It perplexed me why he didn't go to church. I became greatly concerned because I did not want him to go to the hell Jesus speaks about in the Bible.

I was 12 when Granddad had cancer surgery and his right arm and shoulder were amputated. It greatly pained my heart to see my beloved granddad suffer. Alone I cried. Few people lived long after such radical surgery, but Granddad did. He learned to write and drive with his left hand. With the assistance of my teenage cousin Jimmy, he built the second story on my Aunt Lou's house. I watched him lay a cement patio. With the help of only one person he raised and placed a small building onto a flatbed truck and moved it to his property. Granddad never lost his sense of humor and his unstoppable drive constantly amazed me.

When I was a high school student Granddad and Grandma moved a mobile home onto the lot next to my parents. This thrilled my heart. I could now visit them any time I wished. Once in a while I sat with Granddad and read the Bible to him. Although he didn't respond to what I read or said, he politely listened out of respect for me. In my quiet times with God each day I prayed for Granddad to surrender his life to Christ.

Granddad still relished hunting rabbits, so he learned to shoot with his left hand by carrying his twelve-gauge shotgun on a strap over his left shoulder. When game appeared, he'd swing his shotgun up to his shoulder and fire. He seldom missed and usually came home with a rabbit or two. Grandma said he knew more rabbit holes than the rabbits.

One day while hunting alone five years after he lost his right arm and shoulder, a rabbit suddenly appeared. Just as Granddad was ready to shoot, his foot slipped on a rock hidden in the snow and the gun went off. His right foot absorbed the blast ripping it badly. Bleeding profusely, he crawled across a field and onto the edge of a highway. A driver stopped and swiftly drove him to Saint Elizabeth's Hospital in Youngstown.

The doctors examined his mutilated foot and advised that it be immediately amputated. Granddad disagreed and called Aunt Lou's husband Bob to come and take him to the Green Cross Hospital in Warren. I arrived at the Warren hospital only minutes after they did. Looking pale, Granddad was sitting calmly on the examination table. When I looked at his unbandaged foot I understood why the doctors in Youngstown strongly recommended it should be amputated. The doctors in Warren agreed. These were the same doctors who had amputated his arm and shoulder. Granddad pleaded with them to try to save his foot. They looked at each other and finally said, "We will try, but please know there is very little hope that it can be saved."

His right foot was attached to the calf of his left leg in an attempt to graft skin to his right foot. Then a cast was put in place to be sure there was no movement. He would have to be in that position for six weeks.

At that time I was a senior at Howland High. Each day after school I hid behind our family garage and poured out my heart in prayer, asking God to heal Granddad's foot. Six weeks later the cast was removed. To the astonishment of the dedicated doctors, the graft had taken and Granddad could walk again. Awestruck at what God had done, I hugged Granddad as tears of joy flowed freely.

That fall in 1960, by faith I entered Evangel College[1] 800 miles away in Springfield, Missouri, where I had never been and knew only one person. I greatly missed Grandma and Granddad Bedlion and my family. The salvation of my granddad still weighed heavy on my heart. Often at night I slipped into the school chapel and on my knees prayed for Granddad to give his heart to the Lord Jesus. It wasn't unusual for silent tears to slowly course down my cheeks. At times I wrote him long preachy letters which he never answered.

Four years later I graduated from Evangel and enrolled in a seminary near Chicago. One afternoon I sat down in the library and wrote Granddad another preachy letter. When I finished the Holy Spirit spoke to my heart,

Throw away the letter. Your granddad has come into the Kingdom.

Immediately a struggle began in my mind. *Please Lord, am I hearing You correctly or is this wishful thinking? I can't make a mistake about this.* The impression would not go away. I sat quietly pondering this in my heart.

The Holy Spirit spoke again,

Your granddad has come into the Kingdom but he doesn't know how to tell you. Write and tell him that you know.

I crumpled the first letter and then wrote, "Dear Granddad, I know you have come into the Kingdom of God and have not been able to verbalize this to me. I want you to know that I know. Now I am praying differently for you. I have always prayed for your salvation, but now I am praying for your growth in our Lord Jesus Christ. Your grandson David who has always loved you."

It is ironic that my granddad often worried about me because he knew I was constantly concerned about him committing his life to Christ. Neither he nor I had to worry anymore. Not many days after I sent that letter, I received a phone call from my mother in Ohio. She said, "David, your granddad is in the hospital for medical tests. Why don't you call him?"

"I'll be glad to," I responded. Mom gave me his number and I dialed his room. We talked, joked and laughed as we always did during my growing up days. We were not aware of there being any serious medical problem. At the end of our conversation lightheartedly Granddad said, "David, when I get ready to cross the Jordan, I'll send you a letter."

"Granddad," I said, "when you get ready to cross the Jordan you won't need to send me a letter. I'll be there." When we hung up, I wondered whatever caused me to say that.

A few days later my mother called me again. "David, get in the car immediately and come home. Your granddad is unexpectedly dying of cancer." I was shocked. Just a few days ago everything seemed fine. My wife Julie and I quickly packed and started the long eight-hour journey from Evanston, Illinois to Warren, Ohio. I kept praying, "Please God, do not let Granddad die until I get there."

When Julie and I arrived and walked into Granddad's room I was stunned. He groaned in great agony as pain overwhelmed him. He was unable to speak, yet somehow I knew he could hear me. I leaned down and spoke in his ear, "Granddad, it's alright now. I'm here and the Lord Jesus is here with us. You can relax now." I held his hand and prayed from the deepest depths of my heart. The family had told him I was on my way. It seemed he was holding on until I arrived.

Later I walked down a long hall to the waiting room where Grandma and other family members had gathered. Most of them had been there all day.

While sitting quietly talking I became aware of nurses running down the corridor. Instinctively I knew they were headed for Granddad's room. My Aunt Lou and I quickly followed and found three nurses with tears in their eyes as they worked on Granddad. Aunt Lou stood across from me on the other side of Granddad. I placed my right hand on his left shoulder and raised my other hand and began to pray in a supernatural language from God. Probably those wonderful nurses thought I was praying in Greek because Granddad had proudly told them I was studying New Testament Greek in seminary.

Then to my great surprise I began to hear beautiful music. I glanced at the upper corners of the room looking for the stereo speakers from which I assumed the music was coming. There were none. The music was far more magnificent than the finest singing and orchestration of Handel's Messiah. When I looked to my left toward the wall at the foot of the bed, it faded away as deep, rich, bright yet rainbow-soft colors began appearing. The hues were predominately blue tones. The beauty was indescribably beyond anything I had seen on earth. When the colors came into focus I saw groups of angels standing in a field of blue beyond description. They were singing the heavenly music I was hearing.

The exhilaration I felt caused me to stretch up on my tiptoes as far as possible. I longed to go to Heaven with Granddad. While I still had my right hand on Granddad two angels stepped out and came towards us. The very moment they arrived, the music reached its grand crescendo and I heard Granddad take his last breath. Swift silence softly dropped like a curtain at the climax of a splendid performance.

At Granddad's funeral I experienced no grief. Instead unspeakable peace and joy filled my heart. I had seen him go home and knew someday I would join him. I do not know why God in His mercy gave me such an experience but I'm humbly thankful.

Grandma told me later something I never knew. When Granddad received a letter from me, he placed it in his back pocket and carried it around for days. From time to time he pulled it out and reread it. No more letters are now necessary.

THE POWER OF A LITTLE PRAYER

On a crisp fall day in 1967, I drove my green taxi down the hill on Fort Lee Road in Leonia, New Jersey, not far from the George Washington Bridge. It was almost 3:00 PM, the time I picked up lively six-year-old Alex at our taxi station near the bottom of the hill. Each day I parked my cab in a lot across the street from our office. I'd cross the street, take Alex by the hand and walk him to my taxi.

It was always delightful to drive him home. This little blonde-headed boy with beautiful, sparkling blue eyes, chatted all the way to his apartment, telling me about his day at school and asking many questions.

Each day three or four minutes before I reached our office, Alex would happily speak to me over our two-way radio. It made him feel very grown up. On this particular day I was bone weary when, sure enough, over the cab radio came the cheerful voice of first-grader Alex.

"Dave, I'm here. I can't wait to see you! How are you today?"

"I'm fine. Now Alex, listen to me closely. Today I am going to stop on the street right across from the office. Now don't come out of the office until I tell you over the radio to do so. Do you understand?"

"Sure, Dave, I won't come out of the office until over the radio you tell me to."

"That's right, now be careful."

"I'll be careful, 10-4 over and out."

But as soon as I pulled up across from the office, Alex dashed out and into the street right in front of a luxury car. The driver had no time to apply his brakes. I watched in horror as the vehicle hit Alex and threw him high into the air like a hard-thrown baseball. As I watched him fly through the air in his blue corduroy coat, it felt as if my heart literally dropped suddenly into my feet. Alex fell hard onto the street, tried to get up, but fell again. An alert policeman on a nearby corner witnessed what happened and immediately arrived in his squad car. He carefully picked up Alex, placed him in his vehicle and sped towards a hospital. Fighting panic, I followed closely behind. Alex was rushed into the emergency room to be examined. I anxiously sat in the waiting room too stunned to pray.

Finally I was permitted to see him. Sitting up and smiling from ear to ear, Alex said, "Dave, a little prayer is powerful. I prayed for the first time last night."

At first I was so dumfounded by his words I could not find my voice. When I did, I fought back tears and I whispered, "Yes, Alex, a little prayer is powerful." Not even a bruise was found on my little friend. It was as if he had never been hit.

Soon his single mother arrived. Haltingly with a red face I explained what happened. I expected her to be angry with me, but she wasn't. This dignified lady simply said, "It is okay, Mr. Leatherberry. Alex is fine for which I am thankful."

I drove Alex and his mother home. As he hopped out of the car he grinned and called out, "See you tomorrow, Dave!"

"You sure will," I replied trying to sound normal. He had no idea how very glad I would be to see him. As I drove away my stomach churned because I knew Alex could have been killed due to my mistake.

The next three days I was very depressed. I kept kicking myself for being so foolish. I could have caused Alex's death. The evening of the third day while sitting with my wife Julie at our small kitchen table, I hardly touched a thing. I was just too depressed to eat.

Julie quietly asked, "David, did you ask God to forgive you for your mistake?"

"Yes."

"Did you ask Alex to forgive you?"

"Yes."

"Did you ask Alex's mother to forgive you?"

"Yes."

"Did you ask your boss to forgive you?"

"Yes."

"Then David, who do you think you are not to forgive yourself?"

Julie's thoughtful words sunk in. I sat back in my chair and took a deep breath. Her wisdom brought me out of my depression. The next day I looked forward to taking talkative Alex home once again, thankful for the power of a little prayer.

THE COMMUNIST PROFESSOR

Professor Amir, a balding, short, middle-aged man, was stern and unsmiling. In the fall of 1977, I was a student in his class at Kabul University, attempting to learn the Pashtu language. The first day of class the professor picked up a Pashtu history book and instructed us to write in Pashtu the sentences he dictated from the book.

I sat there stunned because I had only begun to learn how to write the Pashtu script. This did not seem to matter to Professor Amir. The University had assigned me to his course and I was expected to do the assignments. Professor Amir had the right to teach the course any way he desired.

Because I always failed his exams, he concluded I was a lazy student. One day he expressed this to my friend Ole, a fellow student from Sweden. Ole was a linguistic whiz who excelled in the class. My friend tried to convince our instructor that I was a diligent, hardworking student. Nevertheless, the professor did not change the demands he placed on me. I completely and miserably failed his course.

Even though Professor Amir was not one of my teachers the next semester, I was still concerned about him as a person. However, I was clueless to know how I could improve our relationship because of his attitude towards me. I did appreciate the fact that he was a sincere scholar who deeply cared about the poor in his country. One day in class he had angrily declared, "One hundred rich families in this country control all the money. Daily the rich become richer and the poor become poorer. There is no justice in this land. Things have to change!"

The professor believed the philosophy taught by Karl Marx was the answer to liberating the oppressed, suffering people of Afghanistan. He did not hesitate to declare himself a communist. This utterly amazed me since at that time Afghanistan was fiercely Islamic and would not hesitate to eliminate such a person who had become an atheistic communist. One thing was perfectly clear, Professor Amir was totally committed to his cause.

One morning during the second semester, I awoke from a sound sleep, opened my eyes, and saw clearly before me the face of Professor Amir. As I looked at his face these words, as if they were a command, came distinctly to me, "Go today to the University and look for Professor Amir. When you find him tell him you remember the day in class when he mentioned that while he was in India working on his master's degree, he looked and looked for a copy of the Holy Bible but could not find one. Tell him you have a copy in his language and you would be glad to give it to him as a gift."

I was surprised at this word of instruction that came from outside of me. I pondered what had just happened and prayed. Then I said, "Yes, Lord," and prepared to go to the University. As I walked onto the campus, I saw Professor Amir not far from me. I walked over to him and warmly greeted him. He did not smile. Instead he gave me a cold reception. I almost lost my courage to speak about the gift I thought I should give him. But rising above my feelings, I awkwardly made the offer. His response was not uplifting. With a grim look on his face he said, "Oh, you have that book in my language, do you?"

"Yes, sir," I replied.

Still looking grim, he said, "Bring it to my office tomorrow afternoon at three," and he walked away.

I stood there with a sinking feeling. *Did I just make a drastic mistake? Will the secret police be waiting for me in his office tomorrow afternoon? I did not want to be arrested and expelled from the country I so dearly loved.*

The next afternoon as I purposefully walked to the University, I knew I was taking a risk. I also knew that without being willing to risk, the Kingdom of God could not go forward through my life.

I knocked on the door of Professor Amir's office. He opened it and invited me into his sparsely furnished room. As I stepped inside I was relieved that no one else was there. After closing the door, he locked it. Professor

Amir was a brisk person not given to formalities. He turned to me and the first thing he said was, "Did you bring the book?"

As I handed it to him I said, "Yes, sir." I had carefully wrapped the Holy Bible in a beautifully colored cloth. I had placed it in a brown paper bag so it would look like any other bag as I walked along.

"May I please open it?" he asked. That was an unusual request because in the Afghan culture it is not considered polite to open a gift in front of the giver.

"Please do," I replied.

With great care the professor opened his special gift and walked to a window. For several minutes he carefully looked through the pages as I quietly prayed. Finally, Professor Amir placed his unique gift on his desk and slowly walked over to me. He put out his right hand to shake mine. When I extended my hand, he firmly gripped it and took another step towards me, placing his left hand on my elbow. Looking straight into my eyes the professor earnestly said, "I want you to know I cannot thank you enough for this gift." I could feel the joy he was experiencing. I smiled.

As I walked home that afternoon joy kept bubbling up in my heart. I was grateful I had taken the risk and obeyed my Lord. The words of Jesus to His disciples, "As my Father has sent me, I am sending you," took on a more profound meaning to me. I rejoiced that I was sent to Professor Amir's office that day. And I was reminded of these words, "The Lord does not look at the things man looks at. Man looks at the outward appearance, but God looks at the heart."

I never again had the privilege of seeing Professor Amir, but then again, I may at the end of time.

THE AMERICAN MAJOR AND THE IRAQI COLONEL

When I awoke before dawn to have my quiet time with God, I had no idea on that day I would witness an amazing meeting between an American Major and an Iraqi Colonel. The evening before, I had received a request from the Allied Headquarters in Zakho in northern Iraq to bring to their office the next morning the passports of the members of my humanitarian relief organization, Shelter Now International.[1]

Early in the morning on my way to the military headquarters in my rented Toyota pickup truck, I collected Bob from another Christian NGO[2] as well as a young Frenchman from a French organization. They too were requested to bring their members' passports. Unfortunately neither Bob nor I could communicate with the French gentleman because we did not know his language.

In the summer of 1991 after the first Gulf War I was the leader of a small team assisting in the rebuilding of the destroyed Kurdish village named Baroshky, located two hours from Zakho. The work was progressing well when I was summoned to the United Nations office in Zakho. I was informed we had two days to leave Iraq. The UN had not been able, as they had promised, to obtain from Bagdad the visas necessary for relief workers to continue to work in the country. The Allied Military had wanted to obtain those visas, but the UN office insisted they would do it. The Allies were not happy with this development. Therefore, they had requested the passports of all the relief workers to be delivered to them the next day.

So there I was outside the Allied Headquarters in my pickup with Bob and the French lad with our passports in hand. A soldier stepped outside the building and came to the window of my truck. He said, "There's going to be a special meeting this morning. You are to represent the relief workers. Please follow the military vehicle parked over there." Soon three military men in uniform came out of the drab gray building and crowded into the green military vehicle with the driver and headed south. I followed, trying to stay up with them as their speed increased.

I looked up into the sky when I heard the noise of an Allied helicopter overhead. On top of the helicopter was a big round red ball.

I said to Bob, "Look, that helicopter is tracking us."

Bob replied, "Do you really think it's following us?"

"I'm sure," I answered. I thought, *How intriguing.*

We drove south up and down rolling hills for about thirty minutes. Suddenly we came up over a hill and on our right was a gate to a large Iraqi military base. The green army vehicle in front of us turned into the installation.

"Bob, do you think we should drive in there?" I questioned.

"We were told to follow them."

So we did, wondering what would happen. We drove deep into the jaws of the base. Finally, we came to a huge building and parked our pickup beside the vehicle we had followed. Iraqi officials opened the doors of our vehicles and politely greeted us. For the first time we met the three Allied soldiers, shook hands, and we were escorted by the Iraqis into the building.

We were led into a large conference room. Behind a beautiful wooden desk sat an Iraqi Colonel. On each side of him were seated other Iraqi military men as well as immigration officials. Everyone shook hands. The Allied men sat a distance across the room from the Iraqi Colonel. Bob, the Frenchman, and I sat in chairs along the wall to the left of the Allied men. Later I learned the three Allied men were an American Major, an American military lawyer, and a US Marine interpreter from the Middle East.

I could not help but notice the contrast between the American Major and the Iraqi Colonel. The American Major, probably in his mid-thirties, was strikingly handsome. He had blue eyes, blonde hair, and a fair complexion. It was obvious he was in top physical shape. The Iraqi Colonel was very distinguished looking with a thick black mustache, olive skin, and dark eyes. He probably was in his mid-forties, and also looked to be in good physical condition.

The visa negotiations began. It fascinated me that when the Major's interpreter spoke, he was the mirror image of the Major. If the American Major leaned forward in his chair, so did the interpreter. If the Major changed his tone of voice, so did the interpreter. I had worked with a lot of interpreters. He was the best I had ever seen.

Every time the interpreter spoke, the eyes of the Major never left the eyes of the Colonel. The American Major knew how to be relaxed and gave the impression he had all day to sit and talk, that time was not a factor. He was humorous at just the right moments. He knew how to shame just enough and yet not be offensive. One would have thought the Major had grown up in the Middle East.

As the negotiations proceeded, I noticed something else very intriguing. The more the Major and Colonel talked, the more it became apparent that the Iraqi Colonel greatly respected the American Major, and that the American Major had a heart full of compassion for the Iraqi Colonel. I could see it in the Major's eyes. The Major was very much aware that if the Colonel made a mistake, it was likely he would be harshly punished or even executed. That is the way Saddam treated his military leaders.

At the same time it was clear to me we would not be leaving without the needed visas. Except for a few questions that were directed to Bob and me, I sat quietly praying a solution would be found. After nearly two hours the Colonel came up with a workable solution. Visas would be granted on a separate official paper properly stamped, but not stamped in the passports themselves.

As I drove my pickup to the gate to leave the Iraqi military base, we saw the Allied helicopter parked across the road. As soon as we were observed, the blades began to rotate as it prepared for lift-off. Later I was told the red ball on top is called a million-dollar ball that can eavesdrop on a conversation 15 miles away.

The next day I had to see Major Kevin Ryan regarding other business. When I first met him I said, "Sir, you were marvelous in those negotiations yesterday. Where did you receive such wonderful training regarding Middle-Eastern people?"

Major Ryan responded, "If anything significant happened yesterday, it was due to the grace of God and the grace of God alone. Are you a Christian?"

"Yes, sir, I am. Bob and I were praying for you during the meeting."

The Major said with a pleasant smile, "I was praying on the way there. My wife, now in Germany, is a woman of prayer. I am not an expert on the Middle East. I am a specialist on the former Soviet Union and fluent in Russian. I have had some training in negotiating. I would appreciate it if you could tell me what I did right yesterday."

For a moment I did not speak because I was so amazed at what I'd just heard Major Ryan say. It was clear that God had used this humble man. Finally I said, "Sir, I will be glad to debrief you." And so I did.

Later I was at another event. To my surprise the Iraqi Colonel was there. He spotted me far on the other side of the courtyard and started to walk towards me. On the way he motioned for the Marine interpreter who had been at the first meeting to come with him. When the Colonel reached me, he stood beside me and held my hand, an eastern custom. Looking into my eyes he quietly said, "I want you to know I am very glad you are in my country. If ever I can do anything for you, I will be glad to do it." Then he quietly walked away.

The Holy Spirit whispered to my heart, "The Colonel is for real. That was not a put-on." Since that time I have often prayed for the Colonel. I am convinced the compassion of Christ which radiated through Major Kevin Ryan[3] softened the heart of the Colonel and showed him a different way.

ANDREI AND EUGENE

I crouched in the darkness on the flat roof of our little mud house in Kabul, Afghanistan, the night of December 27, 1979. Wide-eyed I watched the Soviet soldiers attack the government buildings at the end of Darlaman Road a mile and a half away. I never dreamed 26 years later in my cramped office in Yekaterinburg, Russia, I would meet one of the attackers.

Andrei was 19 years old then and one of the most elite members of the elite Soviet Special Forces. He and his fellow warriors were the first to assault the government buildings. I well remember the attack as I watched flares light up the sky, red tracer bullets fill the air, and heard the piercing sound of machine gunfire and exploding rockets.

In response to God speaking to our hearts, Julie and I had moved to Yekaterinburg on the edge of Siberia in 2003 to minister to the former Soviet soldiers who had fought in the Soviet/Afghan War. We founded and published a specialized national Russian newspaper called *Afganets* for the veterans of that war. More than a million Soviet soldiers had served in Afghanistan.

A friend of Andrei, whom Julie and I had previously met, urged him to visit me. So one afternoon he stopped by my office with his friend Margarita, who had been a young, dedicated nurse with the Red Army in Afghanistan. As I stepped into the hallway to warmly welcome our guests, the size of Andrei surprised me. As his frame towered over me, he appeared to be about six feet six inches in height. This broad-shouldered giant of a muscular man with huge powerful hands and a large open friendly face, smiled at my surprise. He chuckled and said, "I was one of the smallest in my unit." I wasn't too sure I would want to meet his comrades.

In my office I pulled up a chair and sat across from Andrei. Margarita and my faithful interpreter Farida sat nearby. I asked Andrei if he would like to share about his time in Afghanistan. At first he was silent. It seemed he was carefully sizing me up trying to decide whether or not I was trustworthy. I patiently waited for his response. He took a deep breath and began his story. Andrei explained about his basic training and being chosen to be in the elite of the elite of the Special Forces. He went on to say he was among the very first to attack the government buildings on the edge of Kabul the night of December 27, 1979. On hearing those words I sat straight up in my chair utterly amazed.

"Andrei," I almost shouted, "I was there too! I was within a mile and a half of you."

Andrei looked as if he could not believe his ears. "Really, why were you in Afghanistan at that time?"

"Julie and I had returned on tourist visas trying to find a way to serve the Afghan people."

After a moment, Andrei with a serious look on his face leaned forward, "How did you feel about that night?"

I replied, "I did not know what was happening. I thought the Afghan resistance fighters that had surrounded Kabul now had broken through into the city. I was totally surprised the next morning to see a Soviet soldier on every street corner. Julie and I were hoping we did not have to leave."

"Andrei, how did you feel about that night?"

"I thought we had come to liberate the Afghan people," he said with earnestness in his voice.

As Andrei continued to unfold his story, I listened respectfully. The veteran softened his voice and slowed his speech as he told me the hardest part. He said, "One day Afghan fighters ambushed our unit in a gorge. There was a horrific fire fight. All the men in my unit were being slaughtered. I was the only one still alive when I was shot in the leg. I cursed and wished I had been shot in the head. Just then the helicopter gunships arrived and I was rescued."

I sat silently feeling his pain and wanting to cry. Andrei showed me his prosthesis. His left leg had been removed right below his knee. After a long pause I quietly said, "Andrei, God saved you for a purpose. He loves you."

Andrei wasn't convinced. As we talked it became clear that Andrei had a brilliant mind and was an honest, sincere skeptic. After our initial visit Andrei would come by to talk with me from time to time.

Step by step during our visits I laid out the evidence for the validity of the New Testament and how we know Christ is the Savior. We also discussed other vital issues such as the problem of evil. At times Andrei would attend church with Julie and me to check it out.

Andrei had become an alcoholic. He drank to deaden the pain due to his experiences in Afghanistan. He slept little because of the horrible nightmares, nightmares so vivid that it seemed the battles were actually happening all over again. Like many other traumatized Afghan veterans, he resisted falling asleep because of the nightmares.

Constantly Julie, our close Russian friends and I prayed for Andrei to be delivered from alcoholism and healed from PTSD (post-traumatic stress disorder). We knew the One Person who could bring about that deliverance and healing.

One night, perhaps two or three months after Andrei and I became good friends, I received an urgent phone call from Margarita. "David, I am afraid Andrei plans to commit suicide tonight." There was panic in her voice.

"Margarita, please tell Andrei to get over to my office right now, and I mean now!" I phoned our gifted interpreter Farida and asked her to immediately meet Julie and me at the office.

A few minutes after our arrival Andrei rang the doorbell. He walked in very excited. Under his arm was a copy of our latest *Afganets* newspaper, in which I had published a story about Eugene, a Vietnam veteran.

Andrei kept saying, "Eugene's story! That's my story! That's my story! I wish I could talk with him."

I said to Julie, "Please look and see if we have Eugene's telephone number in the States." Julie found it.

Previously I had met Eugene in the States. As a 19-year-old Marine he was sent to Vietnam. His squad was often ambushed and engaged in many fire fights. One day when Eugene was not present, every Marine in his unit was wiped out. He turned to alcohol and drugs to seek relief from the extreme mental pain and pressures he was experiencing. Soon he became addicted to both.

Eugene returned to the States an addict, full of anger. One reason for the anger was due to the discrimination he experienced in the Marines as an African-American. He was arrested for robbery and spent 21 months in prison. At other times he was incarcerated for assaulting others.

Like Andrei, he was a huge muscular man. Eugene became suicidal and was hospitalized. His ex-girlfriend invited him to attend church with her. He went believing he had nothing to lose. When the altar call was given Eugene went forward and surrendered his life to the Lord Jesus Christ. He was immediately delivered by Christ from his addictions and left the church a new person in Christ. The grip of PTSD on his life was broken and no longer enslaved him. He enrolled in college, became a community nurse full of compassion, and completed a bachelor's degree.

I dialed Eugene's number in the States. His pleasant voice answered.

"Hello Eugene. This is David calling you from Russia. Do you have time to talk with me?"

"I sure do. You've caught me just in time. I was just ready to go out the door to work."

I explained to Eugene about my friend Andrei and that he would like to speak with him.

"Great, put him on."

Although they did not know each other's language, I let them greet each other in their mother tongue. It was good for them to hear each other's voice. Then Farida did a wonderful job interpreting.

"Eugene, are you ashamed of your medals?" Andrei asked. Eugene kindly answered this question and many others that were very important to Andrei. After a long conversation they said goodbye.

After the phone was hung up, I said, "Andrei, what Jesus has done for Eugene He can do for you. You need to ask Him to forgive you of your sins and to invite Him into your life."

"I will think about it," Andrei responded.

"No, Andrei you have had enough time to think about it. Now is the time to surrender your life to the Savior."

"Okay."

"Would you like to repeat a prayer after me and mean it from your heart?"

"No, I will pray."

I was surprised because Andrei didn't have a church background. We bowed our heads. This giant of a man, tough as they come, poured out his heart to God. He wept.

Andrei left our office a new person in Christ. Like Eugene, he was delivered from the grip of alcohol and PTSD. This brilliant veteran went back to school, earned two masters' degrees and became the head of a design-engineering department.

It was an unimaginable joyous day when Eugene and Andrei later met in Yekaterinburg, Russia. I cherish the picture I have of their meeting. The memory of Andrei giving to Eugene his Special Forces blue beret will never fade from my mind.

Andrei and Eugene will tell you what the Lord Jesus has done for them He can do for you.

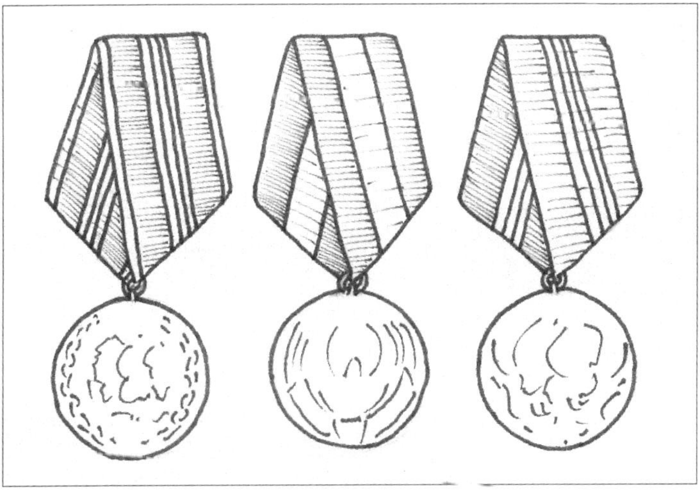

CREATED STORIES FROM MY HEART

THE BULLY

My arms were loaded with books as I managed to close my high school locker. Suddenly the books were slammed out of my hands and crashed to the floor, scattering in all directions.

"Hello you Jesus freak. Remember! You have to turn the other cheek," sneered Billy as he roared with laughter.

A voice from nowhere demanded, "Pick up Jeremy's books. Politely hand them to him and say, 'I am sorry,' or else you're history."

Billy turned and came face to face with Pete, our star halfback. Next to Pete stood Sam, our fastest linebacker. Billy's countenance turned crimson. The school's bully did as instructed and quickly walked away.

Apparently Billy did not know Pete and Sam were my friends. For you see, I was the water boy for our high school football team, the Vikings.

As my friends started down the hall, Pete grinned as he good naturedly called over his shoulder, "Hey, Jeremy, if you're going to win the world for Jesus, why don't you start with Billy?"

"Good idea!" I shouted back.

Then, as they continued down the corridor Sam turned and yelled back, "Jeremy, consider us your angels. If anyone else gives you trouble, just call on us." They both laughed.

"Thanks, I'll be sure to do that," I responded.

I smiled to myself and thought, *I'm ready to accept the help of any angels no matter what form they may take.* For I knew someday I may need their assistance when I would serve my Savior in a far-off distant land.

NAJEEB AND MR. JOHNSON

My name is Najeeb Muhammad. I grew up in an Islamic country in the Middle East. As a child I was proud to attend the local mosque with my devout father. He would tell me stories from our holy book the Qur'an. I was especially fascinated with the stories of the Prophet Jesus (peace be upon him). The miracles of healing he performed, as well as raising people from the dead, captivated me. What incredible power he possessed.

My father told me about people called Christians. They claimed to be followers of Jesus the Messiah, but they corrupted the very book, the Holy *Injil*,[1] he gave to the people of his day. I became curious about the followers of Jesus. I wondered how they wandered from the true path, and why they did not accept our holy book the Qur'an and our prophet Muhammad (peace be upon him).

Although my father did not have the opportunity to receive a formal education, he always encouraged me to study hard so that someday I could enter the university in our capital city. I had a hunger in my heart to learn and diligently applied myself to my studies.

The summer before I was to enroll at the university

my father became suddenly ill and died. For weeks my heart was overwhelmed with grief. I promised myself that I would graduate from the university and fulfill my father's dream for me. *This I must do to honor him.*

At the university I qualified for an advanced English course. I knew if I could become fluent in English it would open doors for me in the business world. My teacher was from America. *How fortunate,* I thought, *to have an instructor whose mother tongue is English.*

I'd never met a foreigner before. To my surprise he was only nine years older than me. I carefully observed Mr. Johnson. Of course I considered him an infidel and knew I needed to be careful.

Mr. Johnson smiled often and spoke clearly but softly. His deep blue eyes and light skin were quite a contrast to our olive skin and dark eyes. It amazed me how at ease he was in a classroom full of young Muslim men, since he was the only non-believer.

As the weeks rolled by I wondered why Mr. Johnson cared so very much about his students. I'd never met anyone so patient. He never embarrassed us when we made mistakes. He did not fit the picture that Hollywood movies portray. Mr. Johnson did not smoke, drink alcohol, eat pork or use bad language. He was always respectful to our culture and religion.

I was surprised to learn that he earned only a small salary as a volunteer with a humanitarian organization. I determined in my heart to get to know this unusual individual.

Mr. Johnson's wife taught English to a class of high

school girls. The word was that she too was of high moral character. I was told she always dressed modestly and wore a head covering as our girls did. Her behavior was honorable, and she did not go to the swimming pool for foreigners. The conduct of this couple caused me more than ever to wonder what they believed about God.

One day I saw Mr. Johnson entering a tea shop. He happened to see me and invited me to join him for a cup of tea and biscuits. I thought, *This is a lucky day for me.* After much small talk I became courageous enough to ask Mr. Johnson about his religious beliefs. "Sir, I do not want to offend you, but could you please tell me what you believe about God?"

He responded, "Why, thank you, Najeeb, for asking. I will be glad to tell you what I believe."

In a most natural way Mr. Johnson told me he was a follower of Jesus. His response caused me to ask many other questions. He thoughtfully tried to answer each question step by step. I studied his face for any negative reaction as I kept asking more pressing questions as well as giving my opinions. There wasn't any. One thing for sure: Mr. Johnson was thoroughly convinced of what he believed and did not feel threatened.

I decided to take another bold step. After first glancing around, I quietly asked Mr. Johnson if he could find for me a copy of the Holy *Injil* in my mother tongue. For a few moments he said nothing. Then he seriously asked, "Why do you want a copy?"

I replied, "So I can read it for myself since it is a holy book even though it is corrupted."

Mr. Johnson leaned forward in his squeaky chair and looked deep into my eyes. I hoped he could see my sincerity. Then he sat back as a smile slowly crept across his face. "Najeeb, please come to my house at 4:00 PM tomorrow and I will have that special gift ready for you."

I was astonished. I knew he was taking a high risk. He did not know whether or not I would report this to the secret police. If I did, he could be arrested and deported. Why did he trust me? I did not know, but I determined I would be worthy of his trust. The next afternoon I received that significant gift and began to read it that night.

Mr. Johnson and I became very close friends. I could tell him everything in my heart and he would not tell anyone. He was at my graduation applauding me. I wished my father could have been there. The next day Mr. and Mrs. Johnson made the long bus trip with me to my village. I stood gazing at my father's grave with my cherished degree in my hand. My teacher's arm was around my shoulder. My eyes were wet. I whispered to my father, "I did it, Father, I did it!"

Three years after my graduation my teacher with his wife attended my wedding. Even though we had become the dearest of friends, out of respect, I could only address Joe and Betty Johnson as Mr. and Mrs. Johnson. Within the next ten years I became a very successful businessman in my country, and God gave to my wife and me three beautiful children. It was a joy to have the Johnsons in our home. Sometimes I sent my driver to pick them up from the other side of the city.

The day came when the fundamentalists in my homeland came to power. I refused to join their party. My life was threatened. With a heavy heart I fled my country with my family. We lost everything.

When we arrived in the United States, the Johnsons came and helped us. Mr. Johnson convinced an international company that I was the right person to work for them. He vouched for my integrity and experience. On his word they hired me.

After five years I was made a chief supervisor in my company. Now I was financially secure and my children were receiving a good education. Once a year Mr. and Mrs. Johnson came to visit us. Often we were on Skype together. They were not permitted to return to my homeland. This was heartbreaking for them. They took positions as English teachers at another university in the Middle East.

Once when I was on a business trip in Virginia, I had a free Sunday morning. I thought about my teacher. I said to myself, *I will honor him and attend a church service this morning.* About 500 people were present. No one seemed to notice me as I slipped into a seat on the back row. The music was lively. *This is a little different from a mosque,* I mused to myself.

After announcements, a baby dedication and another song, the pastor stood to preach, a man in his fifties. His voice boomed through the speakers as he stated his topic: "The Dangerous Threat of Muslims to America!" He had my full attention.

Every eye was focused on the man in the dark blue suit behind the glass pulpit. I took a deep breath. Speaking harshly, the pastor made one inaccurate statement after another amid the "amens" from the congregation. I wondered what my Jewish CEO who recently had my family in his home for dinner would have thought.

After the closing prayer in which the pastor pleaded for God to save America from Muslims, I sat quietly stunned as the parishioners filed out into the large foyer. Finally I made my way through the chit-chatting crowd engrossed with each other. No one took time to greet me. On the way to my car I noticed emboldened on the marquee, "The friendliest church in Virginia."

How ironic, I pondered as I started my rental car. I had quit attending the mosque in my home city in California because of the negative messages against American infidels. I had also become disillusioned due to the hypocrisy of many Muslims from my home country now living in America. I could no longer stand the two-facedness of my own people. I wondered how many professing Christians were also hypocrites.

Months later my teacher and his wife returned to the States for a visit. It had been almost thirty years since I first met Mr. Joe Johnson. I considered him my best friend on Earth. Even after I did not accept his beliefs about God because I could not accept the doctrine of the Trinity, he remained my faithful friend, always caring for me and my family. I never met anyone as loving and dedicated as my teacher.

One afternoon during their visit, my best friend and I took a long walk in a nearby forest. We came across a wooden picnic table and sat across from each other. After a while I said, "Mr. Johnson, you have an extremely hard task trying to convince any Muslim to become a follower of Jesus." Gently I went on to explain the reasons why the task was so difficult. I knew that after thirty years of living among Muslims my friend had seen no more than five become and remain followers of Jesus. Yet, he never gave up. I knew why. He loved them. Daily he prayed for his many Muslim friends.

As we conversed, my teacher and I agreed there had to be absolute truth. It amused us that those who believed there is no absolute truth absolutely believe that to be true. We chuckled as we talked about such an absurdity. Yet within my heart I did not know which was truly the absolute truth. Was it the way of Islam or the way of Christianity?

In the course of our discussion, with all seriousness, my teacher asked if I personally believed it was right for him to constantly try to persuade Muslims to be born anew and become followers of the Lord Jesus Christ. Without hesitation and with great conviction I firmly answered, "Certainly you should, Mr. Johnson. Certainly you should!"

"Why?" he queried.

"Because you believe the Gospel with all of your heart and you live it. That is who you are. I wouldn't want you to be any different," I earnestly responded.

I was unprepared for what happened next. Hot tears coursed down the slightly wrinkled, sunburned face of my beloved teacher. He could not speak.

I sat quietly and wondered if there were other authentic Christians like this man. Maybe I should read his holy book once again as well as my own. Maybe, just maybe, I could find out which absolute truth is the absolute truth. Almighty God knows I truly want to know.

THE SWEETEST WORDS

Afghan veteran Anatoly loved his beautiful 15-year-old daughter Katya even though he did not know how to relate to her. He sat at the kitchen table in his two-room flat with a shot glass of vodka in his left hand and a cigarette in the other. Katya had just left to visit her good friend Tanya.

Anatoly had raised his daughter by himself since she was ten years old. One day five years ago Anatoly had come home from work to find a note from his wife left on the kitchen table. It read:

> I have had enough of your drunkenness and abuse. I have found a man who truly loves me. I never want to see you again. Take care of Katya. I must live my own life.
>
> Lila

From that day onward Anatoly lived for his daughter. She became his only purpose for living.

When Katya reached the age of 15 Anatoly began to constantly worry about her. It seemed all of a sudden she had blossomed into a lovely young woman. She was especially pretty with dark brown hair and beautiful brown eyes. Anatoly knew the boys would notice.

Anatoly didn't know how to talk with his teenage daughter. He only knew how to give orders. He never complimented Katya. He never once told her he loved her. He never once placed his arm around his daughter and said he was proud of her.

One day his worry for Katya became so severe he felt he had to act. He had to say something. So he drank down another shot of vodka and marched from the kitchen into the next room where she sat reading a romance novel. Towering over his petite daughter Anatoly said in a demanding voice, "Katya, you are never to take drugs. You are not to smoke or drink alcohol. You are never to permit a boy to touch you. If he does, I will knock his head off. Do you understand?"

Katya just sat there and stared back at her father and said nothing. Anatoly turned, went back to the kitchen, and quickly drank another shot of vodka. He had said what he had to say, but he still worried.

A few weeks later Anatoly came home from work to find Katya quietly reading a book. She looked up at him and smiled.

"What are you reading?" Anatoly asked in a loud voice.

"I'm reading the Bible," Katya softly replied.

"The Bible!" he exclaimed. "Katya, I don't believe there is a God. The Bible is a storybook full of fairy tales."

"Have you ever read it?" Katya politely asked.

"Where did you get it?" her father demanded to know.

"My friend, Tanya, gave it to me. I've been going to church with her."

"You what?" her father exploded.

"I've been attending church with Tanya. I've wanted to tell you. I'm sorry Papa, I haven't told you earlier. I really meant to."

"Katya, going to church is a waste of your time. Church is only for old grandmothers who need something to do," her father snapped.

Then Katya caught her father completely off guard, "Papa," Katya said in a tender voice, "I love you. Jesus has filled my heart with such wonderful love. I am very thankful to God that you are my father."

Anatoly became utterly speechless. No words would come to him. Tears began to well up in his eyes. Quickly turning away, he headed towards his sixth-floor apartment door.

Anatoly was glad no one was in the lift with him because he could not stop the tears, which slowly began to slide down his cheeks. He bit his lip and quickly wiped the tears from his eyes. *What is wrong with me,* he thought, *I'm a man. Why am I so emotional?* He had to take a walk.

Anatoly swiftly moved his big frame down the street. He headed towards a park. He needed to be alone. Anatoly found an empty bench and sat down. He reached for a cigarette, but then decided not to smoke. He must think. He must control his emotions.

"Papa, I love you," were the sweetest words he had ever heard. But how could Katya love him? He had driven away her mother. He still came home drunk, especially on weekends. He did not know how to relate to his daughter. Deep in his heart he considered himself a failure. He wanted to place his arm around Katya and tell her he loved her, but he was fearful of his own emotions. And if Katya knew his past, she would hate him.

It happened when he was a young 19-year-old soldier in Afghanistan. His unit received a report that Mujahideen were in a nearby village. Anatoly's unit was ordered to quietly surround the village after darkness fell and to shoot on sight any Mujahid fighter who tried to escape. At the break of dawn his unit was to attack.

It was still dark, right before dawn when Anatoly vaguely saw a figure running from the village towards a line of trees. In an instant Anatoly had aimed his weapon and shot. The figure slumped to the ground. Anatoly was elated. With one shot he had hit the target. He considered himself fortunate.

Soon dawn began breaking across the sky. There was very little movement in the village. Then the unit received word that the report was inaccurate. There were no Mujahideen in the village. Anatoly's unit was to withdraw. But hadn't a Mujahid tried to escape from the village?

Anatoly, with another young soldier, cautiously moved towards the fallen body. Anatoly looked down at the form on the ground and was horrified. "Oh God, oh God, what have I done?" he whispered in disbelief as he stared at the pretty face of a dark-haired village girl lying motionless. She was about 15 years old. A pool of blood was beside her. Anatoly dropped his weapon and fell to his knees. He whispered hoarsely to the body, "Please forgive me. Please forgive me." Then he vomited.

Now sitting on the park bench, he placed his head in his hands as once again the horrible scene passed through his mind. Since that tragic day Anatoly had never been the same. Often he would dream about that event and see the sad, still face of the beautiful Afghan girl. He drank to kill the pain. Time had not healed his heart. Yes, if Katya knew her father's past, she would hate him. Anatoly wept.

A few weeks later Anatoly was sitting once again at his small kitchen table drinking a shot of vodka when Katya came in. "Papa," she said, "may I please sit down and talk with you?" Anatoly nodded his head and motioned for her to sit on the stool across from him. Anatoly had to admit to himself that in recent weeks the character of his daughter had drastically changed for the better. He wasn't sure why. Katya quit trying to avoid him, but instead she seemed to want to be with him. Now she spoke kindly and respectfully to him instead of staring at her father in silence when he made demands of her.

Although Anatoly permitted Katya to attend church, he still thought it was a waste of time. But it did not seem to harm her. Anatoly was a little concerned Katya might become some kind of religious fanatic since she read the Bible every day and prayed. On the other hand, he had never seen her so sincere and thoughtful of other people. He would wait and see what happened.

Katya looked across the table at her father and smiled, "Papa," she began, "I have been praying for you and I think I need to tell you something."

Anatoly took a deep breath and felt uneasy.

"Papa, I want you to know something. I forgive you of everything in the past because I love you."

Anatoly looked down at the table.

"I want you to know, Papa, that God will forgive you of anything that may have happened in the past. Papa, I don't need to know your past. God knows it, and that is enough. I just want you to know God will forgive you because He loves you. Thank you, Papa, for listening to me."

Katya quietly stood up and slipped out of the kitchen. Her father continued to look down at the table. *Oh, Katya,* he thought, *I wish what you said were true, but if there is a God, I am sure He will not forgive me.*

A few days later Katya cooked a simple but delicious meal. Anatoly watched his daughter with admiration as she washed the dishes. In the middle of drying a pan Katya turned to her father and said, "Papa, I want you to do something very special for me."

"Sure, Katya, what is it?" Anatoly replied.

"Papa, I want you to go to a special church service with me on New Year's Eve. Please, Papa, will you go with me?" Katya begged.

"Well, Katya," Anatoly responded, "you know I don't go to church, and besides I plan to get together with two or three of my Afghan veteran friends to celebrate the New Year."

"But, Papa, just once couldn't you please go to church with me?"

"Well, Katya, I don't know."

"You aren't afraid to go to church are you, Papa?"

"Well, of course not," Anatoly replied indignantly.

"Well then, why not go with me on New Year's Eve?" Katya said.

Anatoly could see the pleading in his daughter's eyes. How could he refuse her? He knew he would feel awkward in church, but it would please his daughter. And in his heart, he also knew that it would be better than getting drunk with his friends.

As Anatoly stood up he tried to casually say, "Okay, Katya, I will go with you, but remember I don't believe in this God stuff."

"Oh, Papa, how marvelous!" Katya exclaimed as she threw her arms around his neck and kissed her father on his cheek.

Anatoly swallowed hard and tried to speak in a normal tone of voice, "No big deal, Katya, no big deal. Now I have to go and see my friend Volodya.

* * *

Anatoly and his daughter Katya stepped off the crowded tram and headed towards the church. It was New Year's Eve and very cold, but Katya had a warm heart as she slipped her hand inside her father's arm as they walked through the freshly fallen snow.

Anatoly was surprised to be so warmly welcomed by people at the church as Katya proudly introduced him to some of her friends. Anatoly took a seat on the back row beside his daughter. The service began and the people sang with sincerity and joy. The music touched Anatoly's heart. The speaker spoke calmly and clearly as he explained how a person could start a new life in Christ at the beginning of the New Year. Even though he was a skeptic, Anatoly was tempted to believe the message.

Then the congregation stood to pray. Although Anatoly felt awkward, he bowed his head. And to his own surprise he slipped his arm around his daughter's shoulder and found the courage to whisper a silent prayer from his heart. *God, if you are there, and if you can forgive me, please do so. God, thank you for giving me my beautiful daughter, Katya, who believes in You.* He paused, *And God, please help the Afghan family who lost their daughter.*

THE STRANGER WHO KEPT HIS PROMISE

Ten days before Sergei was to leave Afghanistan, a sniper's bullet pierced his neck. He was paralyzed from the neck down and could only lie in bed or be placed in a wheelchair. Others had to provide care for all his needs.

At first his friends often traveled to his village to visit him. But as time passed they went about their busy lives and came to see him less and less. Finally, it was unusual for anyone to stop by or even call or write him a letter. Sergei experienced great loneliness. Only his parents and faithful wife Olga remained true to him.

Olga and Sergei had married one month before he was drafted into the army. Every day Olga wrote to her strong, handsome husband. Together they dreamed about their future. They counted the days until his duty to the motherland would be fulfilled and he could return home. Then tragedy struck and their world collapsed.

Olga was not only outwardly beautiful, but far more important was the beauty of her inward character. When Sergei returned home in a wheelchair, he felt ashamed, robbed of his manhood. Sergei pleaded with his wife to divorce him and to marry someone who could provide for her, but she refused.

"Why, Sergei, circumstances do not change true love, and I truly love you. That's the reason I married you," she would say with an adoring smile.

The disabled veteran would look into her soft brown eyes and in a choked whisper declare, "You are a very foolish woman."

"Rubbish," the loving wife would respond. Then she'd ask, "Sergei, do you love me?"

"Of course I do, Olga. Of course I do!"

"Well, then," Olga would say with her gentle eyes, "that's all I need to know."

Olga worked in a factory about an hour from their village. Sergei's parents, who were pensioners, took turns each day staying with their son while Olga was at work. Sergei was their only child, born to them late in life. They loved their gifted son, who had been an outstanding student and soccer player in high school. It crushed their hearts when they received the news that a bullet had paralyzed him. They had such high hopes for his future.

Because of their love for Olga, Sergei and Olga's wedding day was a very happy time for his parents. They did not know who was happier, the bride and groom, or they themselves. Their son's tragedy did not lessen their devotion to him. They did not allow their sorrow to drown out their thankfulness that he was alive.

Sergei loved his wife and parents, but some days he wished he could die to relieve the burden he felt he was to them. In fact, at times he wanted to commit suicide, but because of his paralysis he couldn't find a way to do so. Sergei felt totally trapped and sometimes his feelings of depression and outrage made him want to scream. He could find no meaning or purpose for his life.

One sunny morning Sergei was sitting in his wheelchair in front of his house, letting the sun warm his face, when a stranger slowly walked up the path towards him. The stranger, a short man with broad shoulders and sandy hair, appeared to be in his early forties.

When the stranger reached Sergei, he cheerfully introduced himself. Sergei slightly nodded his head in response.

"Why are you here?" Sergei asked somewhat suspiciously.

"Well, I am here because I was told you are an Afghan veteran. Is that true?"

"Yes," Sergei answered.

"Well, so am I," the man said.

"When were you in Afghanistan and with what unit did you serve?" Sergei asked.

"I served with the sixth infantry in Herat in 1985-86. How about you?" the stranger inquired.

"I was with the 86th infantry unit in Kandahar in 1984-85," Sergei replied.

Although Sergei felt more at ease because the man was an Afghan veteran, he was still cautious.

"You said you came to see me because you were told I'm an Afghan vet. Who told you?" Sergei questioned.

With a kind expression on his face, the stranger replied, "A mechanic named Vladimir in your neighboring town told me about you. You see, I am a truck driver and my truck broke down this morning. So

I asked the mechanic whether he knew any Afghan vets in this area. When he mentioned you, I decided to visit you to keep a promise I made to God while I was in prison."

Sergei's mouth and gray eyes opened slightly wider upon hearing the stranger's unusual statement. With sarcasm in his voice Sergei asked, "And why were you in prison and what kind of promise did you make to God?"

The stranger was not disturbed by Sergei's tone, but calmly continued. "I was in prison due to my criminal activity. You see, when I returned from Afghanistan I felt rejected by my own society. It seemed to me that no one cared that I had risked my life for the motherland. I became angry and bitter. And when I could not find a job, I decided to make easy money, and to spit in the faces of those who rejected me. But I was caught by the police and sentenced to seven years in prison.

"I'll be glad to tell you about my promise to God, but first would you like to hear how that promise came about?" the man asked.

At this point, Sergei did not know whether or not to be skeptical. As for God, he wasn't even sure if He existed. After a long pause, Sergei said, "So go ahead and tell me how the promise came about."

By this time Sergei invited the stranger to pull up a stool that was near his wheelchair and to sit down. His fellow veteran seated himself, putting his elbows on his knees. Clasping his hands together he began.

"Well, I found prison to be a very restricted, lonely place. At first a few of my friends wrote to me. Some sent cigarettes and two even came to see me. But after several months, the letters stopped coming except from my mother. And she became my only visitor. My friends forgot me and my relatives disowned me. I do not blame my family members. I had been deliberately mean to every one of them.

"After about two years in prison I started to feel terribly lonely and depressed. Outwardly I tried to act very tough, but inwardly loneliness began eating away at my soul like a horrible cancer.

"Then one day a small group of Christians came to our prison to hold a meeting. Anyone was welcome to attend the meeting. I was never interested in Christianity or God, but I was bored, so I went just to have something to do. I was surprised that these Christians weren't arrogant or self-righteous. I have always disliked self-righteous people. Nevertheless, I thought it was easy for them to speak about God. They could freely walk out of the prison. I could not. Besides, my attitude was that God and I had a deal. I wouldn't bother Him and He wouldn't bother me. That was fine with me.

"Two weeks later those same Christians returned and held another meeting. I again attended. I figured, why not. In fact, they continued to come every two weeks. I wondered why. I could not figure out what they were gaining from this. So once when they came I decided to accept one of the Bibles they were always offering us. I thought maybe by reading the Bible I would find out the real reason those Christians made such a long drive to visit us."

Sergei quietly listened to the stranger but was becoming a little impatient. He wanted to hear about the promise.

The stranger continued, "To make a long story short the Bible changed my life. For you see, it told me about Jesus and His love for me. I discovered if I would ask Him to forgive my sins He would do so, and He promised never to forsake me or leave me alone. So one night when I thought everyone else was asleep, I knelt and asked Jesus to forgive me and to make me new inside just like the Bible promised He could do. Sergei, Jesus changed my life and made me new. At times I still had hard days in prison, but I knew that I was never alone because the Savior was with me."

"And what was the promise you made to God?" Sergei interrupted.

The stranger responded, "I promised God when I got out of prison, I would always look for another Afghan veteran who was suffering from loneliness and felt that his life had no meaning. So that is why I am here on your doorstep. I'm keeping my promise."

"And what makes you think I am lonely and that I think my life has no purpose?" Sergei said with irritation in his voice.

The visitor smiled warmly and was silent for several moments. Sergei could feel the compassion he saw in the eyes of this man.

The stranger quietly said, "Are you lonely, Sergei? Does your life have meaning?"

Sergei did not immediately answer. Finally he said, "Do you think there's any hope for me? Is God punishing me? Is that why I'm in this wheelchair?"

Tears came to the visitor's eyes. "No, Sergei, a thousand times no! God is not punishing you for your sins, or the sins of your parents, or anyone else's. God loves you and wants only to forgive your sins. He wants to heal your soul and give you eternal life. He desires to use you."

"How can He use me?" Sergei blurted out as he looked down at his hands and feet.

"Sergei, you are an intelligent and thoughtful person. God is able to use your mind. God has given you a voice. You can use it to speak encouragement to others. Why, Sergei, you may even want to try writing articles or maybe a book by dictating your thoughts to another. I am convinced that if you ask God, He will show you ways He can use you that you haven't even thought about."

The two Afghan veterans continued to talk about possibilities for Sergei's future as well as about their experiences in Afghanistan. Finally the stranger had to leave. They exchanged addresses and telephone numbers.

When Olga returned from work that evening, she found Sergei with his wheelchair pulled up to the kitchen table deeply engrossed in a book.

"What are you reading that has you so deep in thought?" Olga asked.

Trying to sound casual, Sergei replied, "Oh, the Bible, for you see, a stranger stopped by today to keep a promise, and I'm so very glad he did."

A DAUGHTER'S LAST REQUEST

Doctor Bekinsky's words caused Afghan veteran Alexander Petroff to feel as if someone had just kicked him hard in the stomach. The good doctor had just told Alexander and his wife Elena that their lovely 19-year-old daughter Svetlana had only a few days to live. She had contracted a rare fast-acting disease and there was no known cure. Alexander felt completely numb and Elena began to sob. Doctor Bekinsky sat motionless in his chair, his face full of pain.

Svetlana, the couple's only child, was in her second year at the university preparing to become a nurse. Three years earlier she had become a believer. Her faith is what had motivated her to enter the nursing profession. Svetlana's heart had become full of compassion and she especially wanted to help children.

One day while attending classes she began to feel seriously ill. After numerous tests the doctors discovered the cause of her illness but, sadly, could do nothing about it.

Svetlana's (Sveta's) parents felt it would be immoral not to tell their daughter the truth. They knew if they were in her position they would want to know. But how could they tell her. Sveta's mother had become a believer the year before. She suggested that Sveta's pastor, Pavel, should tell her the prognosis. Reluctantly, Alexander, who was not a believer, agreed.

Pastor Pavel respected Svetlana's parents because they had the courage to be honest with their daughter. With all color drained from their faces, the couple stood by their daughter's hospital bed while Pastor Pavel gently broke the news to her.

Sveta's response seemed unreal to Alexander. Sveta had smiled and said, "I know, God has spoken to my heart that He is taking me home to Heaven to be with Him."

Alexander wondered if a drug had affected his daughter's mind. Was she hallucinating? Had she lost all touch with reality? Alexander said nothing but gently patted his daughter's hand as he fought to hold back the tears.

Late that night as Alexander sat in his flat, he was tempted to go out and get drunk to silence his pain. But he decided that would not help. Instead, he let his mind reminisce about his daughter. Svetlana was the apple of his eye. He vividly remembered the day in Afghanistan when he received the joyous news that Elena had given birth to a beautiful baby girl. Along with the letter had come pictures of their new daughter. Alexander was especially pleased that she looked so much like him. He proudly showed everyone her pictures.

It would be another year before Alexander would be reunited with his family. Meanwhile the dedicated soldier purposed in his heart to be the best army officer possible. He personally felt deeply responsible for all the young men under his command. Alexander was determined to get those sons home alive to their mothers. He was well-liked by his troops because they knew their leader put their well-being before his own.

It was a joyous day for Alexander when his parents, Elena and his little hazel-eyed, light brown curly headed daughter met him at the train station. At first little Sveta treated him like a stranger, but within a few days she followed him around like a little puppy. Alexander delighted in his daughter and was thrilled beyond words to once again be with his faithful wife. Every evening Alexander lay on the floor and played with little Sveta. What joy she brought to him. Her laughter was rapturous music to his ears.

Alexander recalled Sveta's first day of school on the 1st of September. She bubbled over with excitement as she bounced down the street between her parents. She proudly held onto her father with one hand and with the other she clutched three roses for her new teacher. Sveta looked beautiful with white bows in her hair and wearing shiny new shoes.

The wonderful relationship Alexander had with his daughter only deepened as Sveta blossomed into a lovely young lady. She always had kind words to say about her father when her peers bitterly complained about theirs. Sveta considered herself fortunate to have such a thoughtful father who always had time for her. Theirs was the kind of warm relationship a father and daughter should have. At times Alexander would catch that special look of love in her eyes for him as her father. Nothing made Alexander feel so proud and happy as the love and respect shown to him by his wife and daughter.

Yes, life had been very good to Alexander. After retiring from the army Alexander became a successful businessman. He considered himself extremely fortunate. He now owned four shops that sold auto parts. He was still physically strong and worked out at a gym four days a week. Though well-liked by others for his kindness, he was a very proud, self-reliant man who felt he needed no one's help. He believed there was nothing he could not handle in life. He believed a person had only to determine in his own mind to be strong and he could overcome any problem.

But now his world had suddenly come crashing down upon him. No father on earth could love his daughter more than he loved Sveta, but now for the first time in his life he felt totally helpless. He knew no way to save her life. Alexander was completely devastated even though he did not want to admit it to anyone.

Alexander never felt he needed God. He considered it a sign of weakness for a man to say he did. However, he believed it was okay for women to pray if it made them feel psychologically better. After all, they were women.

After a long sleepless night Alexander once again sat by the bedside of his pale daughter. Although his heart was breaking, he had decided he must be very strong and brave for her sake.

"Papa," she said with that special look of love reserved only for her father, "I will be going to Heaven soon. It's such a beautiful place of peace and joy and happiness beyond description."

"But, honey," said Alexander through dry lips as he forced himself to control his emotions, "don't you want to live? Don't you want to live with me and your mother?"

"Oh, yes, Papa. I very much want to live with you and Mama, but what I want most is to live with you forever. That is why I want you to truly repent of your sin, and to ask Jesus to be your Savior. If you do so, He will give you eternal life. Then you and Mama and I will joyously live together forever. Papa, I want you to be with me in Heaven."

Alexander took a deep breath while trying not to show any expression on his face.

Sveta continued, "Papa, I want us to live together forever as a happy family. Please try hard to understand."

Alexander slowly nodded. For the sake of his daughter he would try to understand.

Very late that night Alexander again sat alone in the kitchen with a second cup of black coffee in his hand. His heart was full of sorrow beyond any he had experienced. The grief-stricken man could hardly bear the thought of his tenderhearted daughter dying at such a young age. She had such a radiant personality that gave life to her whole being.

Alexander had never liked thinking about death. He believed the only thing you could do when someone died was to preserve the person's memory. He had convinced himself that this present life on earth is the only life there is. At death people went out of existence.

Sveta's words kept running through his mind as he slowly sipped his coffee. *Papa, I want us to live together forever as a happy family. Please, Papa, try hard to understand.*

Alexander wished that was possible, but he considered it only wishful thinking. Besides, who would want to live with a God who took your daughter at such a young age? Alexander felt his heart becoming full of anger at God.

"How very cruel of you God!" the distraught father shouted out. He cursed.

After a long weary night, Alexander once again sat at the bedside of his daughter. He and Elena took turns sitting with her throughout the day. Sveta obviously was becoming weaker. In late afternoon, as if Sveta could read her father's mind, she said, "Papa, are you angry at God because He is taking me home to Heaven? I think you are."

"Of course I am angry, very angry!" Alexander blurted out as his anger erupted. "Only a cruel God would do this to you. A God who only wants to punish us for no reason."

Sveta's soft hazel eyes looked steadily into the sorrowful eyes of her father. "Papa, have you ever thanked God for bringing me into this world and giving me life? Have you ever thanked Him for all the good times He has given us together? Have you ever thanked Him for bringing you home safely from Afghanistan? Have you, Papa?"

Sveta paused and let those words sink into her father's consciousness before continuing. "God feels your pain. He has only one Son and He sent Him into this world to be crucified on a cruel cross for my sins so that I could go and live in Heaven forever. Papa, God is not punishing us. On the cross His Son Jesus took the punishment that you and I deserve for our sins. That's love, real love."

"But Sveta," her father protested, "you really haven't sinned. You have always been such a good girl."

"Oh, Papa, yes I have sinned," his daughter responded. "And one of the sins I have committed is the same kind of sin that you have committed. Until three years ago I was like you, because I always wanted to be like you. I too felt that I was strong, self-sufficient and could handle any problem. I believed as you do that only weak people need God. But now we see that we were wrong. I cannot save my life and neither can you save me from death. Papa, it is sinful pride that makes us think that we are self-sufficient and don't need God."

Alexander was truly amazed at his daughter's ability to clearly articulate her thoughts. He had always tried to teach her to think clearly. Perhaps he had taught her too well. Alexander had never so patiently listened to his daughter. He realized she was talking much because she loved him.

After a long silence Sveta said, "Papa, please don't be angry with God because I am dying. He is the One who has made it possible for me to live forever in Heaven."

Three days later while her mother and father gently held their daughter's hands, Sveta opened her eyes and smiled. In a whispering voice she said, "Papa and Mama, I love you. Please meet me in Heaven!" Then their lovely daughter took her last breath and peacefully passed from this earth.

Pastor Pavel spoke at Sveta's funeral. He said in the midst of deep sorrow we can have great hope because Jesus said, "I am the resurrection and the life. He who believes in me will live, even though he dies.... Do not let your hearts be troubled. Trust in God, trust also in me. In my Father's house are many rooms; if it were not so, I would have told you. I am going there to prepare a place for you."

Four days later it was Easter Sunday. Veteran Alexander Petroff sat next to his wife in church. In his hand he held his daughter's Bible. As his eyes moistened he thought to himself, *Yes, my precious daughter Sveta, I will try to understand, for I long to come to you.*

THE OLD VETERAN AND NADEZHDA

PART 1

Nadezhda, a Medical Academy student, was quietly walking in a hospital corridor when through a partly open door, she saw an old man sitting on the edge of his bed. She had met this elderly veteran during a previous visit and now returned to his room to chat. Peter Alexejevich was nearly 80 years old and she had just turned 21. The lovely young lady had brown eyes bright with kindness and a tender voice full of sincerity. The old veteran wondered why the soft-spoken church girl cared about an old man like him. He had no family and considered the hospital his home.

Nadezhda gently asked Peter questions about his life. He was glad to tell again about his experiences in the Great Patriotic War[1] and proudly showed her his medals. She kindly asked about each one and the old veteran carefully explained. Then with a pleasant smile Nadezhda said, "You have lived a wonderful life. Now what do you think about your future?"

Future, the old veteran repeated the word in his mind. He did not know what to say. He tried not to think about his future. When he was young he believed he had a future. He had gone to war to protect the motherland. After three years of fighting on the front lines he returned home a hero, and believed he had a future. How the years had flown by! And now before he knew it, he had become an old war veteran. Future... he felt he had no future. He and his fellow veterans constantly talked about the past, the glorious past. Now more than ever the Great Patriotic War defined their lives. Usually, no one spoke to them about their future, only about their past.

Nadezhda patiently listened for a reply.

Old Peter took a deep breath and sighed as he ran his hand through his thin gray hair. He felt he had to be honest with Nadezhda even though he would like to have avoided the subject. With sad eyes he looked into hers as he slightly leaned forward and slowly uttered, "I have no future, daughter; everything I have is in my past."

"Oh, but you can have!" Nadezhda said as a warm smile spread across her face.

"How can that be?" the old veteran queried. "Soon I will die and be buried. That will be the end of me. I have no future."

Softly, Nadezhda said, "But you can have a future. Do you know that the Lord Jesus Christ personally loves you? That He died on a cruel cross for your sins? He rose from the dead. He is the Savior. If you ask Him to forgive you of all your sins, He will. He offers you a glorious future, an eternal home in Heaven with Him.

"Jesus once said, 'I am the resurrection and the life. He who believes in me will live, even though he dies.' Jesus also said, 'Do not let your hearts be troubled. Trust in God; trust also in me. In my Father's house are many rooms; if it were not so, I would have told you. I am going there to prepare a place for you.'"[2]

The old veteran with wrinkled skin looked carefully for a moment into the smooth face of Nadezhda before speaking. Then with amazement in his voice he said, "Do you really believe that?" He knew from the look on her face that she did. The old man was puzzled because he knew Nadezhda was an excellent student at the university. In fact, she was studying to be a heart surgeon.

"Yes, I do," said the girl.

There was a long silence as the elderly veteran pondered her words. He thought, *Could it possibly be that what this church girl said is true? If it is true, I could have a future.* The thought of going out of existence had always depressed him. He did not want to hurt the girl's feelings, but once again he felt he must be honest with her. Finally, the old gentleman in a voice just above a whisper said, "I doubt that."

"So did I," Nadezhda admitted.

Surprised, he sat up straighter, "But you are a church girl. You are supposed to believe in God."

"But I wasn't brought up in the church," she responded.

"But you go to church," the old veteran replied.

"I do now, but I didn't until one day another student talked with me about God's personal love for me and gave me a Bible to read. I now have real joy and peace in my heart."

The old veteran was happy for Nadezhda and wished he too could believe, but how could he? He had grown up and lived in a different day. Nadezhda seemed to have read his thoughts and understood his skepticism. With a glow in her eyes she said, "I would like to make a suggestion since I believe you are a sincere skeptic. I suggest you pray an honest skeptic's prayer."

"But I don't know how to pray," interrupted the old veteran. "I've never prayed except once in a fierce battle I cried out, 'God, help me.' I don't even know why I said that."

"It's okay that you don't know how to pray. I didn't know how to pray either. The only time I had prayed before I gave my life to Jesus was one day on a street when I saw a certain young man from my school who I wanted to ask me for a date. I whispered, 'God, please help him to notice me.'" The old veteran and Nadezhda laughed together.

"If it is okay with you," Nadezhda continued, "I'll write out an honest skeptic's prayer for you. And later, after you read it, if you want to pray it from your heart, you can." The old veteran nodded his approval. So Nadezhda reached into her purse and took out a piece of paper and a pen. She carefully wrote out a prayer as the old soldier studied her. *Why does this young lady care about an old man like me? I am not worth much, but for some reason she thinks I am.*

Nadezhda handed the old veteran the sheet of paper. Then she smiled and said, "I must go now to study for an examination. I'll look forward to seeing you next week."

The old veteran nodded his head, shook her hand and thanked her for coming to see him. He hated to see her go and was already anticipating her next visit.

Nadezhda quietly slipped out the door but the kindness of her presence lingered. The veteran sat and thought for a few moments and then slowly picked up the sheet of paper and began to read.

> God, if you are there, and I do not know if you are there, please make yourself known to me. If it is true that Jesus is your Son who died on the cross for my sins, and that He is the Savior Who personally loves me, then I sincerely ask Him to forgive me of all my sins. I ask Him to come into my life and to grant me a future in Heaven with Him. So God, if you are there, please hear and answer my prayer.

For a long time the old veteran thought about the prayer. Then he thought to himself, *Yes, I can honestly pray that prayer. And if God is there, I can truly have a future.*

Peter Alexejevich slowly read the prayer again, only this time he read it quietly out loud and from his heart. Then he paused and added another line at the end of the prayer, "And God, if you are there, thank you for Nadezhda."

THE OLD VETERAN AND NADEZHDA
Part 2

The old veteran, Peter Alexeyevich, sat on the edge of his hospital bed, thinking, thinking, thinking. She had promised she would come today. He knew she would. The old man was greatly anticipating the visit of Nadezhda, the young medical student. Her sincere and pure heart had captured his own. He felt he could be completely honest with Nadezhda and not be rejected.

A few minutes later Nadezhda quietly slipped into the room. With a smile she pulled up a chair and sat down opposite the gray-haired veteran. Her beautiful dark hair set off her youthful face and sparkling brown eyes. To the elderly veteran she looked like an angel. The old veteran and Nadezhda chatted for a while. Then he grew quiet. Nadezhda could tell from the serious expression on his face that there was something on his mind. She patiently waited for him to speak. Nadezhda's eyes told the old man he could trust her.

Finally he began softly, "Daughter, I must tell you the truth about myself. The last time you came, you said something that has greatly disturbed me. After we looked at my medals you said I have lived a wonderful life. I must tell you that is not true. Sometimes young people try to comfort old people by making such statements. But covering up the past with optimistic words is not helpful."

Nadezhda slowly nodded her head in agreement. She felt admiration for the old man. His insight and honesty had just taught her a vital lesson.

The old veteran paused as he summoned up courage to continue. "Nadezhda, my life has not been wonderful. For some reason I feel I can tell you my true feelings."

Nadezhda felt honored that the old man trusted her. She smiled shyly and did not move.

Pausing for a moment, he began again, "I came home a hero but my life has not been wonderful. Two years after my return my only brother cheated me out of a large sum of money. I hated him because of his selfishness. I refused to speak to him ever again and did not attend his funeral. This I regret."

The old veteran looked searchingly into Nadezhda's face for a sign of condemnation. There was none. He looked down at the floor as he continued, "Daughter, once I drank too much and started a fight with another man in a bar. I broke his nose and right arm. Neither ever healed properly. Nadezhda, it gets worse. I was unfaithful to my wife and treated her badly. She was a good woman. I did not deserve her." The old man's voice broke, "I must tell you the truth. I am not a wonderful person. I have not lived a wonderful life."

Nadezhda felt compassion flowing through her heart for the sorrowful man. She wished others would be as honest about their lives. Nadezhda reached out and touched the old man's hand. Almost in a whisper she said, "Papa, I love you no less because you told me the truth about your life. God loves you. He will forgive you if you ask Him to."

The old veteran looked at Nadezhda, trying to absorb her words. He thought *How* can *this lovely young lady so full of life love me so deeply.* The room was very still while the old veteran struggled with his emotions. Finally he spoke, "I prayed the skeptic's prayer you wrote and left with me the last time you were here. But Nadezhda, if there is a God, how can He forgive me of my sins? I have committed so many."

"Because He loves you," she replied. "On the cross His Son Jesus paid the price for your sins so you can be redeemed. When you personally repent and ask Him for forgiveness, He forgives. A verse in the Bible says, 'If we confess our sins, He is faithful and just to forgive us our sins and purify us from all unrighteousness.' Papa, it's a promise," Nadezhda joyously exclaimed.

The old veteran felt hope arising in his heart. To be forgiven. To be made clean. To not be afraid of death. To have a joyous future in Heaven. How wonderful that would be! The old veteran wanted to believe. He lifted his head and looked into the soft clear eyes of Nadezhda and smiled slightly.

Moments later Nadezhda had to go. In parting, she hugged him and promised to visit again next week.

The week passed and it was May 9th, Victory Day. At mid-morning, Nadezhda arrived by bus at the veterans hospital. In her delicate hands she held a bouquet of flowers and a neatly wrapped box of candy. With a happy heart she walked down the long corridor and quietly slipped once again into the old veteran's room. Puzzled, she looked around. He wasn't there. His bed was empty. Then a nurse walked in. "Where is Mr. Peter Alexejevich?" she asked.

The tall thin nurse looked surprised to see her and replied, "Oh, I'm sorry to tell you. He died last night in his sleep."

Tears filled Nadezhda's eyes and quietly rolled down her cheeks. She loved the old veteran. Nadezhda had never known either of her grandfathers. That is what the old man had become to her. Nadezhda lowered her head and prayed silently. When she opened her eyes, they fell upon the Bible, which was on a stand next to the bed. Nadezhda noticed a folded sheet of paper tucked into it. Carefully, she took out the paper and unfolded it. It was a letter addressed to her dated May 8th.

Dear Daughter,

I have never been good at expressing myself, but I want to thank you for giving me hope. When I met you I had no hope for the future. I lived only in memories. Because of you I now have a future. I have come to believe that God is there. I have been reading the Bible you gave me. I understand now that Jesus died for my sins and loves me. Since your last visit I have been reviewing my life, confessing my sins, and asking God to forgive me. Today I woke up feeling completely clean on the inside. I have never felt like this before. I feel as if I have been given a new life. I now have peace in my soul as never before.

Thank you, Nadezhda, for giving a hopeless old veteran true hope. I love you.

Your Papa

Tears fell freely as her heart overflowed with thanksgiving to God. She would miss the old veteran, but in the midst of her sorrow she experienced the joy of knowing she would see him again. Nadezhda thought of the verse in the Bible that says, "But thanks be to God! He gives us the victory through our Lord Jesus Christ!" Yes, she knew the old veteran was experiencing everlasting victory!

As Nadezhda turned to leave, an old veteran shuffled into the room with a hopeless look on his face. He sat on the edge of the other bed and gazed out the window. Wiping her tears, Nadezhda approached the elderly man and introduced herself, "Hello sir, my name is Nadezhda.[3] I would like to congratulate you on Victory Day," she said with a smile, while handing him a bouquet of flowers and a box of candy wrapped in love. Surprised, he asked her if she would like to pull up a chair. She did.

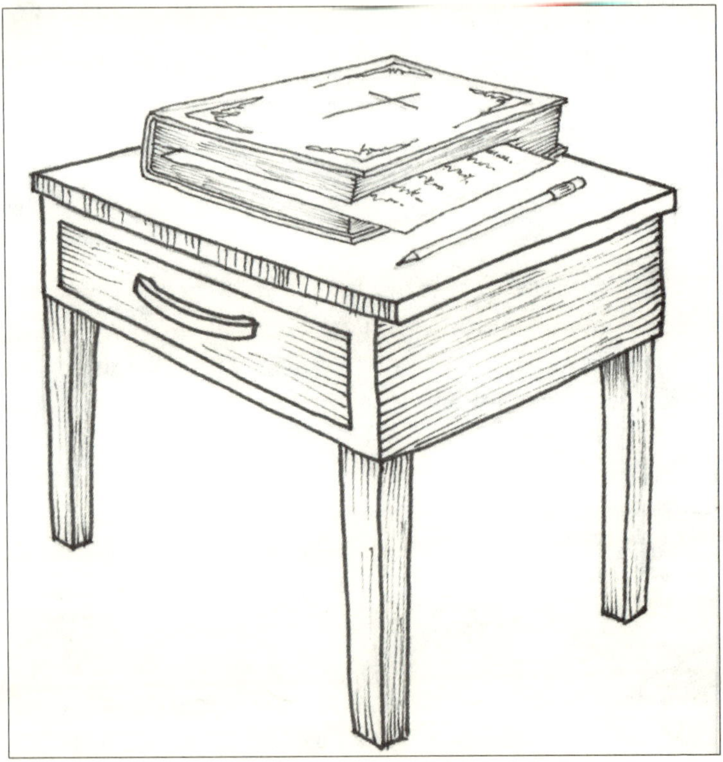

FIVE VETERANS MEET IN HEAVEN

The five veterans were surprised to meet each other in Heaven. Tuan was from North Vietnam, Dima from Russia, Habib from Afghanistan, and Bob and Steve from the United States. The five of them sat together drinking celestial tea.

To his amazement Tuan recognized Bob. He remembered being hidden high in a tree in the dense jungles in Vietnam and looking through the telescope of his sniper rifle. Although unseen himself, he could clearly see the handsome face of a young American soldier. The American was alone, apparently lost. He looked distressed. Tuan was delighted for he hated Americans. Tuan aimed carefully and slowly squeezed the trigger. With one shot he killed his enemy. Tuan felt elated at his success.

The Vietnamese sniper remained motionless until the night's darkness engulfed the jungle. Then he quietly slipped down the tree, and in silence approached the body of his prey. Holding a match as he searched the body, he found a picture of the American soldier with his wife and baby girl. As he closely looked at the photo, Tuan felt a momentary stab of pain in his heart for the dead soldier's family. He thought about his own beautiful wife and baby who lived in a village in North Vietnam.

The war finally ended, but Tuan could not forget the face of the dead American soldier. It haunted him in his nightmares.

In Heaven as Tuan looked across the table at Bob tears of joy filled his eyes. "Bob," Tuan exclaimed, "I am so very glad you are here. For you see, I am the person who killed you. I could never forget your face. I would try to justify killing you, but in my heart I could never quite do so." His voice choking with emotion, Tuan continued, "Bob, will you forgive me for killing you?"

Bob's brown eyes, full of forgiving love, looked deeply into Tuan's dark eyes. Gently Bob spoke, "Yes, Tuan, I forgive you. My heart is full of joy because you are now my brother. Please tell me, how it is that you are in Heaven."

Tuan wiped his eyes and took a deep breath, "Bob, after the war I returned to live in my village. Several years later an American volunteer relief worker arrived with two Vietnamese men to assist us in digging deep wells. I was startled when from a short distance away I saw the face of the volunteer. He looked exactly like you. I was terrified. Fear gripped my heart. Had you come back from the dead to get revenge? I knew you did not know me. But how did you find my village so deep inside Vietnam?

"I quietly slipped away, hoping no one heard the pounding of my heart. I stayed completely away from the person who I thought was you. The other villagers liked the American volunteer because he spoke our language, ate our food and was very kind.

"Once the leader of our village asked him why he had come to assist us. He said because God loves you. No one understood what he meant, God loves you. The people in my village noticed that every morning the volunteer read a book in our language and prayed. One of my friends asked him if he was in the war. He said, 'No, but I had an identical twin brother who was killed in Vietnam.'

"When my friend told me this I thought to myself, *How can this man love us? I killed his brother. What is his secret to life? I want to know.* Bob, when your brother left our village he gave his Vietnamese Bible to our village leader. Later I borrowed it. I thought perhaps it would tell me the secret of your brother's life. It did. Bob, that is why I am here in Heaven today."

Dima, the veteran from Russia, was fascinated by the conversation between Tuan and Bob, but there was something even more amazing to him. It seemed unbelievable to Dima that he was in Heaven sitting across the table from a former Afghan guerilla fighter.

Dima looked at Habib, the Afghan, and said, "I cannot believe we are here together in Heaven. I wanted to kill as many Afghan fighters as possible and to send them all to hell. They killed my closest friend in a fire fight."

"I understand," Habib replied. "I had a burning passion to kill as many Soviet soldiers as possible, for you see, my youngest sister was killed by a Soviet rocket when it hit our house."

Dima was quiet for a moment then said, "I am very sorry about your sister."

Habib responded, "I believe you are."

"Habib," Dima asked, "How is it that you are here in Heaven?"

Habib sat back in his chair and thought for a moment, "After I returned from fighting in the mountains of Afghanistan, I went to Peshawar, Pakistan to take a break from the war. One day as I was wandering about in the old bazaar, I saw a used book shop so I went in to browse. I had graduated from Kabul University with my degree in linguistics. I was very proud of the fact that I had great language ability and could fluently speak and read Pashtu, Dari, Arabic, English and Urdu. I considered myself an excellent scholar and enjoyed reading books.

"While looking through the books, I was surprised to see a copy of the Bible in Urdu on a high shelf. As I opened it, I made another unexpected discovery. This Urdu Bible was printed and published in Pakistan, an Islamic country. I wondered how that could be. I decided to buy it so I could read and refute it, since I believed the Bible had been corrupted. Day after day in the afternoon I sat alone in Khalid Park and read the Bible. As I read about Jesus I found myself captivated by His life.

"However, one day I became angry when I read that Jesus said we are to love our enemies. How could I possibly love the Soviet soldiers who were atheists? God certainly did not love atheists. In fact, I believed I was helping God by killing them. Due to my anger I almost quit reading the Bible, but for some reason I continued. When I read Jesus' prayer of forgiveness for those who were crucifying Him, I was completely astonished. I would have cursed them!

"One night I had a dream. In the dream Jesus came to me. He said, 'Habib, I am the Way, the Truth and the Life. Come follow me. I am the Savior.' Suddenly I awoke and my room was filled with a bright light. I bowed my face to the floor and asked Jesus to forgive me and to save me. When I did, my heart was flooded with joy. I had never experienced such love.

"Later I returned to Afghanistan but no longer could I shoot to kill. One day we were ambushed and a grenade landed in the midst of us. I threw myself on it to save the lives of my fellow fighters. The next thing I knew I was in Heaven. And now, here I am with you."

Habib continued, "Dima, it is your turn to tell us how it is that you are here in Heaven." The other veterans at the table nodded in agreement.

Dima began, "After the war I tried to drown my pain in drink because I survived when several of my friends did not. I became an alcoholic and began abusing my wife. She finally left me for another man. I thought about committing suicide. In fact, once I put a gun to my head, but right at that very moment someone knocked on my door and I put my gun away.

"The next day as I walked down a street, I met a friend I used to drink with. Like me he had been a paratrooper. I said, 'Sergei, let's go have a drink together for ole times' sake.'

"Sergei smiled and said, 'Thank you, Dima, but I don't drink anymore.'

"I said, 'What? You don't drink anymore! Are you sick?'"

"'No,'" he said. 'Jesus has changed my life.'"

"I could not believe my ears. I sarcastically responded, 'What! Have you become some kind of a religious fanatic? What do you mean, 'Jesus has changed your life?'"

"Sergei replied, 'When I was released from prison I knew my life needed to change. I realized I could not change myself. But I did not know what to do. One day I said, 'God, if you exist, please help me. Please change me.'

"A few days later a neighbor invited me to church. I thought, *Why not*? So I went.

"The people were genuinely friendly and the way they sang from their hearts was inspiring. The pastor spoke about God's great love for each of us. That was hard for me to believe since I knew the kind of sinner I was, but I kept returning to the church. The day came when I asked Jesus to forgive me and to change me. And He did.

"I looked at Sergei and thought, *This sounds too simple to be true.*

"Sergei seemed to read my mind. He said, 'Look, Dima, come to church with me and see for yourself.'

"I thought, *Why not? It won't hurt for me to go one time.* So I did. To my surprise I kept returning. And what happened to Sergei happened to me."

Habib warmly smiled at Dima as he continued, "And you know, Habib, God delivered me from my bad habits. But what convinced me the most that Christ had really changed me was that I no longer hated the Afghans. In fact, I wanted to return to Afghanistan to help the Afghans rebuild their country."

Habib reached across the table and firmly shook Dima's hand.

After four of the veterans had shared their stories, they turned their attention to Steve the American veteran who had participated in the Korean War. Steve had quietly listened to the others.

After a long silence, Steve finally spoke. "My brothers, I am very grateful to God you are here in Heaven and we will be brothers forever. Your stories have caused me to marvel at God's love for each of us.

"Maybe I am the one most grateful for God's grace, because perhaps I committed the greatest sin. In fact, due to the terrible sin I committed as a soldier, I believed God would never forgive me. I was absolutely certain I was doomed to spend eternity in hell which I knew I deserved."

The other veterans leaned forward in their chairs as they listened closely to Steve.

"You see," Steve continued, "I was 19 years old when I arrived in the cold and barren land of Korea. Five days after my arrival I was assigned to go on patrol with three other American soldiers. As we drove slowly up a mountain road in our jeep, suddenly three North Korean soldiers came up out of a ditch. They had their hands raised high over their heads. It was clear they were surrendering.

"We stopped.

"The sergeant sitting next to me barked: 'Get out and kill them!'

"I was shocked by his order and objected, 'Sergeant, they are surrendering. They have no weapons.'

"The sergeant snapped back, 'We don't take prisoners. Shoot them!'

"My mouth went dry. I said, 'Sergeant, we are Americans. We don't shoot prisoners.'

"'Shoot them!' the sergeant shouted at me.

"With my voice full of anger I yelled back, 'I will not! I am an American!'

"The sergeant's face turned red as he pulled out his revolver and pointed it at my head. In a low, mean voice he spit out, 'Private, you shoot them or I will shoot you and say they did it.' I knew he meant it.

"Trembling, I got out of the jeep and killed all three prisoners. The sergeant laughed. I was horrified at what I had done. From that moment on I considered myself a coward. I never told anyone because I thought no one would believe me. All my life I lived with that horrible secret. It tormented my soul.

"When I was 74 years old I was diagnosed with cancer. The doctors in the veterans hospital said I only had a few weeks to live. I became terrified at the thought of dying since I knew I would have to face God. He knew my secret. I became so terrified of death that I could hardly speak, and I did not want to see anyone. Not anyone! But something unusual happened. A man with a very kind face walked into my hospital room and sat down by my bed. He was the hospital chaplain.

"Somehow he knew I was full of fear. 'Steve,' he said gently, 'I believe you have a secret from the war that you have never been able to tell anyone. I believe that is why you are paralyzed by fear.'

"I was shocked. *How did he know I had such a secret?* I stared at him.

"The chaplain softly continued, 'Steve, I do not condemn you for your secret. All your life you have suffered from it. I am ready to listen to your secret. I will not tell others. God is ready to forgive you if you will ask for His forgiveness.'

"I mumbled to the chaplain, 'God will never forgive me. I am doomed to hell.'

"The chaplain looked at me with eyes full of compassion like I had never seen before. He said, 'Steve, let me tell you a story. Jesus was dying on a cross between two men who were also being crucified. They were criminals. One thief said to the other: 'We are being punished justly, for we are getting what our deeds deserve. But this man has done nothing wrong.'

'Steve, I wonder what the criminal did that caused him to say he deserved to be crucified? He must have done something very horrible.

'Steve, then the man in his agony turned to Jesus with a truly repentant attitude and said, 'Jesus, remember me when you come into your kingdom.'

'Jesus answered, 'I tell you the truth, today you will be with me in paradise.'

"The sensitive chaplain then said to me, 'There is no sin Christ cannot forgive if we honestly ask for His forgiveness. I think it would help you if you told me your secret. I will tell no one. God wants to forgive you. That is the reason Jesus died on the cross for you.'

"For some reason I knew I could trust the chaplain. Slowly through hot tears I told him my secret.

"When I finished he asked if I would like to ask Jesus to forgive me. I said, 'Yes.' The chaplain nodded, and haltingly in my own words I asked Jesus to forgive me. Then I wept as I had never wept in my life. Peace flooded my soul. One week later I died peacefully, ready to meet God."

Tears of joy filled the eyes of the other veterans seated around the table. They understood.

After hearing each others' stories, the five veterans spontaneously stood, raised their hands and worshiped the One who had redeemed them.

THE OLD MISSIONARY

The old missionary, now in his eighties, began his daily morning walk by the sea. The clear blue sky was beautiful. Sun rays glistened on the perfectly calm sea. The quietness of the sea reflected the calmness of his heart. The old man gazed into the cloudless sky as if he were gazing into Heaven.

As he strolled by the quiet waters, he continued his intimate conversation with his Lord. They had become close friends from the time he was a boy of six. Over the years, the longer the old missionary had lived, the more intimate their friendship had become. The Lord and he delighted in each other's company.

The elderly white-haired man with sunburned wrinkles always seemed to have a twinkle in his deep blue eyes. As he slowly walked tears of joy quietly slipped from his eyes as he reflected on his past. He and his Lord had faced many challenges since he first stepped onto foreign soil 55 years earlier. The old missionary had experienced hardships, dangers, disappointments, illnesses, slander, rejection and ridicule, but the joys he experienced far outweighed the difficulties. Peace flowed through his being because he knew he had not wasted his life. Instead, he knew God had fulfilled His purpose for him. This more than satisfied the old saint's heart.

The old missionary slowed his pace and thanked his Friend Jesus for saving his soul, and for never failing him. He thanked Him for sending Susan into his life. Soon they would celebrate their 60th wedding anniversary. They had sought God with all their hearts and knew He had chosen them for each other. The old missionary loved Susan even more than the day he married her, something he thought wasn't possible.

As the aged man glanced at the crystal-clear sea, a large fish suddenly broke the water and leaped high into the air. Happy memories made him smile as he thought about his boyhood days when he and his father fished from an old wooden boat on Lake Milton. He loved those special times because it was just the two of them. Often with his line in the water he sang the song he learned in Sunday school, "I will make you fishers of men, fishers of men, fishers of men. I will I make you fishers of men if you follow Me." The very words Jesus had spoken to His disciples. It seemed to him he could almost hear Jesus whispering in his ear, "Someday for Me, you will be fishing for men." The day came when as a young man with Susan by his side he followed his Savior to a faraway country to fish for those who had never heard the Good News.

Now as the elderly missionary turned and retraced his steps home, he quietly prayed name by name for his beloved friends in that far off land. Most of them had been his close friends for many, many years. They loved Susan and him even though very few had surrendered their hearts to the Savior. This was a mystery to the old man, but he would never give up praying for their salvation. He would pray for them until he took his last breath.

As he neared home, the old missionary hastened his step. The love of his life was waiting for him. When he opened the screen door of their little cottage, Susan turned, and her eyes sparkled at the sight of her husband. They embraced. The old missionary seated his wife and himself at the table. Joining hands and bowing in prayer, they humbly thanked their Heavenly Father for each other. Joy filled their hearts. Peacefully they faced the future, knowing they would have forever together.

AN ENCOURAGING MESSAGE

HEARING GOD'S COMPLIMENTS

I have a very important question to ask you. When was the last time you heard your Heavenly Father say something good about you to you? This morning? Last night? Last month? When was the last time you heard your Heavenly Father compliment you? A compliment is when someone says something good about you to you.

If a child hears only his parents' corrections and never hears his parents' compliments, you would think there is something wrong with the child's hearing. You would be right. If you, as a child of your Heavenly Father, hear only His corrections and never hear His compliments, you have a hearing problem.

You would not consider parents wise or loving if they only corrected and never complimented their child. You would be right. If a good parent compliments his or her child, how much more does your Heavenly Father want to compliment you, His child!

Why does a parent compliment his child? Because he loves his child. Because he wants to encourage his child. Because he wants his child to see himself as he really is. These are the very same reasons your Heavenly Father desires to compliment you, His child.

There is an amazing statement in God's Holy Word in I Corinthians 4:5 that I would not believe except it is in the Bible. The last sentence of this verse says, "At that time each will receive his praise from God." The dictionary definition of compliment is an "expression of praise."

This verse is talking about that day when you will stand before God. It is saying that on that day, God Himself is going to say many good things about you, to your face, and before many other people. Now if God on that day is going to say beautiful things about you to you, don't you think at the present time He is saying beautiful things about you to you? There is no doubt in my mind that He is doing exactly that, but you must listen and receive those compliments.

Often, we do not hear what God is saying because He is saying things we don't expect Him to say. We need to learn to <u>listen</u> to God's compliments and to <u>accept</u> them. How do you think a parent feels when he genuinely compliments his child, but the child will not accept his parent's loving words? How do you think your Heavenly Father feels when He genuinely compliments you, but you will not receive what He says.

There are many examples in the Bible of God complimenting His children. In Hebrews 11:5 we find this statement about Enoch. The best translation from the Greek says: ". . . he obtained the witness that before his being taken up he was pleasing to God" (NASB). In this verse underline in your mind the word "before."

God said good things to Enoch about Enoch before God took him to Heaven. What is so very interesting about Enoch is that the Bible says so little about him: six verses in the Old Testament, three verses in the New Testament. We have no big success story about Enoch, as most people understand the idea of success. We read nothing about Enoch performing great accomplishments. Yet we are told that God was pleased with Enoch. We read that God told Enoch He was pleased with him before Enoch was taken to Heaven.

Often, we do not hear God saying good things about us to us, because we believe for God or anyone else to say something good about us, we must be successful at doing good works. We must perform! We must produce! We must prove ourselves! We think our worth as a person depends upon our work. This is not true! Our worth as a person is based upon the fact that Jesus loves us!

Was God pleased with Enoch because he could perform, produce and prove himself acceptable? In Genesis chapter 5 and verses 21 and 24 we read why God was pleased with Enoch and complimented him. Twice in those verses it says Enoch walked with God!

God was pleased with Enoch simply because he walked with Him. God is pleased with you because you walk with Him. This is what brings joy to His heart. There is not another person in the whole universe like you. That is why He cherishes His relationship with you. That makes you special, and He loves walking with you. The greatest joy for me on the foreign field was walking and talking with God day after day.

Exodus 33:17 says: "And the Lord said to Moses . . . I am pleased with you." Was Moses a perfect man? The record clearly shows he was not. Do your children have to be perfect before you compliment them? Of course not! Then why do you and I think we must be perfect before God can compliment us?

Do you know that God complimented Daniel? God let Daniel know how highly he was thought of in Heaven. In chapters 9 and 10 of Daniel you will find this said directly to Daniel three different times because God wanted to be sure Daniel heard His compliment. "Daniel, you are highly esteemed!"

I believe this really surprised Daniel. He was feeling very weak. Daniel was praying and confessing his sins and the sins of his people. I don't believe Daniel had any idea he was so highly thought of in Heaven when he heard what he did not expect to hear, "Daniel, you are highly esteemed!" What a compliment Daniel received from God! In fact, probably the greatest revelation to Daniel was not the incredible prophetic revelations he received from God, but the revelation that he, Daniel, was highly esteemed in Heaven.

You would be amazed, my brothers and sisters, if you really knew how highly esteemed you are in Heaven.

In the Gospel of Mark chapter 14 you can read about Jesus complimenting a lady. In an act of love a very devout lady poured expensive perfume on the head of Jesus. There were those in the room who harshly rebuked her for not selling the perfume and giving the money to the poor. It is likely this dear woman felt terribly embarrassed and confused. Perhaps she thought she had made a serious mistake. But instead of criticizing her, Jesus complimented her before others. He said, "She has done a beautiful thing to me.... She did what she could" (Mark 14:6,8). Can you imagine how very surprised this conscientious woman was to hear Jesus compliment her!

If you are doing what you can for Jesus, though few may notice your efforts or you feel limited or misunderstood, Jesus may surprise you by complimenting you in a way you would never expect. Please listen and accept His compliments as His precious child.

Jesus once highly complimented a Roman military officer who did not expect to hear such words from our Lord. He was not Jewish, but a Gentile. He was part of the army that occupied Israel. He was a man of authority. He had to be amazed to hear from the lips of Jesus, "I tell you the truth, I have not found anyone in Israel with such great faith" (Matthew 8:10).

The Lord Jesus sees your heart of faith, compassion, and humility as He saw the heart of the centurion. Do not be surprised if He compliments you.

In the New Testament we find an unknown, faithful village girl being complimented by God. Luke 1:28 says, "The angel went to her and said, 'Greetings, you who are highly favored!'" Mary had no idea God thought so highly of her.

Jesus once publicly praised a man. You can read all about it in Matthew 11. Jesus publicly praised John the Baptist. Jesus praised John when he was depressed, discouraged, confused and full of doubts. At the time John was in prison.

John had sent his disciples to ask Jesus this question, "Are you the one who was to come, or should we expect someone else?"

If I would have been Jesus, I would have chided John and said, "Oh no, John, not you! I am so very disappointed in you. You are the one who identified me and declared, 'Behold the Lamb of God who takes away the sin of the world!' You are the one who baptized me and witnessed the manifestation of the Holy Trinity."

I would have considered John hopeless, a complete failure. I would have criticized him. Not Jesus! First Jesus answers John's question in such a way that John would know, yes, Jesus is the Messiah. Then Jesus complimented the despondent prisoner. Jesus said, "I tell you the truth; among those born of women there has not risen anyone greater than John the Baptist." Can you imagine how John felt when that word reached him! What an incredible compliment which must have blown him away! Those were words John never expected to hear.

What is absolutely amazing is what Jesus has to say about you in Matthew chapter 11: "I tell you the truth;

among those born of women there has not risen anyone greater than John the Baptist *yet he who is the least in the Kingdom of God is greater than he."*[1] What a profound compliment He is giving to you which is almost incomprehensible. But we can know it is true because Jesus said it.

Brothers and sisters in Christ, Jesus thinks highly of you. Jesus is pleased with you! Jesus is saying good things about you to you, but you must open your ears to hear. Please do not hurt the heart of your Heavenly Father by not accepting His compliments.

I would like to share with you my most discouraging time on the foreign field and what my Heavenly Father said to me. Julie and I had to leave Afghanistan after the Soviet Invasion in 1979. For the next 13 months we lived out of suitcases traveling back and forth between Pakistan and India on tourist visas trying to get residence visas for Pakistan. We had just made another trip from India back to Peshawar, Pakistan which is on the border of Afghanistan near the famous Khyber Pass. Again, we checked into room 32 of the little, rustic but functional hotel called Jan's (pronounced John's) Hotel. Nothing was going right, and I was fighting discouragement. I didn't care about diseases, the bugs, the heat or dirt or things like that. But I did care about being able to minister to the Pashtuns. I was discouraged, lonely and depressed, plus, I did not know what to do next.

One morning soon after our arrival again in Peshawar, I took a walk to the nearby Khalid Park. Now what had really made everything bad was that Julie and I had just had a big misunderstanding. This was rare because we are deeply in love and have faithfully worked at our marriage since our wedding day. But it really did happen and what made it worse is that it was all my fault. By the way, if you are married and have never had a misunderstanding with your spouse, you're already in Heaven but you just don't know it!

So I sat in Khalid Park and in my frustration I decided that the only fair thing I could do was to hand in my resignation to God as a missionary. I did not want to do that, but in all fairness to God, I felt I must. My conversation with the Lord went something like this:

"Lord, I just don't have what it takes to be a missionary. You made a mistake when you called me. Lord, I cannot even do what I want to do. I just want to live in a village among the Pashtuns to whom you have called me, but I can't even get a visa to do that. Even if I did get a visa to live among the Pashtuns, it wouldn't do much good. I'm still not fluent in the Pashtu language after hundreds and hundreds of hours of study. I'm not an effective witness for you in Asia. I'm not making it.

"Lord Jesus, I'm certainly not worthy of the people back home who pray for us and financially support us. I don't have the slightest idea what to do next in this situation. And Lord, I've just hurt and discouraged the person I love the most. So, Lord, I'm sorry, but I don't have what it takes to be a missionary. Therefore, this morning I would like to hand in my resignation so I won't be an embarrassment to you and to others. Jesus, please don't take it personally, for it's nothing personal, but, Jesus, you made a big mistake when you called me to be a missionary."

I expected the Lord to agree with me and say, "I understand, David, you're right." But to my amazement God said something like this to me.

"David, I'm the Person who chooses and calls missionaries and I don't make any mistakes. David, I'm not accepting your resignation. You are right in the center of my will. You don't understand this now, but you will later. You have been faithful in answering my call and in being obedient to me. I deeply appreciate that. Don't worry, I'm going to work all things out for your good and my glory. David, just keep being faithful to me as you have been."

Then the Lord said some other beautiful things to me about me. I sat there on the park bench overwhelmed by His love and His presence. I was tremendously encouraged because my Heavenly Father would not accept my resignation. I did not want to resign. All I ever wanted to do was to live among the Pashtuns and share the love of Christ with them. I left the park full of joy! I hurried back to that old rustic hotel and sincerely apologized to Julie.

Then I said, "Honey, I tried to hand in my resignation, but the Lord won't receive it."

Julie said, "I know. I tried to hand in mine while you were gone and He refused to accept it also."

I said, "Honey, the Lord told me we are going to make it."

Julie said, "I know, Sweetie, we are really going to make it!"

I want you to know that you too are really going to make it. It is very important that you realize God is pleased with you and wants to compliment you. It is easy to hear and accept the negative things the devil says to you. It is easy for you to criticize yourself. You rightly expect your Heavenly Father to correct you at times and He does, out of His love for you. But also, your Heavenly Father expects you to hear and receive His compliments because He loves you. You are His child! Please do not hurt Him by not listening to and receiving the compliments He is saying to you.

May I suggest that you quietly bow your head and close your eyes and do not pray. But instead listen, listen quietly and hear and accept the compliments from your Heavenly Father that He desires to speak to your heart.

NOTES

The Little Boy and His Gift

1. Adapted from my book *Afghanistan, My Tears.*

One Step Short

1. Adapted from my book *Afghanistan, My Tears.*

2. Big Jim Nycum made a full and unconditional surrender of his life to the Lord Jesus Christ in 1997. For the last 15 years he has conducted weekly Bible studies for prisoners. Jim and I keep each other encouraged in the faith.

3. Coach George Landis taught me how not to quit, so I never quit praying that he would personally surrender his life to the Lord Jesus Christ. In 1960 I graduated from Howland High School in Ohio. Thirty-six years later when my book *Afghanistan, My Tears* was published, he did not know I had included a chapter about him. Reading his own story "One Step Short" was key to his understanding the grace of God. As a result he entered into a deep personal relationship with the Savior. At the age of 84 Coach Landis continues to be flat out for the Lord Jesus. We stay in close touch.

The Challenge

1. The name is changed.

2. Recommended Apologetic Books:

    Know Why You Believe,
    Paul Little (2008 edition)
    The Case for Christ,
    Lee Strobel
    The Case for Faith,
    Lee Strobel
    Making Sense of God,
    Timothy Keller
    Mere Christianity,
    C.S. Lewis
    The New Evidence that Demands a Verdict,
    Josh McDowell
    Baker Encyclopedia of Christian Apologetics,
    Norman Geisler

Confrontation at Chicago State

1. Name is changed.

The Quarter

1. SALT: Student Activist Leadership Training (presently refers to Matthew 5:13 where Jesus says, "You are the salt of the earth.")

The Day Granddad Died

1. Now Evangel University.

The American Major and the Iraqi Colonel

1. Based in Germany.

2. A non-governmental organization: usually non-profit and independent from government.

3. Major Kevin Ryan, a graduate of West Point, became a Brigadier General. He is now retired and is presently an Associate Fellow at Harvard Kennedy School Belfer Center. I cherish his friendship.

Najeeb and Mr. Johnston

1. Arabic for the Gospels (Matthew, Mark, Luke and John), often used to refer to the New Testament.

The Old Veteran and Nadezhda Part I and Part II

1. World War II

2. John 11:25; 14:1, 2.

3. The Russian name Nadezhda means hope.

Five Veterans Meet in Heaven

1. The Gospel of Luke, chapter 23, verses 39-43, tell the story of the repentant thief on the cross.

Hearing God's Compliments

1. The italics are mine.

OTHER BOOKS BY DAVID LEATHERBERRY

Afghanistan, My Tears

A compelling story of one couple's deep love for the people of Afghanistan. Though danger and chaos were their constant companions, neither could keep this couple from answering God's summons to give their lives in service to the Afghans.

Abdul & Mr. Friday

This book is an account based on a true story about a devout Muslim and a dedicated Christian. Each was willing to die for the other, yet neither could be moved from his faith. These were two men from two different worlds whose bond of friendship could not be broken. Neither wanted to go to heaven without the other.

Julie, My Love

Insightful gems can be found in these narratives about a common girl with uncommon courage. At times Julie Leatherberry lived in great danger, but her faith in God was unshakeable. She felt secure in her husband's love knowing he cherished her as his precious jewel.

How to Order

These books as well as *Strengths from Inspiring Stories* are available at $10 each including shipping & handling.

Please make checks and money orders payable to:

Enhearten Books
3938 W. Madison Place
Springfield, MO 65802

The books can be purchased as e-books on Amazon.

If you would like to correspond with the author, please use this email address: enheartenbooks@gmail.com

David would be delighted to hear from you.